Hunny And The Bear

M. L. SMITH

Book design by Cauldron Press Designs
Editing by Fair Crack of The Whip Editing

Foreward

This is dedicated to my husband.

One

P ressing a hand to her belly, Hunny Russo stared at her reflection in the vanity, eyes wide with shock. The droning of the small TV behind her nearly blocked out the frantic beating of her heart, but she was too anxious to understand any of the words blaring from the device. Too freaked out to do anything but stare at her stomach.

Pregnant.

She was *pregnant*.

"I can't believe it," Hunny murmured to herself, lifting her shirt up a few inches to inspect her flat belly. She couldn't be more than a few weeks along—that's when she'd met Jason, Alpha of the Moon Rose pack, and he was the only one she'd had sex with in recent months.

Her vehicle had gotten a flat tire as she'd driven through Montana and, as fate would have it, Jason had stopped by her rickety old truck pulled over on the side of the road, offering to help. All it had taken was one look into his steel-blue eyes and she'd felt the true mate bond flare with recognition between them. A powerful flood of emotions poured into her very psyche.

And the most prominent emotion? *Lust*.

Hunny shivered, recalling that night so vividly. Jason had nearly ripped her truck door off its hinges in his haste to sink inside her, his eyes glowing a bright blue as his wolf pressed close to the surface. As soon as he'd invaded her space, their animalistic urges had consumed them, flooding them with need. They tugged each other's clothes off right before he'd rutted her, his thick, muscular body pressing her slender form into the cracked leather cushions, both desperately clawing at each other for more.

Afterward, he'd taken her to a little cabin deep in the woods within his pack's territory, promising she'd be safe while he sorted out some issues with his pack mates. He hadn't gone into detail and she hadn't asked, too nervous to overstep. As a lone rabbit shifter, she didn't have a nest and she didn't want to start off in a wolf pack by displeasing her Alpha.

Hunny's brow pinched. Well, he wasn't her Alpha *yet*, as he hadn't formally invited her into his pack. But he would.

He had to. They were true mates.

An uneasy feeling, mostly one of wariness, settled in her belly, the sour emotion growing stronger with every passing day she remained alone in this cabin. She couldn't help wondering, was she being locked away like a dirty little secret?

Life hadn't been the greatest for Hunny. Not so far, anyway. Both of her parents had passed away when she'd been only seventeen years old, and shortly after that, her old Buck, a rabbit shifter equivalent to an Alpha, had attempted to force her into mating him, insisting she needed his protection from the outside world to survive. What he'd really wanted was to prey on her. Disgusted, she'd left her nest, determined to explore the world on her own.

Too bad that at seventeen she hadn't truly understood the harshness of living on her own. She'd struggled to make ends meet over the past five years, moving from one place to the next in the search of something better. Something *more*.

Truth be told, Hunny had almost given up until she'd neared the mountains in Montana, her beat-up truck on its last leg as she'd turned down a road around a cliffside. She'd stared in awe at the surrounding landscape. Mountains as far as the eye could see were enveloped by lush green forests. It was so different to the plain states she'd spent her life in. That day, with the sun's rays poured in through the windshield as if welcoming her home, something inside her had settled.

Now that she knew her true mate was here, it all made sense, though she wished things between the two of them would progress a bit differently.

Jason had come back a few times over the last three weeks, always at night, and always too eager to bed her to do anything else, like discuss their future. She enjoyed his visits, but she longed for him to hold her after sex or tell her something about himself. *Anything*. She yearned for an emotional connection to form between them, not just a physical one.

Would it be so bad to just relax in each other's company and enjoy some pillow talk? Apparently so, because every time she started to converse with him, he hastily pulled his clothes back on as he hurried from the bed, saying he had to go before promising to return soon. Sometimes he came back the next night. But sometimes three to four days passed before he returned to her.

That's okay, Hunny told herself, ignoring the uneasy feeling that grew as she thought of how little she actually knew about Jason. *There will be plenty of years to get to know him. He's your mate.*

Her eyes flicked up the length of the mirror to her bare, unmarked neck.

Well, he was *technically* her mate, although they hadn't made it official with a mating bite. Just like he hadn't officially invited her into his pack ...

When she'd asked him about it yesterday, Jason had assured her that their mating was coming. And then he'd retreated once more, disappearing through the cabin door and into the woods.

Tugging her shirt down over her belly, Hunny ran her hands through her long, wavy lilac-colored hair.

Although she couldn't be happier at the idea of welcoming a kit into this world, and she was eager to share the news with her mate, she couldn't help but feel ... *distressed*.

Nerves had set in days ago—a lurking suspicion that Jason was just using her for sex before inevitably rejecting her. It was rare, but rejections could happen among true mates. Jason was an Alpha to a wolf pack, and Hunny ...? She shifted into their prey. She wasn't dominant where it mattered most, and a fluffy woodland creature wasn't exactly an ideal selection for a pack's Luna.

But if Jason planned on rejecting her, why bring her to his cabin? Why visit her at all? It would be in both of their best interests to cut ties to one another before they bonded; a natural occurrence between mated pairs, where their minds linked and they could feel each other's emotions, though no one knew exactly how the bond formed. It could be because of close proximity or maybe mutual affection, like love. While a bond *always* happened between true mates, it could also occur with chosen mates, though it often took longer to form.

Suddenly, the knob on the front door rattled, breaking through Hunny's thoughts. She jumped, head snapping up to the front of the cabin. Faintly, she heard a key slide into the lock and the door pushed open, revealing Jason standing on the front porch.

He was tall, with powerful muscles, shaggy blond hair and a clean-shaven face that showed off his rugged jawline. His fists were clenched at his side, his blue eyes colder than she'd ever seen. She brushed off a sudden onslaught of unease, focusing on her excitement to see him.

"Hi, Jason. I've missed you." Smiling, Hunny moved toward her mate, only to pause when his scent drifted into the cabin. She inhaled, stiffening as she caught the offensive odor of another female's perfume intertwined with his—like some bitch had rubbed herself against him only minutes prior.

Instinctively, her eyes shot to his neck, widening in horror as she gasped.

There, peeking out halfway from the neck of his t-shirt, was a bite mark. A *mating* mark.

"What is that?" Hunny asked faintly, cringing at how distraught she sounded. If she wasn't in such shock, she would have rolled her eyes at her own question. Instead, she uttered forlornly, "Jason, w-what have you done?"

But she knew what he'd done, didn't she? He'd mated someone else. The truth was clear to see. The proof right there in plain sight. He'd kept Hunny here in his cabin like a dirty little secret because that's exactly what she'd been. Not a revered mate, but a lustful shame. A guilty pleasure.

Her breath hitched and her heart *hurt*, a physical ache that had her pressing her palm to her chest, rubbing hard over her wounded organ as if it would help ease her pain. But it didn't help, and she suspected nothing would.

"You know what I've done." Quietly, Jason stepped into the cabin, his powerful frame filling the doorway. Hunny retreated a step, her legs like jelly as she fought to keep from sinking to the floor in misery. He took a deep breath. "I've mated an Alpha female from my pack. Someone I've had my eye on for a few years. She's the perfect Luna."

Tears pricked Hunny's eyes as she looked up at Jason, her nose stinging as she fought to keep them from falling. "But I'm your true mate. Fate decides who is perfect for you, and it's *me*."

Why can't he see that?

Jason snarled, taking a menacing step toward her. His words laced with venom, he spat, "Fate gave me a weak female. A rabbit shifter, and a submissive one at that."

She flinched as if he'd struck her, her gaze dropping to the bite mark on his neck once more. It taunted her, and nausea rolled through her stomach. "Submissive doesn't mean weak," she replied softly, but her voice wavered, all but proving him right. She felt weak. Useless. *Used.*

Broken.

Jason scoffed, the sound grating on her soul. "You can't even look me in the eye as you say that, Hunny. How could you ever discipline a member of my pack if you can't even stand up for yourself?" He shook his head. "Natasha was the perfect choice for my Luna and my mate. Consider this my formal rejection."

"Why?" Hunny snapped, spinning away from him before she did something pathetic, like fall at his feet and beg him to reconsider. She wanted to run from the cabin, to jump into her truck and drive the hell out of this state. To get as far away as possible. But fleeing the cabin meant brushing past Jason, and she didn't want to be anywhere near him right now.

God, why had she ever felt like Montana was home? This place was nothing to her. She didn't have a home; she hadn't since her parents had died. And now, all she'd have of this place were memories of how completely her heart had shattered here. She regretted ever stepping foot in these mountains.

No, that wasn't exactly true. Her hand slid to her belly protectively. She'd have a kit, someone to love and cherish; even if its father couldn't do the same for her. That was enough to make this last month worthwhile. It had to be.

Jason sighed in resignation. "I've told you why."

"No, I mean, why did you bring me here? Why did you lead me on for weeks? Just to use me for sex?" She bit out the last question through her teeth, some of her sorrow fading as indignant fury replaced it.

"Of course not."

Reaching the bed, Hunny spun back around to face him, content with the distance she'd created. "Then why lead me on? Why do any of this if you never planned to mate me?"

"Because I couldn't just let you go," Jason bellowed suddenly, his features twisting with rage. A second later, he schooled his expression, leaving Hunny to wonder if she'd noticed anything amiss at all. "I'd already made promises to Natasha that I couldn't back out of," he continued softly, the scent of his regret filling the air. "From the moment we met, it was already too late."

"Oh, bullshit," Hunny scoffed, running a hand through her hair. "You talk about me being weak, but it's *you* who's weak," she declared vehemently. "You might have made promises to that female, but when you invited me here, when you fucked me within minutes of us meeting, you made promises to me, too. You were just too much of a coward to act on them. Don't blame the submissive for your shortcomings."

Jason's nostrils flared with anger. Inhaling, he stiffened, gaping at her in shock. "You're pregnant."

Hunny swallowed past the lump in her throat. "Yes. I just found out tonight." Not that it mattered. He'd made his choice already.

"Pregnant," Jason whispered with a shake of his head. "I don't believe it."

Welcome to the club, jackass.

He took another step toward her, and then another. She straightened her spine as he pushed into her space, refusing to cower. Dropping his head to her neck, he inhaled, his nose lightly roaming over her skin. He shuddered then, wrapping an arm around her waist and pulling her flush against him. "You always smell so good," he groaned. "I can't get enough."

"Well, you won't need to think about my scent anymore. I'm leaving here as soon as possible." She was already planning her next steps, calculating how long it would take her to leave the state. Luckily, she'd moved so much in the last few years that it was more or less second nature at this point.

She just needed to walk out—to push him away; she wanted to more than anything. But her body betrayed her, and she dropped her forehead onto his chest, sinking into his embrace. Every time he held her, it always felt *right*. Magnetic, almost.

Only now, his scent was wrong, and his touch didn't bring her any comfort. It just hurt.

"You could stay," he began softly, his breath tickling her flesh. "I've marked Natasha, but I don't love her, Hunny. I don't want her like I want you, and she doesn't need to know about us. Stay here in this cabin, and we can raise our pup together."

"Excuse me?" Hunny asked in dismay. He expected her to live like this for the rest of her life? To take the scraps he offered and be content as the other woman? That would *never* happen. She flattened her palms onto his chest and shoved, but he didn't budge an inch. "Let go." She pushed at his chest again. Jason ignored her, his arm tightening around her waist. His lips landed on her neck, delicately skating over her flesh.

"I need you, Hunny."

"Stop. *Jason!*"

"You're carrying my pup," he murmured reverently, and she almost scoffed at his audacity. Because they were both different animal shifters, their child would either be a wolf or a rabbit. And based on how he'd treated her for being a rabbit shifter, she knew he'd discard her and their child if it took after her.

He kissed her neck again, his teeth grazing over her sensitive skin as if he intended to sink them into her. Like he planned on biting her, giving her a perversion of a mating mark. It was all too much! She felt like she was drowning.

"Get your hands off of me!" Hunny shouted, blindly reaching for his face. The sound of her palm connecting with his cheek sounded so loud in the room, startling her almost as much as it did him. She doubted it hurt. She wasn't at a proper angle to smack him like he deserved, but he broke away from her anyway, snarling angrily as he shot her a glare.

His chest rose and fell rapidly, his eyes glowing brightly as he curled his lip in disgust. "You hit me, you ungrateful bitch. Do that again and you'll regret it."

She flinched from the venom in his voice, but she didn't back down. "You're revolting, Jason. Like I would ever want to stay here with you after you've mated someone else! Like I'd ever want you to touch me again!"

He has to be out of his mind!

He smirked coldly, pressing a hand to his red cheek. "Fine. Raise that fucking brat by yourself. No one's going to want a shifter whore and her bastard, so I hope you enjoy a life of loneliness. After all, isn't that what you were running from when I met you?"

"Fuck you," she seethed, a fresh wave of tears filling her eyes. What had she ever seen in this male? How was *he* supposed to be her perfect match?

"I'll give you an hour to pack your shit and leave my territory," Jason spat, backing toward the door. He kept his eyes firmly on her, like a predator stalking its prey. "When I come back, you better be long gone from here."

With that, he turned and left, slamming the door behind him.

Hunny waited several seconds before she sank to her knees, all her strength leaving her as she sagged against the bed. A small sob left her throat, the tears she'd been holding back finally falling down her cheeks.

She'd been such an idiot. How could she have thought that finding her true mate would turn her life around? That the one person specifically designed by fate to be hers wouldn't destroy her trust, her heart? If she'd learned anything over the last five years, it was that she could only rely on herself.

Wiping at her cheeks with the back of her hand, Hunny took a deep, shuddering breath.

"You're okay," she whispered to herself, repeating it over and over until she almost believed it. Another minute passed before she pushed to her feet, ignoring the way her legs shook as she began moving around the cabin, numbly gathering her things.

She didn't have a lot, just what she could fit into her truck at a moment's notice. It only took about five minutes before Hunny was ready, gathering her suitcase and leaving the cabin, stepping into the crisp night air. She didn't even bother closing the door because honestly ...? She was petty and Jason could go fuck himself.

Maybe she'd get lucky and a bear would wander in there, ready to eat him when he came back.

Her lips twitched as she neared her truck, the image of him screaming in fear and running away from a grizzly flitting through her head.

A twig snapped to the left. Hunny tensed, whipping toward the noise, her senses on high alert.

There, standing less than ten feet away, on the edge of the woods, was a naked woman with a mating mark proudly displayed on her neck. When Hunny's eyes met hers, they glowed an ominous blue, signaling the woman was a wolf shifter. The wind kicked up, carrying a now familiar scent to Hunny's lungs.

Of course, Jason's chosen mate would show up to watch Hunny slink off into the night.

Just perfect, she thought sarcastically.

"Natasha, right?" Hunny guessed, running a hand down her face in exhaustion. "How long have you been lurking out here?"

The female narrowed her eyes. "Long enough to hear Jason's offer."

"Then you'll know I rejected it. And you'll also know that I'm leaving."

Natasha tilted her head, studying Hunny with a calculating look. It made her nervous, and her grip on the suitcase handle tightened until her knuckles went white. "I know that you're carrying his pup, the future of this pack, if it's born a wolf."

"My child won't be the future of any wolf pack, so don't worry," Hunny bit out.

Natasha smiled then, flashing a set of wickedly sharp canines. "Oh, I'm not worried. In fact, I'm here to guarantee it." The wolf held up her hand, and within a second, it shifted, her nails lengthening into deadly claws.

Oh, shit.

Hunny dropped the hold on her suitcase, frantically searching her jeans pockets for her keys. Shit, shit, shit! Where were her freaking keys?! She must have left them back in the cabin. Hastily, she glanced back at the opened cabin door, her eyes locking on a set of keys sitting on the table in the entryway.

You've got to be kidding—

Wrenching her hands from her pockets, she grabbed the truck's door handle, hoping like hell she'd left it unlocked so she could at least get inside. There was a spare key in the glove compartment. She tugged hard, but the door didn't budge.

Fuck!

The wolf stepped from the treeline, calmly stalking toward her. Hunny's mouth dried, fear slamming into her like a battering ram.

She was dead if she didn't do something!

Natasha spoke as she prowled closer, her voice taking on a distorted edge that sent terror skating down Hunny's spine. "I heard rabbits are fond of running. You should try it."

And then Natasha hunched over, fur sprouting over her skin, bones cracking as she began to shift into a wolf.

New plan, Hunny thought desperately. Kicking off her shoes as she quickly backed away from Natasha, she ripped her shirt over her head and unbuttoned her jeans.

And then Hunny shifted, shaking free of her clothes right as the she-wolf lunged for her, jaws opened wide.

Luckily for Hunny, in her rabbit form, she was quick and agile. She bolted to the right, barely dodging Natasha's fangs as she snapped her mouth closed. And then Hunny took off, rushing into the woods like her life literally depended on it.

Terror dogged her heels as she heard Natasha give chase from behind, plowing through bushes that Hunny weaved seamlessly through. She wouldn't last long in an outright chase though; wolves were objectively faster than rabbits, and although Hunny had the advantage of panic and adrenaline on her side, it wouldn't help her keep this grueling pace for long.

Maybe she could find a burrow and use that tunnel system to escape. Nose twitching as she ran, she tried to scent for other creatures, but she was moving too fast and was honestly far too panicked to detect much of anything aside from the foul odor of her own fear.

It filled her lungs, clogging her throat as she kept up her intense pace. She ran hard for several minutes, Natasha's growls echoing in her ears as she bobbed and weaved through any underbrushes she could find, hoping to lose the shifter or at least slow her down. It didn't work, and she had the distinct impression the wolf was toying with her.

Suddenly, Natasha charged her from the side, sharp teeth biting into her front leg, breaking through skin and bone. Hunny screamed, the sound loud and high-pitched, echoing through the woods as blinding agony flared through her leg.

Natasha jerked Hunny backward, the movement too quick to counter. She felt a moment of panic as the wolf released her leg, wind whipping through her fur as she was launched through the air. She slammed into a tree a second later, her side and head smacking against the thick wood with a sickening crack.

With a small whine, the fight went out of her, and Hunny collapsed, landing in a heap on the ground. She tried to stand, but her legs barely twitched, and a pitiful, desperate cry poured from her throat.

Jason really was right. She was weak. And now she was going to die here. Alone. And no one would even remember her or care.

Natasha chuffed, the wolf's version of laughter ringing in Hunny's ears as her vision doubled, black spots flitting in front of her as she struggled to blink. Her head hurt and her body was killing her. As she wheezed, laying there, the scent of her own blood filled her nose.

No, not *just* blood.

She tried to inhale once more through the pain and smelled musk, clovers and berries invaded her senses. What on earth was that smell? It was so distracting, so soothing, that she didn't even notice Natasha approaching, drool dripping from her muzzle as she reached Hunny's side.

The wolf opened her maw wide, lunging for Hunny.

A blur of brown fur filled her vision—was that a giant paw? It slammed into Natasha, batting her body away before she could strike. The wolf yelped and went flying, right as a bear's ominous roar tore through the night.

Great, she'd traded getting eaten by a wolf shifter for getting eaten by a bear. The throbbing in her head increased tenfold, and before she had a chance to feel an ounce of fear for this new predicament she'd fallen into, Hunny fell unconscious.

Two

The last thing Henry 'Tank' Sinclair expected to find on his nightly stroll through the woods was a she-wolf attacking a rabbit shifter. And he damned sure hadn't anticipated knocking the large wolf into some nearby vegetation like a pesky fly, his every instinct demanding he protect the small, wounded creature at his feet.

It was odd—Tank never felt compelled to protect anything that wasn't his family or part of his bear clan. And yet, he knew if that wolf struck again, he'd rip the canine to shreds without a moment's hesitation. In fact, as he inhaled, drawing the two warring shifter scents deep into his lungs, his claws ached to inflict even more damage on the damned beast.

What was a wolf shifter doing in bear territory anyway, preying on a rabbit shifter? Every supernatural creature knew that rabbit shifters, along with other small woodland shifters, were relatively harmless and, by nature, submissive, though there were always some that broke the mold, being more dominant.

At least he'd arrived in time to stop the wolf from finishing what she'd started.

As an enforcer for his brother's bear clan, it was Tank's duty to wander the edge of their territory at night to hunt for intruders. Typically, he didn't find much of anything—his clan was located deep in the woods, more than an hour away from 'civilization,' and although the occasional hiker wandered into their domain, they usually fled in terror after he charged at them, roaring loudly for the entire forest to hear.

It was hilarious watching the humans pale in fright, and scaring them had the added bonus of spreading rumors in nearby towns that the woods weren't safe, meaning fewer hikers to deal with. The fewer people, the better. In his opinion, anyway.

He couldn't stand people; humans especially. They were just all so ... *talkative*. That was part of the reason he enjoyed being an en-forcer—wandering the forest daily for hours left little room for chatter among his clan, and when brute force was needed, Tank was called in to handle difficult situations.

Tank looked down at the blood staining his claws, and then in the direction he'd tossed the wolf. His eyes narrowed suspiciously when all he noticed were a few limp bushes.

Where was the wolf?

He moved his large body protectively over the little bunny as he scanned the perimeter. No wolf in sight, and he heard nothing to indicate the beast was lurking nearby. It seemed it had tucked tail and ran as soon as he'd intervened.

That's just as well, he thought, moving back a step to stare down at the shifter he'd just saved. Covered in blood, the sleeping rabbit let out a pitiful whine, the same sound that had drawn Tank's attention to this location only moments ago. The sound stirred something within him, instinct demanding he pick the creature up and nurse it back to health.

The thought was laughable. No one would ever describe Tank as *nurturing*. Quite the opposite. Brutal, easily irritated, and always quiet, he wasn't the type of male to play nurse for anyone, let alone a stranger.

What was it about this shifter?

He leaned down, his muzzle drawing so close to the rabbit he almost brushed against her fur. He could tell it was a female from instinct alone. Closing his eyes, Tank inhaled again, the scents of lavender, vanilla, and ... *honey* filling his nose. Despite the coppery smell of blood, Tank's eyes nearly rolled back in delight at the rabbit's delicious scent.

He loved honey—and his obsession with the treat was a long-run-ning joke among the rest of his clan, though normally no one brought it up, not to his face at least—unless they wanted to get their skull cracked. He knew his love of honey was a horrible stereotype, but it was too irresistible for him to care. Like a glutton hungry for more, Tank dragged in another lungful of the rabbit's scent.

If his true mate hadn't died years ago, right before they'd both reached adulthood, he'd wonder if this female was his. It would explain his urge to protect her, and his fascination with her smell. Ever since Cassandra had died, though, nothing held his attention for long, and *nothing* was ever fascinating anymore.

That happened a lot with true mates—when one half of your soul died, so did you. Either physically or metaphorically. Because Tank hadn't properly claimed his mate, he hadn't been tempted to end his life to join her in the next—but he'd never been right after her passing.

His nose twitched as another scent, barely there, intruded.

The female was pregnant.

He reared back onto his hind legs, staring down at the rabbit in a new light. Maybe that explained his odd behavior—as a dominant bear, he'd feel inclined to protect a pregnant female in need, especially a submissive.

Not wanting to waste more time, Tank fell back onto all fours, leaning down and opening his maw wide. He scooped up the rabbit's limp body into his mouth, careful not to puncture her delicate skin, before he began moving back to his cabin. Her tail teased one side of his mouth, and her head dangled from the other, but this was the only way to carry her while ensuring they were both protected.

If that wolf came back and he was in his human form, it would only take one bite to snap his neck.

Opening his telepathic connection with Murphy, the clan Alpha and his brother, Tank bit out, *Spotted a wolf shifter on patrol.*

He wasn't fond of talking to people in general, but for shifters, communicating with one's Alpha telepathically was a convenient tool. Luckily, he could close the connection at any time, and it didn't extend to other members of the clan, otherwise he knew the rest of his family would harass him every hour of the day.

There was a brief stirring in Tank's mind before his brother's deep cadence filled his head. *You think it was a member of the Moon Rose pack?*

Tank nearly snarled in irritation at the mention of that dumbfuck Jason, and his pack of nearly rabid wolves. The only reason he kept silent was because of the unconscious female he carried. He didn't want her to wake in his mouth and harm herself if she struggled to break free.

Might have been, Tank answered. *The wolf was attacking a rabbit shifter on the edge of our territory. I intervened.*

Good. We don't want any unnecessary bloodshed on our lands. There was a brief pause before Murphy asked, *Did you send the shifters on their way with a warning to keep their dispute off our territory?*

Tank hesitated, keeping his eyes on his surroundings as he rounded a corner. *Not exactly.* He moved quickly, passing over a fallen tree trunk and heading deeper into the heart of the woods.

What does that mean, Tank? You didn't kill them, did you? I know you're rough, but surely—

No, I didn't kill them. Tank rolled his eyes. *Well, I don't think so. The rabbit was already wounded. The wolf was going in for the kill so I frightened her off.*

Then what does 'not exactly' mean? Murphy asked.

Tank sighed, his body relaxing as he caught sight of familiar claw markings along the bark of several trees he passed. He was nearly home now. Good, he needed to shift and look after the female.

Tank? Murphy grumbled. *Answer me.*

The rabbit is unconscious. Tank grimaced as he stepped onto his driveway, gravel digging uncomfortably into the pads of his paws. The small log cabin stood out impressively among the forest. Two stories in total and with a porch wrapping around his first floor, his home was his haven away from everyone.

And now he'd brought a stranger into his den. One that smelled like heaven but would likely drive him insane as soon as she began harping in his ear. He wasn't used to company.

Did you leave it where you found it? His Alpha's voice interrupted his thoughts.

What? Tank asked, his voice heavy with confusion.

The rabbit shifter. Did you leave it where you found it? Murphy repeated irritably.

No.

Murphy huffed. *What did you—*

Tank slammed his mind closed, effectively blocking his older brother out from communicating with him any further. Murphy was a stubborn bastard, though, and it wouldn't take long before his cell phone began ringing incessantly.

Or the bastard would just show up. Actually, that seemed far more likely.

Making it to his porch, Tank lowered his head toward the first step, carefully placing his wounded companion down. And then he shifted, the sensation of skin stretching and shrinking accompanied by the cracking of bones as his body returned to his human form. As Tank was thirty-two years old and had been shifting since he was a cub, the transition from bear to man was seamless, and it only took two seconds at most.

Now naked as the day he was born, Tank scooped up the rabbit into his arms, casting a worried glance over the small thing as he moved up the steps and into his home. He never locked the door, but the only fresh scent was his, so he pushed confidently inside, closing the door behind him.

It was late, the darkness of the forest peeking through the vast windows of his cabin. Warm lighting poured down from the ceiling fan, though, and a lamp in the far corner illuminated the rest of the living room. The cabin was cozy; the main floor boasted the living room, a small dining room, and a large kitchen.

The bathroom and his bedroom were both upstairs.

Beelining for the massive leather couch, Tank placed his companion onto a cushion. He checked her breathing—steady— along with her wounds and her vitals. A front leg appeared broken, and there were a few puncture wounds on her back and side. That was all. She just needed to shift back into her human form and the wounds would heal instantly.

Until then, he didn't want her bleeding out.

Pushing away from the couch, Tank moved to the stairs to slip on some clothes. He took them two at a time, reaching the upstairs landing. A balcony railing attached to the stairs made up a half-wall for his bedroom, allowing him to look down and observe a majority of the first floor whenever he wanted. He'd built it this way for two reasons: he lived alone, so he didn't need an extra room; and it wasn't a cozy house for anyone but him, so he almost never had visitors and didn't require privacy.

Except now.

Frowning, he walked into his closet and grabbed a T-shirt and jeans from his dresser, changed, and went back downstairs to the kitchen. In a cabinet, he found some gauze, hydrogen peroxide, and a few hand towels. Snatching it all up, he filled a small bowl with warm water and returned to his little rabbit.

She hadn't moved from where he'd left her, still out cold. How long would she be unconscious? Twenty minutes had passed, at least, since he'd found her. He refused to believe she'd sustained a major head wound; he couldn't see any bleeding or obvious trauma.

Did she have a concussion?

"Wake up, bunny," Tank uttered dryly, wincing when his vocal chords strained from both disuse and a long-ago injury. He'd had most of his throat shredded a few years back during an attack on his clan, the damage so extensive he'd actually scarred, and the chords had never quite healed entirely, even after shifting. Luckily, he'd survived.

He couldn't say the same for the fucker who'd wounded him.

"Up," he repeated roughly, sighing heavily when all he got in return was a brief tremble from one of her whiskers. He was used to people doing what he said as soon as he said it, usually out of fear. His harsh voice and massive appearance had that effect on people.

Now a bunny shifter couldn't even rouse herself at the sound of his voice. She had to have scented him by now, even subconsciously. So why wasn't she up and quaking in her fur?

Hesitantly, he sat down beside her, unsure of what to do as he set his medical supplies on the coffee table in front of him. He should have just called his mom, a doctor for the clan, and told her to swing by. She'd be of more help than he would.

But for some reason, he didn't want anyone near his companion while she was so vulnerable—not even his mother. Unfortunately, that just left him to tend to the rabbit. Reaching for the roll of gauze, Tank unfurled a small section, ripping the piece free from the rest. Then, carefully, he lifted the broken front leg—

The rabbit's head shot forward, small blunt teeth biting down on his hand and piercing the skin.

Tank growled in outrage at the sharp sting of pain, yanking his hand back in surprise as the bunny leaped quickly to the furthest end of the couch, turned in his direction, and hissed. Her nose twitched and her whiskers trembled as she opened her mouth, hissing again in warning.

The threat was so ridiculous, a faint urge to laugh bubbled up from within him for the first time in years.

Just what had he gotten himself into?

Three

Where the hell am I? Hunny thought in bewilderment, her nose twitching as she inhaled a strong, delicious scent; a mixture of bear, musk, and cloves filled her lungs. Like an addict, she inhaled again, the trembling in her whiskers giving her away. She eyed the man across from her warily.

No. Not just a *man*. A bear shifter. And damned if he didn't look intimidating.

Even sitting across from her on the couch, one large hand wrapped around the other that she'd bitten, every inch of him was menacing. He was tall and well-built, muscles practically bulging through a tight T-shirt. He was tanned, with unruly brown hair and an equally unkempt beard that could use a trim. And his eyes? They were such a dark brown, they appeared almost black. Objectively, he looked mean as hell, but in a way that would heat any female's blood.

Mentally, she shook herself, hoping to clear that particular thought. She didn't need to be thinking that anyone, *especially* a shifter, had sex appeal. Wasn't that how she had ended up in this mess?

Speaking of ... Was this the same bear she'd caught a brief glimpse of before she'd lost consciousness?

Hunny shifted on her feet, her body immediately protesting against the movement as pain washed over her. Her head ached, her front leg throbbed, and her side was still tender from where she'd hit the tree. The only upside was that her stomach felt fine. She'd once read somewhere that human babies were well protected in the womb, at least in the first trimester, and she suspected that was the case for her as well.

I should shift back. If she did, she'd heal almost instantly. But then, where would that leave her? Naked and vulnerable in an unknown shifter's home. But if she stayed as a rabbit, at least for now, then she'd be faster and have an easier time hiding if necessary, even wounded.

Although, for some strange reason, she didn't exactly feel scared or in danger. Ridiculous, really. All of her years living alone and traveling through the States, she'd learned that even if she felt safe, it didn't mean she *was*. A vulnerable woman was easy prey to the wrong person. And this particular male, even though he'd saved her life, was a stranger.

"Are you planning on shifting or just sitting there like a stuffed animal?" the male asked gruffly, dropping his hands to his knees. The sudden movement startled Hunny.

She hissed again, her bushy tail stiffening in agitation.

A choked noise came from him then, and his lips twitched as if he were trying his best not to laugh at her.

She narrowed her eyes menacingly, her body shaking with indignant fury. How dare he find her threat funny! She might be small, but she was a force to be reckoned with. Well, okay. Maybe not as a bunny. But if he actually did laugh at her, she'd hop her injured ass right on over to the front door and shit into his shoes.

Who'd be laughing then, you smug son of a bit—

The male ran a hand through his disheveled hair. A few strands fell into his eyes. "At least, let me finish bandaging your foot. It's broken, and if you won't shift, I need to ensure the bone is set."

Slowly, he leaned forward, grabbing a strip of gauze from beside him before moving a roll of the cloth onto the coffee table on her left. It was then she noticed a plethora of supplies set there: a bowl of water, hydrogen peroxide, etc. What kind of person saved another one from an attack, brought them to his home, and wanted to patch them up?

A good one. At least, Hunny hoped so.

She didn't move as they stared at one another, trapped in a silent stand-off. Despite the choked sound he'd made only a few moments ago, his eyes lacked any hint of humor. Instead, it was almost like she was gazing into a void. No warmth, no depth, no emotion. But no anger either. Or hatred, nothing like she had seen in both Jason and Natasha earlier.

She'd seen that same blank look reflected in the mirror for years—when she'd felt utterly broken after her parents' deaths, just going through the motions of life day by day, desperate for some semblance of normalcy. It left her wondering; what had broken him? Had someone died that he'd held dear to him? Not a mate, surely. Usually, when one mate died, the other followed.

Her heart twisted painfully, a brutal reminder that she'd just been rejected by her own mate. Not *only* rejected, but hunted down and nearly mauled to death by his chosen mate, Natasha.

"You gonna let me tend to your wounds, little rabbit?" the male asked, his deep, gravelly voice sliding over her like a warm breeze. Whatever thoughts were bouncing around in her head fled, and cautiously, she took a small step forward.

Fine. She'd let him treat her wounds, if he insisted, and then as soon as he went to sleep, she'd shift, heal, and leave.

Mindful of her front leg, she moved a tad bit closer before daintily holding out the injured limb. Grunting, he moved into her space, his yummy scent growing stronger until Hunny felt like she was bathing in it. She sighed audibly, and his brows shot up in surprise before snapping back down to her wound.

Shockingly gentle for someone so massive, the bear shifter took her paw in one hand, tenderly moving the aching limb. She winced, and he paused, giving her a moment before he carefully began again. Once he was satisfied with how it lay, he began wrapping it, ensuring the gauze covered almost her entire leg. The cloth was tight, but not too painful as he tied it off to secure it.

"Now onto your open wounds." He grabbed the peroxide and a towel. "This'll hurt." He paused, eyeing her speculatively. "No biting."

Hunny rolled her eyes but remained still as he began treating the rest of her wounds, the liquid burning several spots on her back and side. She made sure to keep her attention focused on him and not the pain, acutely aware of every move he made. She told herself it was out of protection, but in truth, she kind of found her mystery savior intriguing.

She'd never met a bear shifter before, and despite how massive he looked now, she had a feeling he'd still be an impressive size when she was in her human form. What was he? Six-foot-five? Maybe taller?

"Done." He stood abruptly. Her head tilted back ... and then waaaay back as she tried to take all of him in.

Jesus. It's like looking at a lumberjack gladiator.

Seriously, the guy looked like he could split some wood with his bare hands. And wouldn't that be a sight to see?

The bear shifter cleared his throat, wincing a bit before he spoke. "I'll set out some food and water for you." He moved quickly away from the couch and out of her line of sight. He was quiet, only the sounds of drawers opening and dinnerware scraping lightly together giving away his location. After a few minutes, he returned, holding two small metal bowls.

Setting the dishes down onto the leather cushion in front of her, he murmured, "Bon appétit." She glanced into each one, which looked suspiciously like it was made for a cat or small dog, and narrowed her eyes at what he'd brought her.

Water filled one bowl to the brim, and the other contained lettuce, chopped carrots, and cucumbers. She'd have snarled at him for the stereotypical meal, but she loved salad. Most vegetables, actually. In fact, it looked delicious, and as her stomach rumbled angrily, she dove into the meal.

"Might want to slow down," he suggested. Hunny growled low in her throat at his audacity, chomping down aggressively on a carrot as she locked eyes with him. His lips twitched again. "My apologies, little rabbit. Eat and rest." He pointed to somewhere behind her. "I'll be up there if you need anything."

And with that, her rescuer turned off the overhead light, keeping a lamp on in the corner, and left. She turned her head, watching as he hustled up a flight of stairs to the second story, which appeared to be a small room with a balcony overlooking the rest of the house.

Gaze shifting around, Hunny took in the rest of the house while she ate. It was pretty inside, if small, with a high ceiling and beautiful, lightly stained oak walls and floors. A dark blue rug covered the center of the living room floor, but aside from that, the rest of his home looked bare.

Kind of a waste of such a pretty cabin. He needed an interior decorator or something to make this place a home. If she lived somewhere nice like this, she'd have art on the walls, vibrant plants hanging from shelves, and whatever else she could dream up to make the space more inviting.

But this place wasn't her home. Nowhere was.

With that sobering thought, Hunny stopped eating; the food turning to ash in her belly.

The light upstairs switched off, plunging the balcony into darkness. She stiffened, stock-still for several minutes as she waited for him to fall asleep. After what felt like forever, she heard a soft snore and gingerly jumped off the couch. Moving toward the front door, she shifted, bones popping audibly as the gauze tore from her arm. A few seconds later, she was kneeling on the ground.

Standing quickly, she took inventory of her nude body, pleased that every inch of her had healed. Cocking her head to the side, she relaxed when she heard another snore coming from the balcony, relieved she hadn't woken up the bear.

Quietly, she placed her hand on the doorknob. She needed to go back to her truck, grab her things, and leave. But before she could open the door, a thought intruded.

What if Natasha was back at the cabin? The bear had mentioned nothing about a wolf, so for all Hunny knew, Natasha was lying in wait for another opportunity to strike. She'd been adamant about killing Hunny, so she highly doubted the wolf would give up after one failed attempt. And she definitely didn't want to face that bitch again. Not when the female had been so eager to rip her and her baby apart.

But all of Hunny's stuff was back in the truck. Her ID, her clothes ... her money. She didn't have a bank account because she constantly moved, so she kept all of her cash stashed away in the glove compartment.

She couldn't just leave everything behind. But the thought of going back there and running into Natasha was too much to handle. Or worse, what if she ran into Jason and found out he had sent his precious new mate to kill her in the first place?

No ... he wouldn't do that. Natasha had been hiding out when Hunny had spotted her initially. Why hide if Jason had given his permission to have her killed?

Then again, Hunny hadn't believed her true mate capable of using her and discarding her like yesterday's trash either. She damned sure hadn't expected him to learn of her pregnancy and abandon her. An ache formed in her chest, ruthless in its intensity. She gripped the doorknob like a lifeline, a sense of hopelessness consuming her.

Stop thinking about Jason, she seethed inwardly. *You've had a cry, now it's time to move on.*

But that had been before his mate had attacked her. Before she'd found herself in a new place, with fresh wounds and none of her belongings. Hunny sucked in a ragged breath, her chin wobbling as she struggled to dig up a reserve of strength, an ounce of willpower to keep going. Only, she didn't feel strong. Not right now. She felt beaten down.

Worthless.

Uncertain.

Even if she made it back to her truck without issue, what then? Where would she go? Now that she'd been rejected, she truly had no home. She had belonged nowhere since her parents died, and now she never would. Even her true mate had discarded her.

She was completely alone.

Maybe ... maybe she'd just stay here for tonight. Hunny turned around, shifting back into her rabbit form and jumping onto the couch. Getting comfortable on a cushion, she laid down, facing the balcony.

Tonight, she'd rest. And tomorrow, she'd figure everything out.

Four

A knock on the front door startled Hunny awake. Her head jerked up, and she squinted from the bright sunlight pouring in through the windows. Her nose wrinkled as she caught the scent of a different bear shifter nearby.

She tensed, immediately wary. What time was it?

It had to be early; she never slept for more than a few hours at a time. Another sharp knock had her pushing to her feet, her paws sinking into the soft leather of the couch. She stared at the front door, tension knotting her muscles.

"Fuck's sake," the male upstairs grumbled, his voice thick with sleep. At the sound of his gravelly timbre, some of her anxiety eased.

She wasn't alone. And considering he'd let her sleep peacefully in his home after dressing her wounds, she really didn't think he'd hurt her. Not anymore.

As her bear friend with the sad eyes moved around upstairs, she jumped down from the couch, tucking herself under the coffee table to escape notice. Just because she was beginning to trust him didn't mean she'd blindly trust whoever the hell was visiting.

Heavy footfalls sounded on the stairs, and then she spotted bare feet on the wood floor as her bear shifter moved to the front door. Muttering under his breath, he ripped open the door. "The fuck you want?" he snapped in irritation.

Hunny's eyes widened in surprise. Was he always so disgruntled in the morning? He seemed fine last night.

Someone must have woken up on the wrong side of the bed.

"That's no way to greet your Alpha and brother," an unfamiliar male stated, his voice laced with humor. "Plan on letting me in or will you just stand in the doorway like a dickhead, Tank?"

Hunny wrinkled her nose. Her rescuer's name was *Tank?* It suited him, she guessed. He was a big, buff male who looked capable of steamrolling anyone.

Tank grunted, stepping aside and letting the other male enter. Hunny ducked her head out from under the table, intent on sneaking a peek at Tank's Alpha.

Instead, she caught an eyeful of Tank, and she found herself staring up at the big male in shock. Sweatpants hung low on his hips, and he was shirtless, big, strong muscles on display everywhere she looked. And damn, did she *look*. In fact, she tried to force her gaze anywhere else, but she was stuck, completely riveted on the way his muscles rippled as he crossed his arms in front of his chest.

A chest that had a healthy dusting of hair. Not only that, but he had a happy trail that dipped into his pants, leading somewhere equally impressive—she was sure of it. Realizing that she was drooling, she swallowed thickly.

I should look away before I do something stupid.

Like jumping out from under the table, climbing up his leg like a squirrel, and smashing her face all over his chest. It must have been the pregnancy hormones, or something, because all she could think about was how his hair looked like the perfect fur to build a nest with. But instead of a nest, she could just lay on that warm chest and—

Snap out of it! Hunny shook her head hard before turning her attention to the other clothed and less rugged-looking male.

They looked alike. He had long legs, huge muscles, and the same shade of brown hair as his brother, though his was combed back and his beard kept trimmed close to his face. He wore working boots, blue jeans, and a flannel, but where Tank looked like a sexy lumberjack, this guy looked like a wealthy entrepreneur on vacation in the mountains.

"What do you want, Murphy?" Tank asked, casting a small glance to the now empty couch. His brow furrowed, and he inhaled, like he was trying to hunt her down. She ducked back under the table before he could spot her. Although she was hiding, Hunny felt briefly tempted to stick a paw out, just to see if he'd notice.

Stop acting weird. Seriously, what was wrong with her? She'd seen her fair share of naked men, and Tank wasn't even naked, for fuck's sake!

"What do *I* want?" Murphy snorted. "You never answered me about the rabbit shifter. You found it injured in the woods. Did you leave it there? Did you bring it here?" He exhaled roughly. "It's here, isn't it?"

Tank grunted again.

"Why would you bring an unknown element into our territory? That's not like you."

"Technically, she was already in our territory."

Murphy turned back to his brother. "The rabbit shifter is a female?"

Another grunt from Tank. Hunny rolled her eyes. Was that his primary form of communication or something? She craned her head out from under the table again, wanting a better look at each brother. They were both extremely tall, but from her position, she couldn't see who was taller. Maybe Murphy?

"Pregnant, too. Feisty as hell." Tank scratched his beard. She preened at his last comment.

"Feisty how?"

Tank smirked absent-mindedly. "She bit the shit out of my hand."

"Are you *smiling*?" Murphy asked in surprise. Before Tank could answer, his brother looked around the living room and then nodded toward the upstairs room. "Where is this mystery female? In your bed?"

"Left her on the couch," Tank huffed. "Guess she's hiding somewhere." His eyes shot over to the coffee table, snapping right onto her location. Startled, Hunny jumped, smacking her head against the wood with a tiny thunk. Pain exploded along her temple, and she let out a soft hiss as she turned, hopping fully under the table once more.

Shit, that really hurt!

"What the hell was that?" Murphy asked in bewilderment. Tank didn't answer, and his brother sighed. "Fine. Remain aloof, as always. If the female intends to stay in bear clan territory for any length of time, though, I'll need to meet her. She needs to be vetted properly, otherwise she's a risk to our clan."

"I know."

"And yet you let her stay the night without following protocol," Murphy chided. "Do you know anything about her? Where she's from? What nest she belongs to? For all we know, she could be a lone shifter," he finished, uttering the last sentence like a curse.

She tried not to take it personally. Typically, lone shifters like herself were exiled from their packs, nests, etc. for committing crimes, or for other nefarious reasons. It wasn't common for someone to leave on their own; there was safety in numbers and shifters craved physical touch and care, the nurturing of their pack or clan.

As humans didn't know of their existence, a structured supernatural pack was important to a shifter's health and wellbeing. They were social creatures with an appreciation for a familial presence.

"Could be," Tank agreed. There was a beat of silence before he added, "I'll talk to her."

"Good." Murphy opened the front door and stepped out onto the porch. "Mom wants you to stop by the den later for dinner."

"Not tonight."

"Alright, Tank." The door clicked shut behind Murphy, leaving her and Tank alone.

Her ears pivoted toward the front door, straining to hear any movement from her companion as she hid out of sight. After a few seconds, and feeling incredibly nosy, Hunny moved back to her previous spot, peeking her head out once more.

She saw the door. But Tank was gone.

What? When had he moved? She hadn't heard a thing.

Suddenly, the table lifted, and Hunny was plucked up from the floor, squawking in surprise.

"Gotcha," Tank announced, lifting her up by the scruff of the neck until she was eye level with him. She tucked her legs in close to her body defensively. Before she even had a chance to hiss at him threateningly, he tucked her against his chest, placing an arm under her body to keep her steady. Warmth enveloped her, along with his woodsy scent, his chest hairs tickling her whiskers.

I can't believe he's manhandling me like this, she thought irritably. No one had ever picked her up in her rabbit form and just *held* her. It was frankly disrespectful. At least, it should have been.

Right?

She should just bite him—it would serve him right for treating her like an actual damned animal. Instead, she leaned in against him, soaking up his body heat.

He was so warm. And cozy.

Maybe this wasn't so bad, actually.

"You plan on shifting back anytime soon?" Tank asked. "Looks like you already did to heal. Can't imagine you plan to stay like this forever." Rather than answer, Hunny smashed her head against his chest, shuddering in delight. Yeah, this wasn't bad at all. And no, she didn't plan on shifting in front of him. Then he'd ask questions, and she'd likely end up word vomiting her troubles all over the place. She never could help herself; always preferring to talk things out, sorting it out in her own mind by doing so, if for no other reason.

Besides, as soon as he found out she was a lone shifter, he'd likely send her packing, and she wasn't ready to face the rest of the world. Not on her own. Not again. Not after she'd believed she'd finally found a pack, a family to call her own, and then had it all ripped away from her.

She'd give it another day to wallow in self-pity with this bear shifter, and then she'd gather her resolve and leave.

Tank walked over to the front door, opened it, and stepped onto the porch with her in tow. "Guess you'll need to use the bathroom out here, then."

Oh. Ugh! She hated peeing outside, but he had a point.

As soon as he set her down, she hopped down the porch steps and into a nearby bush to handle her business. She heard him moving around to the side of his house, loud enough so she could tell where he was. Like he wanted her to know where he was, perhaps so she didn't think he was trying to sneak a peek at her, which was hilarious when she was a foot long and covered head to toe in fur.

Gentlemanly, though, she'd give him that.

Once she finished, Hunny hopped out from under the bush, moving toward where she could still hear Tank. Rounding the corner of the small cabin, her eyes widened as she saw him lifting a giant log before dropping it down onto a flat tree stump. An axe was stuck in the ground beside it, the handle facing toward the sky.

Was he about to chop some wood? Without a shirt on? Her mouth watered once more at the thought, a small bit of drool running down her chin before she quickly wiped it away with the back of a paw.

Get ahold of yourself!

Tank spotted her, stopping his task and moving toward her. Her nose twitched in disappointment until he bent down, plucking her off the ground and back into his arms.

"Time for breakfast."

Right then, her stomach rumbled in agreement. She hadn't realized how hungry she was.

Grunting, he walked back into the cabin, shutting the door behind him and moving into the kitchen. Turning on the sink, he grabbed a dish towel and wet it. "Paws up, bunny."

What?

Confused, Hunny hesitantly lifted a front paw, snorting when he began to wipe the pad clean with the warm towel. This was so bizarre. A giant of a male, a freaking *bear* shifter, was carrying her around and cleaning her paws? When he finished the first front paw, she held out the other expectantly, feeling like rabbit royalty.

What was he going to do next? Put some clothes on her?

As soon as he finished with that paw, he flipped her quickly. Startled, Hunny squeaked as she fell backward, her spine connecting with his inner forearm as he cradled her like a damned baby. Bewildered, all she could do was stare up at him wide-eyed as he cleaned her back paws, his face lined with absolute concentration.

This is so weird. And embarrassing.

And ... kind of sweet?

Tossing the towel into the sink, Tank gently set Hunny onto the kitchen counter, right beside a set of barstools.

"Fruit for breakfast?" he asked, staring down at her. His eyes wandered over her before settling on her face, waiting for her response. She nodded eagerly, licking her snout when he turned away, his muscled, tanned back on full display as he moved to the refrigerator.

Opening it, he fished out several pieces of fruit, a carton of eggs, bacon, and a bowl of batter, covered in plastic wrap. Placing everything on the counter in front of her, he went to work, setting cookware on the stove before cleaning the fruit off in the sink. Grabbing a cutting board, he pulled a knife from a wooden block on the counter and cut up an apple, a watermelon, a mango, and several strawberries. He placed them neatly on a small plate and slid it in front of her before returning to make his own meal.

She nibbled on a piece of strawberry, feeling oddly relaxed as she watched him move around his kitchen. For someone so big, he was really graceful, each move he made purposeful. It was kind of hypnotic to watch, and soon enough, he was sliding his own food onto a large plate. Moving around the kitchen counter, he dropped onto the barstool beside her. It squeaked slightly under his weight. He set his plate next to hers.

Tank dug into his meal, and Hunny did the same with hers, her teeth clicking together as she nibbled. After a few minutes, she made a soft purr of gratitude, barely glancing at him. He paused, a forkful of food halfway up to his lips. "You're welcome," he replied gruffly.

They ate the rest of their breakfast in comfortable silence.

CHAPTER II

Five

After a quick breakfast and clean up, Tank set the little cottontail onto the couch, reluctant to let her go. Her fur was thick and soft, and some possessive part of him enjoyed carrying her around in his arms.

"I'll be right back," he said, ignoring the irritation in his throat. He never talked this much, but after the visit from his brother this morning and the little rabbit refusing to shift back, he'd already overexerted himself by chatting with her, as limited as the conversation had been. He often went days in absolute silence, which worked out perfectly, as he relished his solitude.

Usually.

Now he was itching to converse with his house guest.

Hurrying up the stairs, Tank strode to his closet, ripping open the door and stepping inside the small room. He turned to the dresser on the right, opening the top drawer and pulling out a pair of boxer briefs and thick socks. Opening the next drawer, he grabbed a flannel and a pair of worn denim jeans. Dressing quickly, he put on a used pair of steel-toed boots before heading back downstairs.

Tank eyed the bunny, now lounging on the couch, before nodding toward the front door. "Gonna cut some wood."

She raised her head from her paws, jumping down to the ground. Hopping over to the door, she looked at him expectantly.

He stared down at her, brows raised in surprise. She wanted to come with him?

"It'll be boring out there." He gripped the door handle slowly, waiting for her to change her mind. "Won't be talking." He pointed to his neck, his scars hidden by his long beard. She tracked the movement, nose twitching. "Throat hurts after a while," he explained. Even now, his vocals sounded strained, too deep and gravelly, each word a small, painful stab.

In answer, she pawed at the door.

"Alright, let's go."

Opening the door, Tank waited diligently for her to hop through before following her out onto the porch. It was late in the morning now, with the sun shining brightly overhead. Despite its rays, there was a slight chill in the air, the weather brisk enough that even he felt mildly cold. He eyed his bunny carefully.

She seemed unbothered by the weather, so he grunted and moved to the side of the house where he had a large pile of logs waiting for him. Some were from fallen trees in the woods, others from trees he'd cut down in his spare time. As winter was approaching in a few months, he'd planned on stocking up on firewood for himself and his clan within the next eight weeks until winter struck.

But now, after his talk with Murphy, he had a feeling he'd be using this wood for something else. Discreetly, he watched his bunny hop around a few feet from him as he grabbed his axe handle, pulling it free from the earth.

If she planned on staying for any length of time, there wouldn't be enough room in his cabin for her. Not as it was. But he'd built his home all on his own; he was more than capable of adding on a room. He could also build some furniture, so she wouldn't need to sleep on the couch at night.

It'd be better for her and her kit that way.

As he lined up his axe with the center of the log, he wondered why he was being so presumptuous. She likely wouldn't stay within his territory for anything more than another night, at most. And if she spoke with Murphy before then and decided to stay, Tank doubted she'd want to live with him. Why would she?

She barely knew him.

He frowned, suddenly irritated. And then his brows furrowed in confusion. Why did the thought of her leaving piss him off? Did he even want her to live with him? No.

Of course not.

She might smell good, and clearly he found her entertaining, but he enjoyed living alone. He preferred being isolated from everyone—that way he could pretend no one in his family pitied him for losing his true mate. He didn't need a roommate, anyway, especially a pregnant female.

She wasn't his responsibility, nor was her kit. In fact, he'd be doing himself a favor by going back inside and stopping his own foolishness before it even began.

Without missing a beat, Tank swung the axe, cutting through the log like butter. Tossing the pieces of wood aside, he grabbed another log and dropped it onto the stump, slicing it in half just as easily. The bunny stopped her frolicking, finding a thick patch of damp grass and nestling down into it. She watched as he got to work, falling into a pattern and moving like a well-oiled machine until he had a neat stack of wood.

He'd need a lot more wood than this though.

She shivered, drawing his attention as she shifted slightly on her feet before settling down again.

Was she cold? She was tiny in this form, and even though she was a shifter, he doubted she could maintain enough body heat in these temperatures for any extended period.

Propping his axe along the stump, Tank removed his flannel as he walked over to her. With his free hand, he scooped her up, enjoying her sweet scent of honey, lavender, and vanilla. Dropping the flannel onto the ground, he set her on top of it. Next, he crouched down, fluffing the piece of clothing up in case she wanted to burrow into it.

"Good now?" he asked, his eyes locking onto the crown of her head as she leaned forward, nuzzling his palm with her nose.

He'd take that as a yes.

Never in his life had he been so tuned into someone before, and he hadn't even spoken with her. He didn't even know what her name was or what she looked like. Yet here he was, fluffing up a bed he'd made with his fucking shirt because she'd shivered.

Not to mention the need he'd felt to come out here and chop wood so he could permanently alter his home for her. This entire situation was ridiculous. He didn't behave like this. He didn't find stray shifters and go out of his way to ensure their comfort, especially if it deterred his own.

What had gotten into him?

He didn't know. But as he returned to his task, picking up his axe and swiftly cutting log after log, he realized he didn't really care why he was behaving this way. He'd felt protective of her since he'd saved her last night. It was instinctual.

It felt right.

So, if he wanted to prep a room on the off-chance she stayed with him for a while longer, then he'd do it.

He just might not mention it to any of his brothers in case they planned on busting his balls for the rest of his days.

A fter a few hours of grueling work outside, and an interesting afternoon of snacking and watching TV with his rabbit—who had a lot to say about what show they watched considering she couldn't even speak—it was time for dinner.

"You want to change back now?" He nodded toward the plates and silverware he'd set out on the counter in preparation for their next meal. "Maybe eat dinner with some utensils?" he joked.

The rabbit twitched her nose, looking around the room before staring back at him, her eyes wide. He'd placed her on the counter again, mostly just because he enjoyed keeping an eye on her while he completed other tasks.

"Don't know what you're trying to say."

She huffed, hopping over to him. She reached out with a front paw, batting at his stomach. His brows rose until she leaned forward, snagging his T-shirt with her teeth and tugging lightly.

Oh.

"You want clothes first?" Usually shifters weren't shy about nudity, especially not when it came to shifting, so it hadn't even occurred to him she'd want to cover up. Grunting, he pulled the T-shirt up over his head, grabbed her, and moved from the kitchen and around the corner. Setting her and the shirt on the ground, he walked back to the kitchen, leaving her to her own devices.

He remained aloof, though he couldn't deny the way his stomach churned with anticipation, acutely aware of every noise in the cabin as he pulled a few trout from the fridge and began preparing them. He'd just chopped off the last head and tossed it into the garbage disposal when he heard the faint sound of bones popping, followed by a delicate, feminine sigh.

His gut clenched at that one sound, his mouth watering as lust hit him from out of nowhere. His cock swelled in his jeans, desire licking at his balls.

What in the hell was wrong with him?

His fingers were bone white as he clutched the butcher knife in a death grip, his cock harder than he'd ever felt in his life. He pressed himself against the kitchen counter, desperate to hide his erection. She could turn the corner at any second. He needed to calm the fuck down before she scented his lust.

Pull yourself together. All she did was sigh, you perverse fuck.

Tank shook his head to clear it, thinking about anything other than the woman in the other room. Towels, chores he hadn't gotten to yet, artwork that he found boring. Luckily, that did the trick, and his cock no longer felt like it would punch through the denim material.

Releasing a shuddering breath, Tank went back to preparing the fish, forcing his shoulders to relax.

His head jerked up a moment later when he heard the gentle sound of feet moving cautiously on the hardwood floor, every ounce of his being focused on her footsteps as she drew closer.

After a second, a young woman stepped into view, and Tank nearly lost the grip on his knife, his heart thundering in his ears.

She stopped in the entryway to the kitchen, eyeing him nervously as she shifted onto the balls of her feet, his shirt absolutely dwarfing her body, hanging to her knees.

She was fucking beautiful.

Tank felt like a goddamn idiot for gaping at her, but he couldn't look away. She was short, with long lilac-colored hair, fair skin, plump pink lips, and a small upturned nose. A dusting of freckles was scattered over her cheeks and she had the brightest, most vivid green eyes he'd ever seen. He'd known she was a submissive shifter by her scent alone, but seeing her small frame now, it was more apparent than ever.

Aside from her beauty, it was impossible to not notice how thin she looked, or and the dark circles under her eyes, as if she hadn't slept or eaten properly in months.

Tank didn't like that. He didn't like that *at all*.

She bit her lower lip, glancing away from him for a second before she looked back. Their eyes locked, and Tank felt like a bolt of lightning had struck him, his heart picking up a frantic beat.

"Hi," she murmured, her voice almost as sweet as her scent. It was light, and as delicate as she looked. "I'm Hunny," she added after a few seconds of silence.

"Hunny?" Tank's lips twitched as he suppressed a laugh, his beard doing nothing to conceal the action. Her eyes snapped to his mouth and narrowed.

"Is something funny, *Tank?*" she asked sarcastically, raising a dark-colored brow and crossing her arms in front of her chest, all but daring him to answer.

"Just your name." Her lips parted in shock, a small squeak escaping from her throat that had him adding, "Hunny Bunny is funny. Admit it."

"That's not why I'm named Hunny, you—you—*ugh!*" She threw her hands up in the air in exasperation, and the shirt she wore rose several inches, revealing smooth, creamy thighs. "And that's a weird thing for you to say, considering your name is Tank."

"Tank's a nickname, Hunny," he answered, enjoying the easy way her name slid off his tongue. He even enjoyed the way she sassed him.

Some of her ire deflated as she asked curiously, "What's your name, then?"

"Henry."

"Oh."

He smirked. "Still think it's weird?"

She lifted her chin. "Maybe."

With a deep, rusty laugh, Tank looked down at the fish he'd begun preparing. "You eat meat?" A lot of small shifters didn't.

"Only fish, coincidentally. I'm more of a vegetarian than anything else, Henry." He shook his head at her use of his name. Taking a few steps forward until she was standing at the other end of the kitchen island, she eyed the fish hungrily. "It's been a while since I had trout," she added.

"Sit." He nodded toward one of the barstools before continuing his work. He'd fill her with some nice cooked trout, a salad, and some baked bread.

Maybe they'd talk a bit, too. Finally.

His throat would hurt like a son of a bitch by the end of the night, but suddenly he didn't mind so much.

Six

Hunny had a hard time keeping her eyes off of Tank. She'd felt drawn to him all day long, her gaze riveted by the graceful way he moved despite his size. He might have been even taller than she'd originally assumed, now that she was getting a good look at him in her human form. And what a sight he was, standing there half naked in a kitchen while making her dinner.

She bit her lower lip, looking away from his tanned chest as she made her way over to the barstool. At least when he'd been chopping wood like a man on a mission, his chest had been covered. Because if she'd seen his muscles damp with sweat, his chest hairs glistening in the sunlight, she probably would have lost her mind.

Get your head out of the gutter, you sex fiend, she chided silently, doing her best to ignore the delicious smell of cloves and musk that clung to her borrowed shirt. The material hung over her body like a loose dress, but it was warm and smelled just like Tank, which made her feel protected.

"So"—she shifted in her seat before looking up at him—"do you enjoy fishing?"

He smirked, seasoning the fish. "Depends on how you mean, Hunny."

She shivered as he said her name, that deep gravelly voice making it sound like he'd whispered directly into her ear, like a lover might.

And then his words sank in. She cocked her head to the side in confusion. "Usually people use a fishing pole—" Her eyes widened and she let out a small laugh. "Don't tell me you catch fish while you're shifted."

Tank shrugged, turning away from her to place the fish in a skillet on the stovetop. His sculpted back greeted her, and despite her resolve to stop eyeing him like a piece of meat, Hunny leaned forward to get a better look until she was practically on the countertop.

The stool squeaked, giving her away, and he looked over his shoulder, his chocolate-brown eyes heating as they locked onto her. Startled, she dropped back onto the stool immediately, her face flaming with embarrassment.

Oh, God.

He'd caught her looking at him like a perv!

He returned to his task. "My bear enjoys catching fish, and I clean it all thoroughly when I bring it back. I assume it's much like when you feel the urge to nest."

The image of his chest hair popped into her head, causing her cheeks to heat even further. Yeah, her urge to build a nest using his hair had been nearly overwhelming, so she understood what he meant. Luckily, she didn't feel the need to do that now.

Well ...

"I get it," she replied. "No judgment here."

Tank grunted in answer, moving to the fridge and grabbing some things before returning to the stove.

"Need to ask," he began after a few minutes of comfortable silence had stretched between them. "You in bad with the Moon Rose pack?"

She stilled, her face draining of color at the simple question. She should have expected he'd ask something like that, but for whatever reason, she felt completely blindsided by his question. Probably because this entire day, she hadn't thought about Jason at all, too entertained by Tank's mannerisms, the way he completed his sexy lumberjack chores, and how he'd let her boss him around while they'd watched TV.

For a scary-looking male, he'd sat down and watched hours of her favorite reality TV show while she'd snuggled up against his leg, dozing on and off. Every time she'd woken up, she thought the channel would have changed, but nope. He'd catered to her then, just like he'd done every second she'd been here.

Moving her hand to her stomach, she rubbed her lower belly soothingly. "I just came to Montana about a month ago," she responded vaguely. "That's not really enough time to make enemies, is it?"

He turned toward her then, a set of tongs held tightly in his hand. "So the wolf hunting you down wasn't an enemy?"

"I—" Hunny's fingers twisted into her borrowed shirt. "It's complicated, Tank."

She winced when she said his nickname. Was it bad that she'd rather call him Henry? Physically, he might be Tank, but Henry suited his sweet demeanor perfectly.

"You don't have to tell me anything if you don't want to," he finally said, grimacing as his voice wavered. Her eyes shot to his neck, where he'd pointed at earlier in the day. She could just see scarring there, behind his beard, where he had obviously sustained some sort of permanent injury. Not only had he been helping her through everything, he'd ignored his own pain to comfort her. "Just need to know if my clan should expect trouble."

Her heart dropped into the pit of her stomach. "I didn't think about that." She pushed herself from the stool, suddenly uneasy. What if Natasha came back here? Or Jason? She'd learned, *painfully*, that she'd never really known him, despite him being her mate. What if he found out she was here and caused problems for Tank and his family? She didn't want that. Hadn't she been enough of a burden already? "I-I should leave."

She'd barely made it into the living room before Tank was on her, his fingers wrapping around her wrist. He tugged gently, spinning her around. She was so surprised by the action, she bumped into him, her body going flush against his for one, all-too-brief second.

"I don't want you to go," he murmured, his hold on her wrist firm and comforting, something she was so acutely aware of. "Do you want to leave?"

Did she?

Hunny couldn't remember a time after her parents' deaths that she'd ever felt truly at ease. Even during the few weeks she'd spent with Jason, her stupid true mate, it had never been quite right. A constant gnawing in her gut. She'd waited for the other shoe to drop, or for something terrible to happen. And it had, spectacularly.

So far, she hadn't felt like that here, like the world was going to be swept out from under her. She'd slept the entire night without issue, eaten more than she had in a long time, and she just felt ... she didn't know what, honestly. Rested? At peace? Whatever this feeling was, she liked it, and she didn't want to leave, at least not until she'd properly licked her wounds and came up with a plan to move on.

Right now, she had nothing anyway. No means to leave Montana, no idea of where to go, what to do. She was a pregnant lone shifter.

"No, I like it here," she finally told him, staring at his lips.

"Then stay, Hunny. You're welcome to stay." His thumb slid over her pulse, caressing her skin. "As long as you want."

"Here?" Feeling suddenly shy, she looked away from him, staring around the small cabin. "I don't want to be a burden to you. You've already done so much for me, and my needs are only going to compound the further along I get with my pregnancy."

They hadn't discussed that yet, or much of anything, but she knew he could smell it on her. What kind of male wanted a female, pregnant with another male's babies, invading his space? And his home was small—soon enough she'd inevitably take over his cabin, even without intending to.

"Having you here has been ... refreshing." Tank shrugged, slowly releasing her wrist. She kind of hated how cold she felt without his touch. "You can even have the bed. I'll take the couch."

Hunny snorted. "There's no way your feet won't dangle off the edge. No, I'll stay on the couch."

He smirked. "So you *are* staying."

Was she?

He must have seen the indecision warring on her face, because he reached up, cupping her cheek. Her eyes shot to his. Determination shined in his gaze, and she had a feeling that he'd speak until his voice gave out if that's what it took to convince her. "Give it a few days, at least. Figure out what you need to do first and then decide."

"Okay."

The words had barely left her mouth before Tank moved. Placing an arm behind her knees and lower back, he scooped her up and into his arms, moving quickly into the kitchen. She barely had time to brace a hand against his chest before she was back on her stool, gaping at him in shock as he returned to the stove.

"I can't believe you just picked me up like that!" she exclaimed, unsure if she should feel outraged or baffled. She'd gotten used to him carrying her around as a bunny, but now he was doing it while she was in her human form?

He shrugged, plating their food and making his way over to her. "I enjoy carrying you."

She raised a haughty brow, ignoring the way her mouth watered as the smell of cooked trout reached her nose. "You think that now, but if you spoil me, I'll demand you carry me everywhere."

Lips twitching, he sat down beside her, dwarfing her small frame. "Eat. Let me know if you want more."

"More?" She eyed the plate full of fish, salad, and two bread rolls. She didn't even know if she could handle all of this, let alone a second helping. But the delicious smell overrode any doubts and she'd barely had the thought before she dug into her plate, devouring most of it before she'd come up to inhale.

Okay, maybe she was hungrier than she'd realized. She polished off her last bread roll, and before she could even mourn its loss, Tank took the remaining roll off his plate, dropping it onto hers without a word.

Her throat clogged with emotion at the simple yet kind gesture, and she looked over at him. "Thank you, Henry. Not just for dinner, but for saving my life. My baby's, too." Her nose tingled and her eyes watered as gratitude overwhelmed her. He looked at her then, his expression concerned as she struggled to compose herself. "I, uh, I'm just really glad that you found me when you did." Her voice cracked, and a fat tear spilled from her eye, tracking down her cheek.

And then the floodgates opened, and she began weeping, her chest heaving as a barrage of tears ran down her face unchecked.

His eyes filled with alarm.

"Oh shit!" she exclaimed through a hard sob, wiping quickly at her face with the back of her hand. "I ne-never cry. This is s-so embarrassing!"

This had to be pregnancy hormones, right? What a terrible time to have a meltdown! Tank was probably rethinking his offer now, mortified she'd turned into an emotional mess because of a bread roll.

Pull yourself together, bitch!

Instead, she only cried harder.

Tank stared at her in bewilderment, probably just as startled as she was by her outburst. "I'm so sorry, I literally can't stop," she wailed, snatching up a napkin from the counter and covering her face, like she could spare them both from this entire horrible experience by hiding behind it. She probably looked like a freaking lunatic—

He plucked her up from her stool, careful to keep the shirt covering her ass as he palmed her bottom. Instinctively, she wrapped her legs around his waist and her arms around his neck, removing the napkin to drop her face into the crook of his shoulder. She hid there, partly because she was too embarrassed to face the world, but also because his scent helped calm her down.

He made gentle noises in his throat, rubbing a hand soothingly up and down her spine as he left the kitchen, carrying her around like precious cargo.

"Come now, darlin'. We'll watch some more of that housewives show you like," he bargained, the stress evident in his voice nearly causing her to laugh, despite how much she was crying. "Take your mind off things."

"Yeah?" she asked, sniffling into his neck. She laid her head on his shoulder as he sat on the couch, his hand dropping to her hips as he kept her firmly in his lap.

The position was extremely intimate. She should move away, sit down beside him, and apologize for acting so irrationally.

But as he turned the TV on, the theme song of her favorite show filling the room, she didn't do any of that.

Instead, she clung to him a little tighter, letting the warmth of his body and his addicting scent lull her to sleep.

Seven

T ank spent most of the evening with a sleeping Hunny pressed flush against him, the soft swells of her breasts cushioned against the hard muscles of his chest. Her sweet scent enveloped him as the TV droned on in the background, practically static in his ears as he instead listened to her soft breathing, her warm breath skating over his exposed neck. He hated it, or rather, hated how anticipation burned in his gut each time her breath kissed his skin.

It was torture, pure and simple.

At some point after she'd cried herself to sleep, she'd moved to get more comfortable, settling herself more firmly into his lap. He'd gotten hard instantly, his dick like a steel monster trying to punch free of his clothing. It didn't help that every time he inhaled, her delicious scent filled his lungs, keeping his desire simmering for the last few hours. His erection hadn't gone down, not once, but she hadn't noticed it at all, peacefully slumbering in his arms.

Thank fuck for that.

As it was, he was afraid to move, to do anything to alert her to the literal dickhead that refused to take a hint that now was *not* the time. Hunny required tenderness and care, and although Tank was terrible at administering both, he was determined enough to try.

So his dick needed to fuck right off.

He took another deep breath, counting in his head until he reached one hundred. It did nothing to quell his desire. So he counted again, gritting his teeth as Hunny rubbed her cheek along his shoulder in her sleep, her fingers playing with his thick dusting of chest hair. She mumbled something and he lost count, studying the gentle curve of her face instead.

He should get up, put her to sleep in his bed, and go out. As the enforcer for tonight, he needed to do a perimeter check along his clan's territory in the next few hours. The run would help him clear his head. But he didn't move, not yet. Tank closed his eyes, enjoying the faint sounds of his little rabbit.

I'll get up in a minute, he thought lazily, laying his hand on top of Hunny's. *Just a minute.*

A loud bang startled Tank awake.

He jolted forward on the sofa, his arms wrapping around Hunny's back when she almost slid right off of him. She gave a surprised squawk, her nails digging into his shoulders and her thighs squeezing around his waist.

"What the hell was that?!" she exclaimed, her voice thick with sleep. "Henry?"

"Dunno," he rasped, holding her closer as he rested his head in the crook of her neck, breathing her in. He enjoyed hearing his name on her lips. No one ever called him anything other than Tank, so hearing his birth name felt ... *intimate.* Something shared just between the two of them.

Hesitantly, her fingers slipped through his hair, massaging the base of his neck as he cradled her to him. How long had he slept? It felt like more than a handful of hours because, for the first time in years, he actually felt well-rested.

Birds chirped outside, and his brow furrowed in confusion. His eyes shot to the nearest window, at the sunlight streaming in through the glass. "Fuck," he growled.

He'd slept the whole night like this!

"What—" Before Hunny could finish her question, he gently plopped her onto the couch beside him, pushing to his feet.

"I missed my patrol," he answered gruffly, frustrated with himself for his lack of control. He should have known holding Hunny like that was dangerous; she calmed him too much, made him relish the simplest little things—like the sound of her breathing as she slept.

Another loud bang sounded, much easier to pinpoint now that he was conscious. Grumbling under his breath, he beelined for the front door. Aggravated, he ripped it open, fully expecting Murphy to lay into him for missing his shift. What kind of cruel punishment would Murph conjure up for his mishap?

"Oh! There's my baby boy," Tabitha Sinclair declared loudly, gently tapping Tank's cheek as she pushed past him and into the house, her youngest son, Jasper, following directly after her. "I heard you might need some help today, Tank."

"I thought I was your baby boy?" Jasper asked with a frown, nodding at Tank in greeting as the two of them walked into his home like they owned the place.

Tank's upper lip curled in irritation. They knew he despised having his home invaded like this, and yet they'd wandered their nosy asses right on in without invitation.

This had to be Murphy's revenge, the evil fucker. Tank had to hand it to his older brother; this punishment was diabolical.

As much as he loved his mother and his little brother, Tank hated unannounced visitors. He required ample notice to charge his social batteries for any and every occasion, and he *never* interacted with people in the morning, finding it extremely taxing.

So far, Hunny had been the only exception; he felt good when she was near, no matter the time of day. It was odd, really. Her presence in his home didn't feel like an intrusion, but an addition to it. Natural, even.

"Oh, dear, you know you—" Tabitha stopped in her tracks, a delighted squeal leaving her mouth as she spotted Hunny on the couch. "Oh! You must be the bunny shifter. What a beauty you are. Tank, isn't she beautiful?"

Tank's jaw clenched, unsure of what to say. Obviously, he thought she was beautiful. Breathtaking, especially with her hair a slight mess and her eyes drowsy, giving her a sultry appearance. But he certainly didn't want to voice any of that out loud, neither did he want to make her uncomfortable.

Hunny sat awkwardly on the couch, her mouth hanging open as she reached for a throw pillow. She placed it on her lap, hiding her bare thighs from view. "I—" Clearing her throat, Hunny gave a forced smile. "Yes, hi. I'm Hunny."

"Hunny?" Jasper snorted. "No wonder Tank didn't show up for his shift last night. He fucking loves hon—"

"Shut the fuck up," Tank interrupted, smacking the back of his younger brother's head hard.

"Ow!" Jasper hissed. "What the *fuc*—"

"Boys!" Tabitha scolded, turning from Hunny and batting each of their ears. For someone several inches shorter than her sons, she'd perfected her aim over the years, and his ear rang from the impact of her palm connecting solidly. "Behave yourselves!"

Abruptly, Hunny laughed, the sound delicate and pure, erasing whatever retort was on the tip of Tank's tongue. His gaze snapped to her face, seeing a small flash of a smile before she covered her mouth with her hand. "I'm sorry. Laughing is rude. But you're both so big and your mom is this tiny little thing. I didn't think she'd just clobber you like that."

Tank cleared his throat, his face heating. Luckily, his beard covered most of his embarrassment, otherwise he was sure Jasper would use it as yet another thing to rib him for, the prick. Unfortunately, his mom was staring right at him. Her lips parted in surprise and her eyes widened, almost like she'd seen a ghost. His brows furrowed in confusion at her sudden change in demeanor and she looked away abruptly.

"Well, Hunny," Tabitha said sweetly, morphing from a street fighter back into a loving mother before Tank's very eyes. "When you have a bunch of cubs that outgrow you before they're teenagers, you get creative with your disciplinary methods."

"You're not even that short." Jasper rolled his eyes. "I mean, five-seven isn't *tall*, but it's more than average for females these days."

"You're too kind," Tabitha drawled, sending Tank another odd glance. "There's a reason I decided to not have more cubs after you were born."

Jasper furrowed his brow. "Because I was the perfect specimen after four failed attempts?"

"The perfect pain in the ass," Tank grumbled.

Hunny's lips quivered again, like she was trying to hold back another smile. It was a shame, really. He wanted to see her like that again; radiant and happy.

"I'm sorry for barging in here unannounced," Tabitha stated, sending Tank a pointed look. "But Murphy mentioned your guest might need some clothes and a checkup." His mother lifted her hand, and that's when he noticed her holding a plastic bag stuffed full of clothes. Had she been holding that when she'd walloped him and Jasper? She must have been.

He hadn't even noticed.

Hunny jumped up from the couch, reaching for the bag immediately. "Oh wow, I'd love to change into something." She blushed, looking down at her borrowed shirt. "This probably looks like something happened between me and your son, but it didn't."

Tabitha blinked once. "Looks like *what* happened, dear?" she asked, a little *too* innocently.

Jasper smirked. "Like she and Tank just got done fu—"

"I'll rip you apart if you say one more word," Tank snapped at his brother, his fingers itching to do just that. The little shit might be a few years younger, but Tank would have no problem kicking his ass if he embarrassed Hunny.

"Now I see why your mom didn't want more kids. You're a bit of a shithead," Hunny cut in suddenly. She sent Tank an amused look. "Can I watch when you beat him up?"

Tabitha looked between Tank and Hunny quickly and then giggled. "Oh, I like you, Hunny." Ignoring her two boys, she wrapped an arm around Hunny's waist, steering her toward the stairs. "You know, I've always wanted a daughter ..."

Tank watched his little rabbit walk off, his gut clenching with each step she took away from him.

"Someone's a bit riled up this morning," Jasper teased when the women were upstairs. He laughed as Tank grabbed him by the scruff of the neck and hauled him right back outside. "Ouch!" Tank closed the door softly behind him before he shoved the male forward, smirking when his brother almost toppled down the porch steps.

Jasper righted himself just in time, whipping around to grin sheepishly at Tank.

They'd had a tumultuous relationship their entire lives, which happened a lot with bear shifter siblings. Too much testosterone in a house full of males, and they'd always played rough. It didn't help that when Tank had lost his mate at such a young age, he'd closed himself off from everyone. Sometimes it felt like the relationships with his family had frozen at that point, never developing further. Trapped in a kind of stasis.

He knew that was his fault, but it was easier that way. Or at least, that's what he'd told himself for the past several years.

Tank pointed at Jasper, his expression promising death. "You better behave yourself around my—" He cut himself off abruptly, snarling under his breath when he realized he'd almost called Hunny his woman. "Hunny isn't sure if she wants to stay with the clan." *With me*, he silently added. "And I won't have you scaring her off."

Jasper held up his hands in surrender, some of the childish humor fading from his eyes. "Alright, brother. I apologize." He remained silent for all of two seconds before adding, "Do you always sleep on the couch? Or only when hot females are visiting?"

Tank sighed. "I'm going to kill you."

"That's rude, considering I covered your shift last night when you didn't show up. You could thank me for helping," Jasper added with a smug smile.

Tank raised a brow. "Fuck you."

Jasper's smile morphed into a full-on grin. "You're acting different."

"What do you mean?" Tank asked distractedly, his throat already irritating him. He looked back toward the house, wondering if it had been a mistake to leave his mother with Hunny for any length of time.

Tabitha was a force of a woman, and he knew she could be overwhelming. But she was kind and genuine, and part of him hoped that would help sway Hunny with her decision to remain here.

Jasper shrugged. "Usually I act like a prick and you grunt at me once and then ignore me. But you're far more lively today than I've seen you in years. A rude dick, sure, but a lively rude dick."

"Shut it," Tank muttered, his brow furrowing as Jasper's words sank in. Was he behaving differently? He didn't think so, though he had to admit that he didn't feel drained like he usually did at this point in a conversation. Not that he ever really got this *far* into a conversation.

Unsure of what to do with Jasper's comment, Tank moved from the porch and wandered to the side of the house, feeling the sudden urge to chop up some logs. It calmed his nerves. Only, he'd chopped all the logs yesterday, leaving him with nothing but stacks of wood.

Too bad he wasn't holding Hunny in his arms; that seemed to calm him more than anything over the past few days.

Jasper whistled loudly as he spotted the high stacks of wood, some logs far longer than the others. "You've been busy." Tank grunted in answer. "We've got several months until we need this much wood, Tank. So why'd you cut all this up so soon?"

"Might need to build another room," he said eventually, stroking his beard. "Hunny will need a place to stay, and my cabin's too small right now."

"I see. And you've got no problem sharing your space with her and a kit?"

"No."

Uncharacteristically, Jasper remained silent for a few minutes, the two of them just staring at the stacks of wood.

Eventually, his brother replied, his voice thicker than usual, "You know, you'll probably need a spare bathroom downstairs, too. Women love extra bathrooms."

"Yeah?" Tank hadn't thought about that.

Jasper hummed. "Shifters usually carry to term in about eight months, right? Kit will be here before you know it. We should probably chop down some more trees."

"Right now?"

Jasper shrugged nonchalantly. "Doesn't have to be today. You down for some company tomorrow?" Tank grunted in answer, and Jasper clapped him on the shoulder, squeezing slightly before letting go. "Tomorrow it is then, big brother."

Tank nodded absent-mindedly, already thinking of what other things Hunny might need. Tomorrow sounded good.

Eight

Hunny dug through the bag of clothes sitting on the bed, her cheeks burning from Tabitha's constant staring. She knew what the other woman was thinking; Jasper had almost stated it outright until Tank had threatened to kill him. They both assumed something sexual was going on between her and Tank.

But it wasn't—of course not.

Hunny was barely out of a failed mating, and ... and Tank was ... Well, she didn't know *what* he was, exactly, but he hadn't made a move on her at all. He probably wasn't even interested in her like that.

She grimaced at the ball of anxiety that had formed in the pit of her stomach, plucking up a random shirt as she fought herself internally. She didn't even know why she felt upset by the thought of his lack of interest. She was pregnant with *another* male's baby. She couldn't dive headlong into a fling right now anyway, especially with someone she barely knew.

Except ... Aside from the startling way she'd woken up this morning, she couldn't remember a time when she'd slept better. She'd felt warm and safe all night, wrapped up in Tank's arms. It had felt like she belonged there. She'd even fallen asleep with her face buried in his neck, his beard tickling her skin. But she didn't care, too consumed with inhaling his scent with every breath she'd taken.

She couldn't get enough of it.

His scent clung to her even now, and every inhale felt intimate. Stupid of her to think like that, but it was true. And now that she was upstairs, she couldn't escape his natural cologne. This entire upper floor smelled like him—woodsy and strong, with a hint of berries. It was so intoxicating, and the rabbit in her just wanted to roll around in his bed, burrow under his sheets, and never come out.

She'd just bet that if she peeled back those covers, she'd find heaven—

Snap out of it. Hunny shook her head as she grabbed a pair of jeans from the bag.

"Did you hear me, dear?" Tabitha asked, pulling Hunny from her thoughts.

Her head shot up, and she winced in embarrassment. "I'm sorry. I was a little distracted." *Thinking about your son and how delicious he smells.*

God, what was wrong with her? She was like an addict when it came to Tank.

Tabitha smiled politely. "I asked if you intend to stay here long?"

Hunny's eyes widened. "Oh! I, um, I haven't really thought about it."

Mostly because she knew being a lone shifter was a touchy subject. If she had her talk with Murphy, and told him she was alone, pregnant with another Alpha's baby, *and* rejected, he'd think she was defective—that Jason had sensed something broken within her and kicked her to the curb. That she'd been tossed out by her previous nest. He probably wouldn't even believe her if she explained everything. He would assume she was trouble, too much of a problem to keep around.

Could she really blame Murphy for that?

He wasn't her Alpha. His purpose was to protect his clan from threats—even a lone bunny shifter. When that inevitably happened, she'd have to leave Montana with her tail tucked between her legs.

She'd never see Tank again. Her heart clenched painfully in her chest at the thought.

The last few days with Tank had been amazing, some of the easiest days she'd had in years. She wasn't ready for them to end. But how long could she avoid this talk with his older brother? A few more days? A week?

Maybe she should lie about her circumstances, but she was terrible at that, and it would be easy for another shifter to sense her unease and call her out on it.

The older woman's gaze softened. "Do you have a family to get back to? A mate, perhaps? I don't see a mark on you—"

"No mate," Hunny cut in abruptly. She cleared her throat. Suddenly ashamed, she glanced down at the clothes in her hand. "Not anymore, at least."

"Oh." Tabitha sent her a small, sad smile. "No wonder you and Tank get along. His own mate passed away when he was younger, before they could claim each other, but even still; a loss like that changes a person."

Hunny's eyes went wide with shock, and her heart physically ached at the news.

Poor Henry.

Shaking her head, Hunny blurted out, "My mate isn't dead. He just ..." She paused, unsure if she wanted to say anything else. But knowing that Tank's mate got lumped into the same category as Jason didn't sit right with her. Tank's mate had probably been a lovely female. There wasn't a lovely thing about Jason. Not in the slightest. She felt she had to explain.

Her throat clogged with emotion, and she clenched her jaw, swallowing thickly as she tried to calm down. "He led me to believe he wanted to mate with me, got me pregnant, and then he rejected me in favor of a dominant shifter. He said I was too weak to stand beside him."

It kind of felt cathartic to say it out loud.

Tabitha gasped, and Hunny's eyes shot to her face, just in time to watch a flurry of emotions cross over it. Shock, outrage, and then, oddly enough, a bitter fury that morphed the sweet-looking lady into some kind of avenging angel. "What kind of low-life piece of shit would do that? To their *mate?* Abandon you at such a crucial time, and for another female?" Her voice rose with each word until she was practically shouting.

"Please keep your voice down," Hunny hissed, moving to the railing and looking over the side. No one was below in the living room or the kitchen. And she didn't hear anyone moving around on the first floor either. Had the guys gone outside? She turned back to Tank's mom. "I haven't told your son anything yet. It's kind of embarrassing, and honestly, I'm ashamed that I was so blind to my mate's schemes."

"Oh, dear." Tabitha blew out a breath, some of the red draining from her face. "You shouldn't feel embarrassed. You believed your true mate held your best interest at heart, and it's his loss that he didn't. Be grateful that he showed you the type of male he was before he claimed you." She frowned. "I'm sure you don't feel that way currently. But in time, you will."

Tears pricked Hunny's eyes, and she let out a trembling breath. "Thank you for saying that. I feel so weird about everything."

"How so?"

Hunny shrugged, biting her lower lip when her chin wobbled. Great, first she cried in front of Tank, and now she was word vomiting all over his mother. This poor family was going to be more than ready to send her packing when the time came.

"I-I don't miss him. Not at all. And I should, right?" Hunny ran a hand through her disheveled hair, grateful her fingers didn't snag on a tangle. She took a deep breath before continuing, "I mean, he was my mate. When we were together, every thought I had revolved around him. What he was up to, if he missed me, when could I see him again ... But since I came here, I haven't really thought about him. He didn't even cross my mind all day yesterday, not until last night. And even then, I didn't feel sad ... just worried that he'd find another way to ruin my life."

"Ruin your life how, Hunny? Are you in danger?"

"No," Hunny replied immediately. "At least, I don't think so." Not unless Natasha resurfaced, the nasty bitch. "I'm just being dramatic," she added.

Tabitha snorted, placing a comforting hand on Hunny's shoulder. "After what you've been through, and that awful attack in the woods that Murphy mentioned, I think you're more than entitled to a little theatrics. And for the record, I think it's remarkable you've gotten over your mate so easily," Tabitha finished, a twinkle in her eye Hunny couldn't make sense of.

"You do? I feel like there's something wrong with me."

Though getting rejected, propositioned to be a whore, and then nearly killed in the woods all in one night had probably sped up her mourning process far more than her cry in Jason's cabin ever could have.

"There's nothing wrong with you at all, Hunny." Tabitha smiled happily. "Sometimes fate has other plans for us. Maybe this true mate of yours wasn't supposed to be your endgame, but your stepping stone to something better."

Hunny furrowed her brow. "Well, that's a hell of a way to look at it." Knocked up and rejected, just to find 'something better.'

"Oh, I'm always optimistic." Tabitha laughed, shooing Hunny toward the open bathroom door. "Go, get cleaned up. There's a spare toothbrush under the sink!"

With that, Hunny did as instructed, taking a quick shower before brushing her teeth and dressing. Her clothes might not have smelled like Tank anymore, but her body did from his soap, and she sighed contentedly before making her way back to the bedroom.

She'd barely stepped through the door when Tabitha jumped up from her seat on the bed, sending Hunny another happy smile. "Oh dear, you really are a beauty. I see why my Tank kept you to himself."

Hunny blushed, waving her hand in denial. "Oh! Oh, no. That's not—Henry and I—we're not like *that* ... We're just friends," she finished lamely, feeling like she'd just gotten caught lying. But she wasn't. Her and Tank's relationship was strictly platonic.

Isn't it?

Tabitha raised a brow. "Henry, is it?"

Hunny's entire face turned beet red. "I meant Tank."

"If my son prefers you to call him Henry, go for it."

"He didn't actually tell me if he preferred it or not."

Tabitha laughed loudly, like Hunny had just told her one hell of a joke. "Hunny, if my son told you his name, that means he wants you to call him by it. He never tells strangers anything personal about himself. You must make him feel very comfortable."

Hunny shrugged nonchalantly, but she couldn't help the fluttering in her stomach at Tabitha's words. "He makes me feel comfortable, too," she admitted softly.

"Even more reason for you to stay with our clan," Tabitha stated, bringing their original conversation back full circle. "I'll have a word with Murphy on your behalf, if you'd like. Not about your mate, that is private and for you to discuss when you're ready, but just that I think you'd be a good fit for us."

Hunny's shoulders relaxed. "You'd do that for me? You don't even know me."

"Nonsense." Tabitha pulled Hunny in for a sudden hug before letting go. "I feel as if we're family already. That's what a bear clan is: family."

Family. God, the word brought up so many old memories of her parents, of how happy she'd been growing up. How loved she'd felt. For the last five years, she'd missed that aspect of being part of a nest; the companionship, the friendship, the affection.

And now Tank's family was offering a semblance of that, even if it was just for a little while, until she got back onto her feet. Hope blossomed in her chest, the sensation so sudden, so foreign, that it took her a second to process the feeling. When it did, a tear spilled down Hunny's cheek, her emotions too strong to push back.

"Ah, I'm sorry," she mumbled, wiping at her face with the back of her hand. "I'm so emotional nowadays."

"I've been there several times," Tabitha joked. She moved to the desk, grabbing a Kleenex from a box and handing it to Hunny. "Speaking of babies, I'm the clan doctor, so if you're needing a checkup, I'd love to help with that, when you have time."

"That would be really great." Hunny had barely even thought about her next steps regarding her pregnancy. "I'm only a few weeks along at most, so I wasn't sure when I'd need to make an appointment with anyone."

"Well, with a shifter pregnancy, it's imperative to be seen sooner rather than later as our offspring develop faster than a human's. Aside from that, rabbit shifters are prone to carrying multiple kits. And if the one who impregnated you is a different shifter breed than yours, those pregnancies almost always result in multiple offspring."

Hunny blanched, her breath stilling in her lungs. More than one kit? *Multiple babies?!* She didn't even know what she'd do with one, let alone a swarm of them!

No, Tabitha had to be mistaken. There was no *fucking* way. "I'm sorry? I think I misheard you."

"You didn't mishear, and I'm a bit surprised you weren't aware of this beforehand. Did you grow up in a nest?" the older woman asked casually.

"I left before I was eighteen," Hunny mumbled numbly. "I guess I never really questioned why there were so many twins and triplets running around."

Hunny's parents had never had 'the talk' with her, and she was an only child, so she'd never even thought to question how many kits she'd produce.

Oh god.

"Henry's going to kick me out if I'm pregnant with twins," she whispered faintly, anxiety crashing through her. He wouldn't want anything to do with her after this newest shock. And then she'd never see him again, never feel that safety, or his scent—

Tabitha snorted, and then immediately rubbed Hunny's arms in comfort. She barely felt the touch, too focused on the pulse now frantically beating in her ears. The walls seemed to close in on her. "Now, now. I can't imagine he'd do that at all."

"I can't stay here with a hoard of children. This place is so small. Henry will want his space back," Hunny argued, her heart rate sky-rocketing the more she thought about it. "Is it hot in here? I feel too hot." She blinked quickly as she fanned her face, looking around the bedroom frantically. She could already imagine the cribs stacked on top of each other, ready to topple over and crush her at any second. "I-I think the air conditioner is broken."

"Hunny?" Tabitha inquired, her voice filled with concern. "Are you alright?"

"N-no. I-it's too hot. It's too hot and H-Henry won't w-want me here," Hunny stuttered, her lungs on fire. She couldn't breathe.

He was going to toss her out, just like Jason had. He'd decide she wasn't worth the trouble. Just like—

"You're having a bit of a panic attack," Tabitha murmured soothingly, but it did nothing to calm Hunny down. "Take a deep breath for me," Tabitha instructed, but the words sounded muffled, far away, like the other woman was talking under water.

Besides, she couldn't breathe. Couldn't the other woman see that she was trying?

I can't breathe—

"I need to get out of here!" Hunny exclaimed, rushing to the stairs. With every step she took down, she felt like she was being chased, forced out of the only place she'd felt safe in years. It was all going to end. It always did. It was over. Her feet hit the living room floor, and she raced to the front door.

She needed to get out. She couldn't breathe, she couldn't—

Hunny burst out of the cabin and onto the porch. The feeling of cool wood on her bare feet barely registered as she stormed down the small steps and into the front yard. She tried sucking in a ragged breath, but her lungs felt too tight, her airway constricted.

"Tank!" Tabitha shouted from somewhere behind her. Footsteps pounded on the ground in the distance. Or maybe it was her heart threatening to give out.

"Can't breathe," Hunny gasped, her hands shaking as she clutched at her chest, her eyes wild. She stared at the world around her, not comprehending anything as her pulse roared in her ears. Was she having a heart attack? "I can't, I can't—"

Strong arms wrapped around her waist; clovers, musk, and berries invading her senses. Instinctively, Hunny whipped around, throwing herself into Tank's chest with a small cry.

"What's wrong, darlin'?" he asked darkly, his gruff voice ripping through the harsh pounding in her ears until the feeling eased enough that she didn't feel like something foul had swallowed her whole. He ran a big hand down her damp hair, petting her tenderly. She didn't even realize she was shaking in his arms until he murmured, "It's alright, Hunny. You're okay."

"This is my fault," Tabitha muttered softly from somewhere behind Hunny.

"What did you say to her?" Tank snapped, his voice growing harsh.

"Don't take that tone with me, Henry Sinclair," Tabitha replied quickly. She exhaled a moment later. "I didn't realize she was unaware she'd likely have multiple kits. I mentioned it, and ..." Her voice trailed off.

Great, now that he knew, he was going to want her gone.

Hunny burrowed closer to Tank's body, burying her face in the warmth of his bare chest, wanting to soak up this last moment between them before everything went tits up.

"Huh." Tank's arm tightened around her waist reassuringly, and he cupped the back of her neck, holding her securely to him like he didn't plan on letting her go. Then he said the strangest possible thing. "Jasper, we're definitely going to need more wood."

Nine

*T*wins?

That news was surprising, to say the least. Wholly unexpected, actually. Not just to Tank, but to Hunny as well, given the way she trembled in his arms. Adding on one bedroom and an extra bathroom wouldn't be enough. Not for long. He'd need at least two bedrooms. Doable, if he started working on it in the next few weeks.

He sent a quick glance to Jasper. "We'll probably need Murph and the others if we want to get it all done in a timely manner."

Hunny took a shuddering breath, burying herself more firmly into him. He enjoyed holding her, comforting her when she felt upset, though it drove him mad she felt this way to begin with. He didn't want his little rabbit to feel anything but safe and cared for while she stayed with him. Especially in her condition.

Didn't stress cause complications for pregnant females? His brow creased as concern rippled through him.

Unable to help himself, he sent his mother a hostile look, a reprimand on the tip of his tongue. His mom would likely pummel him for berating her, but he was protective of Hunny, and he didn't want another incident like this to occur.

Not from anyone, especially his family.

As if sensing his incoming rant, Tabitha narrowed her eyes, giving Tank a firm shake of her head. Daring him to say something.

Hunny sniffled then, drawing his attention back to her. "It'll be alright," he rasped, tangling a hand into her damp hair. She smelled like his shampoo and body wash, and possessiveness filled him as he dragged her scent deep into his lungs.

The blending of their scents was intoxicating, stirring up several images into his head, and every single one of them was more carnal than the last. Images of her laying in his bed, spending her nights beneath him as he pumped his cock into her—

"What do you mean, you need more wood?" Hunny asked, her soft voice thick with emotion. She lifted her head from his chest, staring up at him with tears glittering in her emerald eyes. His heart slammed into his sternum at that one look. How could she look so beautiful, even when she was so sad? "What does that have to do with anything, Henry?"

Tank flushed at the question. He hadn't intended to mention anything to her about his plans, not until he knew if she wanted to stay with his clan for any length of time. He didn't want to pressure her into an answer if she wasn't ready to give one.

"Tank's building you a bedroom and bathroom downstairs," Jasper supplied with a grin, clearly under no qualms about keeping his fucking mouth shut. "He asked for my help to get it all ready so you won't have to sleep on the couch anymore."

Hunny's eyes widened in surprise, her mouth gaping open as she stared up at Tank. "You want to build me a room?"

"Only if you want to stay," he answered gruffly. "I'd like for you to, though. Stay, I mean. I'd like for you to stay with me." Christ, could he have been any more awkward?

"Are you sure, Henry? My life is a freaking mess—"

"That's alright," he interrupted quickly, his excitement building as he realized she was on the verge of saying yes.

"—and I'm pregnant," she sputtered. "I'd be intruding on your entire life."

He shook his head in denial. "No, you won't."

Hunny wrinkled her nose, the action reminding him of her rabbit counterpart. "You say that now, but we've only known each other for two days. *Barely*. And in that time I've had *two* crying sessions. And a panic attack. It's only going to get worse, Henry. You're going to get sick of me."

"No, I won't." He let out a small, rusty laugh. If that was going to happen, he was confident it would have by now. Usually engaging with others felt like a chore or obligation, but with Hunny it was neither.

Even though she was vivacious and sassy, she didn't grate on his nerves like anyone else would have. He liked her attitude and her bubbly personality. It was a direct contrast from himself, and frankly, she was like a breath of fresh air.

"What if you meet someone, though?" Hunny argued. "Having a pregnant roommate probably won't look good for anyone you want to date."

Tank scoffed, completely taken aback by her line of thinking. Finding a female to date hadn't crossed his mind since he was an adolescent. Sure, he'd slept around when an itch needed scratching, but those occasions were few and far between. And he wouldn't exactly call *that* dating.

"Are those your only concerns? That you think you'll ruin my dating life?" Jasper snorted in the background, but Tank ignored him, continuing seamlessly, "And that your life is a mess?"

"You don't even know me!" Hunny exclaimed. "I could be a complete psychopath."

His brows shot up. "Are you?"

"Of course not," she huffed.

"Then what's really the matter, little rabbit? What's got you running scared?"

Why was she putting up such a fight? From all their time spent together, he hadn't sensed a moment where she seemed homesick or anxious to leave. She could have disappeared that first night while he'd slept. Instead, she'd stayed.

There was a reason she hadn't left; he believed that wholeheartedly. And since the cat was out of the bag regarding his intentions, he planned on getting the truth out of her now.

Hunny bit her lower lip, and his eyes lowered to her plump mouth, their conversation taking a backseat to this sudden distraction. He wanted to bite that lip, to feel her soft skin between his teeth as he—

"I'm also not a part of your clan," she murmured. "What if Murphy doesn't want me?"

For a moment, Tank was confused, and the thought of Hunny belonging to Murphy in any fashion filled him with an unnatural fury, stronger than he'd ever felt before. His bear roared in his mind, the thought of challenging his brother for the little rabbit consuming him.

"Henry?" Hunny asked, her brows furrowing in confusion. She reached up, touching his cheek with her palm. It grounded him, and as suddenly as his need to disembowel his brother had hit him, it faded just as quickly. "Are you alright?"

"What?" he growled, and then he shook his head to clear it. "I'm fine. What did you ask me?"

"Murphy wants to talk to me, but what if he doesn't want me to stay in your territory?"

Oh, *that* was what she meant. *Thank fuck.* "Why would he want you to leave? Is there something that you're worried about?"

She looked away from him, dropping her hands to her side. "I ... He was right about me being a lone shifter. I'm worried that will be a deciding factor in wanting me off his territory."

Tank let out a relieved breath, holding her closer to him. "I'll talk to him. Or we can talk to him together. He's a reasonable male."

"I'll talk with him, too, as I said earlier, dear." Tabitha smiled at them both. "Being a lone shifter changes nothing in my eyes, and I'm sure with a bit of motivation, Murphy will feel the same way."

"That almost sounds like a threat," Hunny replied.

Tabitha winked, causing the rabbit shifter to crack a small smile.

Turning back to Tank, Hunny murmured, "I think we should talk a bit more before you build anything, though."

His mom turned to Jasper. "Well, I think we should leave and give these two some privacy. Besides, you need to help me with several chores around the house."

"Shit," Jasper whined pitifully. "I need to find a woman and build her a cabin. Then you won't put me to work like a dog."

"You could just move out," Tabitha answered, ushering Jasper toward the driveway. She lifted a hand in goodbye.

Without bothering with farewells, Tank scooped Hunny up, carrying her bridal-style back toward the cabin.

"Henry!" Hunny sassed him, pushing lightly at his chest. "We talked about this; you can't just carry me everywhere." Her face flushed with embarrassment as she glanced after his family.

"It's getting cold and you don't have shoes on. Do you want to get sick?"

She rolled her eyes, putting an arm around his shoulders and one on his chest, her fingers playing with the hair there. "We both know you're not carrying me around because you're worried my feet are cold. You like it."

He grunted in answer, seeing no point in denying it.

Once they were safely inside, he moved back to the couch, dropping onto the leather cushion with her still tucked into his arms. Part of him hoped she'd straddle his waist like she had last night. But that would just further distract him, and if she was open to talking about her life, he'd listen to every word.

His brow furrowed. Actually, having her on his lap probably wasn't the smartest decision if he intended to remain present for their conversation.

He put his hands on her hips, on the verge of sliding her onto the cushion beside him, when she blurted out, "I have a mate." He stilled, eyes snapping to hers as the breath froze in his lungs. She wrinkled her nose again. "I'm sorry, I *had* a mate. He rejected me the night you found me."

Suddenly, Tank could breathe again. So he did, inhaling her scent deep into his lungs to calm himself down. "Okay."

Hunny snorted, staring at him in bewilderment. "That's all you have to say?"

"I'm sorry he rejected you," he added after a few tense seconds of silence. And he *was* sorry. Sorry that her mate was clearly a fucking idiot. Who rejected their true mate? Especially someone like Hunny?

She sat up straighter in his arms. "Thanks," she murmured softly. "It was a huge shock when it happened. Actually, maybe I'm still in shock about it all. I thought he was going to make me a member of his pack. He ..." She trailed off, releasing a ragged sigh. "I thought he was going to turn my life around, you know? Instead, he knocked me up and then mated someone else."

Mated someone *else*? The thought was unfathomable. As absurd as rejecting Hunny in the first place.

"Why would he do that?"

"Apparently, I was too tempting to resist, even though he'd made promises to another shifter before we met." She sniffled, but her eyes remained dry, much to his relief.

"He sounds like a prick," Tank supplied grumpily. "Anyone that would use you like that is a piece of shit."

Hunny grinned, nudging her shoulder against his. "You really believe that, don't you?" He grunted again and she let out a small laugh, the light sound something he relished. He enjoyed making her laugh. "Well, in this case, I definitely agree. Jason sucks."

Tank stiffened. "Jason, the Alpha of the Moon Rose pack?"

Now it made sense how she'd stumbled into bear territory during a wolf attack. Had the evil prick sent one of his she-wolves to kill Hunny and their unborn kit after he rejected her? Tank's hands tightened on Hunny's thighs, rage boiling to the surface. He beat it back, schooling his features.

The humor faded from Hunny's face, replaced quickly with panic. "You know him? Is he allied with your clan?"

"Fuck no, he's not our ally," Tank denied, disgusted at the mere idea. "I can't stand the rat bastard, neither can my brother. Jason's entire wolf pack is full of depraved animals. They're terrible people; every one of them. You were lucky he let you go."

But why would he? Jason didn't seem like a male to relinquish any of his toys—the fact that he'd used Hunny for just sex was a clear indicator that the dickhead had viewed her as exactly that, and not as his true mate at all.

Sick bastard.

"Will being mates with Jason count against me when I talk to Murphy?" she asked quietly.

"No." Tank shook his head firmly. "You aren't mated to Jason, Hunny, so that won't matter. He'll likely be more concerned about Jason coming to look for you, and why you initially became a lone shifter."

"Oh." She was silent for a few minutes before she added, "I don't think Jason will look for me. He offered me the chance to be his mistress—" Tank's fierce growl reverberated through the air, fury simmering inside him. "—I turned it down. After he left, his new mate came by and tried to kill me." She sent Tank a soft look, taking his hand from her thigh and placing it over her flat stomach. His growl stopped abruptly, her body heat seeping into his palm. "That's who you saved me and my babies from."

His fingers flexed against her abdomen, his large hand covering the area completely. "I'm surprised you'd even consider staying here, knowing he's so close."

But he felt honored that she trusted him enough to tell him about this.

Her eyes filled with tears then. "I don't have anywhere else to go. All of my belongings are back at his cabin, and I can't go back there."

"I can go for you." It wouldn't be a hardship, and if he ran into Jason, he wouldn't mind beating that fucker into the dirt. Though, wandering into enemy territory and attacking a pack Alpha unprovoked would definitely cause a war between the bears and wolves, and Murphy would be furious.

"No!" Hunny exclaimed. "I don't want you anywhere near Jason. Besides, he probably got rid of everything that belonged to me. It's not worth it."

That didn't sit right with Tank at all. "We can go into town this afternoon and get you some things." Whatever she needed, he'd provide it. He wouldn't even mind venturing into human territory, though he drew the line at conversing with any of them. He could barely stand his family; there was no way he could tolerate humans in any capacity.

But he'd endure them for Hunny.

"I don't have any money," Hunny told him with a wince.

He rolled his eyes in exasperation. "I don't recall saying you'd need any."

She squeaked at him in surprise. "Oh no. You're already letting me stay here and you keep feeding me. You can't buy me things, too, Henry."

"Yes, I can."

"But I don't have anything to give you in return."

Yes you do, Tank thought suddenly, his heart beating hard in his chest as he gazed into her eyes. His hand tightened on her stomach before he wrapped his arm around her waist, pulling her into his chest. He breathed her in, his brain and heart telling him the same thing; she smelled *right* covered in his scent.

"Don't worry about anything right now," Tank responded eventually. "I've got plenty of money, and it's a privilege to take care of whatever you need. You need some help Hunny. Let me help you."

Hunny relaxed against him, resting her head on his shoulder. "You're pretty amazing, Henry," she murmured.

"Just wait until I cook you breakfast," he half joked, warmth blooming in his chest from her compliment.

Her delicate laughter filled his ears as he got her situated on the sofa before standing up to do just that. And after they ate, he'd see about taking her into town.

Ten

Hunny was still unsure of what to make of her entire situation as Tank escorted her from his cabin to the large detached garage on the other side of his home. She'd had several curveballs thrown her way just this morning, each one more surprising than the last.

On the top of the list?

Finding out she was likely pregnant with multiple kits. She still wasn't sure if she'd freak out again if she thought about it too much, so she pushed it to the back of her mind.

For now.

Next: Tank telling her he was going to add extra rooms to his house just for her.

That was insane. Who did something so major for a relative stranger? They hardly knew one another, yet he was going to build onto his home for her?

It was incredibly sweet. It was also too much. Hunny didn't feel she was worth the trouble, and frankly, she *should* have found his idea off-putting—she didn't. She'd learned a lot since her parents died five years ago, and most of it revolved around males. Ninety percent of them didn't do something out of the kindness of their hearts; there was almost always an ulterior motive.

Hadn't she learned that lesson with Jason just a few days ago? Her very own true mate had used and discarded her like trash. In her one moment of weakness, she had let down her guard, and he'd taken what he'd wanted and sent her on her way. That should have been a lifelong lesson in trusting men; even the ones designed by fate to love you only hurt you in the end.

Honestly, after everything she'd gone through, Hunny should have been shifting and taking off into the woods, never to return.

But she didn't want to leave. Her internal alarms weren't warning her there was something off with Tank, not like they had with Jason. Even when she believed Jason would mate with her, she'd still questioned, at least to herself, why he only visited at night. Or why he never wanted to introduce her to his pack. Why he kept her a secret.

It had all felt wrong. In hindsight, she should have listened to her instincts, trusted the warning signs, and gotten the hell out of there.

Hunny bit her lower lip, barely registering the cool breeze on her face as Tank unlocked the garage door, silently ushering her inside.

If she'd been blinded by Jason before, she definitely felt alert and wary of any potential dangers now. So what were her instincts telling her this time?

That Tank was safe. That Tank was a good, compassionate male. That he'd never hurt her. She just wished she could understand why she felt that way so completely. And that she could stop worrying that it was all going to end too soon.

"You're quiet," Tank commented as he closed the door behind him, his gravelly voice causing a pleasant shiver to work down her spine.

"Today's been a lot," Hunny admitted. "I'm just trying to process it all."

"My family has that effect on people."

Hunny burst out laughing, shaking her head as she looked around the large garage. A couple of four-wheelers, a riding lawn mower, and a large pickup truck sat in the garage, taking up most of the interior, along with several tools hung along the walls.

"Your mom is awesome, and Jasper is kind of funny," Hunny informed him.

"Good. I worried they overwhelmed you."

Did he mean his mom? She shook her head. "Not at all. Your mom actually offered to do a checkup for me, and I think that's a great idea."

Besides that, meeting Tank's family was eye-opening. They were all so different from one another. Murphy seemed every bit the strict, stoic Alpha, while Tabitha was a sweet, affectionate mother. Jasper was clearly a clown who enjoyed teasing his family for a few laughs. And Tank ... he didn't seem to know what to do with it all.

He'd been snarly with everyone.

Except me, Hunny thought cheerfully, her lips curving up into a small smile as Tank escorted her to the passenger side of the pickup truck. It looked far newer than the four-wheelers. Opening the door, he helped her inside, and her smile spread into a full-blown grin.

"You carry me everywhere and now you're opening doors, too, Henry? Quite the gentleman," she teased.

His eyes shot to hers, and his face heated beneath his unruly beard. He grumbled a noncommital response and then closed the door gently between them, moving around the front of the vehicle and to the driver's side door. His blush made her wonder; was he embarrassed to be helping her, or just embarrassed by the praise?

Hunny would bet her life on the latter, and it made her want to compliment him as much as possible, just to rile him up. Okay, maybe she just wanted to compliment him because he was a sweetheart and deserved to hear it as often as possible.

She had a feeling Tank didn't spend his time with many people, not outside his family, at least. That meant it was up to her to let him know he was awesome.

Tank shuffled into the driver's seat, closing his door before starting the truck. The engine roared to life, filling the silence of the small cab.

"How far away is town?" Hunny asked, watching as he pressed a button on his rearview mirror. The large garage door opened a second later.

"About an hour."

She bit her lower lip, putting on her seatbelt before turning to face him. "What are the odds we run into someone from Jason's pack?"

"Slim. His territory is about thirty miles from this place."

Oh. So was the cabin he'd kept her in even technically on his territory? Probably not, the douchebag.

"Do you think there will be any job openings?"

Tank's brow furrowed as they pulled out of the garage and onto the driveway. Once they were clear of it, he took off down a dirt road. "Why?"

Hunny rolled her eyes. "So that I can make money to support myself? I can't live off of your generosity forever." Or for even more than a few weeks. She'd been independent for so long, it would drive her crazy to be reliant on anyone else for even the most mundane things.

She needed some fail-safe savings, at the very least.

You had one, she thought bitterly. *Hidden under the front seat of your truck.*

Too bad that was likely long gone.

Tank's grip tightened on the steering wheel, his lips turning down into a frown. "I told you I'd take care of you, darlin'."

"Which is very sweet of you, Henry. But I need to support myself, eventually. What if you get sick of me? Or fall in love with someone? You won't want me around then, mooching off you."

Suddenly, Hunny felt a brief stab of jealousy, quickly followed by a flash of fury that some unnamed, hypothetical *beotch* would catch Tank's attention. Then he wouldn't carry Hunny, or hold her in his arms when she felt sad, or let her use his hair as fur for a nest.

Okay, that last one hadn't happened—*yet*—but it never would if he fell in love with some skanky bitch.

Just as suddenly as those thoughts formed, they fled, leaving Hunny feeling confused, horrified with herself, and furious about this hypothetical situation.

What had gotten into her?

Huffing in exasperation, she crossed her arms in front of her chest, looking away from Tank before she said or did something stupid. She felt like an idiot for being so pissed off. It had to be pregnancy hormones, right? She might only be a few weeks along, at the most, but compared to humans, that would put her at around six weeks.

Was this when the overwhelming emotions set in? She'd already cried a lot, had a panic attack, and now she was pissed off over *nothing*. It had to be.

"We'll see about finding you work within the clan. Murphy needs a receptionist," Tank suggested.

Yeah, if he lets me stay here, she thought grumpily.

"Fine," she snipped. That was just as good, anyway. Most people were completely oblivious to the supernatural world, and she didn't want to bring any unwanted attention to this bear clan by working among humans. Or to herself, for that matter.

"What's wrong?" Tank asked immediately, moving one hand from the wheel and placing it on her thigh. It was warm, and heat spread through her jeans and to her skin, the simple touch calming her down until she only felt embarrassment for her wayward feelings.

If this was how her entire pregnancy would progress, she was doomed. And poor Tank, he'd probably swear off women and babies forever after putting up with her through it all.

Tank squeezed her thigh, waiting for her answer.

"Nothing is wrong."

"Hunny—"

Hunny ran a hand down her face to hide it momentarily. "It's nothing I want to talk about right now because I'm being stupid and emotional, and if I bring up why I feel like this, I'll either laugh at how *stupid* I am or cry because you'll think I'm a lunatic."

Ugh, she even sounded crazy!

She sent Tank a look out of the corner of her eye, waiting to see if he'd comment.

All he did was grunt in acknowledgement, keeping his eyes firmly on the road and his hand on her leg as he drove.

She looked at his side profile in surprise. "That's it? You're not going to pry me for details?"

He squeezed her thigh again. "Not if it'll make you cry."

Her eyes narrowed threateningly. "Are you implying that if I tell you what upset me, you *will* think I'm a lunatic?"

"I walked right into that," Tank muttered under his breath, sending her an apologetic look a second later.

Lips twitching, and no longer in a shitty mood, Hunny asked, "Do you go into town often?"

Tank grimaced. "No. I hate engaging with people."

"Humans specifically?"

"Anyone."

"Why?"

"They all talk too much."

Hunny snorted, patting the hand on her thigh sympathetically. "Oh, you're in for a rude awakening with me then. Contrary to the last few days, I love to talk."

Tank released a low laugh, the sound causing heat to pool low in her belly. "Oh, I've noticed."

She scoffed at him in mock outrage. "*Rude.* And there's no way you've noticed, Henry. The first day I was a rabbit, and then we watched TV and slept."

She blushed, remembering just how nice she'd felt waking up in his arms. How warm and protected she'd felt cuddling up to her very own grizzly bear.

He sent her a cocky look. "You're a talker, darlin'. Got an air about you, even when you can't form words."

"'An air' about me?" She wrinkled her nose. "What does that even mean?"

"You're a yapper. Even as a rabbit, your little body just vibrates when you've got something to say. You squeak almost constantly."

He cleared his throat with a grimace. Shit, she'd completely forgotten he didn't talk a lot because it hurt him, and here she was, *yapping* away.

She leaned over, shoving at his shoulder playfully. "I can't believe you just called me a *yapper*."

Tank smirked, sending her a heated look.

Her breath froze in her lungs, a lightning bolt of desire slamming right between her thighs. Slick pooled from her core, drenching her panties instantly, and her mind went blank as his gaze shifted back to the road, completely oblivious to the fact that he'd just reduced her to a molten pool of need in less than two seconds flat.

Holy. *Shit.*

What the hell was wrong with her? It felt like he'd just ripped her clothes off and demanded she spread her legs for him without even saying a word. At the thought, a naughty image of doing just that formed in her head, and her desire skyrocketed, more of her own arousal spilling between her thighs. Suddenly, she could almost feel his hand moving up her thigh and pushing between her legs, his fingers wandering—

Nope. No! Stop thinking like that! He'll scent that you're horny, bitch. Think about anything else!

But Hunny couldn't think of anything that didn't revolve around Tank, and unfortunately, the only true thought that came to mind was Jasper joking about how much Tank loved honey.

Even more unfortunately, all she could envision was Tank licking honey from his fingers. Only it wasn't *honey*. It was her slick drenching his fingers as he sucked them into his mouth with a delicious groan of need rumbling from his throat—

"Nothing wrong with having a yapper around." Tank's deep voice startled her from her thoughts. She almost shoved his hand away from her, his touch only turning her on more.

"Hm? Oh, oh! Yep. That's me. Certified yapper," Hunny replied hoarsely, reaching toward the vents on the dashboard. "Is it hot in here? Some A/C would be phenomenal."

It would also dilute the scent of her arousal. God, what if he already smelled it in the truck? She'd never be able to look at him again! Before he could answer, Hunny turned the air conditioner on full blast. Cold air smacked her in the face, blowing back her hair and making it difficult to keep her eyes open.

"So much better," she told him, even as she shivered from the icy air, the temperature at war with the rest of her body.

He frowned. "You're cold."

"Me? Oh, no. *Totally* fine. I love being cold, actually. Just ... Ah—"

Hunny was so mortified with herself that she didn't even realize they'd pulled into town, not until Tank drove into a parking lot in front of a large department store. He parked the truck, turning off the engine.

"Oh, thank God!" Hunny exclaimed, ripping off her seatbelt and jumping from the truck as if the devil were chasing after her. She shut her door and raced to his side, prying his door open. "Come on." She hurriedly gestured for him to get the fuck out of the vehicle. "We don't want to be here around all these icky people any longer than necessary," she joked forcefully.

Sending her a perplexed look, Tank hopped from the truck.

She was so caught up with her own dilemma, she didn't even notice the large bulge in Tank's jeans as he followed after her.

Eleven

Tank was hard as a rock as he followed Hunny blindly toward the first department store, the scent of her arousal still filling his senses. He wasn't sure what the hell had caused his little rabbit to become so turned on while he drove her here, but thank fuck for whatever it was.

He didn't even mind that every step he took made his balls ache; Hunny smelled divine. Good enough to eat, and Tank was suddenly starving. Inhaling discreetly, he swallowed thickly as his mouth watered.

Just this morning, he'd come to the realization that Hunny felt *right* in every way, and now, with her delicious scent filling his lungs, he wanted to test that theory. Wanted to know what she'd feel like beneath him, how good she'd look sleeping in his bed, with his arms wrapped around her, holding her close. At the thought, his arms ached as much as his balls, his hands itching to pull her into a hug.

He didn't just want her for a couple of nights, either. He wanted her permanently. Even his bear agreed. The beast had felt just as protective of Hunny since he'd met her, and now his confusing behavior was all beginning to make sense.

He didn't enjoy sharing his space, except with Hunny. Didn't enjoy talking to anyone, except Hunny. Hell, he wanted to build things for her, just on the off-chance she'd move in with him.

And now she is, he thought smugly. A second later, he sobered. He didn't even know if Hunny was interested in him like that. Her heady scent might permeate the air, but he didn't know if *he* was the reason for her desire. And he didn't want to pressure her into anything.

Hunny was vulnerable right now, and he wouldn't take advantage of that, not for anything.

I can work with slow, he reasoned, dragging in another lungful of her sweet fragrance. His eyes almost rolled back into his head, his bear clawing at him to make a damned move before someone else snatched her up. His upper lip curled in fury at the thought.

So consumed with her teasing scent and his own emotions, Tank didn't even realize they'd entered the department store until Hunny whipped around, grabbing his arm and tugging him forward. "I have no idea where to go. Lead the way."

"Where do you want to go?"

"I-I don't know." She released a shrill laugh, looking up at him with wide, *too* innocent eyes. "But you should definitely take me wherever is best."

His brows rose. Was she hoping to keep her scent downwind of him? Lips twitching, Tank opened his mouth, ready to tell her that the cat was well out of the bag and that she shouldn't be ashamed of her desire.

"Can I help the lovely couple find anything today?" a human male said from over Tank's shoulder, interrupting them.

Pissed that another male would dare force his way into Tank's space, would *dare* get close to Hunny while she was aroused, he turned on a dime, getting in the male's face.

"We're fine," Tank snapped coldly, a furious rumble building in his chest as he pinned the worker with a hard glare. "Now *leave*."

Face paling, the worker nodded quickly before he turned and scurried away. Tank relaxed, satisfaction rolling through him as the temporary threat abated. His bear gave his own low growl of approval, content with how they'd handled the situation.

"Oh my God," Hunny seethed, swatting Tank's stomach hard. Surprised, he looked down at her. "You can't just terrify someone like that!"

"I told you, I don't like people," he reminded her.

"That doesn't mean you *growl* at them, Henry!" she whispered harshly. "Seriously, you scared him so badly I thought he was going to pee himself."

Tank shrugged. "Good."

With a huff of frustration, Hunny ran a hand through her hair. Then she gave him a pleading look that sent a lick of desire straight to his groin, her emerald eyes shining in the overhead lighting. "Will you please not scare anyone else? You can just ignore them and let me do all the talking." He didn't answer right away, and she added, "I bet they'll be just as scared, probably more so, with the silent brooding act."

He grunted. "Fine."

Hunny smiled up at him then, and he'd have promised her anything so long as she kept looking at him just like that. Without another word, he took her hand in his, enjoying the feeling of her skin pressed against his as he led her through the department store. Clothes, purses, shoes, perfume, toiletries, *puzzles*; whatever she set her sights on, Tank made sure she had it.

Luckily, no one else got in their way as they shopped, and when he hauled several items up to a register on three separate occasions, intending to come back to pay for it all, no one had told him no. Granted, they'd looked away from him in a panic each time he approached, but as long as his stuff was accounted for, he didn't care.

"Should have brought the SUV," he mumbled under his breath as they unloaded their last armful of goods at the register, ignoring the pain scratching at his throat as he talked. Over the last few days, being more vocal had actually helped overall. Still hurt like a bitch, but his voice hadn't gone out like it used to, and as long as he paced himself, he could talk for extended periods of time without too much discomfort.

Though, truth be told, he would have talked to Hunny even with hot coals stuck inside his mouth, burning him from the inside out.

"Why an SUV?" Hunny asked.

"More storage space," Tank replied, watching as the worker began hastily ringing up items, tossing each one into a bag. He almost snapped at her to be careful, but he'd promised Hunny he'd be on his best behavior, and he didn't want to ruin it now.

Hunny frowned, eyeing all the items with a worried gaze. "I think I overdid it. It's too much, Henry. I-I should put some things back."

"No." He shook his head. She couldn't live in a home without being comfortable. And he wanted her to always be comfortable and happy. "You need all these things."

Hunny rolled her eyes. "I don't need puzzles, Henry. It was an impulse purchase."

"They're on sale," he countered.

"Okay, but I don't need *seven* of them."

"One for every day of the week, darlin'. Makes sense."

Her frown turned into a shy, sweet smile that he couldn't help but fixate on. "You're ridiculous. Next, you'll tell me all the throw blankets I picked out were necessary."

He shrugged. "You said there were different levels of fluffiness with each one. I believe you." And he wanted to cuddle her on the couch under each one, too, but he didn't say that part out loud.

She planted her hands on her hips, sending him a teasing look. "What about the teddy bear for the kit—*babies*?" She sent a worried look at the cashier, but the woman didn't even look up from her task. Reassured, Hunny looked back at him. "I won't even need that for months, so how can you justify it?"

"You smiled when you looked at it," he replied gruffly. "I like it when you smile."

Hunny's eyes widened, and her cheeks turned a delicate shade of red, a blush traveling down her neck and disappearing under her shirt. "Oh."

"Alright," the cashier said nervously. "Your total is two thou—"

"What?" Hunny exclaimed in a panic.

Tank shoved his debit card toward the woman. "This'll cover it."

Hunny gaped at him, a small squeak escaping her throat. She looked at the cashier next. "I'm sorry; *how* much did you say?"

"Don't answer her," Tank warned, taking his debit card back from the cashier along with a long receipt printed from the register, stuffing them into the front pocket of his jeans. Grabbing all the bags, the straps digging into his fingers, he herded Hunny out of the store and back to the pickup truck as she babbled.

"What? No, this has to be some kind of clerical error. There's no way you spent that much on me. Henry, she said two *thousand—*"

"Did she?" he asked innocently. Unlocking the passenger side door after a brief struggle with the handle, he crammed several bags into the floorboard. Next, he piled the remaining bags on top, and then eventually filled the passenger seat.

Hunny watched him the entire time with wide eyes. "Oh wow, I'm going to be smashed against you the whole way home."

Anticipation stirred in his gut. "We can share a seatbelt," he joked.

With a shake of her head, she looked around, eyes lighting up at something she'd spotted. He followed her gaze to a much smaller store beside the one they'd just visited.

"Alright, let's go in there." Tank pointed at the teahouse.

"Oh, no," Hunny argued. "Absolutely not, Henry. You just spent a fortune."

He raised a brow. "Well, I'm planning on going in for some tea," he lied smoothly. He closed the door and locked it. Holding out his hand, he asked, "You going to join me, darlin'?"

Hunny stared down at his palm, indecision warring in her eyes. Finally, she took his hand, intertwining their fingers. He led her into the packed store, for once not even minding the loud voices echoing throughout the small space.

Hunny walked up to a woman with bright blue hair standing behind the counter. She was short, with a tan complexion, brown almond-shaped eyes, a small nose, and a heart-shaped face.

"Hi," his little rabbit greeted with a bright smile.

The woman behind the counter turned toward her, smiling happily. "Hi, I'm Nessa. Welcome to Nessa's Teahouse." She pointed to her name tag with a teasing gleam in her eye. "That's me, in case I didn't make it obvious enough."

Hunny snorted. "I'd be bragging too if I owned something like this. I like the atmosphere here."

"Thanks! I just opened a few weeks ago. I'm pretty proud of it all." She sent Tank a curious look, but she didn't seem unnerved by his size or surly demeanor in the slightest. "Are you two hoping for a romantic table for two? I can see if I can find something for you, though we're a bit packed at the moment."

"Oh." Hunny blushed. She waved her free hand between her and Tank, looking flustered as she said, "W-We're not a couple."

Nessa tilted her head curiously. "Do you hold all your friend's hands?"

"What?" Confused, Hunny followed Nessa's gaze, staring at her and Tank's intertwined fingers. "Huh. I hadn't even realized," she mumbled to herself. He squeezed her fingers in reassurance, silently letting her know she could let go if she wanted to. Instead, she kept her grip firm.

"Get whatever you want," Tank instructed softly. He leaned in close, whispering in her ear, "I came in here because I could see you wanted to."

Hunny blushed harder, her fingers tightening on his as she stared at the human owner. "Um, I'm actually just looking for some different teas. Do you sell any boxes?"

"Absolutely. I've got anything you can think up."

"Okay, I need a box of peppermint, turmeric, and ..." Hunny trailed off, her brow furrowing.

"Chamomile?" Nessa guessed.

"Yes! How did you know?" Hunny asked.

"All stuff to help with colds and inflammation. Figured that's what you were looking for."

"Well, you really know your tea," Hunny joked. "Maybe you should open your own shop one day."

Laughing, Nessa opened a cabinet and pulled out three different colored boxes of tea. She brought them to the register, ringing up each one. After giving them the total, Tank paid, listening to the two of them talk as Nessa packed up the boxes into a bag.

"What's your name?" Nessa asked, handing the bag to Tank while she kept her eyes on Hunny.

"I'm Hunny, and this is Tank."

"Your *friend*."

Hunny blushed again. "Yes."

"Well, it's been a pleasure to meet you both, and I hope you stop by again soon." Nessa pulled out a small rectangular card from her pocket, handing it to Hunny. "That's my business card, if you ever want to call about tea. Or anything, really. I-I'm new here," Nessa blurted out suddenly. "It's been difficult meeting people, and I feel like you'd be a fun friend to have." She wrinkled up her nose. "Not like the hand-holding friendship you two have going on, though." She waved at Tank dismissively, which was more than fine with him. "But still."

"Do you like puzzles?" Tank asked, speaking to her for the first time.

Nessa floundered for a second before asking, "Who doesn't love a good puzzle?"

Tank grunted. Two yappers who both loved puzzles. It was a match made in heaven already. Hunny elbowed Tank in the side, as if she'd heard his thought loud and clear. "I'd love to hang out sometime."

He smirked as they exchanged farewells, waiting until they were outside before he asked, "What's all the tea for?"

"You," Hunny told him simply.

"Me?" He didn't even like tea.

Sending him a soft look, she confessed, "This kind of tea helps with sore throats. I just thought, since your throat hurts after talking too much, maybe it'll help you. And Jasper said you loved honey, so if you mix some in your tea, I'm sure you'll love the taste." Surprised, he stared at her for so long she shifted awkwardly on her feet. "I-It was a dumb idea—"

"No, it wasn't," he replied, tugging her to him. He hugged her then, dropping his head to nuzzle her crown with his chin.

"I forgot to even ask if you liked tea," Hunny admitted on a sigh, wrapping her arms around his waist.

"Love it," he lied, holding her close.

"Thank you for today," Hunny murmured into his chest. "I don't know what I'd do without you." He kissed the crown of her head then, running a hand up and down her back.

"Come on, darlin'," Tank uttered softly. "Let's get home."

With that, he led his little rabbit back to the truck.

Twelve

Six days later ...

S eated in a leather chair in Murphy's office, Hunny fidgeted with a busted seam on one of her armrests, feeling both nauseous and anxious as she waited for the Alpha to begin their meeting. Tank was here, too, lurking in a corner of the room behind her like a dark knight. It was probably for the best that he couldn't see her face, otherwise he'd know how terrified she felt being here.

And then he'd probably tell his brother to fuck off, pick her up, and carry her back to his cabin, insisting they spend the afternoon unwinding with a show on TV while cuddling on the couch under one of her 'cozy blankets.'

That thought alone had some of the anxiety easing from Hunny's shoulders and she relaxed in her seat, taking a deep, calming breath.

It was kind of cute—okay, *more* than a little cute—how protective Tank had become over the past week. He'd made her feel safe since the day he'd rescued her, but this felt different. More intense. And it had started the day she informed him she might carry more than one kit.

Henry's probably just worried about complications during my pregnancy. Given they were now roommates, with no end to their living situation in sight, he likely wanted to make sure everything regarding her pregnancy went smoothly.

It was too bad that she wished it were something *more* than that. Ever since the truck incident, when she'd become so aroused by Tank she'd nearly lost her mind, she couldn't help but look at her roommate in a *very* different light.

Everything Tank did now had her heart racing, her pulse beating wildly, and her pussy aching. The poor male couldn't even slide a puzzle piece across the dining room table without her imagining his fingers slipping between her thighs and sliding somewhere far more erotic. She did her best to ignore the desire constantly swirling around inside her, and if he noticed any change in her scent while they were together, he didn't say anything.

She'd be mortified if he did. It wasn't like he'd made a move on her, or anything like that at all, to warrant all of her pent-up sexual emotions, and she wouldn't throw herself at him. She'd already gotten herself into quite a mess by doing that to the last male to catch her interest. And now here she was, knocked up and rejected.

She refused to act on impulse like that again.

Besides all that, what if she took a leap, hit on Tank, and he turned her down? Why would he want to get with a female who was pregnant with another male's baby anyway? Tank might hold her close whenever she wanted, cook her nice meals, and spend hours listening to her *yap on* without uttering one complaint, but that didn't mean he had any kind of romantic interest in her. Or did he?

Could he?

Ugh, what am I even doing? I don't need to think about this, anyway! I just got out of a shitty 'relationship.'

"Are you ready?" Murphy asked, drawing her from her thoughts. He filed away the last paper on his desk before leaning back in his worn leather chair.

"As I'll ever be," Hunny answered, sending him a small, tremulous smile.

"There's no reason to be nervous. My brother has ensured this is more of a formality than anything else."

Relieved, Hunny sagged in her seat, her hand going to her still-flat belly. "He has?"

Murphy cast a hard glare over her shoulder before returning his gaze to her. His expression softened marginally. "You've gained quite the fan club since coming here, Hunny. My mother is fond of you, and Tank is—"

Tank mumbled something from the corner of the room.

"Be quiet," Murphy snarled at Tank, "or I'll toss you out on your ass. You're lucky I allowed you to attend this meeting, anyway." Murphy huffed before sending Hunny an apologetic look. "*Tank* is forgetting that he's not the damned Alpha of this clan."

So attuned to Tank, Hunny felt more than heard him stir from the back of the room. "I don't want to cause any problems," she interrupted quickly, looking over her shoulder and narrowing her eyes on the bear shifter. *Behave*, she mouthed.

Tank paused abruptly, like he'd just gotten caught stealing from the cookie jar. A delicate shade of red stained the top of his cheeks, just above his beard. After an awkward silence, he sighed loudly, moving back to his previous position in the corner.

"Now that we've settled that," Murphy stated with a snort, "I'd like to talk to you about your plans to stay in our territory."

"I'm not sure how long I'll stay," Hunny replied truthfully. Tank made a deep, irritated sound behind her that had her adding, "But I don't have plans to move on, either." Especially if things went well today.

Please let things go well.

"Well, you've made an outstanding impression on my mother, and she's put in a good word for you." He sent Tank a sharp look before returning his attention to Hunny. "But I do have questions for you, and based on your answers, you may not agree with my decision here today."

Hunny slid her hands from the armrests to her knees, squeezing them gently. "I'm ready," she reiterated.

Murphy nodded. "Good. How old are you?"

"Twenty-two." Even as she said it, she felt like she was two decades older than that. The things she'd gone through in the last five years alone had aged her, at least spiritually. Mentally, also. Suddenly, she realized something. Glancing over her shoulder at Tank, she asked, "How old are you?"

He smirked. "Thirty-two."

"Wow, you're practically an antique," she teased. Figures he was a decade older than her. She'd always loved an older male.

Stop it!

Murphy chuckled, and she whipped back around, raising a condescending brow. She liked to tease Tank, but she didn't want someone else laughing at him for *any* reason. "Aren't you even older than Henry is?" she asked haughtily, pursing her lips in disapproval. "I wouldn't be laughing, if I were you."

Sobering, Murphy cleared his throat. "What nest did you grow up in?"

"Elder Creek." Hunny shifted uncomfortably in her seat, her knuckles turning white from the grip she kept on her knees. "Just outside of Tulsa, Oklahoma."

"You're a long way from home. What made you leave?"

"My parents died," Hunny admitted reluctantly, feeling guilty Tank was finding out so much about her now instead of days ago. Should she have talked to him in depth about all of this beforehand? It had never come up, and he rarely pushed for any answers. He knew she was a lone shifter, but she hadn't exactly specified all the details. Considering how protective he'd become, she knew he'd get pissed when he found out everything.

Murphy stared at her, almost like he could sense there was more to the story. She grimaced. "My old Buck ... he wanted to mate with me shortly after they passed away. I didn't feel safe there after rejecting him, so I left shortly before my eighteenth birthday."

"That rat bastard," Tank snarled. "I'll fucking gut the prick—"

"Enough, Tank," Murphy warned. "Another outburst, brother, and you'll need to wait out front."

Hunny winced, guilt hitting her anew. "It's my fault. I should have told him before now." She looked back at her surly bear shifter apologetically. Tank's eyes found hers, and he relaxed marginally, crossing his arms in front of his chest. Turning back to Murphy, Hunny added, "I haven't joined another nest or anything since. And I rarely stay anywhere for more than a year, at most."

Murphy cocked his head to the side. "Why not?"

"No place has ever felt like home." *Until now.*

The Alpha stared at her pensively, like he was weighing her words. "When my brother found you in the woods, a she-wolf had attacked you. I'd like for you to tell me what happened there."

Taking a deep breath, Hunny did just that, giving him a brief rundown of her time in Montana, Jason ... everything. When she finished, he didn't seem shocked, so she could only assume his mother, and maybe even Tank, had informed him of a few things.

It didn't bother her if they had. They were only looking out for the safety of their clan. She also knew that Tank wouldn't tell his brother anything if he didn't feel it was absolutely necessary.

"I'll be frank, Hunny," the Alpha announced suddenly. "I don't give a shit about your mated status, or why you were rejected. Jason is a piece of work. You were lucky to escape him."

Hadn't Tank said something very similar only a few days ago? Just what kind of wolf pack was Jason running?

"You're not the first one to tell me that." She shivered as a chill went down her spine. "I'm assuming you were about to throw a 'but' in there somewhere, though," she added helpfully, nerves clawing at her gut.

"I don't trust lone shifters," Murphy disclosed bluntly. "A few bad experiences in the past have left me jaded, and that's not including the reputation your kind possesses. Most lone shifters are kicked out of their packs, clans, or nests because they've done something criminally wrong. While it's not unheard of for a shifter to willingly leave their homes, it is unlikely."

She didn't feel offended by his assessment—it was par for the course at this point. "I'm not lying about why I left, if that's what you're hinting at."

Murphy stared at her intently for one long moment. "I'm willing to let you stay in our territory on a trial basis."

Hunny sighed in relief, feeling like she'd just passed an exam she'd forgotten to study for.

Murphy's gaze shifted from her to Tank. "You need to give us a minute, brother." As soon as Tank began to argue, the Alpha held up his hand, silencing him. "The rest of this conversation isn't for you. I've tolerated enough of your outbursts. This'll only be a minute."

Tank walked up to the desk then, standing right beside Hunny. Dropping his hand onto her shoulder, he waited until she looked up at him before he asked, "You good, darlin'?"

She was tempted to beg him to stay, but in the end, she nodded her head, sending him a reassuring smile she didn't feel. "I'll be fine."

Grunting, Tank sent a hostile glare to his brother before storming toward the door.

"I want to be honest with you, Hunny," Murphy began as soon as Tank closed the door behind him, leaving the two of them alone. "I don't like the idea of a lone shifter staying in my territory. I hate it, actually. If you want to join our clan, that's one thing, and I'd only consider it after a thorough investigation into your background. But right now, you're an unknown element. I don't like those."

Her heart clenched, and her mouth dried from panic. "Then why agree to let me stay at all?"

Murphy pointed to the door. "Because of Tank. I haven't seen my brother act like this since he was a teenager."

Her brow furrowed in confusion. "Like what?"

"*Alive,*" Murphy confided passionately, running a hand through his hair as he released a shaky breath. "It fucking guts me to say it, but my brother hasn't been living. Not for a long time. He's been a shell of his former self since Cassandra died when we were younger. And I never thought I'd see the brother I knew again. But he's changed in the last week. Since meeting you."

Cassandra. That had to be Tank's true mate. She had a pretty name.

Suddenly, Hunny recalled the first night she saw Tank. How she'd looked into his big brown eyes and seen a lonely soul; a sad, kindred spirit. She'd seen a broken male staring back at her then. But now?

She didn't see that void in him, not like before. Hardly at all, actually. Only when he seemed lost in thought, or when the silence between them stretched on for too long.

"And you think I have something to do with this change?" Hunny guessed quietly, warmth filling her chest at the notion.

"I absolutely do. So I don't care if you got thrown out of your nest, or if you're some evil bitch and that's why your mate rejected you. I care about Tank. And if you're what's good for him, I'm more than happy for you to stay." Murphy pointed at her then, his eyes growing hard. "But if you hurt him, or harm this clan, then I'll see to it you regret that decision."

Hunny stared at him like a deer caught in headlights for several seconds as tension filled the room, his vague threat hanging over them both. It was tempting to duck her head and nod in acknowledgment before fleeing out the door, but she was tired of Alpha males thinking they could walk all over her.

Submissive didn't mean *weak.*

And she wouldn't let Murphy think he held all the power, not when she wasn't a member of his clan. *Yet.* Hopefully, what she said next didn't fracture her chances in the future. She took a deep, steadying breath before looking him dead in the eye.

"I don't want to hurt anyone, least of all Henry. You can believe what you want about lone shifters, and even think I'm full of shit for telling you why I left my nest; I don't care." She shrugged nonchalantly. "I can leave right now and never look back. I've done it before."

He narrowed his eyes on her, no doubt thinking the same thing she did; if she left now, Tank might retreat into himself again. She let that truth dangle between them for a handful of seconds before adding, "But I don't want to leave. I think your brother is wonderful, and I—" Hunny swallowed thickly. "It's been a really long time since I've woken up and felt genuinely grateful for the direction my life has taken. So I'd love to stay for as long as I'm welcome."

"Great," Murphy supplied shortly. He stood from his chair, waiting patiently for her to do the same.

She did, dusting off her jeans. "What would I need to do to become part of your clan?" she blurted out suddenly, shocking herself as much as Murphy. "I mean, if that was an option. You know, 'lone shifter' status aside." She air-quoted with a roll of her eyes.

"Well, my first suggestion would be to lose the attitude," the Alpha grumbled. "But then, I'd suspect that's part of your appeal to my brother."

Hunny scoffed, crossing her arms and scowling. "I don't have an attitude." And he thought Tank found her appealing? Her heart did a little somersault at the thought.

"Alright, Tank Jr., calm down," he joked dryly.

She raised her brows. "Oh wow, who's got the attitude now, Murphy?"

"Christ, you're already pissing me off. You'll fit right in." He ran a hand down his face in exasperation. "As for your question, we'll see how the next few weeks go before we look at any more permanent decisions."

"I can work with that," she said softly, hope fluttering in her chest. "But don't mention it to Henry. Please," she added, realizing she was bossing an Alpha around. "I just haven't decided anything yet, and I don't want him to get his hopes up. Not that my staying would matter to him—"

"Oh, I'm sure he doesn't care one way or another," Murphy cut in, heavy sarcasm lacing his voice.

"Ugh, shut *up*!" Hunny exclaimed, leaving his office.

His chuckle followed her out.

Thirteen

Tank narrowed his eyes as the door to Murphy's office opened, a smiling Hunny stepping into the reception area. His brother's laughter floated out after her, and Tank's mood soured further.

Great. Not only had that jackass asked to speak with her alone, now he was laughing at something she'd said. What was next? The fucker would ask her out on a date?

Over my dead body. Better yet, over Murphy's *dead body.*

"What's got him squealing like a pig?" Tank asked irritably, snatching Hunny's hand before she could answer. He intertwined their fingers, leading her as far away from his older brother as possible. No way was he going to let anyone else woo her but him.

Pushing through the front doors of the large cabin that acted as the clan's 'bear den,' which acted as the clinic, Murphy's office, and the primary meeting place for the bear shifters under Murphy's rule, he led Hunny toward his truck.

"We were just having a heart-to-heart," Hunny answered with a small laugh of her own, the delicate sound heating his blood even through his bad mood.

"Murphy better keep his heart to his fucking self," Tank snarled under his breath.

Suddenly, Hunny yanked on his hand, pulling on him until he turned to face her. "What did you say, Henry Sinclair?" she asked menacingly, her nose wrinkling adorably.

Tank cleared his throat, his cheeks heating. "I'm glad you're getting along with my brother."

She raised a brow, her green eyes shining at him like gems. "Is that right? It sounded like you said something else."

He shook his head innocently. "Nope."

"Good. I'd hate to demote you from the position as my favorite bear shifter because you were acting like a jerk."

His fingers tightened around hers, and this time he did the tugging, pulling Hunny close until she was flush against him, enjoying the feeling of her softness pressed against the hard planes of his body. He cupped the back of her neck, staring down at her heatedly. "I'm your favorite bear?" he all but purred.

Damned straight, he was her favorite.

She sniffed haughtily, rolling her eyes even as she blushed. "*For now*. But if you get snarly with me again, your ranking could drop."

Tank leaned in, his lips closer to hers than they'd ever been before as he rasped sensually, "Guess I'll have to reserve all of my nice for you, darlin'."

Hunny's eyes widened, and she released a small squeak. "I—Um, *we*—"

The scent of her desire filled the air, and it took all of Tank's strength to keep himself in check. He'd battled this seductive allure for days, and as much as he intended to remain chivalrous for her sake, it was almost impossible. All he wanted to do was breathe her deep into his lungs, to smash his lips against hers and taste her lush mouth as his fingers delved between her thighs, relieving her of the pressure he'd sensed building up inside of her for a week.

He'd figured out days ago he turned her on, and that knowledge was as delicious as her scent, going straight to his head. Now, he couldn't help but find ways to tease her, to see what flustered her. He liked learning all about his little rabbit, even while she remained oblivious to his intentions.

One day soon, when she'd healed from everything and was ready to move on, he'd make his move. But until then, he'd enjoy this tug-of-war between them.

Squirming in his hold, Hunny finally broke free, her face flushed and her chest heaving as she breathed hard. "Di-didn't you promise to take me fishing?" she asked quickly.

"I did." He raised a brow in mock concern. "Everything okay, darlin'? You look a little flustered."

"I-I'm fine." She shifted on her feet, her thighs clenching together. Unashamed, his gaze raked over her figure, settling on the gentle slope of her breasts before moving back up to her face. She gaped at him. "Did you just—" Her mouth snapped shut, and she shook her head. "Nevermind."

Tank shrugged, turning toward the truck to hide the erection straining in his jeans. Luckily, he was standing downwind of her, his scent concealed in the air. "Let's head on home, shift, and then you can help me fish, Hunny."

I t didn't take long to make it back to his cabin from the main house, and it took even less time to shift and head out into the woods. Although shifters rarely bothered with modesty, Tank remembered Hunny asking for his shirt before she changed forms for him the first time, so he ensured she had plenty of privacy.

When he finished shifting, he waited for a small squeak to sound from a nearby bush before he rounded the corner of the house, stopping in front of his tiny rabbit companion. He chuffed in greeting, leaning down to nuzzle the top of her head with his snout.

I forgot how tiny she is, he thought wistfully. *Maybe she'll stay like this and let me hold her later.*

It wouldn't hurt to ask, right?

Hunny, oblivious to his musings, pounced on him, her little paws smacking into one of his giant ones playfully before she jumped away, taking off like a rocket. Not wanting her to get lost, or stumble upon an actual bear, Tank hurried after her, slowing to a brisk walk once he'd caught up.

For nearly half an hour, he let her race around the woods like a bat out of hell, hopping in between his legs, launching herself into bushes and piles of fallen leaves with so much noise, he was sure she'd gain the attention of other predators nearby. She didn't seem to mind in the slightest, though, trusting him to keep her safe from harm while she frolicked around like a nutcase.

Tank couldn't get enough of Hunny acting so ridiculous. And the little happy grunting noises she made as she flew by him? Music to his ears. He loved seeing her happy, such a contrast to the despondent female he'd met only a week ago.

They traveled like that for another half-mile; her zooming around the woods while he followed along protectively. Soon enough, his little rabbit grew tuckered out, and she roamed back over to him, slumping at his feet.

What did she intend to do now? They still had another half a mile before they even reached the river.

An idea struck. With a low grunt, Tank lay down on his belly, resting his head on the ground right by her feet. Waiting. When she didn't get the hint, he nudged her with his snout until she was half laying over the wide bridge of his nose.

Quickly enough, she figured out his intent, her claws digging into his fur as she hopped over his head and onto his back. He felt her shift around, and after a few more seconds, he felt some pressure pull against his fur. Hunny made a muffled chirping sound.

Muffled?

Was she biting his fur to hold on?

Inwardly, Tank laughed his ass off as he pushed back to his feet, wondering how ridiculous this had to look to an outside observer. Luckily, they were alone, otherwise he knew he'd never live this down. Hell, if she told a single member of his family that he'd carried her around on his back, he'd be the subject of emotional blackmail for a decade, at least.

Carefully at first, he began moving at a brisk walk. The fur she held between her teeth tugged against his skin, but it did the trick, keeping her steady. After a few minutes, he kicked up into a run, hyper aware of every slight move she made as he neared the river.

Suddenly, Tank heard a loud rustling in some nearby bushes, too loud to be anything other than a large animal. Slowing to a stop, he released a dangerous growl, but the sound drew even closer. He twisted his body to face the threat head-on, right as something crashed through the bushes and into the clearing.

The giant grizzly bear spotted Tank immediately, dropping onto its ass and planting its front paws onto the forest floor to stop itself from careening into him. Frozen in place for a moment, it then tilted its head, looking right at Tank's face.

No, not at *him*. Right above his head. He felt it then, two tiny paws pressing down on the crown of his head as his little rabbit peeked over him and at this new addition.

The bear across from him chuffed, and then the sound of bones snapping rent the air, the bear shifting into a man a few seconds later.

Jasper, naked as the day he was born, gaped at Tank. "There's a rabbit on your head. Is that Hunny posing as Simba at Pride Rock?" He grabbed his stomach, bending over and barking out a laugh. "Look at you, Tank; just the perfect chauffeur."

Tank's claws dug into the ground, the temptation to smack his brother right in the face rising to the surface. He might have done it too, if the fucker wouldn't have bled. But that might upset Hunny. Tank didn't want her getting mad at him for injuring the damned nuisance. He also didn't want her fawning all over the bastard, offering to patch him up.

But he *really* didn't want another male naked in front of her, either. Tank made a low noise, telling the other male to back the fuck off. His brother ignored him.

"We should get you a little top hat, so the next time you take Hunny for a ride, you're dressed for the part," Jasper wheezed. "Maybe a harness, actually. Equipped with a little throne for her to sit on," he snickered.

Tank snarled in warning, but his brother didn't heed it, still chortling like a dipshit at Tank's expense.

"Now, now, brother, I know I'm naked in front of your girl, but there's no need to get testy." Jasper smirked.

That little shit—

Tank narrowed his eyes, an idea forming.

Tank crouched down, putting his head to the ground as he had before. Taking the hint immediately, Hunny slid down his body and hopped off, giving him plenty of room to handle business.

He charged at his younger brother then, and Jasper let out a shriek of surprise, shifting back into his bear form right as Tank plowed into him. They collided in a tangle of claws and fur, rolling around on the ground like a pair of adolescents.

Fur went flying, roars echoing around the forest as they fought. Still, with each roll on the ground, they made sure to avoid their spectator. Neither bear wanted to accidentally hurt Hunny.

Soon enough, Tank had his little shithead of a brother pinned beneath him, biting down on the back of his neck as he kept Jasper's head firmly pressed into the ground.

Jasper whined in reluctant surrender, but Tank didn't let up, glimpsing a flash of grayish-brown movement out of the corner of his eye. Hunny hopped over, getting in Jasper's face and making a loud chirping noise that sounded suspiciously like her own version of a laugh. Then she bopped Jasper twice on the nose with her tiny paws before tearing off through some bushes.

Clearly, the short rest had amped her battery back up.

Chuffing, Tank released his brother, backing up to let the other male rise from the dirt. With a glower, Jasper sat up on his hind legs, running his front paws over his furred belly in an attempt to straighten up his now matted fur.

Tank turned away from him, his gaze wandering to where he'd last seen Hunny. He expected her to come barreling back into the clearing at any second, but she didn't. After a full minute had passed, he cocked his head to the side, straining his ears to listen for her.

Nothing.

Suddenly uneasy, he lifted his head and sniffed, hoping to catch her scent nearby. And then he smelled it; wolf shifter. It was fresh. Close. *Too* close.

And his little rabbit was nowhere in sight.

Snarling, Tank rushed through the bushes after Hunny, his brother hot on his heels.

Where is she?

Tank released a threatening roar into the forest, hoping to deter the interloper. Hunny would know it was him. She wouldn't run away. She'd come to him if she were in danger. Right?

Unless she couldn't.

Jasper echoed the sound, letting whatever fucker that had entered their territory know Tank wasn't alone. Still, he couldn't find Hunny, trailing after her scent until he smelled blood. His head whipped to the side, following the coppery stench as he picked up speed.

No, no, no—

There, just a few feet ahead, was a bloody lump on the ground, the same size as his little rabbit. His legs weakened, and his heart stalled in his chest as he made his way over to the wounded animal, a distressed sound pouring from his throat.

The creature was almost unrecognizable, its fur completely soaked in fresh blood. Tank nudged the lifeless animal with his nose, a mournful whine leaving his throat.

"Tank."

The sound of Hunny's voice had him jerking to the left, where he spotted his very human, very naked female crouched down beside a bush. She looked frightened, her cheeks pale and her eyes wild, leaves and twigs sticking out of her hair.

Tank shifted into his human form before he even realized what he was doing, prowling over to her. He just needed to hold her, to make sure she was alright. He picked her up from the ground, wrapping his shaking arms around her.

"You're alright," he assured her, but he knew the words were for him, too, anxiety coursing through him as Jasper kept watch.

Tank's gaze returned to the dead bunny on the ground, and his jaw clenched, a tremor skating down his spine. The stench of wolf was strong here, too, meaning they'd only missed the culprit by a few minutes at most.

What the fuck had it even been doing here, so far from pack territory? Hunting? But then why hadn't it eaten the rabbit? Or had it been leaving a message? The wolf's scent wasn't familiar, but that didn't mean it wasn't part of the Moon Rose pack.

Unnerved, Tank held on more firmly to his woman, breathing in her scent to overpower the smell of blood and death.

"I'm alright. I think you scared it off," Hunny murmured, wrapping her legs around his waist as she buried her head into the crook of his neck. She was shaking almost as hard as he was, and it infuriated him that someone had come into their territory and scared her like this. Scared them both. "I want to go home, Henry."

"Alright, baby," he crooned, turning back toward his cabin with her still secured in his arms. "Let's go home."

He'd take her home, get her settled, and make sure she was safe. And then he'd come back out here, hunt down that wolf, and rip it to pieces.

Fourteen

Hunny's trembling eased as Tank carried her into his cabin, his hot, naked body warming her despite how chilled she felt. His grip on her didn't let up, even after he shut the door behind him, or carried her upstairs to his bedroom. He only let her go when he placed her on the edge of his bed, his fingers trailing over her cheek before he walked over to his dresser, giving her a perfect view of his ass.

And damn ... Tank had a *nice* ass.

She'd seen him shirtless plenty of times since they'd met, but she'd never seen him *naked*. Not until he'd shifted right in front of her out in the woods, his expression gutted until he realized she was alright. And then the relief in his eyes had mirrored her own, and she hadn't been able to see past that. Hadn't been able to think about anything other than Tank holding her protectively in his arms.

But now that she was safely tucked away in Tank's home, with his scent permeating the air and relaxing her, she kind of hated that she hadn't thought to sneak a peek at his bare body before he'd walked away. She might be shaken up, but she was still a woman with *interests*, specifically where her big, burly bear was concerned.

And if the back of him looked this nice, she could only imagine what the rest of him looked like.

"Did the wolf see you?" Tank asked gruffly, sifting quickly through a drawer and pulling out some clothes. She watched him like a hawk, the teeniest bit grateful that he was facing away from her, too preoccupied

to notice that she was blatantly checking him out. If he caught her
lusting over him like a cat in heat, he'd probably be mortified.

Rightfully so.

Seriously, what had gotten into her? One sighting of his sculpted
cheeks and she'd morphed into a horny bitch? Okay, she'd been horny
for days, but she'd just been terrified. She didn't need to be thinking
about how well-defined Tank's legs were, or that his ass was honestly
a work of art.

And yet here she was, multitasking like a champion.

"No," Hunny answered, swallowing thickly as he slid a pair of sweats
up his legs, covering his backside. "As soon as I knew another shifter
was nearby, I hid." Now that some of Tank's tantalizing skin was covered, she felt less distracted and more confused by what she'd seen
outside. "What was a wolf even doing here? Is there one in your clan?"
She assumed the answer was no, but it didn't hurt to check.

A deep growl rumbled in his chest as he said, "No, and I don't care
why it was here, darlin'. It'll be dead if I find it anywhere near you
again." His grip tightened on the drawer handle, his back tensing in
agitation. "I thought that—" His gravelly voice broke slightly, and he
took a deep, shuddering breath. "I thought I'd found you dead in the
woods."

Hunny's face softened as she stared at his sinewy back, her fingers
itching to touch him. To soothe him. "I'm okay, Henry."

Tank turned around then, a sinister expression on his face. Despite
how furious he looked, he calmly made his way over to her, gently
lifting her arms into the air and sliding a giant T-shirt over her head that
smelled deliciously like him. Pulling it down until she was adequately
covered, he lifted her back into his arms, turned, and then sat down
on the bed, cradling her against his chest.

He took another ragged breath, and her hands slid up the expanse
of his chest, her lips pressing against the quickly beating pulse in his
neck as she laid her head on his shoulder. "I know you wouldn't let
anything happen to me," she murmured against his skin.

His hands wandered to her bare thighs, holding her more firmly
against him. "I almost did." His fingers dug into her skin. "It took me
too long to find you."

"I was only gone for a few minutes, Henry. And as soon as I felt
threatened, I shifted. I knew I'd stand a better chance in my human
form until you got to me. I promise I'm okay," she reiterated, placing a

light kiss on his frantic pulse, needing to reassure him she was alright. She heard his heart skip a beat, and he seemed to hold his breath. And then he wrapped his arms around her waist, dropping his head into the crook of her shoulder.

She wanted to sink into him, to comfort him and never let him go. She'd gotten used to this level of closeness between them, and she loved it when he held her, just like this. It was so natural. But unlike the other times, this felt so much more *intimate*. The energy in the room was charged, filled with a tension she couldn't ignore.

Was it because he thought, however briefly, that she'd gotten killed? Or because they were in his room together, a place she'd avoided like the plague unless it was to use the connecting bathroom?

She didn't sleep in here; a point Tank had grown irritated with over the last few days, arguing that, until her room was built, he could sleep on the couch while she took the bed. But Tank was literally, well, *a tank*, and the couch was too small for him to sleep on comfortably, so she refused to steal his bed.

Not that her decision mattered. In the end, they'd both taken to sleeping on the couch nightly, usually because they'd fall asleep watching trashy shows on TV, covered by a mountain of warm blankets and cuddled into each other. Hunny didn't mind sharing the couch with him, mostly because she loved feeling his body pressed against hers.

Tank was snuggly, warm, and safe, even while he made her insides melt with desire. Still, she'd never felt this same level of sexual tension between them until now.

Another thought intruded, and she distinctly remembered earlier, when they'd left Murphy's office. Tank had acted jealous over nothing, so she'd teased him about being her favorite bear shifter, just to get him out of his snit.

As soon as she'd done it, it was like a switch had flipped between them. Tank had invaded her space, his scent powerful and addictive as he'd leaned in close. For the briefest moment, she could have sworn she'd seen a carnal hunger shining in his eyes. Her body had reacted immediately, and as he'd leaned in even closer, she'd felt confident he would kiss her.

And she'd been so disappointed when he hadn't.

What did that whole encounter even mean? Did he *like* her? No. She didn't believe that. Sure, he did nice things for her. Like, cook her delicious meals, let her boss him around, indulge her love of puzzles and reality TV, cuddle with her all the time—

As the list piled up, Hunny felt like a damned idiot, and suddenly Jasper's playful jabs at Tank, Tabitha's sly smile, and Murphy's comments earlier today all made sense.

Tank was a dick to everyone but Hunny. Hunny, who he went out of his way to accommodate. Hunny, who he loved to listen to all day long, even though he claimed to despise chatterboxes. Hunny, who he'd asked to stay when she'd thought about leaving. That's why he'd looked at her so hungrily earlier.

Because he *wanted* her.

No ... He can't want me, not like that, she thought ruefully. Wouldn't she have scented his desire if that were the case? But she hadn't. Not once in the last week. Even so, she couldn't help but wonder, *What could he possibly see in me?* Probably nothing more than a female to protect.

So consumed with her thoughts, Tank startled her when he grabbed her hips and squeezed. "Were you listening, darlin'?"

Hunny blushed, her lips brushing his neck again as she asked, "Repeat it for me?"

"I need to go back out there," Tank rasped. "I don't like that a wolf was on bear territory, and it feels like it left that dead animal there as a warning."

"You think it's one of Jason's people?" Hunny shook her head in denial. "That wasn't Natasha."

"Doesn't mean it wasn't another one of his pack members."

"Why would Jason send one of his wolves here?" She shook her head again, leaning back to stare at him. He lifted his head as well, his gaze meeting hers, his eyes dark and broody. "Natasha having it out for me makes sense; she's pissed I'm pregnant. But how would another wolf even know about me at all? I doubt she'd reveal Jason's true mate to anyone, and Jason kept me locked away like a dirty secret. He hated me for being a submissive, so why would he tell anyone about me after his rejection?"

Tank huffed, reaching up and pulling a few leaves from her messy hair. "Maybe it's not someone from his pack, but I'm betting it is. Either way, they aren't meant to be here. If I can hunt down that wolf, I'll get some answers."

Hunny nodded reluctantly, but she wasn't sure she agreed with Tank's assumption. Jason was finished with her, and after the incident with Natasha, that bitch hadn't shown back up here to mess with her. She guessed she didn't have the guts to attack her on bear turf.

So what would be the point now?

"Are you taking Jasper with you?" she eventually asked.

"No," Tank said firmly, absent-mindedly combing her hair with his fingers. "He's going to stay outside to monitor you and the cabin while I'm gone."

Hunny cupped his face then, his beard tickling her palm as she sent him a worried look. "I don't want you going after that wolf alone. What if there's more than just one?"

He was a massive grizzly bear, but several wolves could overpower him. Not only that, he'd told her the Moon Rose pack was full of crazy bastards; she didn't want Tank anywhere near them, especially alone. She still needed to ask him more about that, to learn just how depraved Jason was, but part of her didn't want to know.

She carried his offspring—what if there was something genuinely wrong with Jason and that got passed along to her children? She'd be distraught. Not that going in blind was a smart decision, either, but couldn't she live with the wool over her eyes for a little while longer?

"I talked to Murphy on the way back home." Tank tapped the side of his head, indicating the telepathic connection an Alpha shared with its subordinates. "He and a few others will come with me to hunt."

Hunny sagged against him in relief, but she still didn't like it. He was putting himself in danger for her. "I can't believe it's day one of being allowed to stay in bear territory and you already have to track someone down because you think they're a threat to me."

Murphy was probably ready to throw her out on her ass.

"It's my privilege to care for and protect you, Hunny." Tank leaned into her palm as it cradled his cheek, his eyes softening before he pressed his forehead against hers. "I'm glad you're okay, darlin'."

Her heart squeezed in her chest at his admission, and her eyes burned from the sudden sting of tears.

"I'll always be okay when I'm with you, Henry," she murmured, breathing him in.

And she meant every word.

Tank stood then, cradling her close as he walked into the bathroom. "Come on. I want you to take a nice bath and relax." Setting her on her feet, he moved to the bathroom cabinet, opening a door under the sink. "You haven't tried that bubble bath shit since we got it the other day."

Hunny's lips twitched as she watched him bend over at the waist, opening several plastic bags inside the cabinet to rustle through each one. "They're bath bombs, Henry."

He paused. "No bubbles?"

"No, but they smell good and make the water look pretty." And then, with his touch still warm on her body, Hunny decided to test her new theory, just to see if she was being crazy. "They also make my skin feel really smooth, too."

The rustling noises stopped and his shoulders stiffened. "Oh?"

"Mmhm. Sometimes, after a nice long bath, I just can't help but touch myself. If you want, when you come back, I'll let you touch—"

Tank stood so quickly, his head slammed into the edge of the bathroom counter with a loud thunk. He bit out a sharp curse, spinning around and wincing.

"Holy shit, are you alright?!" Hunny exclaimed, forgetting all about her theory as she rushed forward and grabbed the sides of his face. Worried, she jerked his head down, inadvertently burying his face against her boobs so she could look at the top of his head. Sliding her fingers through his unruly hair, she sighed in relief—no sign of a lump or a cut. "I don't see any blood."

"What were you saying?" Tank asked, his voice muffled by her shirt. His breath was warm, seeping through the material. Her nipples hardened in response, and her core heated as desire flared to life.

"You're not bleeding," she murmured, fighting every urge she had to rub herself against him.

"No, before that."

Her brow furrowed, and then her eyes widened in realization, her heart kicking into overdrive as it pounded against her sternum. Grabbing a handful of Tank's hair, she pulled his head back to look at him. "I said that when you come back, you can touch my arms, if you want to see how soft they feel."

His eyes flashed with an indecipherable emotion, and then he stood to his full height. "Oh. Right. Your arms." He cleared his throat, taking a step back. And then she smelled it in the air; the barest trace of Tank's musk, dark spices, and *arousal.*

Oh.

My.

God.

"I'll be back soon," Tank promised gutturally, rushing from the bathroom before she could say anything.

He left her standing there; bewildered by the knowledge that he was attracted to her and wondering just what she planned to do about it.

Fifteen

Tank waited for Murphy and the others outside, his dick hard as a rock and easily noticeable in his sweatpants. Luckily, no one but Jasper was present just yet, and his younger brother was still in bear form, meaning he couldn't make any sly comments to Tank's face if he did notice his state of distress. Not yet, anyway.

Like distress is even the right word, Tank thought angrily. He wasn't distressed. He was horny as fuck.

Running a hand down his face, he groaned quietly into his palm, his cock aching as much as his damned head as he recalled the words Hunny had whispered seductively to him only minutes ago, conjuring up all sorts of wicked images.

Mostly, those images involved hands roaming over her naked body. But it wasn't just *her* hands; he'd envisioned his own caressing every inch of her silken skin. Touching her sensually as she moaned his name, her delicate flesh soft and perfect under his calloused palms.

He shuddered, squeezing his eyes shut. He needed to push those thoughts away, to concentrate on the task at hand; finding the wolf that posed a threat to his little rabbit and wiping it out.

Immediately, his head cleared, his erection dying down a few seconds later. Although Tank was glad Hunny was fine, he was furious with himself that he hadn't caught the wolf responsible, and anxious about what the entire ordeal meant. Something didn't sit well with him, and his instincts were screaming at him that something was wrong.

The sound of an engine and the crunch of rubber on gravel had Tank's eyes snapping open. He spotted Murphy's large luxury SUV as it pulled to a stop. His oldest brother was in the driver's seat, and a few other bear shifters were crammed into the rest of the vehicle. Colter, who was sitting in the front seat, was a fellow enforcer—bear shifters that acted as security for the clan, enforcing the rules that Murphy set.

Another male that he spotted toward the back, Zeke, was simply a dominant shifter. Two more males were also in the backseat, but he couldn't make out their features enough to identify them.

Murphy turned the SUV off and hopped from the vehicle, nodding at Jasper, who lounged on the porch beside the front door. Then the Alpha's attention shifted back to Tank. "You ready?"

Tank grunted in response, nodding to the males his brother had brought with him as they each exited the vehicle. The last two to hop out were the twins, Marcus and Dante, both trackers. Including Tank, there were six males in total. More than enough to watch each other's backs while they searched.

As they began walking toward the heart of the woods, Tank filled the others in on the situation, careful not to exclude a single detail. It wasn't much, admittedly, but by the time he was through speaking, his throat hurt like a son of a bitch, and he wished he had some of that tea Hunny kept forcing down his throat each morning. It tasted god-awful, but it helped.

"We'll find out who it is." Murphy clapped Tank's bare shoulder. "Hunny doing okay?"

Tank huffed, sending his brother a sidelong glance. "She thinks you'll want her gone after this." She'd joked about it, but Tank knew his little rabbit well enough to know this was yet another worry hoisted upon her shoulders, and he wanted it removed. Immediately.

Murphy shook his head, his hand tightening on Tank's shoulder before he dropped it. "I wouldn't do that, brother. She's not at fault for the actions of another."

He'd known Murphy would say that, but he'd still wanted to make absolutely certain so he could tell his Hunny. Murphy might be a stickler for the rules, but he was a fair Alpha and thoughtful. Unlike some leaders, he took his responsibilities seriously.

They were silent as the other males fanned out. After a few minutes, it was just the two of them, and Tank couldn't help but ask, "Why'd you want to talk to Hunny alone?" His tone was bitter and full of jealousy, he knew, but he didn't bother hiding it.

Murphy shrugged innocently. "I didn't think you'd approve of our conversation, so I didn't want you a part of it."

Tank cursed under his breath, his body tensing as his jealousy spiked. "And just what was your conversation about? Are you interested in her?"

Stopping dead in his tracks, Murphy grabbed Tank's arm and twisted him around until the males faced each other. "No," Murphy informed him vehemently. "Do you think I've got a death wish? I've seen the way you look at her, not to mention what I heard from Mom and Jasper. You barely give her an inch to breathe when you're in the same room, and you glare at anyone who gets within ten feet of her."

Damn straight, he did.

Murphy raised a brow. "You're not even going to deny it?"

"Deny what?"

"That you want her," his older brother stated, lowering his voice into a near whisper.

"No. She's mine."

"And does Hunny know this?"

Tank grunted, resuming their walk. Murphy sighed, racing to keep up with him. "I take it by your silence that's a no."

He almost didn't respond, itching to shift into his bear form and go hunting. To escape this barrage of questioning. But he stopped again instead, facing his brother once more. "I don't want to frighten her off, Murph. She's been through a lot."

"That's true. Plus, her stay with us is only temporary. She could be a bad fit for the clan or decide to leave at any moment. Hell, maybe your overbearing bullshit will frighten her off." Tank growled at that, and Murphy smirked, adding, "But you won't know if you don't make a move, jackass."

"Fuck off," Tank snarled, though his brother was right. "I'm giving her time." It didn't matter that every day waiting was agony; he'd give her as much time as she needed because, contrary to Murphy's assumptions, Tank didn't plan on scaring Hunny off.

He planned on making her his.

"Not too much, I hope." Murphy sent Tank a sly look. "I heard pregnant females need to be satisfied a lot."

Lust hit Tank square in the gut like a battering ram. Hissing under his breath, he ripped off his sweats and shifted. His paws had barely touched the forest floor before he took off at a run, needing an outlet for the emotions pouring into him.

All the while, Murphy's laughter echoed after him.

H ours later, long after the sun had set, Tank wearily made it up the front steps of his porch. He'd searched the woods for so long, hoping to find a trail, a familiar scent, *anything* he could link to the Moon Rose pack. Instead, they'd found nothing but irritation.

He didn't know what next steps would be taken, if any, but that was a problem for tomorrow. For now? He just wanted to climb onto the couch with Hunny and fall asleep with her body and scent surrounding him. This was the longest he'd gone without her since they'd met, and he didn't like the separation. At all.

Jasper was napping by the front door, his jowls shaking as the grizzly snored loudly, completely oblivious to Tank's arrival. Some line of defense he'd been, the little shit.

Quietly opening the front door with a shake of his head, Tank stepped inside, closing the door behind him before locking it. Eyes adjusting to the dark lighting, he looked over to the couch, head tilting in surprise when he spotted familiar blankets folded neatly on the far cushion.

But Hunny was nowhere in sight.

Had she finally slept upstairs? He should have felt relief at the idea; he'd pressed her for days about using the bed because he knew it would be better for her body and would help her feel refreshed and charged for the next day. Although, now that he realized she'd be sleeping up there, he'd be without her at night while he slept down here.

Just great.

His upper lip curled in distaste as a low, indistinct rumble of irritation poured from his throat. He looked up at the railing, faint light shining down from the bedroom.

I should go check on her, just in case she needs another blanket or something. The idea barely formed before he had prowled over to the staircase, eager to at least be near her.

He also needed to grab a change of clothing, considering he'd lost his pair of sweats somewhere in the woods and hadn't bothered to track them down. Ensuring he was quiet, Tank reached the landing, a small lamp on the far nightstand illuminating the room in a soft, delicate glow.

And there, slumbering peacefully on his large bed, was Hunny. Her lilac hair spread over one of his pillows in a thick cascade as she hugged another pillow to her chest, her brows furrowed and her nose twitching as she dreamed. She was still wearing his shirt from earlier, and warmth blossomed in his chest, contentment threatening to burn him alive.

She looked perfect, sleeping in his bed with his shirt wrapped around her body. He eyed the pillow she held with disdain, angry with an inanimate object because she'd cuddled up with that instead of him. It didn't matter that his scent was likely all over the damned thing; what mattered was that *she* wasn't all over *him*.

Moving until he was flush against the side of the bed, Tank reached out, plucking up one of Hunny's stray curls and rubbing it between his thumb and finger. He'd barely let go when she shifted on the bed. Her eyes still peacefully closed, she grabbed his wrist, tugging him forward.

"Henry? Come to bed so I can finally sleep," Hunny whispered, her voice thick and drowsy.

Heart kicking up speed in his chest, and refusing to wait for another invitation, Tank peeled back the covers, climbing in beside her until only the pillow she'd been curled around separated them. "You were sleeping just fine without me," he murmured, glaring down at the pillow.

He didn't want anything separating them.

"Nope," she slurred, haphazardly shoving the pillow away from her as he laid onto his back. Then, moving faster than he'd ever seen, Hunny was beside him, plastering her small body to his side as she spooned him. A small arm stretched across his torso, her hand settling on the center of his chest as she dropped her leg on top of his. She made a small sound of contentment, laying her head on his chest. "Much better."

He huffed out a brief laugh, even as his heart swelled. Then he wrapped his arm around her, bringing her closer still. Her bewitching scent invaded his senses, and his stomach clenched, his cock twitching as it stirred to life. "Better than your pillow?" he asked, clenching his teeth as desire licked up his shaft.

She still hadn't opened her eyes yet, and Tank was pretty confident she was just talking to him in her sleep. She did that sometimes, which he found adorable.

"Mmhm. Smell good and you're so warm." Her fingers sifted through his chest hair with a teasing caress he felt all the way down to his balls. "Want this."

He swallowed thickly as she stroked him again, taking a shuddering breath to keep himself in check. "My chest hair?" he eventually asked, his voice strained.

Hunny hummed, and his erection flexed, the tip smacking against his lower abdomen. The scent of his desire permeated the air, and he stilled, afraid she'd notice and actually wake up.

He watched her like a hawk, his eyes riveted to her face. Her nose wrinkled up, and then she moaned, pushing her leg more fully over his. Her bare pussy pressed against his thigh, her slick dripping onto him as she rocked herself against his leg, inhaling deeply. "So good."

"Darlin'—"

"Henry," she moaned sleepily, and the smell of her sweet desire rose between them.

Oh, fuck me.

Precum dribbled onto his tip, and his hips rocked involuntarily, cock thrusting into the covers as he fought against the urge to roll her onto her back and sink into her hot, wet entrance.

Tank's muscles tensed, indecision warring with his lust. Should he touch her? Wake her up? Leave before she did something she'd regret?

Before he could do anything, though, Hunny settled back into him and began snoring softly against his chest, leaving Tank with a hard-on from hell. He released a trembling breath, wrapping his arm more firmly around her as he stared up at the ceiling, wide awake as Murphy's words from earlier taunted him, daring him to act.

To sate Hunny in all the ways she needed. Before it was too late.

Sixteen

Hunny woke in a cocoon of warmth, Tank's heady scent filling her lungs with every breath she took. Waking up like this, with him being the first thought to cross her mind, was nice. Relaxing and sweet. She'd spent years with survival being her only priority, busting her ass to take care of herself and ensuring she didn't starve. But since coming here, she hadn't worried about any of that.

She hadn't needed to because Tank took care of everything. Considering how independent she'd been for half a decade, it was surprisingly easy to fall into the role of a kept woman, even if they weren't actually a couple.

Tank was just that good at seeing to her needs. Even now, while he slept, he took care of her. She could feel him behind her, his arm thrown around her waist and his legs cradling hers as he spooned her protectively. As always, Hunny felt safe with him. And happy.

She hadn't truly felt like that since her parents died. But now? The warm emotion was always present.

Peeling her eyes open, it took her a second to adjust to the light from the lamp on her nightstand. Blinking blearily, she glanced around for a wall clock, but the room was pretty bare.

What time was it? And when had Tank crawled into bed with her?

She shifted slightly, and he murmured something under his breath, his muscled arm tightening around her waist before he pulled her hips back toward him. Something hard, hot, and thick pressed against her bare ass, and her eyes widened into saucers as realization struck.

Oh shit.

Not only was Tank *very* naked, his erection was prodding her butt. Hunny swallowed thickly, her fingers curling into the bed sheets as he pushed his cock more firmly against her, grinding his hips against her ass with a throaty groan. Instantly, she was wet, her pussy spasming with need. All she had to do was lift her leg and drop it over his hip, and his tip would brush against her entrance.

She'd be open and waiting for him.

Dragging in a shallow breath, Hunny's nails tightened around the sheets, and she vaguely wondered if she'd rip them from how fiercely she held on.

What should she do? Should she do anything? She knew what she *wanted* to do, and that was to turn around, push Tank onto his back, and straddle him. She wanted to take his shaft in hand, guide him to her entrance, and let him sink inside her.

And then she wanted to fuck his brains out, again and again and again.

More slick pooled between her thighs just thinking about it, and her core ached. The last week had been agonizing, dealing with the feeling that she held so much unrequited lust for Tank that she could do nothing about. But she'd smelled his desire yesterday; she knew he wanted her. That knowledge had haunted her all night while he'd been gone, but now he was here.

Was he awake? Did he know what he was even doing?

"Henry?" Hunny asked quietly. His breathing remained nice and even, and his hold on her didn't change in the slightest.

Make a move. Don't be such a coward. You know he wants you, so do something about it!

Emboldened, or maybe just aroused and delusional, Hunny arched her back, planting her ass firmly against the length of his erection. Tank released a deep, needy growl that she felt everywhere, her nipples hardening in response. His lips pressed against the back of her neck, his body coiling around hers. Warm breath teased her skin, and then he licked her, groaning heavily.

That deep sound was her undoing, and Hunny rolled her hips, stroking his hard length with her ass.

Tank stiffened, and then he launched himself away from her like she'd burned him. Hunny whipped around in surprise as the covers came flying off of her, wrapping around Tank's body as he fled from her side. They tangled around his legs, and he pitched forward and off the side of the bed, landing on the ground with a heavy thud.

"Oh my god," Hunny cried, mortified as Tank groaned in pain from somewhere on the floor. "H-Henry, are you okay?"

Hell, was *she* okay? She'd made a move on him and he'd run away like she was contagious. All of her confidence disappeared in an instant, leaving her humiliated and on the verge of tears as he pushed himself up from the floor, sending her a bewildered look.

His beard was a mess, his hair stuck to one half of his head, and his chest rose and fell quickly, his breathing loud and uneven. Tank cleared his throat, his eyes widening in alarm when he noticed the tears filling her eyes. "I'm sorry, Hunny. I was sleeping, and I didn't mean to touch you like that, darlin.'"

'I didn't mean to touch you like that.' The words repeated in her head, slowly moving down and twisting through her heart like a knife. Hurt mixed with humiliation and Hunny looked away from him, swallowing thickly.

Of course, he hadn't meant to touch her. Because he'd been sleeping. If he actually felt attracted to her, that wouldn't have mattered—it never had before with past partners. But based on how quickly he'd tossed himself from the bed, he obviously found her repulsive.

That had been his way of rejecting her, and the message was loud and clear. How could she have been so stupid? Was she really that lonely, that desperate for affection that she'd imagined everything growing between them?

Her heart squeezed like a vise in her chest, and her lungs burned as she tried to breathe normally. The last thing she wanted now was to break down sobbing and only humiliate herself further.

He didn't want her after all. His rejection had been clear. And she didn't know how to react. Didn't know how to feel. With Jason, his rejection had gutted her. But she knew she'd be fine. That she could persevere.

But Tank rejecting her? This was a level of devastation she hadn't felt in years.

'I didn't mean to touch you ...'

She tugged her shirt down, desperate to cover every inch of her body from his gaze as shame joined the party of turmoil swirling around inside her.

How had she gotten her signals so wrong? She couldn't wrap her head around it, but clearly, she was a freaking idiot. Tank didn't want to touch her, and she'd taken advantage of him in his sleep. What kind of person did that make her? What the fuck was wrong with her?

Tank stirred, rising from the floor with the sheets now wrapped securely around his waist. "Are you okay? I didn't make you uncomfortable, did I?"

Hunny snorted, but the sound lacked humor as she slid a hand down her face, keeping her gaze averted. "No, I—" Her throat constricted, and her chin wobbled as she fought to control her emotions, just for a few minutes longer. "*No.* You didn't do anything wrong."

"You look like you're going to cry—"

Her fingers twisted along the hem of her shirt as she struggled to keep her composure, refusing to admit the truth. "It's just pregnancy hormones."

"Okay," he answered slowly, but there was an uncertain note in his voice as he added, "I never want to hurt you, Hunny. Or make you think I'm taking advantage of you. Please believe that."

Oh, great. Now he was consoling her because *he* felt bad. He'd be better off digging her a grave outside and just letting her wallow in it until she died of shame.

The silence between them grew, and the tension was taut and oppressive. Enough so that Hunny mustered up a small smile, sending him a quick, fleeting look. "I don't feel that way. Everything's good between us. I promise."

Tank stayed there for another few seconds and then he put the covers back on the bed for her. She quickly looked away from him, lying back down as she pulled the covers close, wishing they'd swallow her whole.

Tank sighed. "I'm going to take a shower."

"Yup. I'll just"—*cry my eyes out*—"get a bit more rest."

It wasn't until he'd locked himself in the bathroom, the sound of the running shower loud through the door, that Hunny let herself cry, hoping to ease some of her wayward emotions.

It didn't work.

"**H**ow are you feeling, Hunny?" Tabitha asked later that day, ushering both Hunny and Tank into an examination room just off from the clinic's lobby. The building was attached by a long hallway to the den house and just a mile from Tank's cabin, but after a silent drive over, it had felt like an eternity.

Hunny felt Tank crowding in behind her, and her irritation spiked. She was tempted to turn around and demand he haul his big bear ass back to the waiting room. This wasn't his kit so he didn't need to be here. Instead, she ignored his presence like she had all morning. She didn't want to say anything she'd regret later, and right now, she wasn't in the proper mindset to talk to him about anything.

She was still too hurt.

She placed a protective hand over her still-flat stomach, looking at Tabitha. "Pretty good, I think."

It was a lie, obviously, but it was a better answer than, 'Actually, I tried to have sex with your son this morning and he shot me down spectacularly. No, I have not recovered from the emotional trauma.'

Her cry earlier had only caused resentment to build, and instead of feeling better, she was now pissed off *and* miserable. It didn't matter that several hours had passed since the *incident;* Hunny's mood hadn't improved in the slightest.

Probably because Henry ran from me like I was diseased and *on fire*, she thought irritably. Even though she'd read all the signs wrong, including the metaphorical neon arrow pointing to the erection he'd had *no problem* thrusting against her, his reaction this morning was over-the-top.

Completely ridiculous.

Falling out of bed in his haste to get away from her? *Puh-lease.* That aggravating male never let her sleep more than an inch away from him any other night, but now, *suddenly*, she was disgusting to be around? Confusion and hurt warred within her.

She dropped her hands to her side, clenching them into fists to help keep her mind focused on this appointment.

Tabitha sent her a quick smile, adjusting the white doctor's coat she wore as Hunny climbed onto the examination table. "Nervous?"

"No," Hunny grumbled, only to wince when Tabitha shot her a hesitant look. "I'm sorry. I'm a bit hormonal today. And okay, maybe a little nervous," she added at the last second, hoping to placate Tank's mother. It wasn't Tabitha's fault she had a jerk for a son.

As soon as the thought entered her mind, Hunny felt guilty.

Was Tank really a jerk? No, he wasn't. He'd set boundaries, albeit aggressively, and she didn't need to throw a fit just because she didn't like them. He had already done so much for her. He was her friend before anything else, and she needed to be respectful.

Even if it did hurt.

And God, it hurt so much.

Don't think about it. Focus on your kit. Focus on yourself. Deep breaths, bitch. You'll be okay. You're always okay.

"Hormones happen," Tabitha said matter-of-factly, in way of explanation for Hunny's poor behavior, taking a seat on a small medical stool with wheels. A large cart was beside the bed, a sonogram machine sitting on top. "Lie back for me, and we'll take a look at your kit."

Suddenly anxious, Hunny did as instructed, moving her shirt up until it rested just under her breasts. Needing an outlet for her nerves, and still moody, she turned toward Tank, who'd parked himself in a corner, and waved a hand at her bare belly. "Feel free to look away if this is too much for you, Tank. I don't want to freak you out again."

As soon as she said it, she felt like an asshole.

See? This is why you need to keep your mouth shut until you're feeling less bitchy.

Tank's eyes narrowed and his jaw clenched, but he remained silent, crossing his arms in front of his chest.

Clearing her throat to cut the tense silence, Tabitha turned the machine on, grabbing a wand and a tube. "This is some gel I'll put on your belly. It's cold, but it'll help me see what's going on."

Squirting the gel onto her stomach, Tabitha made quick work of pressing the end of the wand to Hunny's skin, moving it around as they both stared at a black-and-white monitor. Hunny had no clue what she was looking at, but Tabitha whistled lowly after a few minutes.

"You've got your work cut out for you, Hunny."

Well, that didn't sound good at all. What kind of news was that?

"What does that mean?" Hunny sat up on her elbows, staring at Tank's mom in dread. "It's twins, isn't it?"

Tabitha sent her an apologetic smile. "Triplets."

There was a beat of silence as her brain struggled to catch up, the wand digging uncomfortably into her stomach. Hunny shook her head quickly. "Can you repeat that? I must have misheard you."

Before Tabitha could answer, Tank was beside the bed, his hand resting on Hunny's thigh as he stared in awe at the monitor. "Triplets? You're sure?"

"Positive." With a sweet smile, Tabitha pointed to three tiny dots on the screen. "You can see each one has its own gestational sac, which is good. It means health complications are less likely."

"Oh. Great," Hunny stated a bit frantically, unsure if she was going to vomit all over the floor or pass out. Both? "I thought maybe, worst-case scenario, *maybe* twins. But triplets? *That's three,*" she whispered faintly, bile rising in her throat as her head swam. "That's three, but I only have two hands. That's not enough hands for three babies!" she exclaimed hysterically, her breathing becoming shallow as a chill swept down her spine.

Oh no, she was going to vomit.

She sat up quickly, swinging her legs over the side of the table. The room spun, and her nausea increased. She needed to get the hell out of here—

Suddenly, Tank cupped her face, his palms warm against her cold skin. He looked down at her, his deep brown eyes radiating a calmness she didn't feel. "Breathe for me, baby," he murmured, taking a deep breath and waiting for her to do the same.

Her vision flooded with tears, and she glanced at the sonogram monitor just over his shoulder. The image was gone. But that didn't matter. It was burned into her brain for the rest of her life.

How could she raise three kits? She wasn't even cut out to be a mother, and she couldn't do this alone. She *couldn't*.

Three?

Hunny gasped, her heart pounding in her ears; the world around her tilting on its axis.

Tank shook his head, tightening his hold on her face until she glanced at him. "Don't look at anything but me. Breathe."

"B-But I c-can't breathe, I-I only have *two* h-hands," Hunny blubbered nonsensically, tears sliding down her face unchecked as she began crying.

She felt every kind of pathetic, and somewhere in the recesses of her mind, a stronger version of herself was demanding she shut the hell up and pull herself together. She'd handled the death of her parents, being rejected twice, and enduring years of self-imposed isolation; she could handle this, too.

Unfortunately, that voice was drowned out as she cried harder, embarrassing herself for the second time in less than twenty-four hours. Could this day get any worse?

"I've got two hands, too, darlin'," Tank pointed out with a small chuckle, wiping away some of her tears with the pads of his thumbs. "That's four between us and more than enough for three kits."

"I know how to count, Henry!" Hunny wailed miserably, her shoulders shaking. "But you don't e-even like me. S-soon enough you won't be here. It'll just be me. It's always *just* me. I'll be alone again—"

"No, you won't," Tank growled, cupping the back of her neck. He forced her head back until she was looking up at him, dominance radiating from every inch of him as it poured over her, his influence demanding that she calm down.

And she did, sucking in a deep, trembling breath. Tears still ran unchecked down her face, but at least she didn't feel like she'd pass out anymore. Or hurl everywhere.

"You won't be alone," Tank told her firmly, his eyes penetrating and possessive. "I'm here with you as long as you want me."

She squeezed her eyes shut and sobbed, knowing that it likely wasn't true. He was just trying to make her feel better.

Tank bit out a sharp curse and then picked her up from the table, holding her tightly to his chest as he ran a palm up and down her back soothingly. "You're breaking my heart with your tears, Hunny."

"At least now we're even," she mumbled in despair, only for her mouth to drop open in horror when she realized what she'd said.

Tank went completely still. A heartbeat passed between them before he asked, "What did you just say?"

Seventeen

W hat the hell did Hunny mean by that? He'd broken her heart? When? *How?*

"Answer me," Tank commanded darkly, his fingers tightening on the back of Hunny's neck as he held her firmly against his chest. His shirt was damp from her tears, and each shuddering breath she took made his heart twist painfully. He wanted her to stop crying, to not be so petrified of the future. To stop feeling like she would always be alone.

But most importantly? He wanted her to answer the damned question.

His mom popped up from her seat, the sudden movement startling him. His head snapped up, eyes meeting hers. "I'm going to give you two a moment," she informed him, her voice more high-pitched than he'd ever heard it before. Pointing awkwardly to the door, she shuffled from the room like a fire had been lit under her ass.

"I didn't mean anything by it," Hunny whispered, returning his attention to the small form huddled against him. She kept her face firmly buried into his shirt. "Can we please not talk about it?"

Not talk about it? Just like they'd barely spoken all day? Hunny had avoided him like the plague since this morning, barely glancing at him, barely responding to anything he said. And for someone like Tank, who thrived on silence, he'd absolutely fucking hated how quiet his cabin had been today.

Fuck, had he hated it.

It had only begun this morning, after he'd woken up with his hands gripping her tight and his cock buried against her ass as he'd thrust against her.

That had to be why Hunny was upset; he'd taken advantage of her in her sleep. It didn't matter that he'd been asleep, too. He should have at least put some clothes on before climbing into bed with her. And though he'd apologized this morning for his behavior, it clearly hadn't been enough.

Had he damaged his chance with her forever?

The scent of her tears made his heart ache, her murmured words of heartbreak echoing in his ears and settling in his gut like a heavy weight.

His little rabbit was out of her damned mind if she thought he'd let that comment slide. He intended to get to the bottom of it, to *fix* it. But he could give her a bit of time to collect herself, at least. She was shaken up from the news of her pregnancy, and he didn't want to stress her out any further.

But how long could he wait? A day? Longer? His jaw clenched at the thought. That was too damned long. The drive back to his cabin, then? Even that felt like an eternity from now.

Eager to return home, Tank palmed Hunny's jean-clad bottom, fitting her more firmly against his chest as he spun around toward the door.

"Let's go, darlin'."

She sagged against him in relief. Did she think this conversation was over?

Tank almost snorted at that, but remained silent, leaving the examination room. He waved at his mother, who was now behind the front desk, ignoring whoever else might be around, and left the building. It was short work, putting Hunny in his truck, getting into the driver's side, and starting the engine. But each second that ticked by felt like an hour had passed, and as he drove home, he thought about pulling over several times and demanding some answers.

Instead, he listened to her breathing, relieved that it had evened out and her tears had finally ebbed. She seemed in better control of her emotions. Regardless, he reached over, laying his large palm on her knee. She didn't flinch from his touch, which he considered a small victory, so he kept it there, needing to be close to her in whatever way she'd let him.

After what felt like several lifetimes, but was actually less than ten minutes, Tank parked his truck in the garage, climbed from the vehicle and moved toward Hunny's side. She'd already opened the door, sliding over the side of the seat. Her feet hit the garage floor, but before she could close her own door, he grabbed it, nearly denting the metal as he scowled down at her.

"You always let me get the door for you," he growled, offended.

She bristled at his tone, sending him a watery glare. "I can open a door for myself."

"I didn't say you couldn't," he argued hotly. "But you don't need to because I'm here to do it."

Exasperated, Hunny ran a shaky hand through her hair. "One day you won't be here for stuff like that, Tank. It's not a big deal if I get back into the habit of looking out for myself."

His hand left the truck door, palming the nape of her neck as he crowded into her space. Nearly pinning her spine against the side of the passenger seat, he pulled gently on her hair, forcing her to look up at him. "Stop calling me that."

"Everyone calls you Tank—"

"Not you," he hissed. He leaned in, resisting the urge to slam his mouth against hers in a claiming kiss. Her lips would be soft, and she'd taste sweet; he knew it down to his bones. His nose brushed hers, and it was all he could do to not close those last few inches between them, his body coiling with tension as he fought to remain in place. She swallowed thickly, her hands finding his chest as he rasped, "Say my name, little rabbit."

Her eyes widened, and the rising scent of her desire had his mouth watering, his cock hardening with need. Her fingers tightened their grip in his shirt, and for the briefest second, he could have sworn she'd pull him down and claim him just as eagerly as he wanted to claim her.

Then Hunny's eyes hardened, and she shoved at his chest. Even though he barely felt it, he released her, taking a step back to give her the space she wanted. "You can't say stuff like that to me." She threw her hands up into the air as she pushed past him and out of the garage. "You're giving me every kind of mixed signal!"

"Mixed signal?" Confused, Tank prowled after her, hot on her heels as she rushed up the porch steps and into his house. "What mixed signal?"

"I said I didn't want to talk about this."

He slammed the door behind him, stalking after her from the living room and into the kitchen. "That's too damn bad, darlin'. Turns out I'm in the mood for a talk."

Hunny scoffed, keeping her back to him as she reached the refrigerator. She ripped the door open, grabbing items at random and dropping them on the counter haphazardly. What the hell was she even doing?

"If you're hungry, I'll cook something for you."

"I can make my own food!" Hunny snapped, looking over her shoulder and glaring at him as she slammed the refrigerator door closed.

"Oh?" He glanced down at the items on the counter in irritation. She'd laid out sour cream, mustard, and a melon. "What the hell are you making?"

"None of your business, *Tank*!" Hunny exclaimed, grabbing the tube of sour cream as she whipped around to face him.

He took a step toward her, his voice dropping several octaves. "I told you to stop calling me that."

"Well, it's a good thing you're not the boss of me," she seethed.

"No, but I made it clear to you last week I want to provide for you, and now you won't even let me feed you?" He asked irritably, completely bewildered by this entire conversation. "Is this about this morning? I apologized for that."

"Trust me, I'm *well* aware." Hunny crossed her arms in front of her chest. Her cheeks heated and she looked away from him. "We don't need to bring up what happened this morning."

"Apparently apologizing wasn't enough, which you made evident when you told me I broke your heart." Tank was confused and desperate to figure out what the hell had gone wrong between them. "I just want to fix—" His voice cracked, and his throat sliced with pain, causing him to grimace.

Immediately, Hunny dropped her arms, her expression losing its hard edge. "I forgot to make you tea this morning."

"It's fine," he grumbled.

Rolling her eyes, Hunny moved to the sink, discarding the sour cream and grabbing the kettle off the drying rack, filling it with water. Next, she moved to the stove, placing it on top of a burner and turning it on. He watched her with a desperation that was equal parts longing and fear.

Had he really fucked things up so drastically? What if she left him over this? He didn't know how he'd handle it. If he *could* handle it.

The silence between them might as well have been a vast canyon, and he didn't know how to cross it. She was shutting him out, and it made him feel out of control. Unbalanced and lost. And given how he'd spent years of his life, always on the outskirts, alone and isolated ... Tank didn't want to go back to that. Never again.

Not after Hunny ...

His heart was in his throat as she placed a tea bag and honey into a mug and then poured piping hot water into it. Focused on her task, she turned to him and handed him the mug, which he took, his attention still trained solely on her.

"I'm really sorry, Henry." Hunny's voice was soft and hesitant. "About this morning and how I've been acting all day." Her lower lip trembled, and she huffed out an agitated breath. "I ... Look, it wasn't you-" She cut her words off abruptly.

Hunny was always ready and willing to talk about anything and everything, but now he'd done this to her: she felt like she couldn't talk openly with him. He never meant for her to feel she had to censor her words in any fashion.

He frowned, his grip tightening on the mug until he thought he might crack the damned thing. "Just spit it out—"

"I thought you were attracted to me!" Hunny blurted out, her eyes widening like she couldn't believe she'd just said it out loud. His eyes mirrored her own expression, widening as he dropped the mug onto the counter with a thud, scalding water sloshing over the side.

"I woke up and you were all over me, and you were ... *aroused*," she explained, her cheeks turning a brighter shade of pink. She glanced away, wringing her hands. "I thought it was because of me, and I made a move on you because I really like you ..." She shook her head, unaware of the way his heart was pounding. "That doesn't matter. You woke up and freaked out. And I-I—"

Hunny turned away from him, moving back toward the stove. She stood beside it, placing her hands on the counter. "I just feel so stupid. And my feelings *are* hurt, but that's not your fault. You can't help that you don't want me like that. And it's fine, even though I'm acting like an absolute idiot about it," she whispered forlornly, her head dropping as she stared down at her hands.

Hunny's shoulders were tense as she waited for him to say some-thing, but Tank was still trying to wrap his head around everything she'd said. "You were coming onto me this morning?"

He'd woken up thinking he'd taken advantage of her, and he'd fled the bed to keep from scaring her. He hadn't known she'd set out to entice him, otherwise he'd have pinned her beneath him and taken her, just like he'd wanted for days.

"Yes," she answered tightly, oblivious to his own thoughts. "I'm so sorry. I shouldn't have assumed that just because you were turned on, it was because of *me*."

"It was because of you," he admitted gutturally, crowding in behind her. She'd wanted him to make a move, and he'd scurried away like some kind of weak fucking dipshit. He wouldn't make that mistake again.

Wrapping an arm around Hunny's waist, he pinned her between himself and the counter, careful to not put too much pressure against her stomach. He dropped his head to her shoulder, his lips roaming over her pulse.

She gasped when he kissed her neck, her desire perfuming the air. Instantly, he was hard, his cock straining in his jeans. "What do you mean, Henry?" she asked softly.

"I've wanted you since the moment I saw you standing there in my shirt, little rabbit." His fingers tightened on her waist, and he pressed himself more firmly against her. He didn't want any signals getting crossed between them this time. "You feel right in my arms, darlin'. Every part of you feels like you're mine."

Her breath hitched, and she grabbed his arm, her fingers digging into his skin. Even though her scent was strong between them, he still caught the smell of fresh tears. "Then why did you apologize this morning?"

"I want to be patient with you. You've been through a lot, and I didn't want you to think I was just using you for sex." *Not like that pissant, Jason.* "I apologized because I was afraid that I'd pushed you too far, and I didn't want you to think that's all there is between us and leave. I care about you. More than you could know."

Still looking down at the counter, Hunny asked, "What do you want from me, then?"

"Everything you want to give me," Tank replied immediately, reveal-ing his intentions without another moment's hesitation. He kissed her pulse again, his teeth scraping over her skin. Hunny shivered from the light grazing, her nails biting into his forearm.

She twisted around in his arms, staring up at him with a heated look that threatened to undo him in every way. "Are you sure? My entire life is a mess."

"I don't care." Tank cupped her face in his hands. "And I don't want you to feel pressured by anything. You've got a lot going on, and I'm willing to wait as long as you want. We can take things slow—"

Hunny moved before he could finish his sentence. Grabbing the nape of his neck, she pulled him down as she stood up on her tiptoes. Her mouth crashed into his, her lips just as soft as he'd imagined. She licked the seam of his lips, and his brain short-circuited, precum sliding over the tip of his erection as Tank let her lead their first kiss.

He'd let her lead him anywhere, let her take things as slow and sweet as she wanted, even if his balls eventually exploded from the pressure.

Pulling back suddenly, Hunny stared up at Tank with a devious glint in her eyes. "Henry?"

He cleared his throat, his own eyes heavy-lidded with lust as he met her gaze. "Hunny."

She smiled, pulling him back down until her lips brushed his. "I don't want to go slow," she murmured against his mouth, licking his lips again. Tank froze, a ringing in his ears, and his body filling with tension as he registered her words.

And then he was on her.

Eighteen

Hunny's lower back barely hit the edge of the counter before Tank grabbed her ass, lifting her up and dropping her onto its surface. His mouth slammed onto hers, and a deep growl of need reverberated in his throat, the sound going straight to her core. Her panties became instantly soaked, and as his tongue teased her lips, demanding entrance, his hands roamed over her thighs, leaving a burning trail of fire through the denim encasing her legs.

She wanted nothing more than for him to rip them off.

Another delicious lick against the seam of her lips, and Hunny opened for him, moaning softly as his tongue swept into the cavern of her mouth, dueling with her own. He tasted perfect, and the scent of his lust rose to meet hers, blending together in an intoxicating aroma that stole her breath. It teased her as much as his tongue and hands, giving her a glimpse of everything she craved.

It wasn't enough, though, and her body screamed at her to get him naked. To touch him *every*where, and to explore him until she'd committed every inch of her big bear to memory. *He wants me*, she thought, giddy and lustful at the knowledge he was as drawn to her as she was to him.

He was hers, even if she wasn't courageous enough to say it out loud. She could feel it, and hopefully one day, she'd be brave enough to have all of him.

Grabbing Tank's shirt, Hunny ripped the material up and over his head, wrapping her legs around his waist and her arms around his neck.

She needed to be closer to him. Yearned for their skin to touch. His erection fit between her thighs, and she rolled her hips, moaning again at the sensation.

"We should get to the bed," Tank rasped in between kisses, his breath skating over her tender lips.

"Fuck me here," Hunny said breathlessly, her hands running down his muscular chest and dropping to his waist. He hissed out a breath, cupping the back of her neck. His hand fisted in her hair as she fumbled with his zipper, and he yanked her head back right as she reached into his jeans, fingers gliding over the hot, thick, velvet length of him.

He's so big.

"If we don't slow down, I'm going to cum much faster than I want," Tank replied, nipping her lower lip. She gasped from the bite of pain as her pussy spasmed, heightening her desire. He licked the sting away a moment later, and then kissed her again, holding her head still as he plundered her mouth like he'd been dying of thirst and finally had his first drink of water. His lips moved from hers, trailing over her cheek and then to her neck, his beard tickling her skin. He nipped her throat and then sucked on her skin, and pleasure shot all the way down to her clit.

"I don't—*oh, fuck*—I don't care," she whimpered, fisting his cock and stroking him as he sucked her harder. "Y-you know the expression 'fucking like rabbits,' Henry?"

He growled against her throat, and she pumped his length harder, tilting her head as much as his hold on her hair would allow to give him better access to her neck. "It's true for rabbit shifters, too," she moaned. "I always want sex, and the last week has been torture. I need you."

Need was an understatement. She was past that, so far beyond it that to even say it was laughable. She planned on wearing Tank out, on riding his thick cock until they were both too exhausted to move. So he could cum early if he wanted this time, it just meant he'd last longer the next round. And the next, and the next.

Fist tightening in her hair, Tank pulled back, his eyes hooded and dark with lust, his lips swollen from their kisses. "What are you saying, little rabbit?"

Hunny smiled, tugging him back down and kissing him. She nipped his lips this time, enjoying the way his cock twitched in her palm.

"Undress me," she murmured against his mouth. "I want you to touch me."

"Fuck!" Tank dropped his hold on her hair, tugging her shirt over her head, leaving her in just a bra and her jeans. He made quick work of them, pulling off her panties right along with the heavy denim until she was naked. He shook his head, his eyes roaming over every inch of her. "You're so fucking beautiful, darlin'."

She blushed, dropping her hold on his cock as he stepped back, pulling his jeans down all the way. Her eyes trailed over him, and her mouth watered as she finally caught sight of him in all of his glory.

And damn, was Tank *glorious*.

She knew his cock was big, but he was wide too, and the veins standing out prominently around his length made her want to fall to her knees and follow each one with her tongue. And then she'd focus on his tip, on the precum glistening all over it, begging her to suck and lick him. To taste him so intimately and coax more of that pearly liquid onto her tongue.

Right as she decided to do just that, he moved back to her, fitting his hips between her legs. He was still too far away, though, and she pouted, pushing her legs open wide in invitation. Immediately, his eyes dropped to her pussy, to the juices she knew were slipping down her inner thighs and onto the counters he kept so immaculate.

She might have felt embarrassed for being so aroused, but Tank's breath stilled in his lungs, his gaze absolutely ravenous as he watched her. With just one look, he made her feel sexy as hell, like a temptress sent to seduce him.

Feeling bolder than she ever had before, Hunny slid her hand down her stomach, her fingers slipping over her pussy lips and teasing her wet entrance.

"Christ," Tank groaned, gripping her knees. He pushed her legs wider apart, eyes locked on her fingers. "Touch yourself, baby. Let me see how you like it."

Biting her lower lip, her cheeks stinging with heat, Hunny did as he demanded, sinking her middle finger into her entrance. Tank growled appreciatively, one hand sliding up her thigh and settling over her hand. She thought he was going to move it away, but he didn't. Instead, his thumb found her clit, circling the small, tender nub as she pumped her own finger into her pussy.

Pleasure, sweet and seductive, wrapped around her, and Hunny gasped, throwing her head back as she worked her pussy faster, her hips rolling on the counter as he kept her leg spread open with his other hand.

Leaning in, Tank kissed her neck, the pressure on her clit increasing before he returned his attention to her pussy. He rasped, "Add another finger, Hunny. You need to be ready for me."

"I can't wait anymore," Hunny pleaded, pulling her hand away. He grabbed it, bringing it up to his mouth and sliding her slick-coated finger past his lips with a deep, needy groan.

His cock twitched as he sucked, and warmth blossomed in her core as she watched, more slick spilling out just for him. As his tongue slid over her finger, she pictured it sliding over the folds of her pussy, sinking into her entrance and filling her. Her pussy was empty and aching, her body needing him in a way she'd never felt before, and as he licked her finger clean, she couldn't take it anymore.

T ank was going to die if he didn't cum soon, and so far all he'd done was watch his little rabbit touch herself and then lick her finger afterward.

And Christ, she tasted as good as she smelled. Vanilla and honey enveloped in the stunning aroma of her arousal. One taste wasn't enough. He needed to lick every inch of her wet cunt, to fill her with his cock and show her more pleasure than she'd ever known. To let her know he was the only male she'd ever need again.

Don't you fucking cum until she does, motherfucker.

"Henry—" Hunny whimpered, her voice full of a sensual need he couldn't ignore.

Tank dragged her to the edge of the counter, fitting his cock against her entrance and slamming home inside her. His snarl of absolute lust filled the room as her soaked, tight cunt surrounded his shaft, welcoming him home in a way nothing else had before. She was hot, and wet, and better than he could ever have imagined, and he'd only just sunk inside her.

He grit his teeth as his balls tightened, precum shooting from his tip and into her, marking her just like he was so desperate to do.

Hunny gasped, cupping the sides of his neck, her thumbs digging under his jaw and her forearms resting on his chest as she leaned into him, shocked arousal stamped all over her beautiful face as she took every inch of him.

"Y-You're so big," she whimpered, her voice choked. She released a trembling breath, rocking into him experimentally as she gave a hoarse cry of pleasure. "I need you, Henry. Please, *please* fuck me," she begged.

Oh, he planned to do just that. He kept a hand on her lower back and slid her right knee under his other hand and onto his forearm, angling her perfectly. He didn't want to keep her waiting another moment.

He pulled out until only his tip nestled inside her entrance. And then he thrust into her, filling her to the brim with one powerful stroke.

His little rabbit moaned loudly, the sound so full of passion, her lips parted on a strangled cry. He wanted more, needed to hear her screaming his name. He pulled out, only to slam back into her. It was like entering heaven, over and over again as he pumped her full of his cock, setting a brutal pace that she was helpless but to accept, pinned to the counter and at his mercy.

Her nails cut into his neck, her pussy spasming around him already as he drove into her. His heart beat hard, his fingers biting into her soft flesh as he filled her, pleasure hitting him like a lightning strike.

"So fucking tight, Hunny," he rasped hoarsely, uncaring of the pain in his throat, the tea she'd made long-forgotten on the kitchen island behind them as he plunged once again into her dripping entrance. "Your little pussy is so wet and perfect, baby. Is this what you needed, little rabbit? To be filled with my cock?"

"Oh my God," Hunny cried out, her breaths coming in shallow pants as she clung more tightly to him. "Yes! Yes, I need you so much." Her hips rocked, her pussy squeezing him like a vise, and it was all he could do to keep himself in check, to not pump his load inside her too soon.

Fuck, when he did, he'd fill her to the brim. And he'd keep it inside her, keep her full of his cum and his cock until his little rabbit was too drained to move. Then they'd shower. He'd take her to bed, let her rest, and then devour her pussy with his tongue to wake her up for another round. He'd make her cum on his tongue, his cock, his fingers ... Everywhere.

She thought she'd wear him out with sex? He almost smiled at her optimism, already knowing he'd keep his female too sated to do anything other than accept him forever.

"You're gonna cum all over my cock, Hunny," he demanded, possession stamped over each word, and her pussy fluttered in response. "I want to feel this tight little pussy claim every inch of me, baby."

"I-I didn't think you'd talk to me like this," she whispered breathlessly, rolling her hips as he pumped harder into her, meeting each of his thrusts with a reckless abandon that he couldn't get enough of. She took everything he gave, enjoying each rough thrust with a sharp cry of pleasure.

He slowed his pace to an agonizing crawl, pulling almost all the way out and relishing in her small shriek of denial. "You want me to quit, little rabbit?" he teased darkly.

"No! Don't stop! Henry, keep going, please—"

He lifted Hunny from the counter, dropping her onto his cock as he slammed back into her welcoming heat. Hunny screamed in ecstasy, throwing her head back as her legs wrapped around his waist. His hands gripped her ass firmly as he worked her up and down on his length, groaning as her cunt fluttered around him again, giving him a glimpse of her impending orgasm.

She clung to him; her nails scraping down his back in a stinging caress as pleasure licked its way to his balls. His cock throbbed, his own orgasm closing in. "Cum for me, Hunny. I want to feel your pretty pussy soak me, baby."

Hunny bit his lower lip, and then she sank her tongue into his mouth, claiming him in a desperate kiss. He devoured her, his needy groan and her heated cry of surrender blending into one sexual sound as her cunt spasmed, squeezing him in a vise-like grip as she orgasmed.

She broke their kiss, screaming his name hoarsely as he bounced her up and down on his shaft, his balls drawing up as a tingle shot from his spine. His heart beat a pulse in his ears, lust roaring through his mind as pleasure consumed him. "Beg me to cum in your pussy," he commanded.

"Cum inside me," Hunny wailed, her breaths fanning his chest as she kept working his length, the vixen bouncing up and down until he grunted with his own need. "Henry, please!"

With a choked bellow, Tank dropped his head onto her shoulder, his teeth locking on her shoulder as thick ropes of his cum shot into her pussy, his balls emptying as he filled her. Everything in him demanded he bite her, mark her as his mate—but he held back. He wouldn't do that until she asked for it, no matter how strong the urge was.

He pumped into her as he came, his groans muffled and his legs shaking as Hunny eased her pace, rocking her hips in a slow, smooth rhythm that had his breath stalling in his lungs.

Before his legs could give out, Tank moved to the living room, dropping onto the couch with his little rabbit nestled in his arms, on his still-hard shaft. His breathing was rough and uneven, his heart stuttering in his chest as she spread her legs wide, her knees planting on either side of his hips.

"Henry," Hunny murmured, her soft lips finding his cheek. She kissed him there before settling on his mouth, giving him one drugging kiss after the other. He cupped the back of her head, feeling lethargic and sated as he returned her affections, sipping from her lips tenderly. She smiled at him mischievously. "Don't tell me you're tired already, my big bear."

He grunted in response, too worn out to even talk. So much for believing he'd be fucking her until *she* passed out. One round like that and he needed a breather, and maybe a nap, before he could do anything else. But how was he supposed to know she'd drain the life from him through his cock?

Hunny rolled her hips, and his half-erect cock stirred back to life, growing harder than it had before. Fuck, just a slight movement from her and he was ready to go again, despite how exhausted he felt. He didn't mind it in the slightest, but he didn't know if she'd enjoy it this time around if he could barely move his limbs.

"I may need a minute," he choked out, his earlier bravado biting him in the ass as he fought to catch his breath. "It's been a long time for me, darlin'."

Hunny pouted and then kissed him again, working her pussy slowly over his erection. He grunted as pleasure filled him, arms wrapping around her waist as she teased his shaft, squeezing him with her inner walls as she rode him leisurely. Just when he was ready to pin her beneath him, she murmured against his lips, "How about you just lay back and relax, Henry, and I'll take good care of you?"

Nineteen

Holy. Shit. This is so much better than I imagined.

Hunny leaned back, her hair spilling down her spine as she gripped Tank's knees. She rode his thick cock desperately, his choked groans of need sending pleasure straight to her core. Each guttural noise he made spurred her on, encouraging her to take him deeper, to ride him faster.

She'd already orgasmed once, and all it did was take the edge off for a few minutes. She needed more. Her body demanded it. She was a glutton for the ecstasy this male could provide. Just thinking about what he'd done to her in the kitchen had her pussy spasming, juices spilling from her and onto his shaft as she quickened her pace.

But now her big bear was tired, and it was up to her to ensure he enjoyed himself. He needed to know that she was perfect for him, that no one else compared to her. She knew, without a shadow of a doubt, that no one else compared to *him*.

"You feel so good," Hunny moaned, tiny beads of sweat sliding down her breasts as she widened her knees on the couch, taking him deeper. The tip of Tank's cock hit her cervix, and she hissed, pleasure and pain mixing together deliciously. Part of her wanted to slow down, to savor the feel of his impressive length stretching her, but she couldn't hold back, desperate for more.

She looked up at him, expecting to see exhaustion lining his features. Instead, Tank's eyes were full of lust as he watched her undulate on his cock, his gaze riveted to their joined bodies. He licked his lips, eyes roaming up her figure before meeting her own lustful gaze.

Her brow furrowed in confusion. "I thought you were tired, Henry."

"Not anymore. You're so fucking beautiful riding me, baby," Tank praised hoarsely, one arm locking around her waist while the other slid down her stomach. He pulled her to his chest, pushing her hips down as he thrust up, bottoming out inside her.

Hunny cried out, so blissfully full she could barely stand it. It was almost too much, but she knew if he pulled out now, she'd scream in frustration. Dropping her hold on his knees, she leaned into him, hands tangling in his unruly hair. With a growl, Tank kissed her, dominating her mouth with his tongue and teeth as he began strumming her clit, taking her pleasure higher than she'd ever been before.

Her pussy fluttered, her orgasm so close she could taste it. She broke their kiss, breathing shallowly against his bruised lips as her orgasm peaked. "Henry, I-I'm—"

"Don't cum until I tell you," Tank ordered, dominance pouring from him in waves as he pinned her hips in place, pumping into her with a brutal precision that had her vision darkening, stars exploding behind her eyes as she held on. She tensed against him, every instinct within her demanding she heed his order. That she obey him.

His fingers plucked her clit, and she whined pitifully from the lightning bolts of pleasure that threatened to strike her down. "Please," she begged, her body winding tighter and tighter with each buck of his hips.

"'Please' what, little rabbit?" Tank nipped her chin hard. "Tell me what you need."

"I need to cum!" she cried, her fingers tightening on several strands of his hair.

"Ask me nicely, baby, and I'll let you cum all over my cock," Tank encouraged, dropping his mouth to her shoulder and nipping her tender flesh.

"Please, Henry," Hunny begged, unsure of when he'd taken over, but loving that he had. As a submissive, there was always some part of her nature that thrived on being dominated. Outside of the bedroom, she hated it, but here, with her bear? She loved it. "Please let me cum!"

His hands locked on her hips, and before she could even squawk in protest, he lifted her off of him, turning her to face the living room. Her hands flew from his hair, and she'd just opened her mouth to scream in outrage when he slammed her back down onto his lap, impaling her in one magnificent thrust.

The moan that left her mouth was obscene, so full of need she barely heard Tank's own ragged exclamation. He grabbed her breast and her clit, pulling her back against his chest as he began slamming home inside her. Her legs draped over his knees and he widened his stance, causing her to sink further onto his cock as he rolled his fingers over her bundle of nerves, driving her wild in just a few strokes.

She grabbed onto the forearm locked around her waist, clawing at him as her head fell back onto his shoulder, her breaths rough and shallow, her heart racing. She couldn't last much longer, didn't know if she could hold on another second before she broke apart in his arms.

"Cum for me, Hunny. Now," Tank ordered, and that was all she needed to hear. Her back bowed against him, his fingers stroking her clit as he filled her completely. Pussy spasming, she cried out his name, warmth exploding through her entire body as she orgasmed all over his length.

Tension eased from her muscles, and she collapsed against him, feeling more sated than she ever had in her life. After the last week, she'd needed this. No, not just the sex.

I needed my Henry.

Tank kissed her shoulder, licking a path up to her ear before whispering, "You're not done yet, little rabbit."

Her eyes widened right as his grip tightened on her. Flesh slapped together as he pinned her to him, giving her no other option but to hold on as he angled her hips just right, driving into her over and over again.

Body still reeling from the aftershocks of her orgasm, he fucked her to within an inch of her life, not stopping even as she felt another euphoric wave crashing into her. She might have even drooled, so lost in her own pleasure to notice much of anything else.

"You're so fucking soaked," Tank rasped, his deep tenor causing her to shiver as he licked her shoulder again. "And your pussy is strangling my cock. Your greedy little cunt needs me, doesn't it, baby?"

Hunny tried to answer, but her brain wasn't working properly, and all she managed was a weird, strangled noise of affirmation.

Tank chuckled darkly. He played with her sensitive clit while he owned her body, his fingers sliding through her slick, the wet sound impossible to ignore. Hell, he was right. She was absolutely drenched.

Bringing his hand over her shoulder, he licked his fingers, groaning at the taste. "In the morning, I'm going to wake you up with my tongue buried deep inside this pussy." He patted her clit possessively. "Every night you sleep in my bed, that's how I'll wake you."

"Oh, fuck," Hunny whimpered, the dirty image of his face buried between her legs, his beard tickling her thighs as he ate her out, sending her right over the edge. She threw her head back against his shoulder as she orgasmed again, her breathy moan blending with his ragged one.

Tank stiffened beneath her, pumping into her with one final thrust. His cock throbbed, and she felt warm and full as he came inside her, marking her in every way but one. His lips skated tenderly over her shoulder and neck as she relaxed fully into him, lethargy setting in.

"Only took you three orgasms to tucker out, huh?" Tank teased, the smile in his deep voice unmistakable.

Pride swelled within Hunny, and she turned her head slightly to the side, noting the sated, mischievous gleam in his eyes. She'd done *that*—turned her sullen bear into a relaxed, cared-for male.

"Be careful, Henry, otherwise I'll show you what a rabbit shifter is really capable of," she warned playfully, stifling a yawn. "Besides, you got tired first."

"I rallied," he countered easily. "I knew I needed to sate my—" His voice cracked, and he grumbled under his breath, the light in his eyes dimming slightly.

Hunny pushed off of him before his scowl could fully form, standing on legs that felt like jello. Immediately, cum started slipping down her thighs, and she grimaced, unsure of what she should do.

Tank reached between her legs, swiping their mixed arousal up onto his fingers. He held it up to her expectantly. "See how good we taste, Hunny."

She blushed, equal parts scandalized and turned on as she opened her mouth. He pushed his fingers gently inside and she sucked as she gazed at him, the heated look in his eyes nearly sending her to her knees just to drink from the source. When he pulled his hand back, his own face was flushed, his eyes focused on her lips as she licked them clean.

Before her legs buckled from that look, Hunny pivoted around, shakily beelining for the kitchen. "Stay there," she called over her shoulder, already well aware that he'd likely started following her. Tank sighed audibly, and then her lips twitched as she heard him sink back down onto the couch.

Shaking her head, she stumbled into the kitchen, each step she took reminding her of the pounding she'd just taken. Her core ached, her legs were shaking, her thighs felt chafed, and it was *magical*.

Had anyone ever made her feel like this afterward? *Nope.* Just Tank.

Smiling, Hunny snatched up the mug, still filled with tea, from the kitchen island, and took a small sip. Ugh, it was completely cold. Wrinkling her nose in distaste, she spent the next few minutes making a fresh cup. She poured a thick glob of honey into the mug, stirring it in with a spoon until it melted.

Then, on legs that shook slightly less, she ventured back into the living room where Tank was still sprawled out on the couch. As soon as he spotted the mug in her hand, he grimaced, though he took it from her all the same.

"No funny faces, Henry." Hunny rolled her eyes, straddling his lap. His erection had gone down, but as soon as she settled over him, she felt it twitch to life, like a zombie rising from the grave, ready to eat her brains. Well, hopefully he'd be ready to eat something *else*.

Grumbling, he took a drink, eyes widening in surprise before taking another larger gulp. "This actually isn't bad," he commented. "Must be getting used to it."

"I added a secret ingredient," she teased lightly, watching him from under her lashes as he stilled.

"What did you put in it?"

Hunny shrugged nonchalantly. "Well, I figured since you wanted me to lick your fingers clean, you might want a taste of *us*, too." She pursed her lips. "It took some effort to put all of our mixed cum on a spoon, but—"

"Fuck me," Tank muttered under his breath, staring down at the mug like it was an alien. And then he downed the rest, sending her a curious look when she gaped at him in bewilderment. "What?"

"I can't believe you just drank that!"

"Why not? It wasn't too hot."

Hunny sputtered, her eyes wild. "Because I told you I put *cum* in there," she whispered dramatically, like it was a dirty little secret.

He shrugged. "I don't give a damn, darlin'. I thought about licking you clean when you stood up. Drinking it from a cup isn't much different."

Desire flared to life, her aching center oblivious to the fact that she'd already orgasmed three times in the last hour. "I was *joking*, obviously. I wouldn't do that!" Hunny exclaimed, feeling flustered and hot. She might have been joking, but he'd drunk it all, fully believing she'd tampered with his tea. "You're such a pervert, Henry!"

And why was that suddenly such a turn-on?

Giving her a teasing growl, Tank pulled her back against him, kissing her sweetly on the lips. "You like it," he murmured darkly, nipping her lower lip.

The scent of their mixed arousal filled the air once more, and Hunny wrapped her arms around his shoulders, her forehead resting against his. "I like it," she whispered softly.

"And you like me."

She cracked a smile. "And I like you."

His shaft swelled between her thighs, and her breath caught as he stood up with his arm cradling her ass, dropping the mug onto the coffee table with a clank. "How about we take a shower, and then I fuck you until you fall asleep?"

Hunny's brows rose, her core tightening with need. "I know you said you wanted pussy for breakfast, Henry, but how about a late-night snack?"

"Christ, you're perfect," he murmured, holding her more securely to his chest. Hunny laughed lightly, letting him carry her upstairs.

Twenty

Tank prowled the border of bear territory impatiently, the moon providing ample light. He wasn't the only bear out on patrol tonight; Colter was at the other end of the perimeter, and Dante was lurking somewhere nearby, hunting for a trace of the wolf shifter they were still attempting to hunt down.

It had only been a few hours since Tank had left Hunny, sated and sleeping in his bed, and already he was eager to get back to her. Not just so they could have sex—which they'd be doing again *very* soon—but also because he wanted to hold her in his arms while she slept. He wanted to feel her breath tickle his chest as he held her to him, wanted to let her adorable little snores lull him to sleep, just like they had all week.

Only this time, she was *his*.

Then, after they'd rested, he'd wake her up just like he'd promised; with his tongue buried in her juicy cunt. He nearly groaned at the thought, remembering the taste he'd had of her earlier tonight before he'd left for patrol. Honey, vanilla, and the sweet essence of woman. She tasted *perfect*.

He licked his snout, the memory an aphrodisiac he never wanted to forget. Having so much of her tonight and then being forced to leave her side shortly after fucking sucked.

Tank huffed under his breath, his paws padding heavily on the ground as he completed another circuit around his section of the woods. The wait to be back at his little rabbit's side was agonizing, but even as he thought about it, his gut clenched, his breath shallowing in anticipation. At least, after another few hours of working, he'd come home and find her tangled up in his sheets, naked and sleeping in his bed.

The image was enough to have his blood heating and his body coiling with sensual tension, begging to be released. Who knew he could crave so much of someone so quickly? That all it would take was a single night of pleasure to turn his entire world upside down.

Although, that wasn't quite right, was it? His world had tilted on its axis just over a week ago, in these very woods, when he'd first found Hunny.

There was a brief stirring in Tank's mind before he heard Murphy ask, *How's patrol going?*

Nothing to report.

Good. Good. And ... how are things? Mom said you and Hunny were having problems in the clinic earlier.

Tank smirked coldly, though it was more of a grimace while he was in his bear form. *Never been better, brother. Why? Were you hoping to ask Hunny out?* he asked, a threatening note in his tone that was impossible to miss.

Murphy snorted, and immediately Tank relaxed. *Not a chance in hell. I know she's yours, Tank. And besides, I like my women quiet and meek. Hunny is far too talkative.*

You have no idea, Tank told him with a smirk. Even as he said it, warmth filled his heart. Not in a million years would he have assumed he'd be smitten with a female so loud and sassy. But sure enough, he was in deep with his yapper, and he wouldn't have it any other way. Turning to walk the perimeter anew, he added, *How inclined would you be for Hunny to become a permanent addition to the clan?*

There was a moment of silence through their bond before Murphy asked, *Things progressing that quickly between you?*

Not quickly enough, Tank muttered. *Hopefully soon. Until then, I want your assurance that she's welcome here indefinitely.*

Tank could practically feel Murphy rolling his eyes. *Like my assurance would matter to you at this point. If I told you no, Mom would beat me over the head with a rolling pin. That being said, if it feels right to you, then I don't see an issue, little brother.* Tank only felt a brief stirring of happiness before Murphy added far more somberly, *Jason contacted me this evening. Wants to set up a meeting.*

What? Tank's claws curled into the dirt as a red haze of rage filled his vision. *What could that fucker possibly want?*

There was only one thing that came to mind, and it was the beautiful rabbit currently spreading her scent all over Tank's bed, right where she belonged. If that wolf thought for one damned *second* that he had any claim to Hunny or her kits—

Apparently, Jason's mate has gone missing, Murphy interrupted, a heavy note of suspicion in his voice. *She was last seen near our border a few days back. He didn't say it outright, but he suspects we've taken her prisoner.*

A few days ago, that wolf shifter invaded our territory. Tank's head tilted to the side as he scoped out the woods around him, remaining alert despite the conversation unfolding in his head. *But it wasn't her. The scent was unfamiliar to me.*

I told him she wasn't here, but he's insistent I meet with him.

In bear territory?

Yes.

Absolutely fucking not, Tank snapped. *I don't want that piece of shit anywhere near Hunny.* But indecision warred within him. He didn't want his brother venturing into Jason's territory either. Not alone or with a dozen bears. He didn't trust the wolves, not for a single second.

We've agreed to meet in town. A neutral location.

Tank almost sighed in relief.

Where?

There's a place called 'Nessa's Teahouse.' It's a human establishment, but apparently the owner is new to the area; likely won't have heard any rumors about our neck of the woods.

Tank grunted. While shifters, or supernaturals in general, hadn't revealed themselves to the human population, the advancement of the internet, technology, and social media had made it increasingly more difficult to remain hidden. Using social media also made it easier for rumors to spread from town to town, city to city, which had pros and cons.

Sometimes, the rumors kept people away. But there was a real reason humans never visited bear territory, and that was because the shifters that lived there scared them off. In doing so, they'd set themselves up for all kinds of dangerous tales, some of which were closer to the truth than were comfortable.

Do you think that's wise? Tank asked. *Jason shouldn't be around humans. The fucker ripped apart the last human, some hiker, that wandered into his territory.*

That wasn't the only thing Jason was known to do with humans, either. Although Tank's clan had never seen it, rumors spread among the supernaturals, too. Apparently, the wolf pack made money by kidnapping humans and selling them to other supernaturals. Sometimes they even sold submissive shifters and loners, though it was difficult to prove illicit dealings when his pack members were just as twisted as he was.

Given that Hunny was both submissive and a lone shifter, she'd gotten lucky with Jason's rejection. That evil piece of shit had never deserved her.

He hated that fate had ever led her to her true mate. Although, even as he thought it, he realized the truth; without her meeting Jason, she might have never met Tank. And then where would he be? Alone, in a quiet cabin, lacking a warmth he'd come to recently relish.

It was a sobering thought.

I'd prefer meeting him publicly than allowing him to set foot inside our territory. Hunny doesn't need the stench of his scent anywhere near her. When we're in town, though, I'll make sure he keeps away from the humans, Murphy assured him. *He'd be a fool to harm them under my protection.*

Tank paused, eyes narrowing in confusion. *You hate humans, and yet you're going to place some of them under your protection?*

I plan to place all *the townspeople under my protection, not just some. It's the least I can do for bringing a predator into their domain,* Murphy replied.

Tank didn't disagree with his older brother, though taking responsibility for an entire town meant that if any of them were affected negatively by a supernatural being, Murphy would be honor-bound to defend them, even if the humans didn't realize it. It also meant that if a human harmed a supernatural, he'd have to answer for their crimes.

When is the meeting?

Two days from now. I'll have to contact the teahouse in the morning and speak with the owner to book the venue for an hour or two.

I can text you the number when I get home. Owner's name is Nessa.

I figured that was her name but why the hell do you have the number? Murphy asked in surprise. *You hate tea.*

Got the business card when Hunny met Nessa the other day. They've been talking on the phone daily. She's a yapper, too. They've got some kind of girl date tomorrow.

Tank hadn't actually been looking forward to Hunny spending more time around humans, but she enjoyed chatting with Nessa. So he'd kept his mouth shut, not wanting to lay his prejudices of humans at Hunny's feet. Looked like it was a good thing he hadn't.

Plus, it now gave him an excuse to explore the teahouse while the females hung out and look for any exits or unusual red flags before this meeting with the Moon Rose pack. Hunny could enjoy her 'girls date' with Nessa, and Tank could give them space while remaining close enough for protection.

I'm dreading speaking to the human already, Murphy answered, and for a second, Tank felt a sharp stab of sympathy for his older brother. Out of anyone Tank knew, Murphy had the most reason to despise humans. Tank didn't think he could ever offer protection to humans if he'd suffered the same way Murphy had because of their kind.

And yet, here Murphy was, doing just that. Not just to protect the clan from Jason, but for Hunny's sake, too. To make sure she felt safe in her own home. He was a strong, honorable Alpha. Tank had always known it, but this only cemented his belief, making him more proud of his brother than he'd ever been before.

Well, just don't be yourself and I'm sure it'll go well enough, Murph, Tank joked over the sudden lump in his throat.

Fuck you.

Tank snorted right as Murphy cut off their connection, leaving him alone to wander the perimeter one final time.

Soon enough, his shift was over, and he practically ran back to his cabin, uncaring of the noise he made as he approached his home. Hunny slept like a log anyway, so she'd be passed out despite the commotion. And if a predator was nearby? They'd think twice about approaching when they heard Tank.

Although there *shouldn't* be any predators nearby—Jasper had sworn to monitor things closely in Tank's absence. He was still unsettled after the dead rabbit incident, and he didn't want to leave Hunny alone and defenseless while he was out.

Shifting back to his human form, Tank pushed up the stairs and onto the porch, stepping over the big grizzly at the top step, blocking him

9 n

from the front door. Jasper, the dipshit, was lounging on his side and sleeping heavily, just like he'd been the last time he'd guarded Hunny.

It should have been irritating as hell to find the guard *asleep* on duty, but Jasper was the fastest and the most observant of them all, believe it or not. Even sleeping, he'd smell an enemy before they got close. It was too bad those same skills weren't as honed when family was near.

Tank moved around his brother until the grizzly was between him and the porch stairs. Then he placed his foot in the middle of Jasper's back, a devilish smirk on his face as he shoved hard.

The grizzly startled awake right as he rolled down the first step, an awkward grunt sounding through the night. His front paws flew forward and his back legs caught onto the railing, causing him to come to an abrupt stop, dangling face-first down the steps. His head slammed into the dirt, paws flailing wildly as he floundered for purchase.

It was a hell of a sight to see.

"Bet you won't sleep on the job again. Now, get the hell out of here, fucker," Tank said with a small laugh. Shaking his head, he stepped into his cabin, locking the door. The slight sound of Hunny's snores reached him, and with his lips turning up into a small smile, he headed up the stairs.

There was no nightstand lamp switched on tonight, not that he needed one to see. The moonlight was bright enough as it shone through the window and it was easy enough to spot his Hunny curled up in bed, blankets snuggly wrapped around her as she slept with his pillow once again clutched to her chest.

His own chest tightened at the sight, and all he wanted was to sink into bed with her. Gritting his teeth, he quietly stomped into the bathroom, taking a quick shower to clean the smell of dirt and sweat from his body. As soon as he had dried off with a towel, he moved back into the bedroom, still naked, excitement clawing at his gut as he lifted the covers.

Hunny's soft, bare skin greeted him; the delicate slope of her back and the gentle curve of her ass were the perfect things to see at the end of the day. It felt like years since he'd seen her last, not hours, and damn, he'd missed her.

Slipping under the blankets, Tank wrapped his little rabbit up in his arms, adjusting himself just right until he had her cradled to him; her ass snug against his groin and the front of his thighs pressed against the back of hers. With an arm around her waist, he dropped his mouth to her shoulder, breathing her in. He kissed her softly, ignoring the way her scent and body teased his cock to life.

As much as he'd love to pin her beneath him and take his fill of her sweetness, holding her like this brought him just as much pleasure. It wasn't just the act of sex with Hunny that called to him; it was the way she relaxed into him in her sleep, the trust she had in him to keep her safe and secure, even at her most vulnerable.

And as she shoved his pillow away from her front, rolled over, and pressed her face into his chest, murmuring his name softly before she began snoring again, he knew he loved these moments most of all.

Twenty One

Hunny's eyes slowly opened as she was tugged down the bed by her hips, her legs dangling over a set of wide, muscular shoulders. The room was dark, and before her eyes could adjust to the lighting, warm breath swept over her exposed, wet pussy.

"Hen—" Hunny's groggy words caught in her throat as Tank licked from her entrance up to her clit with a deep, savage groan. Pleasure exploded from her core as he flicked her clit with the tip of his tongue before sucking it into his mouth and lapping at it hungrily. She arched her back, a startled gasp leaving her as he plunged two fingers into her aching center. "Oh, fuck, *Henry!*"

Hunny looked down the length of her body, finding Tank kneeling on the floor by the end of the bed, his head buried between her thighs. The covers were balled up on his side of the bed, allowing him full access to her, and his unruly hair covered his forehead and part of his eyes. He tongued her lightly, even as his fingers pumped roughly into her, the combination causing her heart to pound and her breath to quicken.

She couldn't look away from him, sitting up on her elbows to watch as he pleasured her. Feeling his tongue and hand work her body was one thing, but seeing it? Watching the need skate across his features as he groaned against her? It made everything a thousand times better. No, scratch that. A *million* times better.

He pulled away from her clit abruptly, his hot breath fanning over the tender bundle of nerves. "You're soaked already, little rabbit." He nipped her inner thigh, the brief sting of pain only adding to the ball of ecstasy forming in her center. She wanted those teeth on her shoulder, biting into her skin until she bled for him. "Were you having naughty dreams?" he asked darkly.

"If I did, they were all about you," she murmured drowsily, rocking into the hand cupping her center. He growled in approval, and she shivered as she fucked his fingers languidly, her hands fisting the sheets as she struggled to speak. "I-I was hoping you'd wake me up like this after the promise you made."

Anticipating it, really. He'd eaten her out last night before he'd gone out, and it had been amazing. He'd left her wanting more, and it had taken hours before she could fall asleep, uncertain if she should play with herself for some extra relief or wait it out until morning.

Waiting was the right choice.

Tank's voice heated to a delicious, gravelly note as he murmured, "Every morning, baby. Just like this." His tongue swept through her folds and upward, circling her clit. He latched onto it again with a hungry groan, and her eyes rolled back into her head as she cried out his name.

Her hands found his head, fingers tangling in the thick strands as he pumped into her, curling his fingers just right until she was shaking beneath him, her hips rolling to meet each of his thrusts. She was still sore from all the sex they'd had last night, but as she felt an orgasm loom over her, she didn't care. This was an ache she'd happily accept as long as her big bear wanted to touch her. He sucked hard on her clit, and her body coiled tight, need coursing through her.

Just as she was about to orgasm, he pulled out of her, releasing his hold on her altogether, leaving her bereft.

"Why'd you stop?" she gasped in outrage, her heart beating hard. She swallowed thickly, certain she'd been only a few seconds away from drooling.

Tank climbed back onto the bed, kissing a trail up from her pussy to her chin as he hovered over her. "I don't want you to come on my fingers," he rasped, mouth finding hers.

His tongue swept over the seam of her lips, and she opened for him, moaning softly as she tasted herself on him, her irritation vanishing in an instant. His hands grabbed her hips, and then he flipped them both, his back hitting the bed as he dragged her up his body until her knees were planted on either side of his head. "I want you to cum on my face," he demanded, his breath teasing her.

"What?" she asked in surprise, tensing. They'd seen every inch of each other already, but this seemed far more intimate than anything else they'd done, which was laughable.

"Grab the headboard," he instructed, slapping her ass cheek when she didn't respond right away. The sting startled her, heating her body as she quickly followed his command. Her back arched slightly, and she hovered over his mouth, unsure of what to do. She'd had a lot of sex, but she'd never *sat* on someone's face before. What if she got carried away and hurt him?

"Are you sure?" Hunny asked hesitantly, biting her lower lip as her grip tightened on the top of the headboard. "What if I smother you?"

"It'd be a hell of a way to go," Tank joked.

"Henry! I'm being serious. What if I get too into it and I break your nose or something?"

"Then I'll pat myself on the back for making you lose control, baby," he assured her, licking her with a deep rumble of satisfaction. Her mouth dropped open as his tongue swirled over her entrance, lapping at her slick. His beard tickled her inner thighs, heightening the sensations stirring inside her. "Now, be a good little rabbit, and *sit.*"

His grip tightened on her hips, and then he pushed her down, his tongue sinking inside her. He groaned beneath her, and instinctively, her thighs clenched around his head, holding him in place as he ate her out. Her head dropped back, hair trailing down her spine as she rode his face. Gently, at first. But another hard slap to her ass and Hunny bucked her hips, riding his tongue faster.

Pleasure whipped through her like lightning, and her body felt too hot, her breathing shallow as she moaned his name. Her thighs trembled, and that ball of tension in her core tightened further, threatening to come undone. Almost as if he could sense it, Tank's fingers found her clit, rolling it in small circles as he stiffened his tongue, thrusting it deeper than before.

"H-Henry!" Hunny cried out, the headboard creaking as she held on for dear life. Her pussy spasmed around his tongue as she rode his face with reckless abandon, heat spreading over every inch of her.

Tank pinched her clit, and that was all it took to send her over the edge. Hunny screamed his name, her orgasm detonating inside her. Tank held her down on his face as he licked her clean, her body shaking around him as her pulse beat a frantic drum in her ears, her breasts heaving as she struggled to regulate her breathing.

After a few more seconds of him licking her overstimulated pussy, he let her roll off of him. She collapsed onto her back with a soft moan, and he followed her, blanketing her with his hard body. His erection pressed against her thigh as he leaned down, teasing her nipple with his tongue. His cheeks were red, and parts of his beard around his mouth were damp from her arousal. She blushed, but he didn't notice, too preoccupied with the boobs in front of him.

Palming one breast, he sucked on the other, sending little zaps of pleasure down to her clit, her body reeling with aftershocks. "Love your tits," he murmured, blowing on the wet peak. It hardened, and he sucked it back into his mouth, teasing it with his teeth.

"Really? I kind of hate that I have small boobs." Well, she hadn't really *hated* it before she'd met Jason, but he'd made a comment once about them being 'too small to hold on to,' and she'd felt insecure about their size ever since.

God, just thinking about it, the differences between Jason and Tank were astounding. How had fate paired her with someone so cruel, so *shallow*? She'd deserved better than that miserable piece of shit wolf shifter.

She'd deserved this surly, gentle bear in front of her. Part of her felt bad for thinking it; she was certain Tank's true mate would have been a better choice for him than she was. But fate had been cruel to both of them, and ironically, brought them both together.

To heal together? To find solace in one another? Hunny didn't care about the reasoning, only that she was glad he was here. She was glad he was hers, in whatever capacity he'd give her.

Tank released her nipple with a pop, his eyes broody as they met hers. "I love your breasts. You're perfect, Hunny. Everything about you is perfect."

Warmth blossomed in her chest at his words, but she rolled her eyes playfully. "You're just saying that because you're a sweetheart."

His brows rose. "Everyone else would disagree with you on that, darlin'."

She shook her head adamantly. "They just don't know you like I do."

With a gruff laugh, Tank kissed his way up her body, stopping to brush his nose against hers. "I'm a dickhead, baby."

"*My* dickhead," she corrected with a small smile.

He grinned. "That doesn't change the fact that you're perfect. And you're only going to get more beautiful with time."

She grimaced at that, a troubling thought occurring. "I'm going to get so big with three babies." She'd always been a small, petite shifter, but there was no way her body wouldn't alter forever after three kits. Even with a shifter's healing and increased metabolism, she wouldn't always look like she did now. Hunny wasn't usually fixated on her appearance, but what if Tank lost interest in her?

"What's that look for?" he asked suddenly, eyes narrowing. "You seem nervous."

"What if I look a lot different after I have my kits?" she blurted out. She didn't add 'and you don't want me' to her question, but it seemed to hover between them all the same.

Tank rolled his eyes. "Is that a serious question?"

"*Excuse me*, Henry Sinclair, but did you just roll your eyes at me?" she snapped in outrage, her fears dissipating for a moment as she shoved at his shoulders. He didn't move an inch. If anything, he sank down further, pinning her more firmly beneath him. She loved it, and despite her irritation, she wrapped her arms around his neck, her fingers sifting through the hair at the base of his head.

"I did. Only proper way to answer a question like that."

Hunny scoffed. "With an eye roll?"

"Yup."

"Be serious, please," she said, a vulnerable note in her voice she couldn't hold back. "It's a genuine question."

Tank's eyes softened marginally, and he cupped her face, staring down at her with a tenderness that threatened to melt her into the mattress. "You're going to look different, Hunny. But that doesn't mean you'll be any less beautiful, and I'm going to want you just as much after kits as I do right now. If I have to fuck you senseless every day to prove how sexy you are," he added with a long, drawn-out sigh, "then I guess that's a burden I'll have to bear."

Hunny glared at him, but her lips twitched regardless and the small laugh in her voice was unmistakable. "You're so ridiculous."

"You love it," he teased.

She stilled beneath him, her heart stuttering in her chest as she met his gaze. "Maybe I do."

His eyes darkened, longing and lust shining down at her from that gaze, making her feel like a million butterflies had taken flight inside her stomach. "I should probably start right now on fucking you sense-less," Tank declared, swallowing thickly before kissing her softly. "That way, when the kits come, you won't even have to wonder if I still want you. I'm always going to want you, little rabbit."

His mouth found hers again, claiming her hard as he spread her legs beneath him, fitting his thick cock against her entrance. And as he slid home inside her, reminding her of how much he craved her, Hunny felt silly for ever questioning it in the first place.

Twenty Two

"**I**s your friend always so ..." Nessa trailed off, sending a curious glance Tank's way as he stalked around the empty teahouse. He must have been on edge about the meeting with Jason tomorrow. When he'd told her about it last night, she'd been on edge too. She didn't want Tank anywhere near that wolf.

Tank grumbled loudly, drawing her attention to the surly male. His entire body was stiff, and he kept huffing every few minutes in irritation. It was kind of comical, seeing him so aggravated, after they'd just spent hours fucking in his bed. How Hunny's male could go from loving and tender in private to sullen and grumpy in public was a mystery, but she enjoyed seeing all sides of him.

Especially when he was naked.

"Nosy?" Hunny supplied with a crooked smile, reaching for her cup of tea. It was decaf, unfortunately. No caffeine for her until her kits were born, although it was a terrible time for it right now, anyway. It was just past six p.m., and the shop had closed roughly an hour ago, giving the two females plenty of privacy to get to know one another while Tank lingered nearby.

Although, Hunny felt like she'd known Nessa for years already. They'd talked almost every day on the phone since they'd met, and although they hadn't delved into each other's personal lives, they had a lot in common, and forming a friendship had been easy.

Her attention turned toward the bear shifter. So far, Tank seemed torn between conducting recon for Murphy and eavesdropping on her conversation with her new friend, which was super rude. Just because the male had enhanced hearing, it didn't mean he had to listen in on *every*thing.

Nessa's lips twitched as she watched Tank rummage through a cabinet along the back wall. "I was going to say 'pissed off,' but sure. We can go with nosy."

Hunny let out a small, surprised laugh, loud enough that her bear shifter turned his head toward them, his eyes softening marginally as they settled on her. She blew him a kiss and his gaze darkened, a sensual hunger crossing his features that had her core spasming with need. "He's actually in a pretty good mood," she mock-whispered to Nessa, sending her a smug smile.

He better be in the best mood of his life after all the sex they'd had in the last twenty-four hours. For all her confidence about rabbit shifters having endless sexual stamina, Tank was definitely keeping her on her toes.

And it is amazing, she thought blissfully. Tank was an exceptional lover; the best she'd ever had, and it wasn't like she'd been a virgin when they'd met. She had plenty of experience with males, and to put it simply; no one held a candle to him. Not just regarding sex, either.

"Oh my God, you slept with him." Nessa leaned forward in her chair dramatically. "I thought you were just friends!" she whispered.

Tank's head whipped toward them, and Hunny shot him a glare that clearly said 'mind your business.' With another huff, he disappeared into a backroom, leaving them alone. Luckily, Nessa had given him permission to roam about when he'd asked, so his leaving to explore more of her shop wasn't weird or awkward. Well, not too much any-way.

Once he was gone, she eyed Nessa warily. "How do you know we slept together? Is it that obvious?"

"Aha!" Nessa slapped her palm onto the tabletop. "So I *am* right. Damn, I should have bet money on it. And to answer your question: you've got this glow about you that wasn't there the first time we met." She grabbed her own cup of tea, taking a delicate sip as she watched Hunny over the rim. "So, did you have a good time? I'm assuming the answer is yes."

Hunny blushed, answering the question without saying a word.

Nessa laughed. "Oh, so he's *good good*."

"Maybe better than that." Hunny's lips twitched.

Nessa whistled. "Makes sense now why you keep giving him the googly eyes every few minutes. You're in love with the grump."

"I-I'm not in love," Hunny sputtered quickly, though as soon as she said it, the truth smacked her in the face like a ton of bricks.

Holy shit. She *was* in love with Tank.

It was wild to think, to even comprehend. Could it happen so fast? She'd barely known him for any true length of time, but already it felt like they'd gone through so much together. She felt more for him now than she ever had with anyone else; including her true mate.

After Jason had rejected her, she'd felt sad, but she'd also known she would move on from him; that she didn't really *need* him. With Tank, it was completely different. He'd wormed his way into her heart so thoroughly, just the idea of being separated from him made her breath stall in her lungs, a swift denial emitting from her very soul. She didn't know what she'd do without him—as if the very notion was so absurd her brain refused to think about it.

Nessa raised a skeptical brow. "Are you sure you're not in love?"

Hunny cleared her throat, shifting uncomfortably in her seat. "I ... I just hadn't thought about it before," she admitted faintly. "This whole situation with Henry, it's all very new, and it seems a little fast, you know?"

But it also felt right. Everything about him felt right.

Nessa shrugged, leaning back in her chair. "Not necessarily. Sometimes the best kind of love blindsides you. It finds you when you least expect it and takes you for one hell of a rollercoaster ride."

"You can say that again," Hunny agreed adamantly. When Nessa sent her a questioning look, she sighed. "I just got out of a bad relationship a couple of weeks ago. I met Henry right after, and I didn't expect to feel so much for him so soon."

"Really? The way you two act together, I just assumed you'd known him for a few years."

"Nope." Hunny bit her lower lip, worry swirling through her mind before she continued, "I didn't think I wanted to be in a relationship or anything like that, not for a while, but Henry's kind of impossible to resist. And you're right, by the way. A-about what you said."

Nessa beamed at her. "I'm thrilled for you, Hunny. Real love's hard to find." Some of her smile dimmed, and she looked away. "A few years ago, I'd have given anything to find something like that; love, marriage, *kids*. But some things just aren't meant to happen."

At the mention of kids, Hunny absent-mindedly touched her stomach. Nessa followed the movement, brows raising in surprise.

"You're pregnant, aren't you?"

Hunny blushed. "Yeah. Triplets, actually."

Nessa's eyes widened, shooting up to Hunny's face and then back to her stomach. "Shut up. Seriously?" She lowered her voice. "You've got to be several weeks into a pregnancy to know you've got triplets, right? Does Tank know?"

Hunny tilted her head, completely forgetting for a moment that humans couldn't smell the same way shifters could. What Tank had known upon first meeting her, Nessa wouldn't know unless she was told or until Hunny began showing. "Oh, yeah, he knows everything about my ex, including that I'm carrying his children. Henry's actually building onto his cabin to make room for us all. It's a bit complicated but we're figuring it out."

Nessa gaped at her. "You're telling me that grumpy bastard"—she pointed toward the backroom Tank had disappeared to—"is giving you great sex, building you a cabin—"

"Building onto an *existing* cabin—"

"—and is completely cool with you having another man's kids?" Nessa whistled again. "You are lucky, Hunny Russo. *Lucky.*"

"Yeah," Hunny agreed with a warm, satisfied smile. "I really am."

"I know we haven't known each other long either," Nessa added, "but please take my advice; you need to lock that man down ASAP. Do you know how many women would snatch up the opportunity to get with a guy like that?"

Hunny stilled. "You think so?" She hadn't met any of the females in his clan besides his mother, but she'd never considered them as competition before. Should she?

Nessa rolled her eyes. "Girl, *yes*. Men like that don't grow on trees, and some women will do anything to take what someone else has."

The thought made Hunny nauseous and territorial. Tank was *hers*, dammit. She didn't start a relationship with him just for someone else to come sniffing around. And Nessa was definitely right; Tank was a catch. She was lucky no other females had noticed it before. What if they did now and Tank was still unclaimed?

It didn't make them a permanent thing just because they were sleeping together. Only a mating mark would make him off limits.

Suddenly, Hunny's canines began to ache, the need to sink her fangs into him and claim him as hers so strong she nearly knocked back her chair to go hunt him down. Instead, she gripped her ceramic cup hard, surprised she didn't crack it as she shook her head, trying to grasp onto reason before she lost her mind. "Henry's not like that, though. He wouldn't leave me for another woman." She knew that with absolute certainty, but it didn't dampen the urge she had to claim him.

"Even more reason to lock him down," Nessa insisted. "The man can barely keep his eyes off you, and if he's happy to raise another man's kids with you, I can't imagine he'd have a problem committing to you." She shook her head a moment later. "I'm sorry. I don't know if I overstepped, Hunny. I don't want to sound like I'm pressuring you into anything, and I don't want to worry you."

"You didn't and I'm not," Hunny assured her, adding with a playful wink, "Besides, Henry *did* say he wanted everything I was willing to give him, so I don't think he'd mind if we took things further."

"Oh, my God!" Nessa fanned herself. "Did I call him a grump? What I meant was, he's perfect."

Hunny smiled widely. "That's what I tell him, but I don't think he believes me."

"Perfect and oblivious to it? Yeah, he's a keeper. And one of a kind, I'm sure," Nessa uttered wistfully.

"He has brothers, you know." Though she wasn't sure if they'd be interested in dating a human.

Nessa grimaced. "Yeah, I spoke with one of them over the phone this morning. Murphy? He called to reserve my shop for some kind of event tomorrow. He seems like a dick, but he offered me a lot of money, so obviously I accepted."

Hunny wrinkled her nose. "Yeah, he has that effect on people." He'd been stern with her, too, during their first and only meeting, but she had the distinct impression that there was more to him than that. Behind his hard edges was someone who genuinely cared about his family, and by extension, her.

"Is it a family trait?" Nessa asked. "They act like jerks but have hearts of gold or something?"

She snorted. "Jasper, that's Henry's youngest brother, is very much a joker. And a dipshit, but mostly just to Henry. I've noticed that Murphy's more serious. He has a lot of responsibilities with his job, though, and I think they weigh on him." She frowned. "Henry's got two more brothers, but I haven't met them yet. Or their dad."

Actually, now that she was thinking about it, she knew nothing about the other members of his family. Tabitha was alive and well, meaning her mate must still be in the picture. So where was he? She'd have to ask Tank about it.

"Sounds like a family reunion is in order." Nessa waggled her eyebrows teasingly.

"I'll invite you so you can have your pick of his brothers," Hunny joked.

Nessa laughed, shaking her head. "I've had my fair share of dickhead boyfriends, so I'll pass. But thank you."

Hunny winced. "That bad, huh?"

Nessa bit her lower lip, a somber expression crossing her features. Running a hand through her turquoise-colored hair, she said, "I mean, there's a reason I moved to the middle of nowhere, Montana. No offense if this was your dream destination," she added hastily. "But this wasn't my first choice. Just the safest."

"Safest?" That didn't sound good at all. "Are you alright, Nessa?"

Nessa's eyes flickered, several emotions crossing over them at once. "I'm fine now. Honestly, I've put the past behind me, and it's nothing I really want to talk about, if that's okay?"

Hunny nodded slowly. "Yeah, of course." Lowering her voice to a soothing tone, she added, "But if you ever decide you want to vent, I'm here for you. Alright?"

"I appreciate that. Seriously." Nessa released a shuddering breath. "Moving away from everything I knew was hard, but opening my shop, having my own freedom ... it's worth everything I went through before, you know?"

"Yeah," Hunny answered firmly. "I know how you feel. My parents died when I was seventeen and I left everything I knew behind to start over. Freedom is scary, but it's empowering, too."

"It really is." Nessa stretched her arms over her head, suddenly letting out a small yawn.

Hunny looked over at the clock on the wall, her eyes widening in surprise. "Oh wow, we've been talking for almost three hours! I should probably head home."

"We need to do this again soon," Nessa said, standing when Hunny did. "I had a lot of fun. Oh, that reminds me." She leaned down, grabbing her purse off the floor and pulling out a small black bag from inside it. She handed it over to Hunny. "I got those trimmers and stuff you asked for. Going to give the grizzly a shave, eh?"

Hunny, startled, nearly dropped the bag. "G-grizzly?"

How did Nessa know he was a bear shifter?!

Nessa sent her an odd look. "Yeah. Tank's like a big grizzly bear. Hairy, tall, growly ... You never got that impression?"

"Oh!" Hunny laughed a little too loudly, the sound high-pitched and wrong. "I thought you meant—*nevermind.*"

Tank prowled out of the backroom, a worried look on his face. "Everything alright, darlin'? It sounded almost like a witch was cackling out here."

Nessa coughed into her hand, smothering her own laugh as Hunny's face heated.

"Yes! Everything is great," Hunny told him quickly, clutching the bag tightly as she moved over to him. She gave Nessa a smile. "I'll text you."

As Tank led Hunny from the shop, he looked down at the bag in her hand. "What's that?"

She blushed. "Well, I kind of have a favor to ask you, Henry."

"Okay," he drawled slowly, eyes moving from the bag to her face in confusion. That look only made her cheeks heat further.

"I want you to give me some of your hair!" she exclaimed in a rush like an absolute weirdo. She waved the bag around like a weapon, the heavy tools clanking around inside. "Just a trim, really. You won't even notice I've cut anything off."

His head snapped back in surprise. "What? Why do you want my hair?"

"For a nest. I keep thinking about it, and the other day when I shifted, I couldn't build it properly. It just felt really wrong, and I realized it's because ..." She trailed off, embarrassed to even be asking him this question. Somehow, it seemed even more personal than him asking her to sit on his face.

"Because you need my hair?" he finished, keeping his lips in a straight line even though the laughter was unmistakable in his voice.

She narrowed her eyes threateningly, stopping beside the passenger side of his truck. "Are you *laughing* at me, Henry Sinclair?"

"Not at all, little rabbit. I just find you adorable."

Some of her ire eased at that, and when he gripped the back of her neck, pulling her in for a drugging kiss, she moaned, forgetting entirely why she'd grown irritated with him to begin with.

"Come on, darlin'," Tank murmured against her lips. "Let's get you home so you can build your nest." Her heart fluttered, and then he narrowed his eyes. "You don't want my pubic hair, do you?"

"*What?*" She sent him a horrified look. "No!"

Although—NO!

Laughing huskily, Tank opened the truck door, helping her inside.

Twenty Three

Tank felt like a fidgety cub as he sat in one of his kitchen chairs, a towel around his shoulders as Hunny finger-combed his hair for the hundredth time. Not that he minded, especially because she was so close. Her breasts pressed into his arm and her honey, vanilla and lavender scent filled his lungs, keeping him content.

If he could bottle her scent and keep it with him all the time, he would. It was like a damned drug, capable of turning even his most agitated state into one of bliss and relaxation. It also made him horny as fuck, especially now that her pregnancy was advancing. Each day that passed, her scent seemed to grow thicker, more potent in the air, and he fucking loved it.

The way it made his balls ache and his cock strain for release ... Fuck, now he wanted to rip her clothes off, pull her into his lap, and—

Hunny inhaled, her fingers tightening in his hair. "What are you thinking, Henry?"

"If I tell you, little rabbit, you won't be cutting my hair tonight. You'll be taking my cock in every position I can think of." And he could think of *a lot*.

"That's not fair." Hunny leaned in, nipping his earlobe before whispering sensually, "You're being naughty while I'm trying to concentrate. Won't you be a good boy for me, Henry?"

Instantly, he was hard, his cock pushing uncomfortably against his zipper as he adjusted in his seat.

Hunny snorted, looking down at his lap gleefully, his erection prominent through his jeans. "Did you really just get turned on by *that*? I didn't think being called a good boy would be your thing."

"It's not," Tank grumbled, cupping his knees to keep from doing what he really wanted, which involved bending Hunny into a provocative position and pumping into her until he came so much he blacked out. His mouth watered just thinking about it. "It's a Hunny thing."

Her fingers paused in his hair. "'A Hunny thing?'"

"Yeah. Everything you do makes me hard as a fucking rock, darlin'."

Laughing lightly, she resumed combing his hair. "Now you've got me wondering how deranged I can get."

"More deranged than cum tea?"

"Oh my God, Henry—there wasn't any cum in there!"

"Not yet," he snickered, just because he knew she'd blush. He snuck a peek out of the corner of his eye, and sure enough, her cheeks were glowing a delicate shade of pink. Regardless of how much he appreciated this banter between them, as soon as she ran her fingers through his unruly mop of hair *again*, he couldn't help but ask, "You planning on cutting anything, darlin'?"

Hunny tugged teasingly on a few strands. "If you actually combed this mess once in a while, I wouldn't have to spend half an hour detangling it."

Tank's cheeks heated with embarrassment. She wasn't wrong—he had never cared about his appearance before, whether it was regarding his beard or his hair. Living in the mountains, relatively alone, it hadn't seemed necessary, which was why every six months he used an electric razor to trim his hair into a buzz cut and took off several inches of his beard.

Self-consciously, he lifted a hand, feeling his long, unkempt facial hair. Shit, when was the last time he'd even done that? Had it been longer than six months? He couldn't remember. So far, Hunny hadn't complained about the length, but what if she hated how he looked?

Frustrated, he huffed, "It's not *that* bad."

"No, it's not," Hunny agreed with another small laugh. Leaning in, she kissed his cheek, her soft, warm lips burning into him like a brand he wanted to wear forever. Just like that, Tank's irritation melted away, replaced by a need so fierce he was surprised he didn't pluck her up and take her to bed right then and there, haircut be damned. Resuming her finger-combing, she added, "But your hair is very thick and silky, so I want to make sure it's brushed out properly."

His brows furrowed as he heard a slight tremor in her voice, and before she could say anything else, he turned in his seat, staring right at her. "You're afraid you're going to fuck up my hair, aren't you?"

She shrugged nonchalantly, but he'd studied her every move for almost two weeks; he could tell by the guarded look in her eyes she was nervous. "Come on, little rabbit. You'll do a great job." And if she didn't, he didn't give a shit. It was just hair; it would grow back. Couldn't get any shorter than a buzz cut anyway.

"Yeah," Hunny murmured faintly. Clearing her throat, she grabbed the scissors from the counter, pursing her lips in concentration as she made the first cut.

"That wasn't so bad, was it? You're practically a professional already," Tank teased gruffly, earning a playful smack on the shoulder.

"I mean, I spent an entire summer working as a dog groomer a few years ago," Hunny commented distractedly, lifting a section of his hair straight up and cutting. She dropped the pieces onto the counter, creating a neat little pile as she continued with her work. "That's kind of the same thing as cutting a person's hair, right?"

"Oh, definitely," Tank replied readily. Although he had to admit, he didn't give a shit about how adept her skills were with a pair of scissors. He was just flattered Hunny wanted to make a nest with his hair.

She wanted a part of *him* with her when she shifted, to snuggle up protectively with. *She said it didn't feel right without my hair*, he thought smugly. If that wasn't enough to make a male feel on top of the world, he didn't know what would.

It was even enough to take the sting out of what he'd accidentally overheard earlier at the teahouse. Even though he'd left the women in the main room while he'd checked out the security features in the back, he'd inadvertently listened in as Hunny denied she was in love with him. As soon as he'd heard it, he felt like his heart had dropped into his stomach, and he'd done everything he could to tune their conversation out, not wanting to experience another blow to his ego and heart.

Even now, a few hours later, he still felt the pain from Hunny's words, but he understood her reservations. He was just lucky she'd given him a chance to woo her, to treat her as she deserved. He'd be patient with her. And soon enough, she'd come to love him like he loved her. To need him like he needed her.

And when that day finally happened, he'd mate her.

His erection hardened further at the thought, his canines aching with the need to lengthen so he could place a possessive brand on her soft skin, to mark her for the entire world to see. Humans like Nessa wouldn't understand the meaning of it. They'd probably think it was a scar or birthmark. But shifters would know that his little rabbit was claimed, and that her kits were his too, even if they didn't share his DNA.

A deep, possessive growl rumbled in his chest, and he didn't bother tamping it down.

"Someone's being awfully vocal," Hunny commented, the smile clear in her voice.

"Got a lot to be vocal about." Clearing his throat, Tank asked, "Did you enjoy your girls' date?"

"Yeah. Nessa's a lot of fun. I think she's had a hard life, though."

"Why do you think that?"

"She made a comment about moving to Montana because it was 'safe,' and that was after she mentioned having a really shitty ex-boyfriend." Hunny sighed, the sound drowning out the snipping of her sheers as she cut more of his hair. "It just gave me the impression she ran away from some kind of abusive situation. She didn't want to talk about it, though, and I didn't have the heart to badger her about it."

"Murphy's claimed the entire town, so she's now under his protection," Tank stated, a slight itch in his throat. He glanced at the counter, to where he'd left his cup of tea. He leaned over, snagging it right as Hunny gasped.

"Henry! Don't do that; I almost messed up."

Grumbling an apology, he took a long drink, enjoying the soothing sensation of melted honey as it slid down his throat. It was the only thing that made this concoction tolerable. Once he finished draining the cup, he continued. "Point is, if she's in trouble, it's Murphy's problem now. He'll handle it, especially if you make him aware of the issue."

"That's good, I guess." Hunny sighed again. "Apparently he was a dick on the phone to Nessa, though, so I can't imagine she'll let him help. Especially since she doesn't know what we are. She'll probably just think he's some weirdo trying to get into her business."

"He is."

Hunny laughed abruptly, the sound warming him from the inside out. "I love the relationship you have with your family, Henry. I always wanted to have siblings, but I wasn't that fortunate."

"Well, you've got a shitload of them now, little rabbit."

"When do you think I'll meet the rest of your family? Your dad and your other brothers?"

Tank stiffened slightly at that, taken aback by the question. "I'm not sure. My middle brother, Reece, ran into a bit of trouble last year, and my dad and other brother have been helping him sort it out for a while now."

"Oh." Hunny tilted her head. "What kind of trouble?"

"It's difficult to explain." Tank hated that he was being so cagey. The situation was as complicated as it was unique, and he didn't want her to think so little of his brother.

"Henry, why are you being so weird right now?" Hunny asked bluntly, seeing right through him. "You can just tell me you don't want to talk about this part of your life."

Tank sighed, running a hand down his face. "I want to tell you all about my life, little rabbit. I just ... I don't want you to get the wrong impression about Reece."

"Hey," Hunny said softly, moving to stand in front of him. She fit between his legs, wrapping her arms around the back of his neck as she gazed down at him. "You and your family have done more for me in a matter of weeks than anyone ever has before. Whatever you're hesitant to tell me, I won't care what it is. I won't judge you or anyone else, Henry. I just want to know more about you. But if you don't want to talk about it right now, that's okay."

"I know, baby." And he did. Placing his hands on her hips, Tank pulled Hunny into his lap, nuzzling her neck. Giving her throat a lingering kiss, he murmured, "Reece has a difficult time distinguishing his baser, animalistic instincts from his more human nature. It makes him more volatile, and quick to anger. Last year, he came to the defense of a human woman who he witnessed getting attacked by a human male. Reece lost control, shifted and ripped the male apart."

"Oh my God." Hunny gasped, pulling Tank closer. "A human watched him shift? What happened next?"

"She agreed to say a bear attacked them and that she escaped. The police believed her. Who wouldn't? Reece's twin, Gunnar, and my dad have been up there with Reece ever since, trying to get him under control."

Hunny leaned back, cupping his face gently. "Why doesn't Reece just come home?"

"He refuses to leave the woman. He's obsessed with her, even though she's terrified of him." Not even Murphy demanding Reece return home was enough to pull the male away. A command from an Alpha should have penetrated the haze of Reece's mind, the compulsion too much to resist. But as a dominant shifter and in his half-feral state, Murphy's command had been all but useless.

"Do you think she's safe with him so close?"

Tank didn't know, and neither did his family, which was why they were currently divided. As if she were in tune with his thoughts, Hunny hummed, giving him a quick kiss before pushing back to her feet.

"Alright, my big bear," Hunny said lovingly. "Let's finish your hair, and then I'll grant you the pleasure of watching me get naked, shift, and put together the most badass nest you've ever seen."

His lips twitched. He could already picture it; Hunny burrowing a small hole in his yard and stuffing it with fur and grass to conceal the opening. She wouldn't put her actual kits in there, obviously, but her instinct to make a nest couldn't be neglected, and he didn't want it to be either.

Tank squeezed her hips gently before he reluctantly let go. "What if, after I watch you get naked, I sat you on the counter and ate your pussy for dinner instead? I'll cook *you* dinner afterward, and *then* I'll take you outside so you can build your nest."

It sounded like a reasonable idea to him, and his dick agreed wholeheartedly.

She narrowed her eyes menacingly. "We both know if you get anywhere near my lady bits, we're not stopping until we're both passed out on the kitchen floor with bodily fluids everywhere."

"Are you suggesting that's a bad thing?" Because it sounded perfect.

Hunny wrinkled her nose dramatically, but it wasn't enough to conceal the lust dancing in her eyes, or the scent of her arousal as it permeated the air. "Alright, fine. You talked me into it. But only *after* I finish cutting your hair."

With that, she began chopping away confidently, whistling lightly as she worked. It was peaceful, and Tank nearly fell asleep before he remembered something from earlier today.

"My mom sent a few links to birthing videos for us to watch when we have time," Tank mentioned.

"*What?!*" There was a loud snip, followed by Hunny's swift, "*Oh, shit.*" That didn't sound good at all. As Tank turned his head to the side, Hunny grabbed his face, awkwardly turning it until he was facing forward once more. "Keep your head straight, Henry, otherwise I'm going to mess up!" she exclaimed.

Brows raised, Tank did as instructed, though he was fairly certain she'd already messed up. "This better?"

Sighing, Hunny began her cutting anew, and after a few minutes she asked, "What kind of birthing videos? Like the whole thing?"

"I don't know," Tank admitted, scratching his chin. "Didn't ask." To be fair, he hadn't clarified exactly what he was after when he'd approached his mother about wanting to learn everything he could about shifter pregnancies, but he knew she wouldn't steer him wrong with the educational videos and books she'd ordered for him to read.

"I don't know if I can watch something like that, Henry. I mean, experiencing it will be more than enough for me," she answered with a small shudder.

Tank shrugged. "I'm interested in seeing the process."

He also didn't want to be unprepared for whenever Hunny gave birth in several months' time. What if something happened while she was in labor and she needed him? He refused to be a bumbling idiot when it mattered most, unsure of how to help when something as simple as a video had been available beforehand.

Hunny stilled beside him. "You're going to watch those videos?" she asked quietly.

Tank shrugged. "At least until the books I ordered come in. They don't have anything on shifter pregnancies, but Mom told me a lot of the information is the same, give or take."

"Henry ... you'd do all that for me?" Hunny's voice held a soft note to it he'd never quite heard before.

Unable to help himself, Tank turned his head right as she cut another section of hair, ignoring the sharp curse that fell from her lips. He gazed at her in adoration. "Of course. I'd do anything for you, little rabbit."

Hunny stared at him with a very long, uneven chunk of his brown hair clutched between her fingers. *"IthinkIloveyou,"* she blurted out in a rush.

Tank's mouth dropped open, and he froze in place, staring at her in bewilderment.

What did she just say? But she'd told Nessa she wasn't—that she didn't—

"Oh God, you're not saying anything. Y-you know what? I didn't mean it. I-it was a joke. Haha, got you!" Hunny declared shrilly, looking like she'd swallowed a bug. She turned away from him, moving into the living room as he stared after her, still bumbling to herself. "Oh wow, I just remembered that I needed to do literally anything else. Alone. By myself. I'm just going to head upstairs—"

Tank didn't let her take another step before he was on her, grabbing her around the waist and spinning her beautiful ass around. He pinned her against the back of the couch, caging her in with his body.

Pressing himself fully against her, he cupped her face, tilting her head upward until she was forced to meet his gaze. She stared at him shyly, and it killed him to see that she'd teared up slightly.

"Tell me what you said, little rabbit," Tank all but growled, his voice thick with a need that stabbed all the way to his soul. "I need to hear you say it."

He might just die if she didn't.

Hunny licked her lips. "I don't know what you mean—"

"I love you," Tank interrupted, not wanting to waste another minute without telling her how he felt. She'd already admitted it, anyway, even if she was nervous to do so again. "I think I knew you were meant to be mine when you bit the shit out of my hand, Hunny. Or maybe when I realized that everything about you calls to me. Your scent. How excited you get over anything and everything. The sweet way you laugh," he murmured.

He watched intently as several emotions crossed Hunny's face. Surprise. Shock. A tiny sliver of fear. And then she melted into him, her vivid emerald gaze softening as her hands found his chest, fingers curling into his shirt.

She opened her mouth, and he could practically hear her confession of love ringing in his ears. Only, it wouldn't be said this time in a rush, followed up by confusion and a hasty retreat. No, this time she'd say those three little words, and he'd let them sink in, enjoying every syllable.

Imagine Tank's surprise when Hunny instead declared firmly, "I want to mate with you, Henry."

Twenty Four

There was a roaring in Tank's ears as Hunny looked up at him, hope and love shining in her eyes as she asked, "Will you, Henry? Will you be my ma—"

Tank plucked her up into his arms, her small squeak of surprise muffled as he planted his lips on hers, his tongue invading her mouth as he moved to the stairs. She tasted sweet, and as he swallowed her soft moan of need, she tasted like *his*.

He wanted her, needed her more than anything else in this world. And he wouldn't give her a chance to change her mind; Hunny was his forever. He'd felt it since he'd first drawn her scent into his lungs. He just hadn't realized it then. But he did now, and he wouldn't squander this opportunity.

As he fumbled his way up the stairs, Hunny ripped the towel off his shoulders, reaching for his shirt next and yanking it clumsily up and over his head. The cloth separated their lips for barely a second before he was crushing his mouth back to hers, tasting her again like a starved male finally given nourishment.

He wasn't sure how they made it upstairs without him tripping over his own feet, but they did, and he moved straight for the bed, the urge to mate her dogging his every move. Making him desperate, needy.

Dropping her gently onto the bed, Tank tugged on the waistband of his jeans, nearly breaking the zipper in his haste to get the damned thing off. He couldn't take his eyes off his little rabbit, his gaze riveted to Hunny as she grabbed the bottom of her shirt—*his* shirt that she liked to wear around his cabin like a nightgown—and lifted it, exposing the apex of her naked thighs.

Before she could take the material off, he ordered, "Don't."

Her brow furrowed in confusion, but that changed as soon as he stepped out of his jeans, his erection jutting out in front of him, precum already nestled on the tip. She'd kept him hard for damn near an hour, but soon enough, he'd have his relief.

Her eyes became heavy-lidded with desire as he stepped into her space, her hands automatically finding his hips and holding on. "I want to undress you, darlin'."

Hunny swallowed thickly, moving her eyes slowly from his erection and up to his face, her expression filled with trust and a sensual hunger that had more pearly liquid dribbling onto his cockhead. "Okay," she breathed.

Slowly, he grabbed the shirt she wore, pulling it over her head. Excitement knotted in his gut as he did so, like he was unwrapping the greatest gift he'd ever received. In a sense, he was. Dropping the material carelessly to the floor, he stared down at Hunny's lovely body, his heart pounding and his mouth watering.

Her nipples were hard, the twin peaks practically begging for his kiss. His tongue. He couldn't wait to see how they'd look in a few months, and distracted, he wondered if she'd let him have a taste when she started producing milk.

Was that perverted, that the thought of tasting her sweetness in every way made his dick ache more than ever? Probably, but he didn't really give a fuck.

"What are you thinking?" Hunny asked quietly, a curious note in her voice. "Your scent ... it's stronger, but not just from lust. It's almost like—"

"Do you know much about mating a bear shifter?" he asked huskily, planting his knee on the bed beside her. Immediately, she scooted back, getting more fully onto the mattress. He followed her, not stopping until she was flat on her back and he was looming over her, his hands roaming over her soft skin.

"No, I don't know much of anything except we're going to mark one another." Hunny's eyes moved to his neck, and she licked her lips, humming softly. "I know it's different when it's a chosen mate instead of a fated one, but regardless, a bond will form between us.

We'll eventually be able to sense each other's emotions, even from a great distance."

Tank nodded. "Bears differ from most other shifters. When we're about to mate someone, chosen or fated, our scent thickens as it seeps from our pores." He could smell his musk enhancing even now, and he slipped a hand over one of her breasts, fingers finding the stiff peak and pinching it.

Hunny gasped, her cheeks heating as she arched her back, pressing more firmly against his hand. "Why?"

"Because when I make you mine, when my teeth sink into your neck and mark you, my scent will linger afterward." Cupping the underside of her breast, he bent down, licking her nipple. He popped it into his mouth, sucking hard as she whimpered beneath him.

Her hands fisted into his hair, pulling him in closer. "How long does your scent last on me?"

Regretfully, he released her nipple, blowing on the rosy tip before answering. "Forever, Hunny. Traces of my scent will always linger on your skin, so that any shifter you encounter knows who you belong to. *Me*," he declared heatedly, lifting his head and taking her mouth once more.

Hungry for her, Tank pinned her beneath him, careful of her tiny baby bump as he devoured her with his tongue. Grabbing her hips, he ground his erection against her, shuddering as pleasure whipped through him, demanding more, urging him to spread her pretty little thighs and take what belonged to him. And Hunny belonged to him. Every inch of her body, her heart, was *his*.

She returned his kiss just as eagerly, and he bucked his hips in surprise as she fisted his length, brushing his tip with her thumb and smearing his cum over the surface. Spreading her legs, Hunny tried to fit him against her entrance, but he pulled back, breathing hard as he looked down at her.

His female, his lover, his *mate*.

"Don't make me beg for you to fill me," Hunny whined, biting her lower lip as she gripped him harder, stroking him with a tight fist when he didn't budge. Tank hissed out a strangled breath—the sound caught between a groan and a feral growl.

"If you keep this up, I won't be able to go slow, little rabbit." And he hadn't even prepared her yet. "The pleasure from the mating bite is going to make this over with quick enough." Although he'd never experienced it, he'd heard of it—how each partner was so overcome with pleasure from the claiming bite that it was impossible to last long.

"I don't want slow. I want *you*." Hunny wrapped her legs around his waist, his cock brushing against her soaked entrance. He groaned, sinking his tip into her tight, wet heat. His canines lengthened dangerously, his gums aching as he brought his mouth to her throat, kissing her soft skin.

Tilting her head to the side and exposing her neck just like the perfect little submissive she was, Hunny whispered, "Make me your mate, Henry. Claim me."

A growl, more bear than man, erupted from him. He thrust forward, his cock shoving home right as his teeth pierced where her neck met her shoulder. Warm blood filled his mouth, and she cried out, her nails finding his back and scratching down his spine, leaving her own mark on him while he took her.

Tank was barely aware of his hips slamming against hers, flesh slapping together as pleasure assailed him, her hoarse, desperate cries ringing in his ears each time he pumped inside her. His teeth sank deeper, and his eyes rolled back into his head as she gripped his ass, rocking her own hips to meet each of his thrusts.

"Don't stop, it feels so good! Harder, bite me harder!" Hunny whimpered, her nails piercing his skin as she clung on tighter. A shudder raced down his spine, and he picked up his pace, plunging into her over and over. "Henry! Yes! Just like that—" She threw her head back into the pillows as she orgasmed, her body stiffening as her pussy gripped him, spasming around his shaft until he nearly blacked out. His balls drew up, his own release seconds away.

Removing his teeth from her flesh, he licked over the bite mark, possessive satisfaction thrumming through his veins at the sight of it. It would never fade, a symbol to everyone that Hunny was a claimed female. *His* claimed female.

Unable to resist the temptation, Tank plundered her mouth with his tongue, each pump of his hips causing Hunny to moan raggedly, her thighs cradling him close to her body. He devoured those small sounds, filling her to the brim with all that he had, all that he was.

"Your turn, baby," he murmured as he felt a familiar tingle start in his spine. He drank softly from her lips before angling his neck for her, his body coiled with anticipation.

Hunny looked up at him then, sending him a sated smile that threatened to steal his breath, her eyes drowsy with passion as she traced a spot at the base of his neck with her finger. "Here?"

Blood heating, and his cock twitching, Tank shook his head. "Higher," he commanded huskily.

Her brows rose as her fingers moved a few inches up the side of his neck, so light that another tantalizing shudder raced through him, threatening to set him off. "Right here?"

"Can everyone see it there, even with a shirt on?" he asked through gritted teeth, his control threadbare. But he didn't want to cum yet. He refused to fill her with his release until her teeth were sinking into him, claiming him like he'd claimed her.

"Yes."

"Then I want it there, Hunny. I want everyone to know who I belong to."

He steeled himself as she licked her lips, a possessive gleam in her eyes that matched what he felt in his heart. Cradling the back of his head, Hunny leaned forward, her mouth caressing his neck. His arms banded around her, holding her tightly to him as her teeth sank into his neck, marking him.

Ecstasy exploded within him, overriding the sting of pain, and his cock jerked inside her tight cunt. He fucked her hard into the mattress as the pressure from her teeth piercing his flesh amplified, driving him right over the edge. His pleasure skyrocketed until he was nothing but sensation, floating on an endless wave of euphoria. He never wanted it to end, but all too soon, his balls drew up, his release shooting from him in waves.

Spurts of his release filled her, and as she sucked on his neck, her moans vibrating against his skin, he felt her claim throughout his entire being, all the way into the darkest parts of his soul.

"Fuckin' hell!" Tank exclaimed, rolling his hips as he pumped into her. He didn't know how much longer he could go until his erection waned, but he didn't care, fucking his cum deeper inside her hot sheath. If she hadn't already been pregnant, he would have filled her to the brim, over and over again, until she was pregnant with his cubs.

"My mate," Tank rasped, fisting her hair, holding her captive so her lips remained on his neck as his orgasm finally subsided. He collapsed into her then; all the strength had been zapped from him as she pulled her teeth free.

Nuzzling his cheek, Hunny murmured into his ear, "I love you, Henry."

His heart stuttered in his chest as he rolled onto his back, taking her with him until she was lying on top of him like a blanket, his cock still nestled inside her. "I love you too, baby." Fingers sifting through her hair, he kissed the crown of her head, peace washing through him as their mixed scents filled his lungs.

Several minutes passed before his eyes began to slide shut, sleep calling to him. Just before he could drift off, Hunny touched the scars along his throat. "How did it happen?" she asked softly.

"Bear fight," he answered, instantly awake as distant memories plagued him.

Hunny sent him a haughty look. "I already know that. But why did you get into a fight with another bear? Was it someone from your clan, or a loner?"

Tank sighed heavily. "Years ago, when the old Alpha died, Murphy was the strongest among us, and almost everyone assumed he'd step up to take his rightful place. But another bear challenged him to become Alpha, and they fought."

"What does that have to do with you?" she asked.

"The male he fought refused to submit, even though Murphy was clearly stronger." And if a challenger didn't submit, they either died in combat or accepted exile ... "Every time Murphy let him up, Tyler attacked again, going for a killing blow even though their fight was rightfully over."

Hunny sat up, resting her hand on his chest, subconsciously caressing his hair. She tilted her head to the side, and her hair slid from her shoulder, giving him a tantalizing view of her mating mark. Fuck, his bite looked good on her. "Murphy ended up killing him, didn't he?"

"He had to," Tank answered, wrapping his hand around her wrist. He massaged her pulse, taking a deep breath to steady himself. "At that time, Murphy was courting Tyler's daughter, Sachi. He intended to mate her, but it's hard to move on from something like that."

"Well, yeah, I can only imagine." Tank's lips curled into a smile at her response, but it was hollow, and her eyes softened. "What happened after that?"

"She and her brother contacted some hunters. Paid them to take care of Murphy."

Hunters were humans that knew of the supernatural world and tracked them down; killing, mutilating or selling them off to other depraved individuals.

"That freaking *bitch*," his mate seethed furiously. "I get being upset over the death of a parent, but Tyler lost his life in a challenge. Murphy tried to spare him!" Her breasts heaved with each breath she took, and her anger on his brother's behalf was comforting in ways Tank had never realized he needed. He liked that she was protective of his family.

"Sachi led Murphy out into the middle of nowhere under false pretenses, and he was taken. By the time I realized what had happened, he'd been gone for hours. I had to kill Sachi's brother in order to discover Murphy's whereabouts, and when I did ..." He trailed off, his throat clogging with emotion as he recalled the days it took to find Murphy and bring him home. The bloodshed, the dead look in Murphy's eyes, the betrayal and defeat his eldest brother had felt. "There's a reason Murphy hates humans," Tank murmured, his voice now scratchy.

"Please tell me someone wiped the floor with Sachi."

Tank shook his head. "She disappeared right after I killed her brother."

"That's who almost ripped out your throat, isn't it? Her brother?" Tank nodded. "I'm glad you kicked his ass, Henry."

"Did more to him than that. But he's long gone now," he reassured her, pulling her back down until she was cradled next to him Contentment filled him. "Go to sleep."

"I have to fix your hair. It's really messed up," Hunny mumbled against his chest.

"Tomorrow, little rabbit."

They'd deal with it tomorrow.

Twenty Five

"I 'm nervous about today." Hunny turned off the clippers, running her hand over Tank's freshly buzzed hair. His beard was relatively the same length, but trimmed and shining from 'beard oil' she'd massaged into his facial hair. He'd never heard of it before, but he'd let her do anything to him as long as it kept her hands on his body. "I know I'm not going, but I don't like the thought of you meeting with Jason, either."

"It won't just be me," Tank replied tenderly, pulling her into his lap and kissing her. "Murphy and a few others will be there." Not Jasper, though. His younger brother would be in the cabin with Hunny, and *awake* for fucking once or he'd strangle the little shit.

"I'm not mated to them. I'm mated to you," she countered, cupping his face. She kissed him again before pushing up from his lap. "You said Jason was a dangerous male. What if he does something stupid?"

"You think he'll act out once he realizes I've mated you?"

Hunny rolled her eyes. "I think you're overestimating my value to Jason." She furrowed her brow a second later. "Wait, is that why you didn't shower after we had sex earlier? So that he'd scent me on you?"

Tank raised a brow at her question, his gaze going immediately to her mating mark. "I want him to know you're mine." He'd already ensured her scent covered him after hours of fucking this morning, and with the claiming bite prominently displayed on his neck, that wolf prick would be a fool not to put two and two together. "And I hope he does do something stupid, so I can snap his neck and call it a day."

Would he regret killing the sperm donor to his mate's kits? Not for a single second. In fact, he looked forward to doing the honors, if he could get the chance. Murphy would probably protest with that course of action though.

Hunny propped her hands onto her hips as she narrowed her eyes on him. "Isn't this meeting because he thinks we're hiding Natasha in bear territory?"

"Or he's using that as a lie to find out where you are. I'm not convinced the wolf that tracked us in the woods a few days ago didn't belong to him."

And he intended to find out today.

Hunny threw her hands up in exasperation. "But that doesn't make sense. Jason rejected me, mated someone else, and clearly," she added haughtily, pointing toward the bite on her neck, "I've more than gotten over all that."

"I'm well aware, darlin'." Tank smirked as he stood to his full height, towering over her.

"My point is this: Jason won't care enough about me, or our kits, to send someone to hunt me down, and I'm more than okay with that, believe me." Releasing a long breath, Hunny ran her hands through her hair. "I haven't wanted to ask, mostly because I'm terrified of your answer, but what exactly has Jason done that makes you hate him so much? You held a grudge with him since before you met me."

Tank pursed his lips, and as her hand fluttered to her belly, moving in a small circle over her bump, he wasn't sure he wanted to tell her the truth. He wanted to spare her the gory details of how sick and twisted the father of her kits was. He clenched his teeth to keep from snarling. No, Jason *wasn't* the father to Hunny's kits—Tank was. Even if he didn't share DNA with a single one, they were his, just as Hunny was.

"The Moon Rose pack is known for their illegal dealings," he began slowly, choosing his words more carefully than he ever had when it came to that fucker. He didn't want to upset Hunny with the truth, but he didn't want to keep it from her either. He planned to approach the subject gently, though.

She swallowed thickly. "What kind of 'illegal dealings' are you talking about exactly? Just spit it out, Henry, please."

"His pack kidnaps humans and sells them to other supernaturals for money, favors, whatever he needs. It's not always humans, either. Sometimes lone shifters and submissives, too."

Hunny's hand pressed down on her belly and she paled, looking like she was close to vomiting. "And you know that for sure?"

Tank shook his head. "No. It's only speculation, but Murphy's looked into every shifter community near us since he became Alpha. It isn't unnoticed that human women go missing near Jason's pack. Everything fits; we just don't have the proof. And I've met Jason and some of his wolves before. There is something off about them."

"What do you mean?"

Tank shrugged, clearing his irritated throat. The amount of time he could talk without it hurting improved daily, likely because of his little rabbit and the large quantities of tea she shoved down his throat. Even still, long talks like this wore out his vocal chords. "He feels wrong. Evil. You never felt it?"

"I—" Hunny closed her mouth, looking away from him as she thought. "I don't think he let me around him enough to see what he was really like, not until that night you found me. And then I just remember thinking how cold, how cruel he really was. How I didn't know him at all, and I was going to have a stranger's baby."

When she rubbed her belly again, Tank slid his hand over hers, his other going to her nape as he kissed the crown of her head. "He might be a sick bastard, but he gave us three precious gifts, darlin'."

Her fingers intertwined with his, holding on tight. "Just be careful today, alright?"

"I will."

A few short hours later, Tank stepped onto Murphy's porch, knocking on the door. His brother answered quickly, narrowing his eyes as he inhaled in surprise. His gaze flickered to Tank's neck and then back to his face. "You mated Hunny?"

Crossing his arms in front of his chest, Tank nodded, unable to keep a possessive smirk from dancing on his lips.

"I wished you'd informed me of your intentions to mate her," Murphy said stiffly, stepping onto the porch and closing the door behind him. He wore black slacks, a turtleneck sweater, and dress shoes, looking more like the damned mayor than a grizzly. But Tank didn't say anything—he knew the real reason his brother kept so much of his skin hidden.

"Do you want me to inform you the next time I bend my mate over and—"

"Shut the hell up," Murphy demanded, clapping Tank on the shoulder. "That's my sister-in-law you're talking about." He grinned before pushing past Tank and moving toward his SUV. "Have you told Mom yet?"

"No."

Murphy whistled. "She's going to lose her mind. Her and Jasper took bets on how long it would take you two to mate. Jasper bet three days, Mom bet four weeks."

"Jasper didn't say anything when I left him with Hunny earlier." *That little fucker.*

Murphy shrugged. "You know he's a sore loser."

Stepping over to the passenger side of the SUV, Tank pulled open the door, climbing inside. "I'm surprised you didn't make a bet," he said once his brother started the engine, settling into his own seat.

"Who said I didn't?" Smirking, Murphy drove to the main lodge, where they picked up Zeke, Colter, and Marcus.

"No Dante?" Tank asked Marcus in place of a greeting as the shifters piled into the vehicle.

"Nah. Murphy didn't want to bring the scrawniest bear to the meeting," Marcus joked.

Colter, sitting in the back middle seat, leaned forward. "Tank, why do you smell like puss—oh shit, brother!" He practically pressed his face to Tank's neck, ignoring the warning growl that rumbled from the grizzly's chest. "You mated your rabbit? Congrats, man!"

The other males in the vehicle issued similar well wishes, each of them praising his good fortune, and Tank didn't hide the excitement from his features, relaxing in his seat as he told them smugly how Hunny had been the one to approach him about mating.

He still couldn't believe it, even though he'd woken this morning with their combined scent filling his lungs, her sweet body pressed against him and the bite he'd placed on her staring proudly back at him.

"You dirty little bear," Zeke teased from behind him. "Letting the lady do all the work in your relationship."

Tank rolled his eyes, but his usual irritation was difficult to find. Instead, he felt grounded. Happy. It had been a long time since he had felt this way. Had he ever?

"You don't even look like you want to beat the shit out of anyone," Marcus commented, clearly impressed by Tank's swift change in mood. "What did your mate do to you? Suck the frustration out through your di—"

Tank turned around before Marcus could finish his sentence, slamming his fist into the male's gut. Marcus hunched forward in his seat, grunting in pain.

"Say another word like that about Hunny again, and I'll rip your fucking head off," Tank snarled.

"Duly ... noted," Marcus wheezed, his face a bright shade of red as a vein stuck out prominently on his forehead.

"No more talk about my mate," Tank told the rest of them, turning back in his seat with an angry curl of his upper lip. His brother smirked, shaking his head as he focused on the road ahead.

The car was silent for the rest of the drive. As Murphy parked the SUV in front of the teahouse and Tank climbed out of the vehicle, he heard Zeke mutter from within, "Smart fucking idea that was Marcus, you goddamn idiot."

"I was just joking," Marcus hissed back, shoving Zeke's shoulder. "You know I didn't mean any disrespect."

"Hell of a way to show it, fuckface."

Glowering, Tank walked into the teahouse first, scanning it for any patrons. Murphy had rented the space for a few hours to ensure their privacy, and it looked like Nessa had kept to her end of their arrangement. Murphy and the others piled in behind him, each looking around curiously.

"Nice place," Murphy commented to no one in particular, almost like he couldn't fathom humans creating anything that wasn't completely disgusting.

"Thanks! I just put the finishing touches on the interior this morning." Nessa came out from around a corner, smiling brightly at their group. Tank nodded his head in greeting while the others released a mixed chorus of 'hellos.'

Everyone but Murphy. Instead of greeting her, the Alpha crossed his arms in front of his chest, sizing her up like he'd spotted a new enemy.

Quickly, the smile slipped from Nessa's face, and she stiffened her shoulders, taking equal measure of the male. "Murphy, I take it?"

"Yes," the Alpha stated coldly. A beat of silence passed between them before he asked reluctantly, "How did you know?"

"You look just like I pictured you from our phone call the other day," Nessa told him happily. Moving past him and getting behind the counter, she muttered under her breath, "Like a dickhead."

Colter snorted before covering the noise with a booming cough. "Allergies," he explained when she turned back around, eyeing him with concern.

"Oh, no. I hate allergies. How about you all have a seat at a table and I'll bring you some tea while you wait for your associates?"

Zeke, Colter, and Marcus thanked her before doing just that, leaving Tank and Murphy standing at the front counter.

Nessa smiled at Tank, pointedly ignoring his older brother. "How's Hunny?" Her gaze drifted to his mating mark and widened. "Good, apparently, if she's biting you like that."

"She's good," Tank confirmed.

Nessa's lips twitched. "Talkative as ever, I see."

Tank grunted, and she laughed, shaking her head at him.

"Are you always so loud?" Murphy snapped, glaring right at her as he awaited her answer.

"As opposed to what? Sullen and grumpy? You seem to have that covered for the both of us." She glared back at him with no small amount of disdain, and despite the tension filling the air, Tank almost laughed. No one ever really went toe-to-toe with Murphy, but leave it to Yapper Number Two to take on the challenge.

"I don't appreciate your disrespect, hum—Nessa." The Alpha uttered her name harshly. Tank's humor fled, and he shifted his body subtly, moving closer to the human in case ... well, he wasn't sure, but usually Murphy behaved better than this.

"And I don't appreciate your attitude," Nessa snapped back. She smiled again, but there was nothing comforting in it. "But I enjoy your money, so thank you for renting out my establishment, and don't forget to tip your server." She winked. "That's me."

"It's always the same with your kind," Murphy scoffed. "All you want is money."

She shook her head, pinning the Alpha with another cold smile. "Well, it makes the world go around. Go take a seat, Murphy."

Instead of listening to her, the Alpha slammed his hands down on the countertop, leaning toward her menacingly. "I don't take orders from you."

Nessa flinched away from him, her face draining of color. Immediately, Murphy dropped his hands, taking a step back as a panicked look crossed his face. "I apologize. I didn't mean to frighten—"

Just then, the front door opened, and a familiar stench clogged Tank's nose.

The fucking wolves had finally shown up.

Twenty Six

J ason strolled in through the door like he owned the place, four
wolves following after him. Three males, one female. The males
had greasy hair, stains on their jeans, and cocky expressions on their
faces, as if they were untouchable. The female's eyes were hard and
wary, like she'd grown up quick and had been dealt blow after emotional blow until she'd fully adjusted to pack life.

Tank knew most of them through a bit of digging. The taller male
of the bunch was Ben, Jason's Beta. The shortest was Kenneth, one of
the more vile, perverse fucks of the pack. The female and the last male
were unknown to him.

Were they newer additions to the Moon Rose pack?

Jason glanced around the room, studying each piece of furniture
while studiously ignoring Murphy and Tank, like he didn't have a care
in the world. Like he wasn't outmatched in every way that mattered. A
wolf might be faster, but bears were stronger. Sturdier. It would take
several wolves to successfully take down a bear, and that was if they
could get close enough.

Jason's indifference was a clear sign of dismissal, letting Murphy and
the others know they didn't intimidate him. Unfortunately for him,
bears didn't give a damn if another shifter found them threatening or
not. Jason's lack of fear wouldn't stop Tank from ripping the wolf's
head from his shoulders while wearing a smile on his face.

In fact, that idea sounded perfect.

"Welcome to Nessa's Teahouse," the human female began, startling Tank out of his rampant homicidal thoughts. He turned toward the counter, keeping tabs on every person in the room as she continued with a polite smile, "I take it you're here for the meeting ..." Nessa trailed off as Jason's eyes shifted to her and narrowed.

Her heart skipped a beat, the sound loud in Tank's ears. The wolf heard it as well, and a predatory smile crossed his face. "You must be the owner of this fine establishment." Jason inhaled, taking a step toward her. "And might I say, you smell divine."

"Thanks, I think?" Nessa responded with a grimace, absent-mindedly straightening a few business cards on the counter between them. Her hands shook, belying her nerves.

She might not know shifters surrounded her, but she could sense the dominance in the room on a subconscious level. Her instincts were probably screaming at her that something was amiss, that she was in danger.

Jason noticed her unease as well, his smile taking on a sinister edge as he took another step toward her. Right before he could reach the counter, though, Murphy blocked his path, shielding Nessa from the wolf's view.

"This town is under my protection." Murphy growled, his eyes changing from brown to piercing gold. He was a few inches taller than Jason, and he used that to his advantage as he moved forward, stalking into the male's space and herding him away from the human.

"No need to assert your dominance, Murphy. I can be friendly with the sweet, little thing." Jason looked over Murphy's shoulder, winking at Nessa. She made a comically disgusted face and turned away from them all, discreetly sniffing her shirt.

Murphy's shoulders stiffened, and his frame rippled once, as if his bear was fighting him, trying to rip its way to the surface. "I suggest you keep your eyes away from that female before I pluck them out of your goddamn head."

Jason stiffened. "Are you threatening me?"

"About fucking time someone did." Tank stepped up beside his brother to stare the wolf down with nothing short of disdain. As soon as he neared, Jason's attention shifted to him. The wolf's nostrils flared, eyes widening before they locked onto his neck. Onto the delicate mating mark Hunny had given Tank last night.

He stared at the brand, dumbfounded.

Smirking, Tank couldn't help but ask, "See something interesting?"

Jason's jaw clenched. Before he could say anything that Tank could use as an excuse to knock the miserable fucker out, though, another wolf hissed, "We're losing sight of this meeting."

"Ben's right," the female wolf agreed, sending both Alphas assessing looks. "Let's just get this shit over with."

Murphy's eyes flickered, shifting back to their normal brown color. "Let's all sit down."

"That's a great idea," Nessa murmured. Murphy and Tank turned toward her as the wolves moved further into the teahouse, sitting down in the back corner with the other bears. She sent Murphy an odd look. "Did you just say you were going to pluck that guy's eyes out?"

"It's rude to eavesdrop," he bit out.

Nessa raised a brow. "I don't think it's technically eavesdropping if you're saying all of this literally in front of me. Also, who the hell was growling?" She shook her head in confusion. "Sounded like a wild animal got in here."

Murphy sighed, pinching the bridge of his nose in exasperation. "Just ... Stay here. Don't serve tea or sandwiches, or whatever the hell you were planning."

Nessa scoffed, propping her hands onto her hips. Her earlier fear toward him seemed to be forgotten as she glared at him. "Who's being rude now? You can't just tell me what to do in my shop. The sign out front doesn't say 'Grumpy's Teahouse,' does it?"

"I'll tip you a grand," he offered through gritted teeth.

Nessa pursed her lips, as if she had to think long and hard about her answer. In fact, the human waited so long to respond that Murphy looked like a vein would burst on his forehead. It was only when he opened his mouth to bitch about something that she cut in, smiling brightly. "Well, I can't refuse an offer like that. I'll add the charge to the credit card I have on file."

"Great," Murphy muttered, turning toward the group of people waiting.

"Hey, Murphy?" Nessa called quietly. Even though she wasn't talking to Tank, he paid close attention as his brother turned back around, eyeing her warily. "Thank you," she commented softly. She gestured subtly toward Jason, shuddering visibly. "For getting in his face like that. Guy gives me the creeps."

Murphy nodded once, and then he and Tank left to join the others.

Placing himself between his brother and the wolves, Tank took a seat beside Colter, his senses on high alert as the meeting began.

"My mate is missing," Jason announced without preamble. "She disappeared a few days ago, and one of my wolves tracked her trail to your territory."

"None of my bears have picked up her scent while they've been out on patrol, otherwise they would have reported it," Murphy answered. "Though we had a wolf enter our territory at around the same time you say your mate entered ours."

"That had to be her," Ben guessed, concern etched across his features. Tank eyed him warily. He seemed more worried about Natasha's welfare than her own mate. Just who was this male to her?

"It wasn't," Tank responded, crossing his arms in front of his chest.

"And how the hell would you know that?" Jason asked sharply, sending Tank a cold, deadly look. In return, the bear shifter smiled, relaxing his stance.

"Because the night I met my mate, the stench of yours was all over her," he replied, satisfaction creeping into his voice as Jason clenched his jaw. The Alpha was pissed that Hunny was a claimed female. Good. He wanted the fucker to know she was off limits forever. "The wolf that invaded our lands recently was someone else. Male, by the scent of it."

Jason stared at the mating mark on Tank's neck, a muscle jumping in his cheek. "Natasha told me about her fight with Hunny. I was sad to hear Hunny would attack my chosen mate out of jealousy."

Tank scoffed. "Is that what your mate told you happened? We both know that's not true. Hunny has more self-worth than to get into an altercation over some male."

Unless that male was Tank. Then he was pretty confident his mate would wipe the floor with someone like Natasha—not that he'd ever put her into a position to find out.

"I'm not *some* male," Jason snarled, slamming his hand down onto the table so hard the glass surface cracked. Murphy cursed under his breath as the wolf continued, "I'm Hunny's fated—"

"You're not Hunny's anything." Tank's voice boomed around the room. His throat stung from the effort, but he didn't give a damn. He'd shout those fucking words until his voice box gave out, if only to watch the look of rage crossing Jason's face like it did right at that moment.

Jason pushed to his feet, his face turning a deep shade of red. "You think she gives a fuck about you? She's pregnant with my fucking pup—"

Tank grinned, flashing sharp canines. He hoped the wolf never found out Hunny was carrying multiple kits. He'd never divulge the truth to this slimy dick. "Make no mistake, wolf, Hunny and that kit growing in her belly are mine. Not yours. *Mine*." He stood as well, hoping like hell Jason would take a swing at him. This pathetic male needed to be put in his place, and if it wasn't out of deference to Murphy, Tank would have made the first move by now. He would have beat him black and blue for the pain he had caused Hunny.

"You motherfuck—"

"My sister is gone!" Ben yelled roughly, snarling at each person in the room. "I don't give a fuck about whatever bullshit this is. We know you've taken her, and we want her back!" When the female reached out to touch him, he jerked his arm away from her. "Fuck off, Angela." She frowned, dropping her hand.

"Maybe she left your pack," Colter added. "Wouldn't be the first time a female tried to escape you all, I'm sure." Angela flinched like she'd been struck, averting her gaze from everyone in the room, and Colter frowned.

"You'll give me back my mate, or there will be hell to pay," Jason spat, his words laced with venom. He glared hard at Tank. "I know you have her."

"For the last time, my clan has done nothing to Natasha," Murphy responded calmly. "My answer hasn't changed since we spoke over the phone. If she tried to enter our territory then whatever other wolf intruded was likely responsible for what happened to her. I'm sorry, but that's the truth."

"Why was she even around our territory to begin with?" Tank asked gruffly. "The only reason she'd have to come near would be to finish what she'd started with Hunny."

And for that alone, if he found her, he'd kill her.

Jason rolled his eyes. "Natasha knows better."

"She didn't before," Murphy pointed out, remaining cool-headed despite how heated this meeting had gotten. "And if we find her on our land, attempting to harm a member of our clan, you won't need to make vague threats of war to get a rise out of me, wolf. I'll come after you myself."

With that, Jason rose abruptly, storming from the room, his group of wolves trailing after him. Kenneth was the last one to leave, but he stopped by the counter before he did so, leaning over and saying something to Nessa. The words were so low Tank couldn't hear, but Nessa didn't look too worried as she sent him a shy smile.

Regardless, Murphy's calm demeanor melted away as he watched them talk, anger radiating from him in waves as he practically charged up to the counter. Kenneth left through the front door before the Alpha arrived, chuckling lightly as he went.

"What did he say to you?" Murphy asked aggressively, rounding on Nessa and planting his hands on the countertop. His fingers smudged the glass, and she scowled.

"That he'd love to take me out for coffee."

"He asked you out on a date?" Murphy asked, brows snapping down into a hard line of aggravation. "And what did you say?"

Nessa looked around the room dramatically. "Not that it's any of your business, but I told him no, Murphy. If I liked coffee, I'd have opened a knock-off Starbucks. And do you honestly think an offer to go out for some coffee by one of the creepy guys sounds enticing?"

"Well, I ..." Murphy huffed, looking like he'd tasted something foul.

Deciding to intervene, Tank grabbed his brother by the arm, steering him toward the front door. "Thanks for putting up with all of our bullshit," Tank muttered. Before the door closed behind them, he called over his shoulder, "A glass tabletop got ruined. Tack it onto Murphy's tab."

"Thanks for that," Murphy grumbled sourly, wrestling his arm free and walking toward his car. "I've racked up a small fortune in less than two hours."

"Who gives a shit? What's gotten into you?" Tank whispered angrily into his brother's ear. "I know you hate humans, but you acted like a complete dickhead to Hunny's friend."

Murphy glowered. "It's nothing I want to talk about right now."

"Fine. I've had enough of today, anyway." Despite rubbing his new relationship with Hunny into Jason's face, the day had been long and drawn-out. All he wanted was to return home to his mate and to hold her close.

It wasn't until the males had all piled into Murphy's SUV that anyone spoke up.

"Well, that entire meeting was a clusterfuck," Marcus said with a shake of his head.

Zeke snorted. "Which part? Where Jason couldn't decide if he gave more of a shit about the fact that his mate is missing or that Tank stole his true mate?"

"I didn't steal Hunny," Tank argued. "And you're right; he didn't give a shit about Natasha at all. Her brother showed more concern for her welfare than he did." Though, was that really surprising?

"I think Colter's theory back there was right," Murphy added, sending the bear an appreciative nod in the rear-view mirror. "If Jason made it that apparent to us he still considers Hunny's child as his," he stated, ignoring Tank's warning growl, "then Natasha likely sensed his interest in her was waning and wanted out. My bet is that she ran away and led a trail to our border to throw him off."

"It would buy her time to get a good distance away," Marcus mused.

"Let's hope that's it." Tank leaned back in his seat, staring at the clock on the dashboard. It would be another hour before he arrived home. He hated being away from Hunny for any length of time, and after hearing Jason speak about her in any capacity, he was eager to reassert his claim on her, if only to appease his bear. "Regardless, we'll need to remain alert for any danger. If Jason and Ben are positive we've got Natasha, they might attack us in the hopes of finding her."

"Part of me hopes they do," Murphy admitted quietly.

Tank couldn't help but agree.

"How much longer do you think they'll be gone?" Hunny asked, earning an exaggerated sigh from Jasper. The male was relaxing on the other side of the couch from her, his feet kicked up on the coffee table as he watched football on Tank's TV. For someone who *should* be guarding her, he looked like he didn't have a care in the world.

Must be nice, she thought with a little snarl. Meanwhile, Tank had been gone for just over two hours and she felt like she was going stir-crazy. She knew he'd be fine, but that didn't make her feel any better. It also didn't help that she'd been nauseous for the last few hours. Was it from her kits or nerves? Knowing her luck, probably a combination of the two.

When Jasper didn't answer right away, she grabbed a throw pillow, tossing it at the side of his head. It connected with a small thud before dropping uselessly to the floor. He shot her a disgruntled look. "Why are you being so mean to me?"

"Because you're not answering the question," Hunny replied, mockingly whining back at him. He scowled, crossing his arms in front of his chest.

"I already answered you twice. They'll get here when they get here."

"That's a terrible answer." And considering how anxious she felt as each minute ticked by, she really didn't think she could handle not at least knowing how close they were to being done. "Can't you just do your little mind meld with Murphy and find out how long they'll be?"

Jasper rolled his eyes. "Clearly, you don't know how Murphy operates. He isn't going to respond unless it's important. He needs to keep his wits about him while he's near any potential threats. Didn't Tank give you a cellphone? Why don't you just text your mate and find out?"

Hunny couldn't help the small smile that tugged on her lips at the mention of Tank being her mate. "The phone Henry gave me *is* his. He said he never used it, so I could have it to talk with Nessa."

Well, *technically*, he'd told Hunny she could have it because he didn't want to talk to any 'damned humans anyway,' or something like that.

Jasper snorted. "I wish I'd thought of pawning my phone off on someone else. Murphy insists we keep them around in case there's a national weather emergency or some human catastrophe happening, so we're in the loop."

"Oh, that's smart. I've lived among humans so long I think it kind of slipped my mind how secluded shifter communities generally prefer to be from the rest of the world." Though, she had to admit, she really enjoyed the freedom of being able to shift whenever she wanted without fear of being spotted. This far up in the mountains, the bears had their own little slice of shifter heaven.

"Well, this is your life now, little sister. Tank's going to keep you locked in his cabin so you don't wise up and run away from him." When she rolled her eyes, he continued, "He even mentioned something about picking a few chains and locks up while he was in town. Didn't say what he needed them for, though."

Hunny grinned. "You're so full of shit."

"I know." Jasper winked playfully before his eyes slid to the fresh mating mark on her neck. His expression softened. "Still can't believe you mated with my brother."

Her hand slid up to her neck, cupping the mark tenderly. "I know. I feel like it happened so fast and took forever at the same time. I don't know if that makes sense," Hunny finished with a small laugh.

"It doesn't, but I've always known it would take a delusional female to mate with any of my brothers," Jasper joked. "If you were smart, you'd have known I was the best choice all along. I'm handsome, funny, and my mom loves me the best."

Hunny wrinkled her nose. "A momma's boy? Gross. I prefer my males broody and independent."

Jasper clutched his hand to his chest as he gasped loudly. "Hey! There's nothing wrong with loving my m—" His words died in his throat as his eyes shifted from piercing green to gold. His head snapped toward the front door, tension lining his body. Immediately, the anxiety Hunny had been feeling returned to the forefront, and she placed a hand on her stomach as it roiled. He stood quickly to his feet, standing between her and the door.

"Jasper, what's—"

"You need to go upstairs, Hunny," he instructed from over his shoulder, his voice holding a furious, deadly note she'd never heard before. "*Now.*"

She pushed up to her feet, doing exactly as he'd asked. She'd just made it to the base of the stairs when something slammed hard against the front door. Hunny flinched, whipping back around to watch as Jasper ripped open the front door. He roared in warning; the sound vibrating through the house and out into the woods.

A few seconds passed and he looked at the ground right as Hunny smelled it.

Blood.

"Oh, what the fuck?" Jasper bent down, snatching something off the front porch. He turned back around, stomping into the house and slamming the door closed. "I'm telling Murphy our territory has been breached right now," he assured her as he held up his arm, something dangling from his hand.

Hunny didn't understand what he was holding at first, her brain taking forever to process it. A second passed, and then another, before she realized he was holding hair. Human hair. No, not *just* hair; a severed head.

Natasha's vacant, dull eyes were half-lidded, her jaw hanging at an awkward angle.

Hunny leaned over the railing and vomited.

Twenty Seven

"Oh, God," Hunny wheezed, the stench of her own vomit filling her nose. Her gut churned, and her forehead was damp with sweat as she struggled to breathe.

"Holy shit, are you alright?" Jasper bit out a sharp curse, rushing toward her. Natasha's severed head swayed back and forth in his grip, the strands of hair twisting together as the dead she-wolf's face circled back into view.

"Get that thing away from me!" Hunny exclaimed, covering her mouth as more bile rose in her throat. Without another look at the bear shifter, she darted shakily up the stairs, racing into the bathroom. She slammed the door shut behind her, barely making it to the toilet in time.

Dropping to her knees, she bent over and vomited again, retching until she was sure there was nothing left in her stomach. With a soft moan of despair, Hunny wiped at her mouth with the back of her hand, feeling more than a little light-headed as her vision swam. When she was confident she wouldn't be sick again, she plopped onto her ass, scooting back until the porcelain tub pressed against her spine. It was cold, seeping into her clothing after a few minutes as she waited for her stomach to stop cramping.

She'd gotten lucky so far with her pregnancy and had hoped she wouldn't get sick at all for the foreseeable future. Now her streak was ruined, and Jason's dead mate was responsible.

As soon as the thought crossed her mind, Hunny felt like an asshole. Wasn't it taboo to think ill of the dead? At that moment, it didn't matter that Natasha had tried to kill Hunny. The she-wolf must have died horrifically. She'd only caught a few glimpses of Natasha's detached head, but it looked like someone had torn it clean off—

"Shit, don't think about it," Hunny whined out loud as nausea reared its head once more. Dragging her legs up, she dropped her forehead to her knees, squeezing her eyes shut and taking a deep, shuddering breath, hoping like hell she could calm down.

Unfortunately, that was much easier said than done, mostly because she'd never seen a dead person before. Or ... *part* of one. Hunny groaned pitifully. She couldn't get the wretched image out of her head. Who'd killed her? And possibly worse—who'd thrown her head at the front door? Jasper didn't seem concerned with chasing anyone down, but it was probably because he didn't want to leave her alone while a threat remained outside.

A shiver raced down her spine. Was the killer still lurking about on Tank's property? Who was it? *What* was it? Could it be Jason? No way. Since they were bonded, he would have felt every moment of her death, so it couldn't be him. Then who? Someone else from his pack? Natasha had clearly been a warning—what if they were coming after Hunny next? What if they got into the house and hurt her babies?

Logically, she knew shifters killed people; it happened all the time in skirmishes and when they went to war. But that was *war*, not some kind of sick, senseless slaughter, and definitely not the same thing as chopping off a head and tossing it onto the front porch. What kind of disturbed freak did that?

Fuck! She wanted Tank—needed him here with her. Now more than ever before.

There was a soft knock on the door, and she whimpered in fear before she registered Jasper's scent just on the other side of the wood. "Hey, how are you feeling?"

She grimaced, ignoring the knot of fear twisting in her gut. "What kind of question is that, Jasper? Someone threw a severed head at the front door!" Just saying it out loud caused her mind to create an image of what must have happened, and she swore she could hear a squelching sound as the head hit—

"Murphy and Tank are on their way, and the rest of the clan is on lockdown. Hopefully, we can find whoever did this before they escape."

At the mention of Tank, Hunny's eyes watered, and a heavy weight settled on her chest as she fought back the urge to cry. "How soon before Henry gets here?" she asked, despising the tremor in her voice.

Don't cry! You're not some weak female. It's just pregnancy hormones; nothing to do with the fact that a murderer is lurking outside.

She let out a small, pathetic sob. Oh God. There was a *murderer* outside—

"I don't know. Maybe another ten—"

"Get the hell out of the way." Tank's muffled voice was little more than a snarl on the other side of the door, and immediately, that weight pressing on her chest eased. Hunny's head snapped up just as the doorknob twisted, the door pushing open softly despite the menacing aura her mate brought with him as he entered. As soon as he spotted her, some of the tension drained from his shoulders. His eyes softened, too, but that did little to eliminate the furious gleam in his gaze as his impressive form filled the doorway. "Ah, little rabbit, don't cry—"

Hunny's chin wobbled. She let out another small sob, throwing herself at her mate as soon as he knelt down beside her. Tank scooped her up into his arms before standing to his full height and carrying her into the bedroom. Sitting on the bed, he readjusted her until she was straddling his waist, her face now buried in the crook of his neck as she cried.

She absolutely hated losing control of her emotions, but it seemed like every slight inconvenience made her hormonal lately, and if this wasn't a good reason to cry in her mate's arms, what was?

"You're alright," Tank whispered tenderly, his large palm sliding up and down her back in a soothing caress. "You're safe, baby. I won't let anything happen to you or the kits."

"I know," she wailed against his neck, her lips tracing over the mating mark she'd given him less than twenty-four hours ago. She inhaled deeply, dragging his scent into her lungs to help steady her racing emotions. "I-I'm just freaking out because I've never seen a dead body before, let alone a-a severed *head*."

Tank stiffened before releasing a harsh growl so fierce it vibrated against her chest. "You showed her the goddamn head?"

"Hm?" Jasper asked innocently, a nervous note in his voice. "I mean, I *might* have come back inside with the head in my hand."

"You showed my *pregnant mate* a severed head?"

Hunny's stomach flipped, that unfortunate familiar burn creeping back up her throat. "Can you please stop saying that?" she begged, swallowing bile back down as she hugged Tank tightly to her. "I don't want to be sick again."

"Of course, baby," Tank crooned, rubbing his palm up and down her back once more. To Jasper, he snarled, "I'm going to beat your fucking ass."

"What did you want me to do, Tank? I had to watch Hunny!"

"You keep the goddamn he—*object*—outside!"

"Oh, that's easy for you to say," Jasper argued. "You weren't here. You were off at your meeting, and I did what I thought was right."

"And what exactly was that? Scaring my mate until she was sick?"

"No, getting the fuck back inside to protect her in case we were attacked."

Tank fell silent, but he kept his hand running gently over her back.

"Jasper's right," Hunny murmured against his skin. "It's not really his fault I saw Nata—"

She pushed away from Tank, nearly tripping over her own feet as she raced back into the bathroom, her mate hot on her heels. This time, as she retched into the toilet, he was there with her, pulling back her hair to keep it from falling across her face. He spoke softly to her, little words of encouragement that were both ridiculous and incredibly sweet as she dry heaved until she was exhausted.

Her head pounded by the time she was finally finished, and she was more than a little thirsty as she slumped against the wall in a heap. Crouching down beside her, her mate ran the pad of his thumb over her cheeks, wiping away her stray tears.

"How about a nice bath, baby? Those little bath bombs will help you feel better, and afterward, I'll get you something to drink." Tank stood, turning toward Jasper, who still lingered in their bedroom. "Wait downstairs, yeah? I'm going to get Hunny settled, and then Murphy will be back in with the others by the time I come down."

Jasper nodded. "They hunting down the fucker who did this?"

"Yeah, they are."

"I'm surprised you didn't go with them, Tank." Jasper tilted his head curiously to the side. "Figured you'd want their head on a silver platter—"

Hunny gagged.

Tank released her hair and lunged at his brother, shoving so hard he sent the male flying backward. Jasper hit the edge of the bed, bouncing awkwardly off the side before slamming onto the ground with a heavy thud.

"Rude," he wheezed, pulling himself up from the undignified lump he now was. "I'll just go wait downstairs," he groaned roughly.

Once he was gone, Tank re-entered the bathroom, closing the door hard behind him. He crossed over to her side, running a hand through her sweat-dampened hair. "You think you'll get sick again, darlin'?"

She really hoped not.

Hunny shook her head, letting him pull her to her feet. "I need to brush my teeth," she muttered as he turned the tub faucet on. Moving over to the vanity, she did just that, grabbing her toothbrush and applying a heavy amount of toothpaste to the bristles.

She'd just gotten done scrubbing her entire mouth when Tank plucked the toothbrush from her hand, rinsing it off and placing it into the holder.

"Hey! I wasn't done with that," Hunny groaned forlornly. She needed another five minutes at least to wash the acidic taste out of her mouth.

Tank narrowed his eyes at her in exasperation. "You scrubbed any harder and your teeth would have cracked."

Hunny sighed. "It wasn't *that* bad." She ran her tongue over her teeth, just to prove a point, and then winced at how sensitive her gums felt. Okay, maybe he was right, but she wouldn't admit that out loud.

Grunting, Tank tugged her shirt over her head, dropping it carelessly to the floor before reaching for the waistband of her leggings. His palm slid over her lower belly reverently before he undressed her the rest of the way. Lifting her up, he carried her the few feet to the bath before he began lowering her into the warm water. "Into the tub, little rabbit."

She sank down gratefully into the blissfully warm water as he moved back to the sink, grabbing a bath bomb from the cabinet and unwrapping it before crouching down beside the tub.

"I need to talk about something, anything, to take my mind off of earlier.".

"Yap away, baby."

Hunny cleared her throat, struggling to find a topic that wasn't related to Natasha. Unfortunately, the she-wolf was at the forefront of her mind, impossible to forget. She floundered before giving up and asking, "How was the meeting, Henry?"

Tank snorted, sending her a knowing look. "Jason was a prick. Noticed we were mated almost immediately." Her brows rose in surprise, and he shrugged, sending her a small smirk. "I might have stated it outright. He seemed more concerned about you than his own mate." He dropped the bath bomb into the water, and almost immediately, it began to fizz and dissolve.

Hunny made a face. "Well, he'll probably regret that when he finds out what happened to her." Tank hummed noncommittally in response, grabbing a washcloth and her shower gel container. He squirted some of the liquid onto the cloth. "Who do you think did that to Natasha?" she asked hesitantly. "It wasn't someone from your clan, was it?"

She doubted it, but did she really know anyone besides Tank's family?

Tank shook his head, bringing the wet, sudsy cloth to her bare shoulder. He ran it down her skin, eyes locked on his task as he answered, "No one within *our* clan would do something like this, Hunny. Maybe we'd take down an intruder, but we wouldn't defile their corpse. Or deliver them to someone like that."

"How long do you think she's been dead?" She ignored the way her nipples pebbled as the cloth slid over her breasts, staring up at his handsome face instead. "Jason had to feel her die. They were fully mated; it would be impossible for him to not feel it."

Even if they hadn't bonded fully—emotional connections usually took months or longer to form between chosen mates, and sometimes it took even longer still before they could communicate telepathically—he'd still feel her death. It would be like his soul had split in two.

And if Tank believed him to be crazy and unpredictable before this, what would Jason be like now? He'd essentially accused Murphy of kidnapping Natasha, and now, on the same night, she was dead in bear territory.

"From what I could smell, the blood was fresh. She couldn't be dead for more than an hour."

Hunny shivered. Tank frowned, turning the faucet back on and adding more hot water to the tub. She didn't have the heart to tell him the chill she felt was soul-deep.

"Can you imagine if she'd died while Jason was with you all? He'd have lost his mind. It could have caused a war," she muttered.

Tank swore under his breath as his head shot up, eyes meeting hers. "Maybe that was the plan. I need to talk to Murphy."

Twenty Eight

As much as Hunny wanted to hide in bed, tucked away from even the thought of Natasha's untimely demise, she got dressed after her bath, ignoring Tank's grumbling as she headed for the stairs. Murphy was out hunting down the killer right now, but she knew he'd be back soon to discuss everything with Tank and Jasper. And when he did, she wanted to be there.

Right before she could grab onto the railing to descend, Tank grasped her wrist, his thumb sliding over her pulse point. "I don't know if I like the thought of you coming down there and dealing with all this," he admitted. He scratched at his chin with his free hand, eyes meeting hers. "It can't be good for the kits that you got sick like that. You should be resting."

Hunny tilted her head to the side, sending her mate a soft look as she placed a hand on her belly. She loved how much he took her needs into consideration, and despite the attention he had shown her over the last few weeks, it still felt wild to her that someone cared about her enough to do so.

"They're fine, Henry. But I already feel pathetic enough for getting so sick. Someone could have barged in after Jasper earlier and attacked, and I'd have been too busy puking everywhere to help him. I don't want to be useless. I don't want to crawl into bed."

Okay, yes, she *did*—a nap sounded phenomenal—but he didn't have to know that. The first glimpse her mate caught of her fatigue, he'd have her dressed in one of his T-shirts and tucked under a mountain of blankets in bed.

Tank eyed her like she'd just told him the sun was green. "Taking care of our kits isn't being useless."

Our kits. Hunny preened at the acknowledgement, tugging Tank to her. Pushing up to her tiptoes, she gave him a light, lingering kiss. "I only mean that if there's a way I can help, then I want to do just that."

Tank palmed her nape, holding her in place as he kissed her again. He wasn't chaste as she'd been. He sunk his tongue past her lips, devouring her until her knees went weak. The arm he wrapped around her waist was the only thing holding her up when he eventually moved his mouth from hers, placing a gentle kiss on her forehead before hugging her to him.

"You constantly amaze me, darlin'," Tank murmured, his chin resting on the top of her head as he held her a little more tightly. "If you want to go downstairs, we will. But if it gets to be too much when Murphy shows up, I'm bringing you right back up here and putting you to bed."

"But—"

"No buts," he argued, cutting her off. "My job as your male, as your mate, is to look after you. You come first, always."

Hunny kissed his chest through his T-shirt. "Fine." Without warning, Tank grabbed the backs of her thighs and lifted her up, waiting until she wrapped her limbs around his torso before heading downstairs. Despite the stress of the day, she snorted. "You know I can walk, right? Puking my brains out doesn't make me an invalid."

"No, but I don't want you getting dizzy. You need to hydrate and eat something before you move around too much."

The thought of eating anything had her grimacing into his shirt, but she didn't argue, knowing he wouldn't hear a word of it. Instead, she snuggled into his chest, relishing in his warmth and delicious scent as it wafted around her. Luckily, she couldn't smell any trace of blood or death anymore, otherwise Tank would have to march right back up those stairs to the bathroom.

As soon as they hit the landing, Jasper jumped up from the couch, the TV remote clasped firmly in his hand. He shot Tank a narrow-eyed look before smiling at Hunny. "Feeling better?"

Tank grumbled under his breath and then cut in before Hunny could even answer. "Did you get rid of *it*?"

"The—" Jasper cleared his throat. "Yup. Put it outside and sprayed some odor neutralizing spray around the place afterward. It's practically as good as new in here now."

Ah, so that's why she couldn't smell anything.

Grunting, Tank walked past his younger brother and into the kitchen, keeping a palm on Hunny's ass as he poured her a glass of water and then began making her a quick meal. She was half tempted to wriggle out of his hold and go sit down on a barstool while he made her some food, but she'd been through a lot the past few hours, and if he wasn't going to complain about her practically being Velcroed to him, she wouldn't either.

All too soon, he'd whipped up a small salad, placing the bowl onto the kitchen island before dropping her gently onto a stool. She set her now half-empty glass of water onto the countertop, eyeing the food warily. Surprisingly, she didn't feel sick anymore. In fact, she was more than a little hungry, snatching up a fork and digging in while Jasper entered the room.

The two males spoke more in depth about the meeting while she ate. It sounded like it went about as terrible as she'd expected, but when Tank mentioned Nessa and Murphy verbally accosting one another, she perked up, more than interested in hearing more.

Unfortunately, Tank didn't get a chance to elaborate further.

She'd just finished her salad when she heard movement outside, followed by the pounding of footsteps on the front porch. Based on Jasper's and Tank's relaxed postures, she could only assume it was Murphy.

Less than a minute later, the bear clan Alpha stepped into the house, followed by three males she vaguely remembered seeing after the dead rabbit incident last week. Each of the new males was tall and muscular. They were almost as large as Tank and his brothers, with wide torsos and thick legs, which she was beginning to suspect was standard for male bear shifters.

Murphy and the new males filed into the kitchen, spreading around the island. The Alpha gave her a firm once-over before sending her a small nod, silently asking if she was alright. Hunny gave him a thumbs-up. He relaxed marginally, running a hand down his face.

"Marcus, Colter, Zeke," Murphy began, pointing each male out to Hunny. "This is our newest addition, and Tank's mate, Hunny." They'd barely waved at each other in acknowledgement before he continued. "We couldn't find whoever killed Natasha."

There was a brief moment of tense silence that cut through the room like a knife before Tank exhaled roughly. "Did you at least glean anything from the scent? What kind of supernatural are we dealing with?"

Murphy pursed his lips, shooting the male he'd called Marcus a long glance. "There wasn't a scent."

"What?" Hunny exclaimed, leaning forward in her seat until her chest touched the edge of the kitchen island. "Natasha just died. There's no way her killer's scent disappeared that quickly."

Especially with their enhanced senses. It would take hours, days even, before that scent could evaporate completely. Maybe if the weather was bad, but ... She cocked her head to the side, glancing out the kitchen window. The sun was just setting, but there wasn't a cloud in the sky.

"Be that as it may," Murphy argued, "there's no scent other than the she-wolf's, and she didn't do this to herself."

Jasper rolled his eyes. "Well, fucking obviously."

"Watch it," Murphy snapped, his body stiffening until the younger bear apologized quickly. When he did, Murphy continued, "Marcus is our best tracker, and even he couldn't pick up on anything."

Hunny's eyes wandered over to Marcus. When she'd spotted him last time, another, almost identical male had been with him. Was Marcus a twin? Why wasn't that guy here now?

"So what are you thinking?" Tank asked. "The killer used scent blockers?"

The drug? Hunny's brows shot up to her hairline. Scent blockers weren't commonly used among shifters, most considered them unnatural, but it would be perfect for someone trying to remain hidden.

"Had to be. Natasha's scent was faint even at the scene of her murder, and as soon as we got a mile from your property, it disappeared altogether." Marcus shrugged. "My guess is that her killer kept her and themselves drugged with it, waited until we were gone, got her close enough, and then killed her when her scent began to reappear."

"Christ." Tank eyed Jasper. "And you didn't hear anything? Not a scream or a whimper?"

"Not a damn thing," Jasper clarified, sounding far more serious than he had a few minutes earlier. "Hunny and I were watching one of those human shows, the ones with the housewives with the Botoxed faces, and just talking. I heard someone approach the house, and then there was a thud at the door. You all know the rest."

Zeke shuddered. "Yeah, we saw the head outside. Gruesome shit."

Expecting bile to rise in her throat at the mention of Natasha's head, Hunny was relieved when all she mustered was a mild grimace of disgust.

"I called Jason," Murphy added. "He didn't answer, but his Beta, Ben, did. Apparently, Jason felt Natasha's death a few minutes before they reached their territory. He isn't handling it well."

"I don't buy it," Colter stated with a firm shake of his head. He glanced at each person in the room before explaining. "We all saw Jason at the meeting. His concern for Natasha was minimal at best, and it seemed fake. He only focused on her after Ben brought her up. And now the Alpha's suddenly distraught that his mate is dead?" He scoffed.

"I don't think Jason loved Natasha," Hunny replied, biting her lower lip when everyone turned their attention to her. She'd never been someone who enjoyed the limelight, especially considering the topic revolved around her ex's dead mate. "When he rejected me in favor of her, he told me it was because she was a strong, smart choice as his Alpha female. He didn't mention anything about caring for her. So maybe he didn't."

She could still remember how easily he'd discarded *her* after weeks of them being together. He'd used her, made her think he cared for her, and then tossed her aside easily. And she had been his true mate. Why would he care any more for Natasha than he had Hunny?

"So you agree with me," Colter inferred, smirking at the others. "I knew I was right."

Hunny shook her head. "I didn't say that. You're forgetting the fact that they were still a mated pair," she added. "Just because he didn't care about her emotionally doesn't mean her death didn't cause him grief. It would have snapped their bond in half. I've heard it's one of the most painful things a shifter can endure."

And one day, either she or Tank would have to live with that kind of agony and decide whether they could handle the separation. Her pulse spiked, and her mouth dried, anxiety swirling in her gut at the mere thought of never being with her mate again.

As if he could read her thoughts, Tank slid his hand over hers, intertwining their fingers and squeezing in reassurance. Immediately, she felt better, releasing a small breath she didn't realize she'd been holding.

"Is Jason accusing one of us of killing her?" Tank asked. "Doesn't help that we threatened to do just that if we found her lurking around."

Oh, shit. That didn't sound good at all.

"I wouldn't blame him if he did," Murphy muttered, leaning back against the counter by the stove. He crossed his arms over his chest, staring blankly ahead. "His pack was adamant they'd scented her at our border, and now she's dead in our territory. This is justifiable grounds for war. But to answer your question, no. He was losing his shit in the background of the call, and Ben told me now wasn't a good time to talk. He's supposed to get in touch with me in the next few hours."

"Do you think Jason planned this?" Marcus asked curiously.

"Somebody did," Tank replied roughly. "I refuse to believe it was a coincidence that Natasha's body was delivered to our door right after the meeting. Someone was sending Hunny a message."

"More like a 'you're welcome,'" Jasper joked. "We can't forget that Natasha tried to kill Hunny. Maybe the killer thought this was an act of service."

Hunny's mouth dried. "That implies I *know* the killer." She held up a hand before anyone could say anything. "I know Jason's a shitty person, but I can't imagine why he'd do this, especially since he now knows I'm mated. What would be the point?"

"You didn't see him at the meeting, though," Colter remarked. "He looked at Tank like he wanted to kill him. Maybe he wants you back."

Hunny recoiled at that thought. *Ew. That's a hard pass.*

"To be fair, he looked at everyone like that," Zeke pointed out, scratching the stubble on his chin. "Jason's a twisted individual, and while he didn't want to mate Hunny, that doesn't mean he wants someone else to mate her, either. Regardless, Natasha's been missing for days, according to him, and Tank and Hunny just mated last night. Do we really think he kidnapped his own mate, hid her in bear territory without any of us knowing, and planned to kill her on the off chance Hunny was claimed? And all *after* she tried to kill Hunny? That's a stretch to assume."

Hunny pointed right at Zeke. "Exactly." Finally, someone else understood where she was coming from. "And it's not like Jason even knew for sure I was staying with your clan before then, right? He'd only have known from Natasha that she chased me into your territory. For all he knew, I was states away by now."

"That's true. We can't rule anything out at this point though." Tank looked at Murphy. "We also need to consider that someone might have planned to kill Natasha while Jason was at that meeting. If he'd felt her death while he was with us, he would have lashed out. Her death could be a setup for him as well as for us."

"To pit us against each other?" Murphy's brows furrowed. "That's an interesting thought."

Jasper nodded. "And it means we'll need to look at our own enemies as well as those of the Moon Rose pack. See if someone other than Jason could be responsible for this."

"That makes more sense to me," Hunny chimed in, though she knew Tank wouldn't agree.

Just as she suspected, Tank growled lowly. "No one throws a goddamn head onto our porch if it's not personal, darlin'. We'll do our due diligence, look into other possibilities, but my money's on Jason."

And with that, the males departed, leaving Tank and Hunny alone.

Twenty Nine

"I still can't believe you were watching those videos this morning," Hunny commented, scrunching her nose in distaste as Tank led her into the foyer of Murphy's home. His brother had contacted him earlier, asking to meet at his place to go over some things that had been overlooked yesterday.

Not wanting Hunny out of his sight for any genuine length of time, Tank had woken her with a firm tongue buried between her sweet thighs, giving her a few orgasms before making her breakfast while she got up and ready for the day.

Tank grunted in response as he closed the door behind them.

"What?" Hunny asked, a slight laugh in her voice as she looked around the large room, her brows rising in surprise before she turned to look at him. "You can't tell me watching a vagina entrance expand to accommodate a baby's head isn't horrifying."

"It's not horrifying at all," he reasoned with a shrug. "A baby has to come out somehow." Plus, the more he knew about the birthing process now, the more prepared he'd be later. And considering he planned to be up close and personal as Hunny delivered their kits, he didn't want to be taken by surprise by *anything*.

"Well, let's hope 'somehow' is as painless as possible when the time comes." She grimaced, clutching her belly protectively. Turning back to the main room once more, she let out a low whistle. "Murphy's place is massive." The awe in her voice was unmistakable.

Tank crossed his arms over his chest as he studied the room critically. Even though it was a log cabin like Tank's, there was nothing modest about it. Giant floor-to-ceiling windows covered one wall almost entirely. The oak ceiling itself was vaulted, with a massive chandelier in the center dangling impressively above the living room. Expensive leather furniture filled the space in front of them, completing the sophisticated look.

For a split second, he regretted taking Hunny with him on this little trip. Why didn't he just have Murphy meet them at the bear den? At least the main house, where the clan gathered together, wasn't ostentatious like this. What if Hunny decided she wanted to move? He was already building onto their home, but he hated the thought of her finding it lacking, especially compared to the amount of money his brother had funneled into his own luxurious space.

"It's fine, I guess," Tank muttered under his breath, earning a snort from his mate. She shook her head at him in dismay before walking over to a leather couch and plopping down onto it.

She shimmied her hips over the cushion before sending him a sweet smile. "I prefer ours. Much comfier."

Tank dropped his arms to his sides in surprise. "Really?"

"Oh, yeah. This seems super stiff, like no one actually sits on it or anything. Not to mention the view dead ahead." She pointed toward the windows with exasperation. "What's the point of all these windows if it doesn't even face a clearing? I know we're in the woods, but the view is literally just tree branches. And no TV?" Hunny made a displeased face. "Who doesn't have a TV nowadays?"

"I fucking love you," Tank admitted, warmth filling his chest as she let out a small laugh.

Tucking her lavender hair behind her ears, Hunny sent him a heated look, a glimmer of laughter in her eyes that he never grew tired of seeing. "I love you, too, but I'm dead serious. This couch feels terrible."

"Well, it cost me ten grand," Murphy explained irritably, stepping out of his office and into the hallway connected to the living room. "It's meant to look good, not to be sat on."

"Mission accomplished then." Hunny popped up, sending Murphy a finger wave as both males walked over to her.

"Let's go into my office. The chairs are more comfortable there," Murphy commented dryly. "Cost me about a hundred dollars each, so I'm sure they'll be right up your alley."

Tank growled at the insult, but Hunny just rolled her eyes, trailing after the Alpha. When they were all seated inside the spacious room with the door shut, Murphy let out an aggravated sigh.

"Well, that doesn't sound good." Hunny leaned forward in her chair, propping her elbows on the top of Murphy's desk. "Is it Jason? Did he get ahold of you?"

"Yes." Murphy ran a hand down his face. "He hasn't outright accused us of killing her, but he's demanding his mate's body be delivered to him as soon as possible."

Tank's brows furrowed. "Convenient that he wants us away from our own territory." Tank didn't like the idea of that one bit. The last time he'd left bear land, someone had thrown a fucking head at his front door.

"That's what I thought too. Until we figure out who's responsible, I don't want any of us leaving bear territory for any length of time."

"So what do we do then?" Hunny asked. "We can't just leave Natasha's body here. As much as I hated her, that's not fair to her family."

"I'm not interested in getting caught by the human authorities hauling a dead body around, either," Murphy replied. "The only genuine option is to have him come here and get her."

"Absolutely not," Tank bit out through clenched teeth.

"You are not in charge." Murphy's jaw clenched, equally irate. "We'll ensure Hunny is protected, and that only Jason and his Beta come into our territory. But it needs to be done, and it will be."

Hunny slid her hand over Tank's forearm and squeezed it gently as she looked at Murphy. "When will he arrive?"

"Nine a.m. tomorrow morning. He'll bring his Beta and one other pack member, though he hasn't specified who yet. We're meeting them at the border of our territory and escorting them to the bear den. Mom's got Natasha's body at the morgue."

"There's a morgue on your territory?!" Hunny exclaimed.

Murphy nodded. "The clinic attached to the den has a room in the back. It's small, but it's equipped to handle a few dead bodies, if necessary."

Hunny let out a small breath. "Okay, Henry and I will stay back at our cabin until he's gone. Right?" she asked Tank, narrowing her eyes on him.

Tank grumbled his acknowledgement. There wasn't a chance in hell he'd leave his mate alone, even though he wanted nothing more than to keep tabs on Jason the entire time he was here. He'd just have to trust his brother would keep the wolf fucker in line.

Murphy leaned back in his seat, the supple leather groaning slightly with his movement. He looked away from them both, staring at a small crack on his desk for what felt like an eternity, his brows pinched, and his shoulders hunched.

"What else do you need to say?" Tank asked abruptly, breaking the silence and cocking his head to the side as Murphy's gaze shot up to meet his. "Just spit it out."

"The human is my mate," Murphy announced harshly, glaring back down at the crack in his desk as if it had somehow wronged him.

Tank blinked in surprise. "What?"

"The human? Wait—*Nessa*?!" Hunny exclaimed, standing up abruptly. Just as quickly, she collapsed back into her seat, gaping at the Alpha. "That's who you mean, isn't it?"

"Yes." Murphy pinched the bridge of his nose before turning his attention to Tank's mate. "I don't like her."

"You don't *like* her?" Hunny scoffed in disbelief. She crossed her arms, pinning the Alpha with a look that brooked no argument. "That's absurd. Nessa's awesome."

"A bit of a yapper," Tank cut in, hoping to divert some of Hunny's attention for the time being. Now that the truth was sinking in, Tank felt like a fool for not realizing it sooner. Murphy, while he hated humans, never acted out of character around them.

But with Nessa? He'd been a grumpy, insufferable dickhead. Now it made sense why. His inner bear had likely been clawing at him, demanding he claim the female right then and there, completely oblivious to all the reasons that match was unacceptable.

First, Nessa was human, so the odds of her knowing anything about the supernatural community were slim to none. Second, even if she *did* know about shifters, Murphy despised her kind. It was no wonder he'd sought every opportunity to argue with Nessa back at her teahouse. He'd likely been conflicted about what to do. Humans as true mates weren't unheard of, but they were rare.

"You love yappers," Hunny said indignantly, sending a haughty look in Tank's direction.

Tank's expression softened. "I love when *you* yap. There's a difference."

"Look," Murphy cut in, his frustration evident in his voice. "I thought it was important to tell you both since you know the human—"

"Nessa," Hunny corrected with a scowl.

"Right." Murphy ran a hand down his face. "Regardless of her name, or who she is to me, I'm not going to claim her."

This time, Tank was the one to gape at his brother in disbelief. "Are you serious, Murph?"

"Yes. It wouldn't work. Nor do I want it to. I have no care for humans, and the thought of mating one ..." He shook his head in disgust. "No. Absolutely not."

Hunny leaned back in her seat, staring at Murphy like he was a foul-smelling stranger. "It's not her fault she's human, Murphy. And what happened to you a long time ago ... it's definitely not her fault, either."

Murphy's shot Tank a furious look. "You told her about that?"

Tank shrugged. "Hunny's my mate. Of course, I told her."

Seething, Murphy pushed to his feet, wandering over to an extravagant bookshelf littered with rare books written by the same humans he despised so much. But once upon a time, Murphy loved humans. He'd found them fascinating. Marvelous in just how different they were from all things supernatural. Reaching out, his brother ran his fingers gently over one book spine.

"Mating is supposed to be a joyous occasion. Whether it's fated or chosen," Murphy murmured, pulling the book from the shelf and opening it to a random page. His eyes roamed over the pristine, if old, paper. "As an Alpha, I've always known that when I found my mate, I'd likely have to work hard to ensure she was the perfect match for me. I need someone strong to stand by my side, someone reliable. Trustworthy."

"Nessa is a good person," Hunny argued, moving from her chair to stand by his side. She reached for the book in his hand, and surprisingly, the Alpha let her pluck it from his grasp. She closed it with a loud thunk, and Murphy clenched his jaw as she added, "You don't even know her. She could literally be perfect for you. Fate seems to think so, but you aren't even willing to give her a chance."

"Your mate didn't give you a chance, and now look at you. Happily mated to my brother. Things seem to have worked out for you."

Hunny blinked at him in shock before waving the book around in exasperation. "So you want Nessa to find someone else? I figured you'd be possessive of your mate. Not disinterested."

"He was possessive back at the teahouse," Tank supplied helpfully from his seat, ignoring Murphy's snarl. "He was furious when she told him one of the wolves asked her out."

"Because she's under my protection—as is the town. I would have felt the same way toward any human in her position," Murphy argued through gritted teeth.

"Oh, that's such bullcrap." Hunny snorted. "Just ask her out on a date, or go back to her shop and feign an interest in tea. Get to know her before you cast her aside, at least."

"I already know enough about her to know she isn't for me," Murphy exclaimed roughly, all but yanking the book out of Hunny's hand. Reverently, he placed it back on the shelf, ignoring the warning growl Tank sent his way.

"What does that mean?" Tank stood, pulling Hunny to his side. "You run a background check on her?"

"Yeah," Murphy all but snarled under his breath. "That was all I needed."

"What the hell does *that* mean?" Hunny reiterated. "Was her credit score too low for you or something?"

"I couldn't find anything," Murphy exploded with exasperation. Running a hand through his hair, he took a few deep breaths to calm down. "Her identity is a sham. Nessa probably isn't even her real name."

Hunny shook her head slightly. "Yeah, I wondered about that. She mentioned that settling down in Montana was the safest option. It made me wonder if she was running from someone. Not that you give a shit, apparently," she muttered under her breath.

Tank smirked despite the tense situation. Given to him by fate or not, Hunny was fucking perfect.

Murphy narrowed his eyes on Hunny, a hard edge flashing in his eyes as they turned gold for the briefest second. "Did she tell you specifically that's why she came to Montana?"

"Well, she said—" Hunny threw her hands up in the air. "Actually, you know what? If you're interested in why she's here, how about you do something crazy and ask her about it?"

"You know I'm your permanent Alpha now, right? Since you've mated my brother, you're bound to the same rules and laws that govern this clan as he is." Murphy raised a brow, his voice laced heavily with irritation. "I can command you to tell me everything you know about her."

Hunny laughed a little too loudly at that, the sound carrying a hint of mania that made even Tank feel wary. This conversation with his brother had gotten out of hand, and although his mate was a submissive shifter, he wouldn't want his worst enemy going against her verbally, let alone Murphy. "Oh, really? Go ahead then, *Alpha* Murphy. Command me."

Stiffening his shoulders, Murphy demanded, "You'll tell me what you know about Nessa."

Hunny narrowed her eyes as she opened her mouth. "Suck my dic—"

Tank popped his hand over Hunny's mouth before she finished her sentence. "How about we all just calm down?"

"You're both dismissed," Murphy commanded, his voice trembling with barely contained anger. "And you'll keep what I've told you to yourselves. Am I understood?"

Hunny's voice was muffled by Tank's palm, but Murphy didn't even spare her a glance. Instead, he left the room immediately, his footsteps echoing down the hall and into one of the bedrooms near the back of the house, the door slamming behind him.

Thirty

The next morning, Hunny was up earlier than Tank. Kind of surprising, considering how deeply she'd started sleeping since discovering she was pregnant. Ever since she'd come here, to the safety of this cabin, to this *male*, she felt at home. Peaceful and safe, like she could finally truly rest after years of loneliness.

But right now? Hunny didn't feel like resting. She felt like doing something far more *pleasurable*, like waking her mate up the same way he usually woke her every day.

Grinning, Hunny slid out of Tank's arms, careful to keep her movements light so she didn't wake him as she slid under the blankets. Next, she shimmied down the bed on her hands and knees until Tank's thick cock was in her face. Biting her lower lip, she cupped his balls with one hand, taking his half-mast shaft in the other.

His cock was hot and heavy in her hand, and all it took was one long stroke before it stiffened, lengthening to the delicious size she loved so much. Refusing to wait another second, Hunny leaned forward, swiping her tongue over his tip. Musk, salty precum, and the heat from her male hit her senses all at once.

Excited, Hunny opened wide, slipping him into the heat of her mouth and sucking. She'd only taken him a few inches when he hardened further, becoming velvet-wrapped steel in her mouth. With a small, needy moan, she tightened her grip on the base of his shaft, stroking up and down in time with each bob of her head. Tank shifted on the bed, his legs tensing as she swallowed another inch of his cock.

He tasted delicious, and a possessive, sensual part of herself wanted to feel his release fill her mouth. She wanted his cum to slide down her throat and fill her belly.

Talk about breakfast in bed, she thought happily, sucking on Tank's cock eagerly. Her pussy clenched with need, and she had half a mind to play with herself as she played with him. But, not wanting her attention to be divided, she tended to her mate instead, more than ready to please him.

Slick spilled from her entrance, and she moaned hungrily, working her mouth over his cock faster. Another bob of her head and she released him, only to lick up the underside of his erection, her saliva coating his veiny length.

He flexed in her palm, his tip bumping against her chin in a silent demand for more. Not one to deny her male, Hunny sucked him back into her mouth, taking several inches at once. She choked as he hit the back of her throat, but refused to stop. Relaxing the muscles in her throat, she took him deeper until her nose brushed against his lower abdomen. And then she swallowed, her throat tightening around the length of him.

"Fuck," Tank groaned gutturally, his voice thick with sleep. Morning light pouring in from the bedroom window hit her eyes as Tank ripped the blankets off of them both, exposing her to his heated, drowsy gaze. He groaned again, his hand finding the back of her head. His fingers fisted in her hair. "Morning, baby."

In answer, Hunny lifted her head, kissing his leaking tip tenderly. She stroked upward, closing her palm over his tip and massaging his cockhead. "Morning, Henry," she purred. "How'd you sleep?"

"Pretty go—" Hunny deepthroated his cock before he could finish his sentence, keeping her eyes locked on his. A deep groan exploded through the room as Tank bit out a sharp curse, using his hand to guide her head up and down the length of him. "Look at you, taking my cock like a good little mate," he preened, his body lining with tension as she sucked harder.

She pushed up more fully onto her knees, arching her back to give him a tantalizing glimpse of her ass. The scent of her arousal filtered through the air, her slick spilling down her inner thighs with every lick of his cock. His eyes flickered to a glowing gold, and waves of his dominance poured into the room.

Hunny whimpered as his power slid over her, licking and sucking eagerly to please him. Sitting up on an elbow, Tank's grip tightened on her hair, holding her still.

"I'm going to fuck this pretty little mouth, Hunny." To emphasize his point, Tank thrust upward with his hips, his tip hitting the back of her throat roughly. She moaned, her desire so strong she felt a brief twinge of discomfort in her womb. It was there one second and gone the next, giving way to a heat that blossomed in her core and spread.

She squeezed her eyes shut as Tank began pumping into her mouth, holding her still as he rasped out her name. "Look at me," he demanded, his tone filled with need.

Her eyes shot open and locked onto him; to the flush staining his cheeks and the lust-filled haze in his gaze as he watched her lips spread over his shaft. "Fucking Christ. Suck me, baby. Just like that. Watch what you do to your mate," he growled, the veins in his arms bulging as he held her still, creating a steady pace with his hips until he was fucking her mouth. She swallowed his cock greedily, taking him deeper than she ever had before.

Tank grunted as she cupped his balls once more, gently rolling them between her fingers. A hungry look crossed his features, and then he began moving her head again, up and down with every pump of his hips. "You want me to cum down this tight little throat, baby, or do you want me to fill your pretty pussy with my cock?"

Hunny moaned, more than eager for both. Tugging gently on his heavy sac, she hummed in answer; the noise vibrating against his length.

"Tight little throat, it is. Swallow every drop of my cum, Hunny," Tank commanded, rocking into her mouth with reckless abandon. He gasped for breath, and his legs trembled as she met each of his thrusts eagerly, sucking and licking until she felt his balls draw up in her hands. His cock throbbed, and he bellowed her name, the sound echoing in her ears. Hot, thick ropes of his cum hit the back of her throat, threatening to choke her.

"Take it, baby," Tank panted, driving into her mouth with one final pump. He held her head in place as he came, his chest rising and falling rapidly as he fought to breathe. More cum filled her mouth, spilling down her throat. Hunny drank him down, reluctant to pull away from him even as he began to soften in her mouth.

With a low rumble, Tank moved, pulling Hunny up the bed and into his arms, adjusting her until she was resting on his chest, her thighs straddling his waist.

"Morning baby," Tank crooned thickly, his eyes losing their golden hue and returning to the chocolate brown she adored.

"Morning," Hunny murmured, sending him a small smile. Cupping the back of her head, Tank pulled her down for a kiss, sinking his tongue into the cavern of her mouth. He rolled, pinning her to the bed beneath him as his hands slid over the curves of her body. He touched her breasts, pinching her nipples hard.

Gasping, Hunny flinched from the bite of pain, only to moan loudly as he rolled his thumbs over the stinging peaks, turning that small amount of pain into a delicious pressure that traveled down to her clit. Tank moved his lips from hers, following his hands down her body. His tongue slipped over her breast right before he sucked her nipple into his mouth, teasing it with his teeth.

"H-Henry," Hunny whined, running her hands through his thick hair. "I need you inside me. Please."

In answer, Tank grasped her thighs, spreading her legs apart as he began kissing his way down her stomach, nuzzling her tiny bump affectionately before his mouth traveled lower. His breath skated over her lower lips, and she shivered in anticipation. "Gonna fuck this pretty pussy with my tongue, darlin'." He sent her a cocky smirk before looking down at her exposed center. "And once you've come all over my face, I'm going to shove my co—"

Tank froze, the look on his face transforming from one of pure rapture to one of horror. He shot up from the bed, rushing to the dresser. He slipped on the comforter that had fallen onto the floor, nearly slamming into the ground before he caught himself on the bed.

Alarmed, Hunny sat up, her heart beating hard as he made it to the dresser. She watched in alarm as he yanked open the top drawer and started grabbing items haphazardly. "Henry, what's wrong?"

He turned to her, a look of panic written all over his face. Before he could answer, she inhaled, a metallic odor filling her nose. Wrinkling her brow in confusion, she looked down, recoiling in horror when she spotted bright red staining her inner thighs and the sheet under her.

"Oh, my God!" she exclaimed hoarsely, an icy chill sliding down her spine. She was bleeding? No, no, she couldn't be—

"Up, little rabbit," Tank urged, reaching her side in an instant. He pulled her to her feet, cupping her face tenderly. Whatever panic she'd seen on his face before was now gone, replaced by a deadly calm she wished she could feel. "It's okay. We're going to go to the clinic and have my mom take a look. Alright?"

Hunny nodded jerkily, but as soon as he released his hold on her, she let out a ragged breath, her chest feeling suddenly too tight. Tears stung her eyes. "I don't understand what's happening, Henry. I don't understand. I didn't—"

Immediately, Tank's dominance washed over her, and the tightness in her chest eased, allowing her to drag in precious oxygen. He tapped her leg, holding out a pair of his sweatpants for her to slip into. She did so robotically, clinging to the waves of power that he released in steady increments, focusing on that instead to keep her from unleashing the scream that echoed in her mind, shouting at her that something was wrong with her babies. She'd done something wrong—

"Other leg, little rabbit," Tank commanded gently, all but lifting her up and into the sweats before setting her back down on her feet. He slid one of his shirts over her head, dressing her while she stood there, too numb to do anything but let him lead her through this. Whatever this was.

Hunny slid her eyes shut as the word 'miscarriage' slithered into her mind like a snake.

She opened her eyes in time to watch Tank dress faster than she'd ever seen before in her life. It was like she was watching him through someone else's eyes, stuck on some weird kind of autopilot. Then he was sliding house slippers onto her feet, picking her up, and hustling them down the stairs. Grabbing the keys to his truck by the front door, he tore out of the house with her, running to the garage and racing inside.

She felt useless as he placed her in the cab of his truck, buckling her up and giving her a quick kiss before he made it to the driver's side door. It was only as they tore down the road, Tank driving far too fast, that Hunny noticed the time on the dashboard, glaring at her in a bright neon green. She blinked rapidly, coming back to herself.

"Henry, it's just past nine a.m.." Her voice sounded off, even to her own ears as Tank fumbled with his cellphone, mumbling irritably to himself as he pressed a number on the screen. The phone rang and he sent her a confused look. "Jason's going to be there to get Natasha, isn't he?"

"Fuck," Tank spat, right as his mom picked up the phone. He looked at the road ahead. "Mom, Hunny's bleeding ..."

Thirty One

Tank thought he'd felt terror before, but it was nothing compared to now. Hanging up the call with his mom, he tossed his phone onto the dashboard before taking Hunny's hand in his. Her touch was like ice, and her skin was paler than usual as he looked over at her, his brow furrowed with concern. The scent of her blood mixed with her own usual scent was unnerving, causing his inner beast to roar and claw at his insides, demanding to be set free in order to help their mate. The animalistic side of himself didn't understand what was happening.

Not that his human side fared much better. Fear and uncertainty were riding him hard, though he was doing his damndest to keep those emotions locked up tight, at least until he could get his mate to his mom. Losing his shit wouldn't do Hunny or himself any favors; not when she was relying on him to get them through this.

His stomach was twisted into knots, his limbs shaking as he fought to pretend that everything was fine. Hunny was checked out beside him; the only thing keeping her from sobbing was the gentle waves of dominance he sent her way every few minutes. Thank fuck he was a dominant shifter. All he could do right now was get her there quickly and try to force back the overriding panic pushing against her.

It was a strain to exert his dominance in waves like this for any length of time, though, but he didn't care. He'd seen the look of pure terror on her face, had caught the scent of her utter despair as she'd realized at the same time he had that something was terribly wrong.

She thought she was losing the kits. Hell, he thought she was losing the kits. There'd been so much blood, he didn't know what else to think.

He didn't know how to help his mate other than to minimize her anguish, to keep her calm. It was a temporary solution until he could find someone to help her. His mom was already at the clinic, just a few minutes away. She'd know what to do. How to help them.

Fuck, he thought almost desperately. *Please let Mom know what to do.* These kits might not be his by blood, but they were his just as much as they were Hunny's. He'd vowed to love and protect them, to keep them safe and raise them. If Hunny miscarried, he'd be devastated. But he knew that was nothing compared to the heartbreak his mate would feel.

Tank's hand tightened on the steering wheel, the leather and metal creaking ominously.

"We're almost there, darlin'," he assured Hunny, pressing down on the gas pedal. If she heard him, she didn't answer, only mumbling something about the time. He knew what she meant—what she'd said as he'd called his mom a few minutes prior.

Jason and his Beta would be at the den house, picking up Natasha's body. The very thing he'd wanted to avoid—exposing Hunny to that prick ever again—was coming to fruition. He didn't want Hunny, nor their kits, anywhere near that sick son of a bitch. But there was nowhere else to take her. It would take too long for his mum to grab all her stuff and get to his cabin. And if she needed more ... surgery or something ... then Hunny needed to be at the clinic.

No matter who they'd encounter there.

"I think I'm in shock." Hunny's voice was off. Hollow. She blinked hard as if to clear her vision. "I feel like I'm not really here, like I'm just detached from this entire situation."

"It might be my power," Tank admitted, hating that his attempt to help could be causing her more distress instead. "Do you want me to ease it back?"

She shook her head, her fingers tightening on his. "No. N-Not yet, okay? Not until we know ..." She trailed off, looking out the passenger side window.

"Whatever my mom says, little rabbit, we'll be okay." Lifting his hand, he kissed the back of her palm. "It could be nothing."

Even as he said it, acid burned in his gut. There'd been a lot of blood between her thighs. On the sheets, too. Was bleeding normal at this stage of her pregnancy? Fuck. He had no goddamn idea.

He clenched his jaw, furious with himself that he hadn't picked up those books from his mom yet. They'd been delivered yesterday. If he'd gone to get them, he could have read up on this very thing. He could have been prepared for any kind of difficulty—

Hunny cleared her throat, drawing him from his thoughts. "You're right. Maybe this is normal," she agreed faintly, swallowing thickly. But he didn't miss her small whine of discomfort.

Not a moment too soon, the den house came into view, his mom's vehicle one of the first he spotted in the parking lot. Tank let out a relieved breath, pulling into a parking spot quickly. Less than a minute later, he had Hunny in his arms and was inside the building, prowling toward his mom's office. He didn't see the wolf or any of his pack, nor did he smell them, which he filed away to give a damn about later.

Hopefully, the fuckers hadn't shown up. Or they had arrived earlier in the morning, sparing Hunny from further distress. Heart in his throat, Tank carried his mate into the clinic.

"**I**'ve got some good news for you both." Pointing at an image on the ultrasound screen, Tabitha sent Tank and Hunny a reassuring smile. "Everything looks great. Kits are nice and healthy."

Tank leaned over the bed his mate was lying on, all but sagging into her in relief as he placed a kiss on her forehead. He closed his eyes as his lips pressed against her skin, and he just breathed her in. His mom had cleaned Hunny up a few minutes ago, removing the scent of blood and replacing it with the stench of chemicals that stung his nose, but in that moment, he didn't give a single fuck.

The last half hour had been a nightmare that he was unsure if he'd woken up from yet. Who knew the best blowjob of his life would turn into the worst morning he'd ever gone through?

"You're sure everything is alright?" Hunny asked quickly, the fear in her eyes dissipating as she laid her hands on her belly. He followed suit, needing to touch her, to touch his little family and reassure himself that everything was actually okay. She looked at the screen and then back at his mother. "Nothing's wrong? Why was I bleeding so much then?"

The reminder had Tank growling low in his throat on instinct. Luckily, Hunny had stopped bleeding on the drive over, not that he'd noticed, as stricken as he'd been.

"Some females bleed irregularly during their pregnancies. It's more common with multiple fetuses, but a bit of spotting, or in your case, bleeding, isn't always a bad thing. Have you two been sexually active recently?" Tabitha asked clinically, rolling away from them both on her stool. Removing her gloves, she tossed them into the hazardous waste bin before turning back to face them.

"I mean, uh, well, we're mated," Hunny began awkwardly, a delicate blush staining her cheeks. Tank nearly collapsed at the sight, relief coursing through him as she regained her normal, healthy glow. She'd been so pale, he wasn't sure he'd ever get the image from his head.

Tabitha sent Hunny a pointed look. "That doesn't really answer my question, dear. You smell like Tank, but that could be from the mating bond itself and the bite. Nothing else."

"Yes, we're having sex," Tank answered hoarsely. "Did I hurt her? Did I hurt the kits?" Dread churned in his gut at the thought, self-loathing roaring through his head. If his dick needed to steer clear of his mate for the rest of her pregnancy, he would make sure the horny bastard remained firmly contained in his pants.

Tabitha snorted, shaking her head. "No. Sexual intercourse isn't something that will cause harm. But the cervix is more sensitive during pregnancy, so if you've been having more sex than usual, it could cause bleeding like this."

Hunny bit her lower lip before adding, "We had sex last night."

"That's probably what caused it, dear. But as I said, the kits are healthy and so are you, so please don't stress over today any more than you already have. To be honest, your panic might have made the bleeding seem worse than it was." Tabitha rolled back over to their table, gently patting Hunny's knee through the privacy sheet. "It was good of you to come as soon as you noticed it, though. It never hurts to be safe with matters like this, so you both did the right thing. Do you have any more questions for me?"

Hunny wrinkled her nose, something Tank noticed her doing whenever she had a distasteful thought. "Do you think I'll bleed like this again every time after sex?"

Tabitha shrugged. "It's hard to say. Every female is different. Ideally, this won't be a recurring issue, but even if it is, make sure to either come in or call me so we can discuss if any action needs to be taken. Okay?"

"Yeah, absolutely." Hunny reached out, giving his mom a quick hug. "Thank you."

Standing from her stool, Tabitha gave his mate another sweet smile before she cast a hard glare his way. Immediately, he was on edge, narrowing his eyes at her.

"Congratulations on your mating, Tank." She sniffed dramatically, dusting off her clean shirt. "It would have been nice to hear the news from *you*, but hearing it from one of my other children was fine, too." She muttered under her breath, "I suppose."

Tank sighed, running a hand down his face. "Jasper told you, didn't he?"

"Of course, he did." Tabitha threw her hands up in the air. "At least one of my boys cares about his mother's feelings and wants to keep her in the loop. I swear, getting you and Murphy to talk to me is like pulling teeth. You never tell me anything."

"It's not like that," Tank argued. "Of course, I planned on telling you, but the last day hasn't exactly been uneventful."

Tabitha raised a brow. "And your phone wasn't working *at all* yesterday? Just this morning?"

"I didn't think about calling. I wanted to tell you in person," he told her reluctantly, his gaze moving from his mom to Hunny as she slipped from the table, straightening her clothing and dropping the privacy sheet back onto the table's surface.

Tabitha walked over to an oak desk in the corner, grabbing a small stack of books. Bringing them over to Tank, she dropped them into his hands. They were heavier than he'd expected, and he looked down, glancing at the various titles.

"Start with the purple book. It's the most detailed and goes over each trimester. I crossed out the information that wouldn't pertain to a shifter pregnancy and highlighted the parts that you'll want to pay close attention to. If you have any questions, call me." Cupping his cheek tenderly, Tabitha waited until Tank looked up from the books. Her eyes swimming with happy tears, she whispered, "Congratulations, my darling boy. Hunny is a perfect choice for you."

Tank's throat tightened with emotion, and he nodded. "I think so too."

Patting his cheek again, Tabitha dropped her hand, sending Hunny a grateful look as the rabbit shifter stepped up beside Tank. "Welcome officially to the family! I can't wait for Phillip to meet you. He'll be so proud to see such a wonderful female on his son's arm."

Hunny smiled, only a brief hint of her previous stress still lining the corners of her mouth. "Thank you. I'm a bit nervous to meet the rest of Henry's family, but I'm excited too."

"There's nothing to be nervous about. Phillip will love you, just like I do." Tabitha announced firmly. She pointed a threatening finger at Tank. "And if this grumpy old bear gives you any trouble, you just let me know, dear."

Laughing, Hunny assured her she would, and that one simple statement, combined with the sweet sound of his mate's laughter, vanquished the last of Tank's fears.

Tabitha waved them both toward the closed office door. "You should get out of here before our *guests* arrive." She hissed out the words, referring to the Moon Rose pack. "They're late, and it's made Murphy's mood foul, but I'm sure they'll show up at the most inopportune time." Tank pulled open the door for his mate, following her out into the lobby as his mother continued, "And again, if you have even the slightest concern regarding the health of your kits, call me right away—"

"*Kits?*" a grating, masculine voice interrupted from across the room. Tank's head jerked up right as he scented the obnoxious odor of several wolf shifters permeating the air. With his free hand, he grabbed Hunny, pulling her protectively behind him.

Jason stepped forward, Ben and Angela following closely behind him. "You're pregnant with multiple pups, Hunny?"

Thirty Two

I f Hunny hadn't been on the verge of vomiting after all the chaos of this morning, she definitely was now as the putrid stench of wolf filled her lungs. She'd only glimpsed Jason for a second—*two at most*—before Tank tugged her behind him, his menacing growl filling the clinic's lobby.

She'd never wanted to see Jason again, let alone on the heels of such a harrowing experience for her and Tank. She was completely on edge and still feeling shaky; the last thing she needed was this.

God, why did they have to run into him? Couldn't she just catch a break once in her damned life?! She knew Jason would come here this morning to collect Natasha's body, but she'd also thought he'd stop at the main portion of the den house and speak with Murphy first. Wasn't he meant to be escorted anyway? Not just waltz in like he owned the place.

"Answer me, Hunny," Jason demanded, a harsh bite to his voice accompanied by a wave of dominance that had her flinching, her throat itching with the need to obey. It had been so long since another shifter had used their power over her to force her obedience that she'd forgotten just how oppressive it was.

Tank had never tried to use her submissive nature against her or to coerce her into something she didn't want. He'd only ever exerted his dominance to help her, to act as a shield or to protect her and hold her up in times of need, such as this morning. Even Murphy hadn't wielded his dominance over her when he'd demanded she answer him about Nessa the other day. He'd been considerate even while irritated.

But Jason hadn't even batted an eye to overthrow her will. "You're having multiple pups?" he demanded again.

She opened her mouth as he compelled her to answer. Her knees weakened as Jason's dominance oozed over her like quicksand, threatening to take her under. She always preached that being a submissive didn't make her weak, but right now, it was hard to feel otherwise. Now, she felt like a puppet dangling from a string, awaiting its master's call.

"Back the fuck off," Tank snarled, his hold on Hunny's wrist tightening. She focused on the feel of his skin touching hers, breathing hard through her nose as she tried to resist Jason's Alpha compulsion. "And that little dominance display you're emitting? End it now, or I'll rip you apart and make sure you meet your mate sooner than later."

Jason ignored him, adding more waves of dominance to his power. Hunny whimpered, but right before her knees buckled, Tank's own dominance swelled around them, so powerful it was almost unbearable. It wrapped around her, growing and growing. Suddenly, the pressure from Jason popped like a balloon, and Hunny sucked in a deep breath of air, sagging into Tank's back in relief.

"I ... Forgive me, it's been a rough few days," Jason stated angrily, and that was when she risked a peek over Tank's shoulder.

Hunny blinked in surprise when her eyes truly took in Jason for the first time since he'd rejected her. His short, light brown hair was a mess, like he'd run his hands through it a thousand times over the last day. His vivid blue eyes were hollow. Even his clothing was a wrinkled mess, and his skin was pale, dark circles under his eyes giving away how hard he'd taken the separation from Natasha, even if emotionally he hadn't.

Part of her had been worried that seeing him again, even though she didn't love him or want him back, would cause some old emotion to well up inside her. Some echo of the mating bond wanting to be formed. Instead, all she felt was pity, and a healthy dose of fury that he'd tried to control her.

Dead mate or not, who the hell did Jason think he was?

"I don't give a fuck what kind of day you've had." Another fierce growl followed Tank's words. "If you, Ben, or that female you're with, try *anything* like that with my mate again, it's over for you all."

Hunny felt more than heard another presence beside her, turning her head just in time to spot Tabitha standing stiffly on Tank's left side, sending a menacing look at the wolf trio as she silently backed up her son.

"Is that what happened to my sister?" the other male shifter asked angrily, drawing Hunny's attention. He looked about as good as Jason did, if not worse, with a slim nose and high cheekbones that matched Natasha's. "You rip her apart?"

The she-wolf looked between the group of them, swallowing thickly. "I-I don't think this is the time for this discussion, Ben. We promised Murphy we'd behave—"

"You can collect your friend," Tabitha interrupted firmly, her tone brooking no argument. "But you'll do so when Murphy arrives and not a moment sooner. You weren't even supposed to be here without him and another bear escorting you."

Jason scoffed, sending Tabitha the same cold look he'd given Hunny the night he rejected her. Like she was a fly that needed swatting. "I don't take orders from anyone."

Tank stiffened, and then he released his grip on Hunny's wrist, squaring his shoulders. Every muscle coiled with tension, and he moved towards the wolves with deadly intent. Jason unleashed his own furious growl, pushing past Ben and moving right toward her mate with a dangerous, maniacal glint in his eyes that terrified her.

He looked like he wanted Tank to attack him.

All of Tank's warnings about the Moon Rose pack came rushing back to the forefront of her mind, and the very thought of her mate brawling with Jason caused a shiver of dread to race down her spine. "Henry, don't—"

Suddenly, the door to the clinic burst open, and Murphy's scent spilled into the lobby a second before the male did. Marcus and Dante followed closely behind him, each male radiating a dark energy that screamed to not fuck with them.

"What's going on in here?" Murphy asked coolly. "You were supposed to meet with my enforcers at a specific location on the edge of bear territory. But you didn't show up, Jason, and now I find you here, harassing my brother and his pregnant mate."

Hunny released a relieved breath, grabbing Tank's arm and yanking him back to her side. For a second, he didn't budge, but he must have sensed her desperation, because when she tugged again, he let her lead him backward. He repositioned himself until he was standing protectively in front of both Hunny and Tabitha.

Jason scoffed. "I don't trust your clan, so no, I was never going to do as you instructed and risk an ambush. One of you killed Natasha, and until you deliver me the bear responsible, you're all my enemy."

The she-wolf looked away from her group, her eyes finding Dante for a second before skittering away again.

Murphy raised a brow. "That's a heavy accusation and a bold threat to make when it's just the three of you here."

Jason smirked. "Who says it's just the three of us?"

Tank stilled, and Hunny's heart skipped a beat, half expecting a slew of wolves to burst into the room past Murphy and the twins.

"We came alone," the female muttered, looking toward the twins again. Ben snarled something at her from under his breath, and she flinched before looking down at the ground once more, hunching her shoulders inward.

"I want Natasha returned to me. Now," Jason ordered with a furious jerk of his head toward Hunny. "And I want to talk with the mother of my pups. I'm entitled to this."

"The fuck you are," Hunny spat, pushing past her mate and giving Jason a snarl of her own. Her heart was beating hard, the ghostly remnants of his dominance still slithering over her skin, but she ignored it, instead choosing to focus on the sweet heat from Tank's own dominance as it cradled around her protectively like an invisible force field. "You have nothing to discuss with me."

"Easy, darlin'," Tank murmured, wrapping an arm over her shoulder and pulling her back against him. He kept his eyes focused on Jason, a sinister curl to his upper lip, practically daring the other male to set him off again.

Taking a deep breath, she tried to calm her racing heart. Tank was right. Losing her shit on Jason wouldn't help the situation at hand, and after she'd glimpsed that crazy look in his eyes, did she really want to anger him? No, she sure as hell didn't. She wanted him to collect his horrible mate and leave forever.

"The hell I don't," Jason argued, crossing his arms over his chest. "My mate is dead, and now those pups are the future of my pack—"

"You are insane," Hunny interrupted hotly, her body vibrating with rage. "My *kits* are nothing to you. Do you understand? Not your future, not part of your pack, because *Henry* is the father of my kits, you arrogant prick. You have no say and no rights to our—"she pointed between herself and Tank"—children."

Tank leaned in, his lips brushing over the crown of her head. "I fucking love you, little rabbit," he whispered, so low that only she could hear it. If she wasn't so furious, she might have blushed. But right now? She just wanted to punch something. Preferably, *someone.*

She also wanted to run far away from the oppression his very being brought back into her life. The feeling of inferiority and repulsion he instilled in her very being. How had she never noticed before just how terrible he was?

Jason's face turned an unflattering shade of red, his eyes skittering wildly around the room before settling on her once more. He took a step toward her. "I have rights, you little—"

"Knock it off," Ben snapped, grabbing Jason's shoulder and holding him back. "This isn't the time or the place. Angela, grab his other arm."

Murphy cleared his throat, moving further into the room with the twins at his back. Stepping between Tank and Jason, he rounded on the wolf, bumping against Jason's chest.

"Jason, my offer to help you discover what happened to your mate has expired. Dante," Murphy called, waiting for the male to acknowledge him. When he did, he nodded toward the wolves. "Take Angela to the morgue with Tabitha. Secure Natasha's body and bring it out here for her mate and brother to collect." When Dante nodded, and Angela quickly made her way to his side, Murphy continued, staring blankly at Jason. "You'll receive an escort from my territory as soon as your mate is in your care."

"This isn't over," Jason spat, getting in Murphy's face. "I won't rest until I handle whoever took my mate from me. I'm owed my vengeance."

"If you step one foot into this territory after today, I'll consider it an act of war," Murphy warned, refusing to move an inch. "And if you refuse to take that seriously, then you'll pay in blood."

Jason's chest rose and fell heavily, his nostrils flaring as if he were fighting the urge to attack Murphy regardless, consequences be damned. Hunny waited with bated breath, clinging to Tank's side as tension filled the air, almost as palpable as his display of dominance had been. Just when she thought the wolf Alpha would attack, Dante and Angela came back into the room, carrying a body bag between them.

"Dante, Marcus. Escort our guests outside. Make sure they find their way back home," Murphy ordered.

After what felt like forever, but couldn't have been longer than a few minutes at most, Jason and his wolves left with the twins trailing after them. As soon as the doors to the clinic closed, Hunny let out a relieved breath, sagging into her mate. "Thank God that's over with," she muttered.

Murphy turned toward them with a shake of his head and a resigned look on his face. "Unfortunately, I don't think that's it. Not until we can figure out what happened to Natasha."

"Any leads?" Tank asked gruffly, kissing the top of Hunny's head again.

"Not a damned one. Zeke's looking into the scent blocker; specifically, where a shifter can acquire it in our region, and we'll go from there."

Hunny wrinkled her nose. "I feel like I need a hot shower to clean off this entire day."

Murphy raised a brow, looking between the two of them as if truly seeing them for the first time. "I'm sorry. I should have asked how you were feeling before anything else. The kits are good? You're all fine?"

"Yes." Hunny sent him a small smile. Then, just to provoke him, she added, "Turns out your brother is just too good at giving my vagina a pound—"

"That's enough of that," Murphy cut in dryly. Grimacing, he took a step away from them. "I'm going to pretend I didn't hear anything past 'yes' and go talk to Mom and see if Angela disclosed any information while she was collecting the body."

Tank released his hold on Hunny as Murphy walked toward the morgue, crouching down and picking up the books that had fallen to the floor at some point during Jason's *visit*.

"Fuck," Tank grunted, stacking them before picking them up.

"What's wrong?"

"Bent the damned cover," he said with a put-out sigh. He sent her a pointed look. "You still think Jason doesn't give a damn about you?"

Begrudgingly, Hunny shook her head. Then she crowded back into her mate's space, wrapping her arms around his waist and holding him close. She rubbed her nose against his chest, relaxing as his scent filled her lungs. "I think he's a freaking psycho. I still don't think he wants me, though, but I didn't like the way he acted so entitled to our kits."

Cupping the nape of her neck, Tank breathed her in. "You set him straight, darlin', and that's all that matters. But on the off chance he comes back and tries to play parent, I'll do the honors of putting him in his place."

Hunny shivered, unease piercing her chest at the thought of seeing Jason again, of him ever trying to come close to her babies again. "You promise?"

Tank chuckled darkly. "Abso-*fucking*-lutely, baby."

Thirty Three

T ank did his best to ignore Hunny as he hoisted up a long, heavy
log that he'd just debarked. Keeping his gaze solely focused on
the stack of debarked logs ahead of him, and not on his tempting
mate wearing barely any clothes, he moved toward the half-built wall
outside of his home.

Roughly a month ago, though it felt like so much longer, Jasper and
Murphy had helped him cut down dozens of trees, and he was only
just now building on to the cabin.

It was mostly to distract himself from the female who'd done everything in her power to entice him for the last few days. Soft touches,
heated glances, blatant propositions. He felt bad for neglecting his
proper duties as her male, but ever since he'd rushed Hunny to the
clinic, he'd been afraid to touch her sexually with anything more than
his mouth.

Hunny hadn't noticed right away, mostly because he still kept waking her up each morning with his tongue buried in her cunt, starting
her day with a few orgasms. But he hadn't taken it any further than that.
She hadn't said anything to him about their lack of physical intimacy,
yet, but his little mate was keen. And given the fact he found an excuse
to disengage every time she initiated sex, she was bound to realize
what he was doing.

To make matters worse, Jason and his little band of bitches were constantly on Tank's mind. Every day, he expected to hear some news on the dickhead, or for him to breach bear territory and declare war. So far, though? Radio silence. Tank didn't like it. Not at all.

Small arms wrapped around his bare stomach from behind, and Tank melted into the touch as Hunny's delectable scent filled his nose. "You're working so hard, you didn't even hear my question," she said, a small teasing note to her voice that had him instantly on high alert. Warm breath skated over his spine, and just like that, lust hit him like a battering ram.

Cock stiffening, Tank cleared his throat, determined to ignore the neglected fucker in his pants. "What'd you ask, little rabbit?"

"If you were hungry for anything."

Tank squeezed his eyes shut, careful to keep his booted feet rooted to the ground instead of spinning around, ripping Hunny's clothes off, and burying himself inside her.

Fuck yes, he was hungry. Starved, actually, but not for food.

His dick flexed in his jeans in agreement, brushing uncomfortably against his zipper like it was trying to break free. He didn't blame the damned nuisance. He'd gone from stuffing it into the most perfect female any chance he could to abstaining from his mate cold turkey.

Warm, soft lips pressed against his spine, and Hunny's fingers tightened on his abs, only enticing him more.

"You want me to make you something, darlin'?" he asked thickly, all too aware of her hands sliding over his stomach. He'd taken his shirt off a little over an hour ago, desperate to feel the cool air on his sweat-slicked skin as he worked, but now he regretted it. Hunny touching him, being so close like this, was complete torture. He didn't know how he'd lasted this long, and he wasn't sure how much longer he could.

Ideally? The rest of her pregnancy. Realistically? Maybe two more days before he caved in some fashion. Jerking off in the shower hadn't helped slake his lust, no matter how many times he'd done it over the past week. One look from Hunny, one brush of her fingers against him, and he was harder than steel.

The little temptress had to know what she was doing to him. Didn't she?

"I was actually hoping I could whip you up something, Henry."
Hunny gave him another light kiss and then removed her hands from
his body, stepping away from him entirely.

Surprised that she hadn't tried for more, his eyes popped open as
he turned to face his mate. "Like what?"

Hunny tucked her hair behind an ear, sending him a coy smile. "I
want it to be a surprise. I have everything I need in the kitchen, and
I really want to treat you to a meal since you're always taking care of
me, but if you're not hungry, I can just make us dinner later."

Touched by her care, and slightly disappointed she hadn't been
trying to lure him with sex, Tank grabbed the nape of her neck and
pulled her back into the heat of his body. Leaning down, he captured
her lips in a tender kiss. It wasn't enough, and it hadn't been for days.

Eager for relief, he rubbed his erection against her lower belly,
hating how little control he had when it came to Hunny. How could
he resist her if he rubbed his dick all over her like a sex-starved fiend?
But he couldn't help it; the lack of sex between them was killing him,
even though he was the reason behind it.

Hunny pulled away abruptly, surprising him even more than before.
He knew she'd felt his erection, but instead of reaching for it like she
had several times over the last few days, she only patted his bare chest
lightly, her fingers running through the tuft of hair there.

Dropping her hand again, she turned back to the cabin, sending
a sweet smile over her shoulder. "I'll have it ready in the next ten
minutes, okay?"

Nodding, he watched her walk away, clad only in one of his long
T-shirts and a pair of house slippers with cartoon bears all over them.
Her smooth legs taunted him as she moved. Before she turned the
corner of the house, she lifted her arms up into a high stretch, causing
the shirt to slide up her thighs, exposing the underside of her naked,
fucking *beautiful* ass.

God, he just wanted to take a bite out of those pert cheeks, to spread
her apart like a feast and shove his co—

Mouth watering at the sight, Tank took several steps after her before
he realized what he'd done. Stopping, he dropped his head, releasing
an irritated grumble that vibrated in his throat.

Deciding to distract himself until it was time to head in, he got to
work debarking more logs, and soon enough, ten minutes had passed.
Moving to the hose hooked up to the side of the house, Tank turned

on the faucet, cleaning off his hands before making his way inside. Stepping into the entryway, he closed the door, kicking off his boots before wandering into the kitchen.

He looked up, jaw going slack as he stopped dead in his tracks.

"Are you ready for your meal, Henry?" Hunny purred, sending him a bewitching smile from where she sat on the counter of the kitchen island. She was completely naked, her breasts covered in a glistening, thick drizzle of honey that dripped down her chest, smearing over her belly and the lower lips of her cunt.

"I—" Tank cleared his throat, Hunny's arousal mixing with the honey coating her body combined into the most intoxicating scent he'd ever experienced in his life. His balls ached, his cock throbbing hard as he tried and failed to remember why going anywhere near his mate was a bad idea. His tongue was thick in his mouth as he swallowed hard, subconsciously taking a step toward her. "What—ah, fuck me. Darlin', what's this?"

Hunny looked down innocently at her naked body, and then back at him. Without wasting another second, she dipped her index finger into an open jar of honey sitting on the counter beside her. Popping her finger into her mouth, she sucked slowly, cheeks hollowing. She released a little moan of pleasure that sent a bolt of lust straight to his dick.

He took another involuntary step toward her, and then another, damn near drooling as she scooped up another glob of honey. Expecting her to suck on her fingers again, his eyes widened as she instead slid the honey all over the mating mark at the base of her neck.

Fuck, he wanted to lick her clean. No, he wanted to fuck her covered in that goddamn honey, and then suck every drop of it off her skin. His resolve weakened, lust clawing at his insides, demanding that he act. That he let go of the fears that had plagued him for a week straight now and just give in to his little rabbit.

"I think you've avoided me long enough, Henry," Hunny told him smoothly, sliding her thumb over her hard nipples. They shone in the overhead light, giving a soft, yellowish glow against her creamy skin. "But you can't avoid sex with me forever."

Startled at being called out on his behavior, he stumbled over a response. "I-I don't ... I'm not avoiding—"

"Yes, you are," she cut in confidently. Her eyes briefly flashed with hurt, and then she blinked, a steely determination replacing it. "I get that you're afraid you'll hurt me, but you won't. You didn't last time, either. And the only way to prove that is for you to screw my freakin' brains out."

"Baby," he rasped. "I want to. Believe me, I do." But he couldn't get the image of her bloody thighs out of his head, couldn't forget how terrified he'd been as he'd driven her to the clinic. What if something like that happened again because he couldn't keep his dick in his pants?

"Then let's do this," Hunny whispered, the sensual notes in her voice replaced with a vulnerability he couldn't ignore. "You've been reading those books. You heard Tabitha, too. You know everything's fine—"

"But I was the reason you bled! The reason you were so scared you'd lose our kits," he bit out roughly, the memory of it all rushing back in. Some of his desire ebbed, and with a shake of his head, Tank backed away from his mate. "I can't do that to you again. I won't."

"You didn't do anything to me, Henry. And I know you were as scared as I was, but you can't hold yourself back from me out of fear." When he didn't answer, she threw her hands up in exasperation, her breasts catching his attention as they swayed. "So you're just not going to have sex with me at all for the next several months? That's your grand plan?"

"I think that's best," he acknowledged, wanting to shove the words back down his throat when her breath hitched and the scent of her hurt overrode the delicious notes of sweet honey in the air.

"But we just didn't know what to expect, and now we do," Hunny added, a soft whine in her voice that pierced his heart. "I won't freak out next time, if it even happens again, I promise—"

"I can't." Tank ran a hand through his hair, looking away from her before he could give in. His resolve was hanging by a thread, and he was so close to snapping, to giving Hunny what she needed. Hell, what they *both* needed. But she was right; fear kept him in check when nothing else could.

Turning around, he hissed out a frustrated breath, beelining for the front door. He had no idea where he was going, but he needed out of this cabin before Hunny tore down his defenses completely.

"You can't just leave in the middle of this!" Hunny exclaimed behind him, her feet hitting the tile as she jumped down from the counter.

"Discussion's over, Hunny," he grated out through clenched teeth, reaching the front door. He bent down to pick up his boots, only to grunt in surprise when something smacked his ass. He shot up and spun around, grabbing Hunny's small hand before she could land another blow. Her breathing was shallow, her breasts heaving as she glared up at him. "Did you just *spank* me?"

"You're lucky I didn't clobber you upside the head just to knock some sense into you!" She tugged on her wrist, trying to break free of his hold, but it was no use. He wasn't letting her go. Not yet. "Ugh!" Hunny pushed at his chest with her free hand, letting out a little shriek of outrage when he didn't budge.

"Stop struggling, little rabbit. I've made up my mind on this."

Hunny rolled her eyes, tugging on her arm again. "When it involves both of us, you can't just decide things. We have to talk it out, you big oaf!" She looked up at him, uncertainty shining in her eyes. "Unless you don't care about me and my feelings?"

His head snapped back in shock. "Of *course*, I care. You think I don't want to bury myself inside you every second of the day? I do! I wake up hard as a rock, and I walk around with a goddamn erection all day long, aching for you." Tank growled, working overtime to catch her other hand before she could swat at him again. She wasn't hurting him at all, but he was worried she'd sprain her hand if she kept at it.

"Then you have got to stop fighting this—fighting me," Hunny pleaded. "I was scared too, Henry, but we can't just tuck tail and run from something like this."

He wanted to deny that he wasn't running away from anything. But he was, wasn't he? He'd been assured multiple times from various credible sources that spotting was normal, but he refused to believe it. It hadn't looked like spotting to him, but then again, he'd thought the worst as soon as he'd seen the smear of red on the bedsheets. "I won't be able to forgive myself if I hurt you," Tank uttered, his voice rough with emotion.

Hunny stopped struggling, her eyes softening on his. "Oh, Henry. You'd never hurt me."

"Not on purpose."

"*Not ever.* Just look at this entire week. If sex had caused any kind of genuine issue, I'd still be cramping and bleeding, and yes, I might have miscarried, but I've literally felt perfectly fine and nothing else has happened. No spotting, no cramping, nothing." As he opened his mouth, ready to argue, Hunny glared at him. "Before you say anything, I read one of the books you brought home *and* I called your mom this morning. Both are backing me up here. And you know that. I know you do; you even highlighted the same page I read about this."

Tank's throat tightened, his resolve weakening. She was right, and logically, he knew that. "You're everything to me, little rabbit. I just can't lose any of you."

Hunny wiggled out of his hold, and the sudden separation was jarring. Cupping his face, she whispered, "You won't. But you have to trust me to know my own body. If I feel like something is wrong, I'll tell you. Okay?"

Sighing roughly, he nodded. Of course, he trusted her. He just needed to trust in himself, too.

"Good." Before he could react, Hunny jumped at him, her breasts slamming against his chest as her arms wrapped around his neck. Sticky honey splattered against his torso as she lunged for his throat. He felt a sharp sting at his neck, his knees nearly buckling from the jolt of mixed pleasure and pain that infused his very being.

She bit him!

Lust roared back to life, and Tank grunted, his hands finding Hunny's bare ass and kneading the soft flesh as she wrapped her legs around his waist, grinding her honey-coated pussy over his abs. She dug her little fangs in deeper, sucking hard at his skin, and the last of his resolve crumbled into dust. He fell back against the front door, panting hard as his dick strained for freedom.

Fuck, he'd missed this. He'd missed it so much, and he wasn't even inside of her yet.

Pulling her teeth free of his neck, Hunny licked a trail up to his ear, nibbling on the lobe. "I need you, Henry. Please, please fill me with your cock." Her warm breath skated across his skin, and the muscles in his stomach knotted, sexual tension lining every inch of his body.

"Fucking hell," he groaned, his brain short-circuiting as all the blood rushed to his throbbing erection.

Hunny nipped his neck again and then peppered bites and kisses along his jaw, working her way to his mouth. She bit his lower lip almost frantically, splitting the skin. Just as blood pooled, she kissed him, her tongue pushing into his mouth. The taste of honey and his mate exploded across his senses, his two favorite things in the world blending together into the most alluring concoction.

All of his concerns, his excuses, and fears became nonexistent in an instant.

Spinning around, Tank pinned Hunny against the door, taking over their kiss. His tongue pumped into her mouth, dominance stamped into every lick, every caress. He swallowed her sensual moan, shivering as her hands ran through his hair, nails scraping at his scalp.

He needed her; he couldn't take the separation any longer.

Slow, he commanded himself silently. *Just go fucking slow!*

Mindlessly, he fumbled with the button on his jeans, accidentally popping it off in his haste to remove the obstacle. He ripped his zipper next, shoving his pants down until his cock popped free, jutting out against her entrance. The juices from her cunt slipped over his erection, and a growl, more beast than man, poured from his throat.

"Hurry, Henry," his little rabbit begged, fingers tightening in his hair as she kissed him again, parting her lips in invitation. Tank collared her throat, nipping her lip roughly when she tried to pull his mouth back to hers.

"I need to prepare you—"

Hunny shook her head, rolling her hips and teasing his cockhead. "I just need you." Shimmying her hips, she lowered herself down onto his cock, taking one thick inch, and then another. "Oh God," Hunny whimpered, sinking in another inch. "I missed this, Henry. Didn't you miss this?"

Fuck yeah, he missed this. Tank grit his teeth, his fingers tightening ever so slightly on her throat as he fought to keep himself in check. This was slow—this was fine. They'd just take it a little bit at a time—

Hunny slammed herself down onto his length, releasing a sharp cry of bliss as he bottomed out inside her. Slick, tight warmth surrounded him, her inner walls gripping him lovingly. Arms banding around her, Tank dropped his head into the crook of her neck, breathing heavily as he fought to keep from moving. He'd needed this so much, craved this type of intimacy between them for what seemed like forever.

Had it been only a week?

"See, Henry?" Hunny moaned, her pussy spasming, taking him impossibly deeper. Tank grunted, his legs trembling as pleasure coursed through him. "Everything's good, my big bear. Everything's—" Hunny rolled her hips, crying out as he gave a shallow thrust, his hips meeting hers. "So good. Oh, Henry. It's so good."

His little mate moaned again, whispering for more, and Tank couldn't deny her a second longer.

Snapping his hips, he filled her up, over and over, each pump punctuated by the door creaking ominously behind her. Hunny writhed on his length, her soft cries spurring him on until he lost all reason, pistoning inside her as he lapped at the honey coating her mating mark, sucking hard on the skin.

Each time he tried to slow down, to pull out, Hunny clawed at his back, driving him right back to the edge until he pounded into her pussy with reckless abandon. He didn't stop when she spasmed around his cock, her orgasm drenching him. He fucked her through it, only moving from the door when he suddenly realized it might hurt her back.

Dropping onto the couch with Hunny seated in his lap, he smacked her ass firmly, urging her to ride him. His heart pounded fiercely in his chest, his breaths becoming ragged. She leaned forward until they were skin against skin. Nothing separated them. And then she was kissing him sweetly as she began riding him nice and slow.

"I love you," Hunny murmured.

"I love you, Hunny, so damned much." Tank held onto her hard, his palms sliding up and down her back, needing to touch her anywhere he could. This was perfect. He didn't give a damn that they were covered in honey, or that he'd probably spend half an hour scrubbing them both clean later.

They were going to be alright; *all* of them. He had to believe that.

Thirty Four

"I'm so happy you could make it out here!" Hunny exclaimed, taking Nessa's hand. The human's car was parked in Tank's driveway, a pickup truck behind it containing either Marcus or Dante, though Hunny had no idea who was who.

Waving at one of the twins as he backed out of the driveway and headed down the road, she pulled Nessa from the front porch and into the cabin, ecstatic the human had taken the long trip up here from town. She hadn't seen her friend in over a week, and with the threat of Jason and his pack looming still, no one was allowed away from bear territory for the next few weeks.

Even if Murphy hadn't decreed they were on lockdown, she highly doubted Tank would have been okay with her gallivanting into town to chat when Nessa could just drive out here. It made the most sense, and since Nessa had been fine about being escorted from the start of their territory to the cabin, it was honestly a relief.

She'd had to come up with a ridiculous reason for the escort to placate Nessa's curiosity, but now the human was convinced Murphy was some kind of eccentric billionaire who had interesting security measures in place.

"Yeah, of course. I've heard a lot of wild stories about these woods, so I was honestly dying to come visit." Nessa kicked off her shoes at the front entrance, looking around the small living room as she took off her jacket. "This place is awesome. Tank's, I take it?"

"Mine now," Hunny joked, closing the front door. She grabbed Nessa's jacket and purse from her, surprised by the heavy weight of the bag. Maybe Nessa was one of those humans that fit her life into her handbag. Smiling to herself, she placed both items on a coat rack mounted on the wall.

"Where is your man, anyway? Lurking silently nearby?" Nessa looked around again, but Hunny had the distinct impression it wasn't *Tank* she was searching for.

Deciding to play on a hunch, she pointed to the left. "He's with Murphy in the kitchen."

Nessa's eyes widened, the sound of her heart pounding loud in Hunny's ears as she whipped her head in that direction. "Oh?"

"I'm kidding." Hunny snorted. "Murphy's not here. And Tank's taking a quick shower upstairs." He'd been working on the spare room all morning, and since he was adamant about spending a little bit of time with her and Nessa before Jasper showed up to help him work, she'd insisted he clean up beforehand.

"Ah." Nessa nodded, pursing her lips and looking somewhat disappointed.

"Were you hoping Murphy would be here?" Hunny asked hesitantly. When Nessa narrowed her eyes on the rabbit shifter, she quickly added, "I heard you two got off to an interesting start."

"Ha! That's a hell of a way to phrase it." Nessa followed Hunny into the kitchen, dropping into a kitchen chair with a huff. "I've honestly never been so irritated by someone in my life."

"I'm thinking the Sinclair men have that effect on people," Hunny commented dryly, taking her own seat across from the human. "Irritating dicks, the lot of them."

"Seriously? Gross." Nessa rolled her eyes dramatically and then smirked, drumming her fingers on top of the table. "And to answer your question; no. I wasn't hoping Murphy would be here." She slammed her mouth shut, running her tongue over her teeth like she wanted to say something but had changed her mind.

Hunny cocked her head to the side. "What is it? You can tell me, especially while Henry is in the shower." Her big bear was a nosy male, but he should be too far away to overhear them, and the spray from the showerhead should drown out their voices anyway.

Nessa sighed in agitation, propping her elbows onto the table and leaning forward. "I just ... I don't like Tank's brother, okay?"

Hunny blinked, wondering just how true that was. "Okay."

"It's just—I don't know. I couldn't wait for him to leave after we met, but now I keep thinking about him, which is weird. It's weird, right? I wake up every morning and he's the first thought on my mind. And I swear I can ..." Nessa huffed, looking around as if trying to find someone eavesdropping. She glanced back at Hunny and whispered, "I can *smell* him."

Hunny stiffened, eyes going as wide as saucers. "You smell him?"

Nessa ran a hand through her brightly colored hair. "Yeah. Does that sound weird? I just can't get it out of my head. I feel like I'm walking around all the time with his cologne shoved up my nose."

How could that possibly be? The only explanation Hunny could even dream up was that Murphy had somehow bonded to Nessa, like Tank had bonded to her when they'd mated. He'd told her that when bear shifters mated, their scent attached to their mate. But how could that have happened so quickly? When they hadn't even touched?

"That's so interesting," Hunny replied faintly, unsure of how she should approach the subject.

Nessa groaned, covering her face with her hands. "I knew you'd think I was crazy."

"No, I just ... I didn't expect you to say something like that." She took a cursory sniff of the air, wondering if she'd be able to scent it as well. Nope. Nothing other than Nessa's own perfume and the chemicals from the products she'd used recently. "Did you and Murphy touch at all? Like a handshake, a hug? Maybe he got mouthy and you swatted his arm."

Nessa peeked at her from between her fingers, puzzled, before dropping her hands. "No, there was definitely no touching."

"Are you sure? It could have been just a brief—"

"No," Nessa cut in hotly, pursing her lips.

Hunny held up her hands in surrender. "Alright, I'm sorry for pressing the issue."

Nessa leaned back in her chair, worrying her lower lip. "No, *I'm* sorry. It was rude to cut you off like that."

"You have nothing to apologize for," Hunny assured her.

"I used to be in an abusive relationship," Nessa blurted out suddenly. Her gaze skittered over Hunny's head and to the wall behind her. "I-I don't really want to talk about it, but, um, I haven't let another man touch me at all since ... Yeah, I just haven't, so I-I would know if one did. That's what I meant before."

Hunny's heart clenched at the admission, even though she'd suspected something similar. "Thank you for telling me that." Not wanting to leave her friend hanging, she added, "That guy Murphy and Tank met with at your shop? Jason?"

Nessa's brow furrowed. "Yeah, that guy was a creep."

Hunny winced. "That creep is my ex."

"What!" Nessa exclaimed, gasping audibly. "That's the father of your babies? Oh no, that's horrible!"

"I know." Hunny slid her hand over her belly, rubbing it soothingly. "That's why you needed an escort out to the cabin."

"I thought you said Murphy was just some crazy billionaire."

"Well, yes," Hunny added hastily. "But he's also trying to protect me. There's been a bit of drama with Jason lately, and so the guys are being extra cautious on who comes and goes."

"Oh wow, that's really scary. I'm glad to see it's to help protect you. Have you thought about getting a restraining order against Jason?"

Hunny shook her head. "No, it wouldn't do me any good."

"I definitely understand that." Nessa stared at the rabbit shifter with a mixture of astonishment and concern, each emotion ping-ponging across her face, before she eventually asked, "What on Earth did you ever see in him?"

She scrunched her nose in distaste. "I have no idea, honestly." Looking back on it now, a mating bond was the only true allure, and thankfully, Jason had ended that. It all felt like a bad memory. "Now that I have Henry, I just can't believe what an idiot I was before. I mean, Jason? He's so gross."

"I'll second that," Tank grumbled, stepping quietly into the kitchen. Surprised, Nessa jerked in her seat, the scent of her fear filling the kitchen. Tank pretended not to notice, walking over to Hunny and dropping a tender kiss onto the crown of her head. "I miss anything fun?"

Hunny smiled coyly, looking up at her mate and giving Nessa a chance to collect herself. "Just girl talk."

Tank grunted, giving a brisk nod in Nessa's direction. "Afternoon Yapper Two."

Nessa arched her brow. "Yapper Two?"

Hunny raised her hand. "Yapper One present and accounted for."

Nessa burst into laughter, and the scent of her unease faded just like that. Tank draped his arms over Hunny's shoulders, hugging her from behind. "I was just going to make some lunch. Jasper won't be here for another hour—"

A hard knock sounded on the front door.

Hunny tilted her head to the side, staring toward the living room in confusion. "I guess he's here early."

"Guess so, the little fucker." Tank kissed Hunny again before making his way out of the kitchen.

Nessa looked around the room. "So how about a house tour?"

Tank huffed as he opened the door, brows rising when he spotted Dante on his porch, a scowl on the tracker's face. It was early in the afternoon, but the sun had hidden behind clouds all damned day, casting the world in grayish hue.

"What are you doing here?" Tank looked around. Was Jasper not with him? That was odd; no one but family ever visited him. "Everything alright?"

Dante rolled his eyes, his shoulders stiff with a tension that Tank couldn't help but notice. "No, man." Dante shook his head, a sorrowful light flashing in his eyes before it disappeared altogether. "I was hoping we could talk about the Moon Rose pack. There's something I think you should know. Can I come in?"

Instantly, Tank was on high alert. He stepped out onto the porch, forcing Dante to back up a few steps as he closed the door behind him, creating a barricade between the females inside and the male.

Murphy, Tank called out to his brother. *Dante's here. Something doesn't feel right.*

"Hunny's wanting some girl time with her human friend," Tank commented dryly to the male in front of him, not wanting it obvious that he'd reached out to his brother. "Probably best we stay out here."

There was a stirring in his mind, a brief fluttering of the Alpha's consciousness before Murphy spoke. *What do you mean? You want me to reach out to him?*

No.

Murphy's sigh echoed in Tank's head. *Okay. Did he say why he's visiting?* he asked, an agitated note in his voice. The Alpha knew his mate was with Tank and likely didn't want an unmated male near her, despite his best efforts to not care.

Dante nodded quickly, his eyes not quite meeting Tank's. "Yeah, this is fine."

He wants to talk about the Moon Rose pack, but why come to me and not you? I don't like it. Tank discreetly looked around the clearing surrounding his house, inhaling to catch any stray scents. There was nothing other than Nessa's on the breeze. He grimaced, his unease growing. That was wrong too, wasn't it? *Just get here, Murph. Don't come alone.*

Tank inhaled again, hit with another stirring of wrongness. What the hell was it?

Dante ran a shaky hand through his hair. "Everything that's happening, I just want you to know; nothing was personal, man. You haven't deserved any of this."

Tank stiffened, his bear pushing to the forefront, urging him to shift. "What are you saying?" His eyes widened as realization struck.

Dante's scent was missing.

Almost like the male could sense the direction Tank's mind had wandered to, Dante lifted his head, sending him a pleading look. "I'm so sorry, Tank. There isn't another way. They're going to kill her if I don't cooperate."

"Kill who?"

Dante lunged at Tank, shifting into his grizzly counterpart as their bodies connected, launching Tank backward. His back slammed into the porch as his own shift began, the wood creaking as his increasing weight caused a strain on the boards. His skin rippled and fell away, replaced by thick brown fur. His body elongated simultaneously, growing wider and taller as his own grizzly rose.

Before Dante could sink his claws into Tank's gut, Tank roared, slapping him in the head with a mighty paw. His claws scored a hit on Dante's snout, and the male reared back onto his hind legs with a dull groan of pain. Tank sent a brief, hurried warning to Murphy as he threw himself at the other male, sending them both careening off the porch.

He needed to get Dante away from Hunny and Nessa, needed to protect his mate and their kits from danger. Blood scented on the air as he opened his maw wide and bit down on Dante's shoulder, thrashing his head in an attempt to sever the muscles connecting his opponent's arm. Hot, metallic liquid exploded on his tongue.

He expected the other bear to fight back, to swipe at him in retaliation. But Dante did neither, taking the brunt of Tank's attack in stride. Why wasn't he defending himself? He'd attacked Tank, but now he refused to fight back when his life was in danger? It didn't make sense. What was his end game?

A howl sounded off in the distance from somewhere behind Tank, but it was the other, much closer canine growl that had him twisting around, giving Dante his back instead of this new threat. His eyes locked onto four massive wolves now standing between him and the cabin, blocking him from his mate.

Just beyond the wolves, Jason stood proudly, a smug, sinister grin on his face. "For Hunny's sake, my wolves will make your death quick."

Fear twisted his gut into a tangle of knots, and his heart jumped into his throat. He was outnumbered, and his mate was all but defenseless.

Tank roared in fury right as the first wolf launched itself at him.

Thirty Five

H unny froze at the base of the stairs, startled by the animalistic roar of rage outside. It shook the walls, and the familiarity of it made her heart clench. Was that Tank? What had happened?

She dropped her death grip on the railing, taking a worried step toward the front door. The sound of wolves howling split the air, slightly muffled by the walls of the cabin. Her heart leapt to her throat.

Wolves?

Her mouth dried, panic clawing at her throat as icy tendrils of fear slid down her spine. Her hand flew to her mouth, covering a strangled whimper. *Oh, God!* They were being attacked, and Tank had stepped outside into the thick of it, completely unaware of the danger lurking just beyond the walls of their cabin.

Who'd even knocked on their door? It must have been someone Tank knew, someone he trusted, otherwise he never would have gone out there. And now he was at the mercy of monsters.

Her mate needed her!

"What the hell was that?" Nessa asked, her voice taking on a higher pitch than usual. Head snapping to the front door, the human took a step closer to Hunny until they were both standing side by side, staring nervously ahead. "Did you hear that roar? And the howling? Why did it sound so close?"

Hunny moved around the couch, on autopilot as she raced toward the front door. "I-I have to go out there. Henry's outside—"

Nessa grabbed her arm, yanking her backward. Hunny collided into the other woman, who kept a firm hold on her. "Are you out of your mind? No, I'm not letting you rush out into some kind of crazy animal fight. I'm sure Tank's fine." Nessa's heart beat as wildly as Hunny's as another roar shook the cabin, followed by a wolf's sharp yelp of pain. "Perfectly fine," she added tightly.

"You don't understand. He's *not* fine. I-I need my phone!" Hunny exclaimed, stumbling over her words as she dragged Nessa along with her toward the kitchen. Had she left it on the dining room table? "I have to call Murphy." He'd know what to do.

God, she wished they'd bonded her to the bear clan a week ago. It involved a blood exchange between both herself and Murphy, but Tank had been so distraught over everything, she hadn't wanted to bring up another instance where she'd end up bleeding. And because of that, her mind wasn't linked to Murphy's; she couldn't contact him through anything other than human means.

What if it was too late? What if, in her attempt to spare her mate's feelings, she'd doomed him? Doomed them both? The dark thought was too much to take.

"What do you think Murphy is going to do about *wolves* outside? What is he, some kind of animal whisperer?" Nessa asked incredulously, as they reached the doorway to the kitchen.

Something struck the cabin with a loud bang, and a wolf growled from somewhere behind them. Both women flinched, startled by how close it sounded. It was so close, like it was prowling the porch, searching for a way to come inside. Soon after, they heard a heavy thud, like something had slammed into the ground.

"O-Okay, yeah, maybe we call Murphy," Nessa agreed immediately. "And like a-a forest ranger, or animal control—"

The front door flew open with a loud smack as it hit the wall, nearly coming off its hinges.

Letting out a yelp of surprise, Hunny spun around, hoping like hell it was Tank rushing into the cabin. Nessa followed her movement, and the stench of the other woman's sudden fear mixed with her own as they both spotted the male.

It wasn't Tank standing in the doorway, but Jason, wearing a cocky smirk on his face. More animalistic noises sounded outside, though they seemed further away than they had only seconds before.

"Ah, my darling mate," Jason crooned, stepping confidently into the house. The door slammed shut behind him, and he slid the deadbolt into place, the sound jarring as silence momentarily descended on them.

"You shouldn't be here," Hunny uttered nervously, casting a quick glance around for a weapon. A deterrent. Anything. Nothing was within range, and she didn't know what she'd use against the shifter anyway. A cushion from the couch? Nessa's heavy ass purse? Maybe she could swing it around and use it like a flail.

Nessa stiffened, sending a sidelong glance to Hunny. Jason took the rabbit shifter in, ignoring the human altogether, as if she were insignificant. "Is that any way to greet the father of your pups?"

Hunny heard Nessa mumble 'pups' questioningly under her breath. Steeling her spine, Hunny shouted, "Get out of here, Jason! You are not welcome."

The smirk on his face dropped. Eyes narrowing, he took a menacing step forward.

"Quiet," he hissed, and she felt waves of his dominance crash into her. Her legs trembled, knees nearly buckling under the pressure of his power. "You're going to come with me, Hunny, and we'll discuss our future together. Now."

"No!" Hunny cried, her mind in denial even as she took a step forward, unable to evade his command. She took another step, moving closer. Before she could make any true distance, though, Nessa grabbed her arm again, tugging her backward.

"She told you no, asshole, now back the *fuck* off!" Nessa yelled, her voice wavering as she pushed Hunny behind her. She stood tall, a protective barrier between them both. Shocked, Hunny could only gape at her friend. Why hadn't she felt the effects of Jason's dominance? Even though it had been directed at Hunny, Nessa was human. She should have been cowering in fear, at the very least.

His eyes lit up with surprise, and the control he'd held over Hunny dissolved instantly as he glared at the human. A moment later, hatred replaced his features. Nessa didn't flinch, but Hunny heard her heart kick up into a frantic rhythm, and she saw a slight tremble run through her body.

Hunny dragged in a shuddering breath, taking in the scent of Nessa's growing fear and determination at the same time the wolf did. He cocked his head to the side, giving Nessa a cursory glance up and down. "You're brave for a human. Rebellious, too, but I can beat that out of you in time. Nessa, wasn't it?"

"I said it once, and I'll say it again!" Nessa spat. "Fuck off! Tank is going to kick your ass into next week for coming here—" Jason snarled, his eyes flashing an icy, glowing blue. Nessa gasped, backing up so quickly she bumped into Hunny. "What the ... what was that? What are you?" she asked faintly.

"Nessa, get back," Hunny warned, trying to force the human behind her. She didn't think Jason would hurt her while she was pregnant with what he assumed were pups, but a human? He'd already threatened to beat her into submission. What would he do if she defiantly stood between him and what he wanted?

Something heavy slammed against the front door before landing on the porch with a heavy thud. A pained whimper sounded, and for the briefest second , she looked away from Jason and toward the nearby window, desperate to see if it was Tank who'd made the wounded noise.

There was a flash of movement from the front door. Jason lunged forward, hands outstretched. Reflexes much faster than a human's, he grabbed Nessa before she even had a chance to react, shoving her roughly out of his way. With a startled scream, she flew into the small living room, hitting the side of the couch and tumbling over it. Hunny heard Nessa's head hit the coffee table with a sickening crack as she disappeared from view.

Smirking once more, Jason prowled toward Hunny, malevolent energy dogging each step. She stumbled backward to evade him as he herded her into the kitchen. "Now, where were we?"

"Why are you doing this? Just leave, please!" Hunny pleaded, her pretense of bravery fleeing with Nessa. "No one killed Natasha, Jason! Whoever left her body here was setting the bears up!"

He kept moving toward her, a predatory gleam shining in his eyes as she moved around the kitchen island, desperate to keep as much distance between them as possible. She didn't know if she could outrun him, but if she could stall him, it would give Tank time.

Please, please come back, she wailed in her mind.

"I know all of that, Hunny. Are you really so dense? I killed Natasha for you. For *us*."

Hunny's heart stilled, all of Tank's words rushing back at her about just how crazy and depraved Jason was. She'd started to realize it on her own after the clinic, but this ... this was complete madness. Not to mention the pain he had willingly put himself through.

To kill his own mate ... Who could do such a thing? Who would risk possibly killing themselves in the process? Only a psychopath.

"Why would you do that? You rejected me, Jason. You chose her!" Hunny shook her head in denial, sidestepping further around the island, making sure she kept it firmly between the two of them. He followed her until they were caught in an awkward, twisted dance; her running backward and him chasing after, tauntingly, like a cat stalking a mouse.

"I warned her to leave you alone, Hunny. Even though I cast you aside, I didn't relish the thought of the mother of my pups coming to harm. But Natasha couldn't obey. She hated the fact that you were carrying my heirs. That you would always hold some advantage over her. So she came back here to kill you. I couldn't let that happen."

Bile rose in her throat. "You knew she was here that day in the woods. That wolf we saw wasn't the only one ..."

"*That wolf* was monitoring Natasha for me, to ensure she did what she was told. But she didn't. She came after you," Jason scoffed, slamming his fists down so hard onto the kitchen island, the countertop cracked. "I wanted Natasha because she was dominant; strong-willed. But ever since you left me, I've come to realize just how beneficial it would be to rule with a submissive by my side." His eyes locked onto hers, staring at her in such a disturbed manner she flinched away from it. "You are who I need."

"I'm mated to Henry," Hunny answered with a calmness she didn't feel. She wanted to scream at Jason that she would *never* be his again, but he was clearly deranged, and she was afraid of setting him off. What would he do if provoked?

"If I can kill my own mate, I can kill yours just as easily," Jason said with an abrupt laugh. "In fact, my wolves are taking care of him as we speak."

Instinctively, her head started to turn toward the doorway, to the last place she'd seen her mate.

Henry—

She only saw the briefest tensing of Jason's muscles out of the corner of her eye before he launched himself over the kitchen island, heading straight for her. Hunny shrieked in terror, turning toward the doorway leading into the living room with a burst of speed rabbit shifters were known for. She reached for the deadbolt, her fingers brushing against the cool metal.

Jason's hand wrapped in the hair at the back of her head, a hard arm banding around her chest as he yanked her back and into his arms, pulling her away from the door. "Did you know that Angela, one wolf I've gone through great pains to teach obedience, recently discovered her true mate was right here within this very territory?" Jason whispered harshly into her ear, his hot breath blowing free strands of hair into the side of her face.

When she didn't respond, his grip tightened in her hair and he pulled it roughly. "Answer me," he hissed.

"I-I didn't know," Hunny whimpered, her mind reeling. Jason was too close, his presence a sinister threat. Her mind screamed at her to get away. To protect her kits. To erase his presence from this cabin. From her home. From her life. And the only person who could do that was Tank, but he wasn't even here.

What was more terrifying than even Jason himself was the knowledge that her mate would be here with her if he could. He'd never let Jason near her, never let him get close enough to breathe her air, let alone touch her. But now, this maniac was all over her.

God, please let Henry be okay.

Unfortunately, the sounds of fighting outside had begun to die down, and he still hadn't charged inside. Where could he be? Her heart twisted, and it hurt to breathe, but she forced herself to relax. If he were dead, she'd feel the mating bond sever. She'd know he was gone, so she needed to hold on. He was alive. She just had to just buy enough time until he got back here to her.

Jason turned them away from the living room and back toward the kitchen, forcing her to walk ahead until he had her pinned against the farthest wall from escape, covering her back with his rigid body.

"I missed you, Hunny," Jason crooned, rubbing his groin against her ass.

She nearly gagged, bile rising in her throat. Every instinct demanded she fight, that she raise hell to get him off of her. But what if he hit her? What if he hurt her babies? For that reason alone, she remained still, frozen in place by terror and the unknown.

Desperate to keep his mind focused on anything but her body, Hunny asked the first thing she could think of. "Who's Angela's mate?"

"That bear traitor." Jason licked the side of her face, groaning deeply. "Imagine Dante's surprise when he intercepted a handful of wolves hunting down Natasha right on these very lands, and then found out that one of them was his mate. Poor bastard didn't know what to do, and suddenly, I saw the future for us all mapped out."

Hunny swallowed thickly, ignoring the way her voice shook as she asked, "You did?"

"Yes," he breathed, rubbing his cheek against the side of her head, like he was determined to remove Tank's scent and replace it with his own. "I told him I'd rape, torture, and kill Angela if he didn't do everything I demanded." Jason spoke nonchalantly, as if rape and murder were normal activities he pursued. It made Hunny even more nauseous.

"He folded easily, especially after I promised I wouldn't hurt you. Then I forced him to keep Natasha in his home until the time was right to kill her. A few days later, I reached out to that pathetic excuse of an Alpha, claiming my mate was here. Demanding a meeting. I let them play right into my hands, but I have to admit, Hunny, I was furious to see that you'd mated someone else. And so soon, too! Naughty girl. You let some filthy fucking bear put his hands on you, *his dick inside you*," he grated out angrily.

Jason spun her around so fast the back of her head smacked into the wall. She grunted in pain, wheezing when he pushed his body flush against hers. No care or consideration of the pressure he applied to her stomach. Her eyes stung with tears, and she fought back the urge to sob. Terror consumed her at the thought of what he might do to her and her babies.

Jason molded himself to her, grabbing her face in one large hand and squeezing until she cried out in pain. "When we get home, I'll replace that disgusting mating mark with the right one and get this rancid scent off you. Then I'll make sure the only dick you remember is mine."

Hunny slapped him hard across the face, the action so sudden, so surprising, she hadn't even realized what she'd done until she felt the stinging burn of her palm. Jason dropped his hold on her, taking a startled step back. "Did you just hit me, you ungrateful slut?" he snapped, his eyes wild.

A loud bang exploded through the room, and Jason suddenly bellowed in pain, bending at the waist and clutching his thigh. Not wasting the opportunity, she rushed away from him and toward the exit, desperate to escape.

There, standing frighteningly still just inside the kitchen, a pistol raised in her hand and pointed right at Jason, was Nessa. Her forehead was bleeding, but if she was in pain, she didn't show it, keeping her eyes trained on Jason. "I believe I told you to fuck off." She jerked her chin to the side. "Hunny, get behind me."

"Absolutely." Relief coursing through her, Hunny did just that, ignoring the acrid scent of gunpowder burning her nose. "When did you learn to shoot a gun?" she murmured, her voice shaking.

"When I was twelve. I'll tell you about it later."

"You won't get a later," Jason snarled, his eyes glowing blue once more. "I'm going to gut you like a fucking fish—"

Nessa shot him again, the bullet sinking into his shoulder. "I wouldn't really threaten the person holding the gun, you arrogant prick."

Jason hunched over and groaned, and for the briefest second, Hunny thought it was in pain. But then she heard it; the sickening sound of bones popping; breaking and snapping as they reformed.

"Shoot him again!" Hunny exclaimed, terror unmistakable in her voice. "He's a fucking werewolf! Shoot him before he shifts!"

Nessa gasped, her bravado fleeing in an instant. "Are you out of your fucking mind, Hunny? Werewolves don't ... don't exist." She trailed off, backing up quickly as Jason's clothing exploded into tiny chunks of fabric, fur covering his skin entirely as he completed his change. "Oh, holy shit—"

Jason growled.

Nessa took aim again, though she was shaking like a leaf as she fired, missing him as he dodged with an inhuman speed. He rushed her as she fired again, tackling into her with his full weight. The gun left her hand, sliding across the floor. Hunny tried to catch the woman, but Jason rolled his prey away from her, swiping his claws at Nessa with one fierce motion.

Nessa cried out in pain, the scent of her blood filling the air as her skin tore from her shoulder all the way down to her chest. The human went limp, her eyes fluttering closed. Enraged, Hunny screamed, drawing Jason's attention before he could attack her friend again.

"You want me, you piece of shit?" Hunny yelled, her voice hoarse with terror and a blaze of fierce anger. She looked frantically around at the ground. Where the hell was the gun?! "Then come get me!"

Jason huffed at her antics before looking down at Nessa in contemplation. Hunny could tell the instant he decided to kill her friend; it was in the way his muscles bunched beneath his fur, his maw opening wide to reveal sharp, lethal teeth.

The cabin floor rumbled beneath her feet a second before a bear—*Tank*—roared. And then the entire front of the cabin split apart, taking the front door with it. Chunks of wood flew in every direction as her big bear, and several more of equal size, filled what remained of the front entrance.

Thirty Six

A few minutes earlier ...

S tanding on his hind legs, Tank swatted at the massive wolf that lunged at him, hitting it on the side of the neck. Claws sliced through fur and flesh, the scent of blood permeating the air. The wolf yelped, flying to the right before it hit the ground, paws scrambling for purchase.

As the wolf pushed slowly to its feet, another five crept out of the woods, their heavy breathing alerting him to their presence instantly. Nine wolves and a traitor surrounded him. Fuck! This wasn't good. Not good at all. Several howls rent the air mockingly. They had him dead to rights, and they knew it.

Tank cast a furious look around, eyes snapping onto the newly injured wolf. The strike he'd made, although painful, wouldn't put a shifted wolf down for long. He'd need to rip out its throat, at the bare minimum, to kill it. With the other wolves closing in on him, and Dante standing too close for comfort, Tank didn't have the luxury of completing the kill.

Time was of the essence. Hunny, their kits, and Murphy's mate were relying on him for protection, and he was failing them. Anxiety and fear tore through him, the force of it so severe, so powerful, it was almost impossible to beat back. But he had to focus.

Murphy and the others were on their way. He knew that. He had to buy time. But Tank already felt doomed to fail. He wasn't sure if he could take on so many adversaries alone and survive. But he had to try.

For Hunny, he would. He'd do anything.

Jason walked casually up the stairs to the porch, reaching for the front door. Fury overrode everything else, and Tank unleashed a primal roar, warning him away. Warning Hunny of the danger. Although, where could she go? How could she defend herself against an onslaught like this with only a human at her side?

Ignoring him, Jason turned the knob, shoving the door open. The wolf looked toward the kitchen and smiled. "Ah, my darling mate."

Jason stepped into the house, closing the door behind him.

Whatever tether of control Tank had been clinging to snapped. Dropping onto all fours, he rushed the wolves blocking him from Hunny, slamming into one with a roar so loud it made his throat burn. He ignored the pain, relishing in the wolf's yelp of surprise as he trampled it.

A wolf sprang at him, launching onto his back. It bit down, catching mostly fur in its hasty attack. The wolf slid off, landing on the ground as another one jumped in, replacing the first. This time, its fangs sank into the fat on Tank's back as the wolf mounted him, another quickly joining in. Fire blazed through him as his skin split, warm blood drenching his thick fur.

Tank didn't acknowledge the pain, instead lunging at another adversary that had come too close. Maw opened wide, he bit into a front leg, yanking his head back and forth until he heard a pop. The wolf yelped in pain, struggling frantically to break free. Tank didn't let it go, instead swiping at the underside of its neck with his claw. He hit at it repeatedly until his claws tore through muscle, severing the wolf's spine. The creature went limp, and he dropped the dead shifter to the ground.

Another sharp bite pierced his back and he grunted. Shaking himself, he attempted to dislodge the two wolves tearing into him. It wasn't enough, though.

More wolves attacked Tank in unison, claws and fangs ripping into him. He roared in pain, completely overwhelmed. Desperate to escape the onslaught, he bit one wolf, blood filling his mouth. He yanked his head to the side, flinging the fucker off him. Another one replaced it instantly, and resignation filled him.

He couldn't fight them all off. Not alone.

He could only pray that he killed enough before he was taken out. That he could make it easier for Murphy and the others to kill Jason and save Hunny. His family would look out for her after his death. Would keep her and their children safe and help her raise all three of them.

God-*fucking*-dammit. That should have been Tank's job. His honor and his privilege to watch their kits grow, to become the family Hunny had always deserved. That he'd always wanted. But now, he was going to die because of some delusional fucknut.

Tank's throat thickened with emotion as he struggled to swallow down his anguish. Hunny would survive his death. She was strong and resilient. They'd only been mated for a short while; if anyone could survive the mating bond snapping, it was her. But the pain ... The loss ...

Fuck. He wished he'd had more time with her. More time to love her in all the ways she deserved. He'd give anything for another day. Another hour. Another second.

The ground rumbled as Dante entered the fray, charging right at Tank. He didn't have time to react, instead bracing himself for the inevitable assault, for his untimely end. Dante swiped at Tank with a mighty paw.

But the blow never struck him.

One wolf latching onto Tank whimpered in surprise, its heavy body disappearing off his back as it hit the ground with a hard thud. Dante struck again, and another wolf clinging to Tank's back let go, leaping away from the bears and out of danger. The others followed suit, the lack of their oppressive weight pinning him down filling him with a bittersweet sense of hope.

Baffled, Tank looked at Dante in confusion. Why had that asshat helped him? Did he think this meant they were allies? It didn't. He'd gut the male if given the chance. But if the traitor wanted to help him out of guilt, Tank wouldn't turn him away.

Despite how much fury burned in his chest for this traitor, the male had saved his life. Regardless, Tank released a low growl, just to let the piece of shit know they weren't on good terms. Once this was over, he planned on settling the score between them.

Dante huffed, turning toward a wolf separated slightly from the others. It was smaller than the rest, one of the few that hadn't attacked yet. A cursory sniff in that direction told Tank it was Angela.

Dante growled in her direction. Stiffening, Angela whined once in protest, staring at the bear with a startling intensity. After a moment, she turned and fled, disappearing from sight. Before Tank could make any sense of it, Dante hurled himself at one of the injured wolves.

Bleeding profusely from several wounds, Tank turned back toward his cabin, coming face to face with an uninjured wolf. Ben's scent filled Tank's nostrils, and he growled deeply. More growls came from behind him, all familiar, and all as equally furious as Tank. He felt a jolt course through his veins.

Reinforcements had arrived. And not a moment too soon. Relief, so sweet it was nearly nauseating, filled him as he caught Murphy's scent. And then Jasper's. Marcus and Colter were there, too. He was sure there were more, but nothing else registered.

Gunshots echoed through the air, and Tank's attention snapped to the cabin. Who brought a goddamn gun? Nessa?

As if he'd reached the same conclusion, Murphy charged past Tank, slamming into Ben. Head down, he got under the wolf before throwing his head and shoulders back, launching their enemy into the air. As Ben hit the ground, Jasper and Colter ripped into him, tearing him to shreds in a matter of seconds.

Good.

Tank raced after Murphy as the Alpha bulldozed his way onto the porch. He rammed into the front door, but the solid wood held, even against his impressive size. Jasper and Colter followed them, and the porch groaned underneath their combined weight.

This close, it was impossible to not smell blood coming from within the house.

Fresh human blood. Hunny screamed, her voice slightly muffled. "You want me, you piece of shit? Then come get me!"

Murphy and Tank roared in unison, launching their full weight at the door again. This time, it and a large portion of the wall exploded inward, debris flying in every direction.

The living room came into view.

Tank spotted Hunny across the room, eyes shining with angry tears, but unharmed. The fear, the panic that had held a death grip on his heart, his very soul—it all melted away. They were okay. They were going to make it out of this.

Maybe Tank's first instinct should have been to look for the threat to his mate, but he didn't. He thundered into the room instead, the tips of his claws sinking into the hardwood floor for purchase as he raced toward the only person who mattered in that moment.

He stopped right in front of Hunny, looking her over as he took a ragged breath; the first real one since the Moon Rose pack had attacked.

She's really okay, he thought, ignoring the shudder that swept through him.

Murphy snarled, and Tank turned on a dime, placing himself protectively in front of his mate. Hunny gasped, but he didn't look to see what had caused her reaction; his focus was entirely on his brother.

Murphy lumbered into the living room and crashed into the wolf—Jason—standing right over Nessa. She lay unconscious on the ground, blood covering her upper body. Rivulets of red dripped from her torso and onto the floor, her skin pale and damp with sweat.

Murphy dragged Jason away from the human, the wolf giving a hoarse, panicked yelp as he scrambled for purchase. The bear ended the Alpha wolf before he even had a chance to fight back.

One ferocious bite on the back of his neck, and Murphy's teeth snapped clean through the bone. Jason went limp, but Murphy didn't stop. He pinned Jason's body to the ground beside Nessa and clawed through what remained of the wolf's neck until the head separated from the body.

Tank felt a brief flare of anger that his brother was the one to kill that rat bastard. He'd wanted to do the honors, to wipe out the threat to Hunny. But it was done. The fucker was dead.

The last of the fighting in his front yard quieted down, and when he glanced outside, all he could see were bears, mostly shifted, standing tall in victory.

The attack was over.

"Y-Your back is really messed up, Henry," Hunny whispered tearfully behind him, erasing every other thought from his head. He turned toward her, shifting as he did so until he was naked, healed, and standing in his human form in front of his beautiful mate.

With shaky hands, he pulled her into his arms, not even thinking about the blood and grime still covering his body as his fingers sifted through her hair, his arm banding around her waist. She was warm, her softness molding to his hard frame until he worried he'd smother her with how hard he held her against him. But he just couldn't let go, and as she wrapped herself around him just as tightly, he knew she didn't want him to.

"Are you hurt?" he asked, his voice hoarse, his heart beating hard.

"Me? Look at you! You're covered in blood!" she exclaimed with a soft whimper, burying her face against his chest. She inhaled roughly, dragging his scent into her lungs just as he did the same to her. And then she began crying. Heartbreaking, wrenching sobs that hurt him more than anything else had over the last several minutes. "I thought you were dead," she bawled, clinging to him harder.

Tank squeezed his eyes shut, everything else melting away but her. "We're alright, baby," he uttered softly despite the fire burning in his throat. He lifted Hunny into his arms, anxious to hold her as close as possible. She wrapped her legs around his waist, arms circling his neck as she crushed herself to him.

Turning back to face the room, Tank saw Nessa stir. Her face twisting with pain, she opened her eyes slowly, staring blankly up at Murphy, who hovered over her, still in his bear form. She choked on a breath, the stench of her fear mixing with the powerful scent of her blood.

"It's okay," Tank murmured. Nessa didn't hear him, her breaths coming in frantic puffs of air as she tried to move away, but she couldn't. Her torso was too ravaged. He hadn't inspected her injuries, but she was bleeding too much. She needed treatment immediately. "You need to shift, Murphy. We have to get her to the clinic."

Mom's already on her way, Murphy informed him, though his voice trembled with fear. *She'll stabilize Nessa here before we move her to the clinic for surgery.*

Nessa's eyes widened in horror as his brother heeded his advice and shifted. Only a second, maybe two, passed before Murphy stood over Nessa, completely naked, his face a mask of fear and concern as he examined her. He kneeled down, hands hovering over her shoulder and chest like he wanted to staunch the flow of blood but didn't know where to start. "My mother is a physician. She's on her way. She can help you. You're going to be okay, Nessa."

Murphy reached for her, but Nessa recoiled, only to cry out in pain.

"Get away from me," she whispered frantically, her terror increasing as Murphy reached for her again.

"I know this is a lot, Nessa, but you need to calm down—"

"Get away! You're a monster!" Nessa screamed in alarm. "You're a monster. You're a monster," she repeated faintly, her voice breaking as tears began coursing down her face. Her breaths became labored and her pulse raced. "Someone help ... me. Some ... one ..."

Jasper crowded into the room. "Back up. Give her space, Murph."

"Don't tell me how to handle my mate!" Murphy bellowed in distress. Running a hand through his hair, he looked back down at Nessa, his face tight with worry. "I won't hurt you, Nessa. I would never hurt you. But you're really hurt, and you have to let me help you."

The human shuddered, looking away from him. Her eyes latched onto the blood leaking from her wounds, which stood out in stark clarity against her torn shirt. Nessa gasped, the sound full of hysteria, and then she passed out cold, her eyes rolling into the back of her head.

Murphy bit out a sharp, panicked curse right as Tabitha's car pulled into the driveway. They heard her slam on the brakes, not even bothering to turn her engine off before she was racing across the lawn, up the porch, and into the cabin. She dropped a large bag onto the ground beside Nessa, pulling out several medical items before she set to work stabilizing the human.

"Nessa's going to be okay, right?" Hunny asked quietly, clinging to Tank just a little harder.

He didn't answer. He couldn't stand to voice his concerns and make things worse for his brother or his mate. Honestly, he wasn't sure if Nessa would make it.

Sudden movement drew Tank's attention back to the gaping hole in his wall as Marcus stepped inside.

"He left while we were distracted." The tracker pushed into the thick of their group, his eyes red-rimmed and his body shaking with rage. He sent Murphy a hollow, dejected look. "I tried to track him, but his scent is missing. Dante's gone."

Tank and Murphy's eyes met across the room.

Fuck.

Thirty Seven

A little more than an hour later, Hunny, Tank, and several others filled the lobby of the clinic, anxiously waiting for Tabitha to finish working on Nessa. Apparently, a lot of the lacerations from Jason's attack were minor; only a few deep enough to hit her shoulder bone. No major arteries or organs had sustained any damage, which was a huge relief.

It was the blood loss that was Tabitha's main concern. While she kept blood on hand for the clan, it wasn't human—giving any to Nessa could have catastrophic side effects.

Contrary to the myths circulating the world, being bitten or scratched by a shifter wouldn't convert a human—and a shifter blood transfusion wasn't an option.

Luckily, Murphy had put in a call to a vampire he knew at a human hospital located over an hour away. Vampires could travel great distances in half the time a shifter could, and a few pints of blood had arrived nearly thirty minutes before Hunny and Tank had even made it to the clinic.

Hunny didn't know what kind of deal the Alpha had made to get human blood delivered so quickly, but she suspected he'd paid a hefty price for it, whether monetary or otherwise.

Right now, that didn't matter. All Hunny cared about was her friend's recovery. While what had happened to Nessa was horrific, she couldn't help but feel grateful that no one else had sustained any severe injuries. Tonight could have been a lot worse. They all could have died. Miraculously, none of them had.

Hunny, sitting sideways on Tank's lap, rested her cheek against his chest. He kept a firm arm wrapped around her waist, his palm protectively cupping her lower belly as if he were holding on just as adamantly to their kits. She needed this closeness, this connection to him after everything they'd gone through tonight.

She closed her eyes, taking one deep breath after another, drawing Tank's scent into her lungs. Even though he'd rinsed off before they'd met the others here, he still smelled faintly of blood, reminding her of just how bad his own wounds had been.

He's okay, Hunny reminded herself, but that did nothing to ease the anxiety she felt, or to erase the memories of the wounds she'd seen. His back had been a bloody tapestry of torn skin and missing fur before he'd shifted, and even though he'd healed during the transformation, she couldn't get the image out of her head.

She didn't know if she ever would, to be honest. She'd come so close to losing him.

All it would have taken was a few more attacks, a few more minutes, and Tank might not have survived. Her breath hitched at the thought, and she pushed her ear closer to his chest, listening to the steady beat of his heart, as if searching for proof he was still here despite it being so obvious.

What would she have done if she had never heard that sound again? If she'd never had another chance to feel his arms around her, his lips on her skin? If she'd woken up tomorrow and his side of the bed had been empty and cold?

Hunny shivered, tears blurring her vision for what felt like the thousandth time that night. Tank pulled her in closer to the heat of his body. "It's alright, little rabbit," he crooned. "I've got you."

"I know." Hunny sniffled, swallowing hard to keep herself in check. Needing a distraction from her morose thoughts, she looked at Tank's oldest brother.

Murphy hadn't been able to stand still for more than a handful of minutes, and he was now pacing the length of the lobby, his shoulders slumped and his eyes downcast.

Hunny didn't know if she'd ever seen the male look so distraught. Not that she blamed him. Nessa was human. She didn't have the luxury to heal as rapidly as they did. And when her body did eventually heal, she'd have scars, a constant reminder of the trauma she'd endured.

But it was the emotional scars that worried Hunny the most. She could still hear Nessa's screams as Murphy had tried to comfort her. She'd called him a monster. She thought shifters were *monsters*. When she woke up, would she feel the same way toward Hunny?

Would she want anything to do with any of them?

While Hunny understood how terrifying it must have been for her friend, a stab of hurt and sadness hit her as she remembered the look of horror on Nessa's face. Hopefully, Nessa gave them all, especially Murphy, a chance to explain things. To ease her into their world after such a painful introduction to it.

"I can't believe Dante escaped," Murphy snarled under his breath, finally pausing long enough to turn toward Tank. "Getting away from what he did scot-free is unacceptable. He needs to pay for his actions."

"I agree," Tank answered harshly. "Fucker should die."

Hunny lifted her head, staring at her mate in bewilderment. She'd told them all what Jason had said about Dante's part in this entire fiasco, and considering the situation, she hadn't expected they'd still want him dead. "What Dante did was wrong, but if you'd both been in the same situation, would you have reacted differently?"

She didn't know if she would have. Tank mattered to her more than anything else, and if his life were on the line, could she really put it at further risk by going to someone else for help?

Tank clenched his jaw, but it was Murphy who grated out, "I don't care what his reasons were—Nessa almost died!"

"Lower your voice when you speak to my mate," Tank snapped, tucking her more firmly against him. "Now isn't the time to discuss this. Not until you know Nessa is recovering. You're not thinking clearly."

"Maybe not." Marcus looked on solemnly from his chair near the front door. Jasper, seated beside him, was uncharacteristically silent. "But Murphy is right. Dante has to pay for his betrayal against the clan. We're a family, and he just—" Marcus's voice broke, and he looked down at the ground dejectedly. Hunny felt a flare of remorse for the male. She couldn't imagine what he was going through, what *any* of them were going through.

Jasper clapped Marcus on the shoulder before pulling him into a side hug, staring angrily ahead. "We'll find him," Jasper promised. "And one way or another, Dante will make this right."

They all went quiet as light footsteps sounded down the hall, moving quickly toward them. Tabitha stepped into the lobby from behind a set of double doors, sending Murphy a hesitant smile. "She's going to be alright."

Murphy sucked in a deep breath, his entire face crumbling with emotion. He looked away to collect himself before returning his attention to his mother, his expression now a stoic mask. "Is she awake? Should I go see her?"

"I have her sedated for now, but it should wear off in the next few hours." Tabitha pursed her lips. "And I think, based on what you told me, it might be for the best to give her a few days to adjust to this new world before you visit."

"She's my mate," Murphy bit out through clenched teeth. "I have every right to be there for her."

Tabitha's face softened. "Of course, you do. But before tonight, Nessa didn't know that shifters existed. And not only did she just barely survive an attack from a wolf shifter, she watched someone she knew change from a bear into a man. That would be a hard pill for anyone to swallow when you don't know this world. You have to prepare yourself because she might not want to see you for a long time."

"She's my mate," Murphy reiterated softly, like he couldn't believe what he was hearing.

"Nessa doesn't know what that means. And if you bombard her as soon as she wakes up, she might not give you a chance to show her, my darling boy. Is that what you want?"

Murphy shook his head.

"I think you should take a few days as well," Hunny added hesitantly, grimacing slightly when he looked at her in confusion. She nestled closer to Tank, drawing on him for some strength before she continued. "Not just for Nessa's sake, but for yours, too. You didn't want to claim her at all, remember, Murphy? Now you're referring to her as your mate and you want to see her. If it's only your instincts driving you to care for her because she's injured, and not genuine interest in *her*, then being near her right now will only cause more turmoil later on when you have a clear head."

Murphy stiffened, and then finally he nodded. "You're right." He looked toward Tabitha. "Mom, please let me know if you need anything, or if ... the human's condition worsens."

Tabitha's eyes shone with compassion. "I will."

Murphy cleared his throat. "Tonight's attack will likely bring conse-quences down on our heads from the shifter community. I need to get ahead of that if I can, so I'll be in my office at the den house, if I'm needed." With that, he moved to the exit as if a hoard of demons were chasing him, disappearing into the night a moment later.

"Should I have kept quiet?" Hunny asked the room nervously. She wanted Murphy to be happy, but Nessa was her friend, even if that might not be the case tomorrow. Regardless, she didn't need to have a territorial male hovering over her if he didn't plan to let her into his life. If he didn't plan to earn her trust and love through patience and genuine care.

"You did the right thing," Tank told her gruffly, rubbing his palm over her tiny bump in comfort. "Murphy knows that, or he wouldn't have left."

Tabitha nodded, walking over to them both. "I haven't had a chance to check in on you, Hunny, but I'm assuming you're okay since my son hasn't caused a fuss."

Tank huffed. "I don't *fuss.*"

Snorting at the blatant lie, Hunny slid her hand over his, sending his mom a small, grateful smile. "I'm okay. Thank you, Tabitha."

"I'm glad to hear that. If something changes, or you feel even the slightest bit unwell, I'll be in my office all night and tomorrow." Tabitha paused before adding, "Whether or not Murphy mates with Nessa, she's family, and I want her to be treated as such while she's in my care."

"I really appreciate that." Hunny smiled again. "Nessa is a good person, and she's been through a lot, and not just tonight. If anyone deserves kindness, it's her. Without her, I might not even be here."

Tank stood up, setting Hunny gently on her feet beside him. "Since Nessa is going to be fine, we'll head out. Hunny needs to rest."

"If she's up for it, I'd love to see her when she's ready," Hunny added, her heart in her throat as her fingers intertwined with Tank's. "I'm sure she probably suspects I'm not human now, but she hasn't seen me shift, so she might be more open to my company while she's here."

At least, Hunny really hoped so.

After a few more minutes of conversation, Tank led her to his truck, and they headed to Murphy's large cabin. He'd given them a room to stay in until their own home was cleaned up and repaired. The truck ride there was quiet, but she didn't mind, allowing the silence to process what had happened until her shock and anxiety slipped away.

It wasn't until they were in the ensuite, naked and in the shower, that Tank said anything.

"I'm glad that this is over and that Jason is dead, but I fucking hate that it happened like this." Soaping up a wet cloth, he ran it over Hunny's body, cleaning her thoroughly as he spoke. "I just keep thinking how much worse it could have been. Dante could have killed me on that porch, and I wouldn't have suspected anything. I was an easy target."

"I don't think Dante wanted to hurt anyone," Hunny explained again, even though they'd had this talk already tonight. "He was put into a bad situation, and he didn't know how to get out of it while keeping everyone safe. What he did was wrong, but he was screwed no matter what he did. And he did try to help you."

"I know." Tank cupped her cheek. He leaned in, pressing his lips firmly over hers. His tongue slid into her mouth, tasting her urgently, like each kiss might be their last. He breathed roughly, pressing her back against the tiled wall as he sagged into her. Dropping the cloth with a wet plop, he curled his arms around her, shuddering hard.

"We're both okay, Henry," Hunny murmured when he broke their kiss and settled his mouth on her mating mark in an act of comfort. She ran her hands over his smooth back, seeking her own reassurance. "I don't know what I'd do without you, and I'm so grateful I won't have to find out."

They stayed like that, his back protecting her from the hot spray of water, his body sheltering hers as they held onto one another, neither one willing to let go.

"I thought about what you said earlier," Tank admitted a short while later, his voice taking on a dark edge. "If Jason had captured you, and threatened me like he did Dante ... I would have betrayed *anyone* if it meant keeping you safe. Nothing—*no one*—else would have mattered to me but you. Not my brothers. Not my parents. Only you."

"Dante saved my life after putting it in danger. But running away like that after everyone was safe ... He took the coward's way out instead of facing the consequences. Nessa almost died, and as much as Murphy wants to fight the pull he feels toward her, I wouldn't want him to suffer through that kind of loss. The kind of loss I have felt. Dante needs to answer for that."

"He will," Hunny assured her mate, her fingers sifting through his hair as she clung to him. The spray of the water beat down on his healed back, helping to wash away the misery and pain they'd both endured. "What Murphy mentioned earlier; do you think another wolf pack will retaliate against us for killing Jason and the others?"

"I don't know. The Moon Rose pack is larger than just the wolves who showed up tonight. But if many of the remaining pack are like Angela, scared and abused, they'll probably flee and never look back."

Hunny could only hope that was the case. But whatever happened, they'd face it together. If tonight was any kind of example, then the pair of them could withstand almost anything as long as they had each other.

"I love you, Henry," she whispered against Tank's neck.

He eased back, kissing her again. Harder than before, and just as intensely, as if he needed to recommit every inch of her to memory. As if he needed her presence to linger on his skin long after they parted. "I love you too, little rabbit. And as soon as we're both cleaned up, I'm going to show you just how much."

She sent him a coy look from beneath her lashes. "Why wait?"

Epilogue

Hunny rubbed her hands over her swollen belly, her back aching as she leaned against the large porch Tank had rebuilt what felt like ages ago when he'd upgraded their cabin, adding several more rooms and furnishing it to accommodate their growing family. Staring out at the front yard, she watched her mate roll around on the ground, wrestling playfully with three small shifters, all under four-years-old. When one kit launched at him, Tank let out a dramatic yelp, catching the tiny male in his arms.

"I'm under attack!" Tank exclaimed, laughter thick in his voice as the two children on either side of him shrieked in delight.

"Surrender!" Henry Jr. yelled from the safety of Tank's arms, only to shriek gleefully as Tank launched him high into the air, catching him a few seconds later. Despite Hunny's sudden nerves at seeing her first-born fly a few feet into the sky, she couldn't help the smile that stretched across her face as Henry Jr. exclaimed, "Higher, Daddy!"

She loved watching her mate play with their children, and she always felt like a fool that there was ever a time she worried he might not want to be their father. He'd taken to parenthood so naturally, so wholeheartedly, that her heart ached. Life had thrown a lot Hunny's way, but she'd do it all a thousand times over to get this same outcome.

Tank might not have been her true mate, but he was her heart and soul.

"My turn, my turn!" Blake insisted, barely giving Tank a chance to sit up before the second kit threw himself at the burly male. Tank adjusted quickly, scooping him up and tossing them both into the air while their little sister watched, eyes wide with fascination.

Beonca was the quiet child among the three of them, more content to watch her brothers play than join in, like right now. Maybe it was her wolf's instinct to sit back and observe—Hunny didn't know; she'd never been an apex predator.

There were times Hunny found it overwhelming, raising a wolf shifter among rabbits, if only because she worried she was doing something wrong. Neglecting her daughter in some unknown way.

Tank wasn't concerned about it, though, likely because bears were predators, too. He understood Beonca in a way Hunny didn't, and that had bonded the father and daughter more than blood ever could.

Hunny still remembered the day she'd given birth to the three of them. Henry Jr. had come first. Healthy but disgruntled. He'd frowned at every noise, every tiny bit of light. Blake had followed soon after, ready to take on the world with a hearty wail as soon as his lungs had cleared. Both rabbit shifters had Hunny's light, lavender-colored hair, and they'd looked almost identical.

Tank had let her choose the names for both boys, and he'd cried, smiling through tears as she'd handed him Henry Jr., and then again with Blake.

But their daughter had been different from the moment Hunny had laid eyes on her. Not only was she a wolf shifter, she'd looked like a replica of Jason. Blonde hair, steel-blue eyes, even the same nose shape and complexion. Although it pained Hunny to admit it, the first time she'd held her daughter in her arms, she'd worried about what Tank would think.

Stupid on her part, really.

He'd barely given Hunny a chance to hold their daughter for more than a minute before he'd scooped the baby girl into his arms, staring down at her little scrunched-up face like she'd hung the moon and the stars in the sky. He hadn't just cried when he'd held her, though.

Hunny's big bear, her stoic, grumpy mate, had wept, crooning softly and rocking Beonca gently as he proclaimed her the most precious baby girl in the entire world.

After Tabitha collected the boys and placed them back into Hunny's arms, Tank had leaned over all of them, kissing her damp forehead tenderly. He'd cried as he'd thanked her for giving him their kids.

Looking back on it now, he might have just been trying to butter her up since he'd wanted to name their daughter.

Beonca wasn't Hunny's original choice for a name, but the first time she'd heard Tank utter their daughter's nickname, she'd understood *exactly* why he'd chosen it, the sneak.

Hunny smiled as Tank pushed himself up from the ground, setting the boys on their feet. He looked down at their daughter, smiling gently as she tilted her head back, staring up at him with a small pout that was guaranteed to get her anything from the male. "What do you say, Honey Bee? You want to fly?"

Beonca shook her head.

"No?" Tank gripped his heart like she'd broken it. "What could my little wolf want?" he asked his sons, pursing his lips in thought, like he didn't already know the answer. It was comical and endearing, seeing him like this. Around anyone else, Tank was a grumpy, snarly force to be reckoned with. But here, with them?

He was as sweet as the honey he loved so much.

"Chase!" Blake chanted, grinning when Henry Jr. repeated it.

Tank held out his hand, pulling Beonca up from the ground when she put her small palm in his. "Are you heathens ready to be chased through the woods by a ferocious, savage bear?" he growled menacingly.

Beonca smiled brightly. And then the three children burst into action, racing around the front yard in opposite directions. Tank chased after them, making ridiculous sounds in his throat as he caught each child. Once he'd collected them and the chase was over, he set them down to run around and turned toward Hunny.

Sending her a heated look, he moved to the stairs, up the porch, and wrapped a possessive arm around her waist. Careful to not squish her belly, Tank kissed her thoroughly, not stopping until her legs trembled and she was breathless.

"How's my little rabbit doing?" Tank murmured the question against her lips, kissing her again.

Moaning lightly, Hunny pulled back as she felt a strong flutter in her womb, followed by a pang against her rib. "Good, except one of your sons wants to say hello."

Tank's brows rose. "Not both of them?"

"Ha. Ha." Hunny narrowed her eyes. "You're lucky one is being polite to his mother, otherwise she might snip you somewhere unpleasant while you're sleeping tonight."

Smirking, Tank cupped her belly, his large hands moving tenderly over her. "Can't have that. I need all my parts in working order if I'm going to give you more kits later."

Hunny gasped in outrage. "You are a menace, Henry Sinclair. There will be *no* more babies after these two."

He frowned, sending her a forlorn look. "But Honey Bee said she wanted a little sister."

Hunny snorted before she glared at him again. "No, she didn't, you glutton. She loves being the only girl because you're wrapped around her finger."

Tank grunted. "What if I just want another little girl to spoil?"

"Is that the case?" Hunny asked primly.

"It might be."

"Well then," she began, wrapping her arms around Tank's neck. Bringing his head down to hers, she kissed him once. "I might be inclined to try again. Just to see if we can even out the numbers. Five kids just aren't enough," she teased.

"True. Evening them out with eight is our best bet," Tank agreed.

"Eight?! I meant six!"

Tank shook his head. "Six isn't happening, darlin'. We both know it. Eight sounds perfect to me. If we have another set of twins, we'll shoot for ten."

"Ten?! No way, Henry. Absolutely not—"

Tank swooped in for another kiss, slanting his mouth over hers. His tongue explored her mouth until she could barely remember her own name, let alone what they'd been arguing over. "How about I have my brother watch the kids and give us a little alone time?"

Hunny smiled. "I already called earlier while you were trying to send our kids into orbit. They'll be here in about five minutes."

"God, I fucking love you."

Grinning, Hunny hugged him. "I love you too."

Author's Note

Thank you so much for reading *Hunny And The Bear*! I hope you loved reading this book as much as I loved writing it. Paranormal romance is a favorite genre of mine, and I hope to release more books like this in the future.

If you would be so kind to leave a review of my work, and to share this book with others, I would be so thankful!

Other Works

Interested in reading more of my work?
Find them here:

Standalone:
Captive Of The Dragon Warlord

Aragnokan Mates Series:
The Monster In My Bed
The Monster Inside Me
Taken By The Monster
Mated To The Monster
The Monster In My Basement

About the author

M. L. is an avid reader and writer of all things romance/erotica, specializing in sexy monster aliens with a penchant for worshiping their women. She believes spice is the foundation of a good romance, and uses it wholeheartedly while writing stories. When she's not spending too much money on books, she's cuddling with her dogs, watching horror movies with her husband, or gaming. Guilty pleasures include: poorly made movies with terrible dialogue, playing video games when she should be writing, and drinking insane amounts of caffeine.

To stay up to date on what M. L. is writing, you can follow her on Inkitt @mlsmithwrites or on Instagram @mlsmithwrites

www.ingramcontent.com/pod-product-compliance
Lightning Source LLC
Chambersburg PA
CBHW031204020726
47499CB00002B/477